Jaguars and Other Game

Jaguars
and Other
Game

Brynn Barineau

ORANGE BLOSSOM PUBLISHING

Maitland, Florida

Orange Blossom Publishing
Maitland, Florida
www.orangeblossombooks.com
info@orangeblossombooks.com

First Edition: November 2022

Edited by: Arielle Haughee
Formatted by: Autumn Skye
Cover design: Sanja Mosic

Print ISBN: 978-1-949935-47-9
eBook ISBN: 978-1-949935-48-6

Printed in the U.S.A.

To My Husband
Who never said if, only when

Table of Contents

Chapter One 1
Chapter Two 18
Chapter Three 30
Chapter Four 40
Chapter Five 51
Chapter Six 62
Chapter Seven 74
Chapter Eight. 86
Chapter Nine 99
Chapter Ten. 110
Chapter Eleven 120
Chapter Twelve 138
Chapter Thirteen. 153
Chapter Fourteen 169
Chapter Fifteen 181
Chapter Sixteen 189
Chapter Seventeen. .201
Chapter Eighteen. 216
Chapter Nineteen. 234
Chapter Twenty. 252
Chapter Twenty-One. 263
Chapter Twenty-Two. 279
Chapter Twenty-Three 286

Chapter Twenty-Four. 297
Chapter Twenty-Five. 309
Chapter Twenty-Six. 318
Chapter Twenty-Seven 330

Discussion Questions 343
Author's Note. 346
Acknowledgements. 353
About the Author 357

Chapter One

Maria

Maria was welcomed home by the distant boom of cannon, a twenty-one-gun salute to vanity and stupidity.

It wasn't *for* her—thank god. Since Prince João and the entire Portuguese court had fled from Napoleon to Rio de Janeiro a year earlier, twenty-one guns saluted every ship that entered port. It had been a noisy year. Maria was thankful to have spent most of it trekking through the mountains.

She rode to a break in the trees, ignoring for the moment the raised voices behind her. The lush, emerald forest flowed down the mountain right up to the white walls and rippling roofs of Rio. The bay was dotted with ships. A whale carcass stretched along the sand, and Maria thought she smelled a hint of sun-rotting blubber on the breeze. Parrots flew by squawking in complaint, probably about the cannon.

Home filled her senses, and a knot tightened in her gut with every cannon blast. She couldn't say if it was longing or dread.

"Oi, Maria!" Isabel, her sister, rode up. "You could survey from under the canopy. It's not quite hot as hell there."

"Harder to spot an ambush under the trees." She pulled a spyglass from her bag and scanned the trail ahead.

"We could relax in the shade then see what lies ahead. Washed out trail. Thieves lying in wait. Nossa Senhora, I'd welcome some excitement."

"Even if an ambush costs us a few crates of gold?"

"Small price to pay for a good fight," Isabel said. "The story I'd tell would earn back our losses in drinks. And who doesn't love surprises?"

Maria grinned from behind the spyglass. "Me."

"Then you might want to know that Zé is about to shoot Berto."

She snapped the spy glass shut and shoved it in the saddlebag. After weeks in the forest, everyone's supply of patience was low, but she wouldn't tolerate murder this close to home, no matter how damn hot it was. Plus, as captain of the mule train, shooting people was her prerogative.

Maria spurred past the tethered mules with their faces buried in foliage to where her team surrounded Zé and Berto. Mateus, her partner and second-in-command, stood between the men trying to calm them, but the men's shining faces and the shirts plastered to their backs told her they were beyond the reach of reason.

"I'm not apologizing to that thief!" Berto, the newest man, spit at Zé's feet.

"You calling me a thief, boy?" Zé bellowed.

"A thief and a goddamn cheat. Maybe I'll see if your wife cheats as much."

Zé yanked his pistol free.

Crack!

Her whip sliced open the back of Zé's hand before he leveled the gun. The pistol dropped. Maria landed a second blow at Zé's feet. He leapt back, and Mateus snatched up the pistol.

Maria rode to the edge of the circle, the men parting in front of her. "Berto, if you play cards with a man wearing his sleeves down in this heat, you deserve the loss. I wonder if you'd notice a jaguar gnawing on one of your mules." She hung the whip over her shoulder but kept a grip on the handle. "Zé, you've been with the train eight years. Can you tell Berto who pays for the shot and powder loaded in your pistol?"

Zé dropped his eyes to the ground. "Dom Joaquim."

"And who buys the supplies in his name?"

"You do, captain."

"And the powder is to shoot thieves after gold and animals after you. Not members of this team. So all pistols, rifles, shot, and powder will be coming down the mountain with me, along with the men who want their pay. If you two want to kill each other, fine, but you'll do it alone with your bare hands."

Maria caught Mateus's gaze and without a word he held out his hand for Berto's rifle. The new recruit hesitated. His grip on the rifle tightened. Her back went rigid at the small defiance, and the last of her patience evaporated.

She spurred her horse forward until it was nose to nose with Berto then turned so the gaping tooth-filled snout of the caiman shot that morning stared him in the face. She rested her whip against the black scales of the carcass draped across her saddle and glared down. "Fall in line or hand over the rifle."

Berto's eyes widened and flicked between the reptile's tooth-filled snout and his rifle. Mateus clapped him on the shoulder, grinning.

"Don't worry about the caimans, Berto," he said. "The trail doesn't pass any rivers from here on. Worry about jaguars, pumas—"

"Mateus, you're going to get him killed," Isabel called from her horse. "Jaguars and pumas hunt at dusk. The jaguarundi attacks during the day."

"Nothing more than a big house cat. Berto could handle a jaguarundi."

"Small can be deadly. I'd rather meet a grown boa constrictor than a baby viper. You get a fighting chance with the constrictor."

Mateus draped his arm across Berto's shoulders and leaned close. "My advice is: be careful what tree you nap under."

"And where you step," Isabel chimed in.

"And where you stop to drink."

"Might be easier to let Zé kill you right here."

"He'd be faster than a constrictor," Mateus muttered in the new recruit's ear.

While Isabel and Mateus listed increasingly gruesome ways to be eaten or poisoned on the trail, Maria assessed Berto's reaction. It had been an unusually quiet trek with only clouds of mosquitos to fight off, and the new recruit hadn't been tested. When men joined a mule team, many often assumed they knew the forest simply by growing up next to it. As if watching a house burn and escaping it were equally instructive.

Berto was stubborn and willing to stand up for himself. She could use that. Stubborn in the face of fear would keep a man and his teammates alive. But stubborn and arrogant were a liability. Stubborn, arrogant, and inexperienced—she might as well shoot him and drape him over her saddle with the caiman.

She needed to know if Berto was smart enough to fear the trail.

"Enough," she interrupted. "Berto, I'd rather have a full team handling the mules, but if you need revenge, I won't stop you. But hand over my rifle." She reached down for the gun and locked eyes with Berto. "We're in sight of Rio. With luck, you might make it back."

There was no hesitation this time. "I'll stay with the team, captain."

"Good," she nodded, then arched an eyebrow at Zé.

"Sorry for the delay, captain. Won't happen again."

"Let Isabel bandage your hand. Now load up," Maria barked. The men immediately scattered. As Zé walked past her, she leaned down and caught his shoulder. In a low voice she said, "Even up with Berto, and never draw on a member of this team again."

Zé nodded and headed for his mules. Maria coiled the whip on her hip. She fanned her shirt. Almost home.

Mateus walked up, lifting a hand for her filly to nuzzle. "Next time I get to decorate *my* saddle with the body of giant man-eater and terrify men into submission."

"Here I thought my leadership commanded respect."

"The caiman helps. That would have gone differently with a string of armadillos across your saddle."

Maria laughed and gave the reptile a pat. "I might make her part of the team."

"How about a live one to eat men who try to shoot their teammates?" Isabel rode up in a huff. "For the love of *Santa Helena*, Maria, can't we toss Zé in a river? Lying, cheating, trying to shoot people. He's more trouble than a troop of starving monkeys."

Her chest clenched, protective of one of her oldest trail companions. "He's also loyal. He rode three years with Papa and didn't hesitate when I asked him to ride for me." Maria shook her head. "He's probably trying to pick up a little extra with the card games. His wife's expecting. I'll talk to him."

"Does any man on this team have a secret from you?" Mateus asked.

Maria shrugged, pretending not to notice the hint of worry on his brow. She'd gotten good at feigning ignorance in front of her second over the last few months. It felt like lying, which wasn't something Maria wanted to do to her oldest friend, but she was the captain. The captain protected her men from any threat on the trail. Apparently, that now included their own misguided romantic intentions. "I'm sure there are a few secrets I've missed."

"I doubt that. My sister knows everything." Isabel winked at Mateus.

He cleared his throat, and his smile dimmed for an instant. "Then I should get to the front before she uncovers something about me even I don't know." He tipped his hat before heading to ready his horse.

"Poor boy." Isabel clucked her tongue. "Does he really think it's a secret?"

"Don't you have a wound to tend?"

"Ugh. We need a doctor or nurse or anyone else who can do this. I'm the cook. I rip skin off, not stitch it back together," Isabel grumbled, trotting off to find Zé.

Maria smiled at her sister's muttering. For all the complaining, she knew with absolute certainty that Isabel would bandage Zé's hand to the best of her ability. Not because her sister cared about Zé, but because Maria had asked her, and Isabel's loyalty was one of the few things in life she never questioned. It was a relief and a responsibility that she worked constantly to be worthy of.

When everyone was in position she whistled, and with a crack of her whip, thirty-five mules, seven men on foot, a sister, a second-in-command, and two dozen crates of gold began snaking down the mountain through the forest toward the gleaming white city below.

After years of traveling between the mines in Minas Gerais and the ships in Rio de Janeiro, the first sight of her city nestled between mountain and ocean still thrilled her. The mining towns in Minas had their gilded churches adorned with sculpted saints, but Rio was a work of art by God himself. Any mark man made on it only took away from the perfection.

That included His Royal Highness the Prince Regent and his court.

Maria hated to admit that her home of mountains and ocean could succumb to the whims of foreigners, but the Portuguese had changed Rio. Since the court's arrival, she frequently found herself caught off guard in her own city. She walked the streets anxious and pensive, as though retracing a trail from childhood that had overgrown. She recognized the trees but could no longer be sure where to step.

Rio de Janeiro had always been a city that demanded a glance over the shoulder, but now the danger marched right up to you, more often than not with a uniform and rank, and walking away wasn't an option. Neither was the butt of her whip against a nose. She didn't know the rules anymore, and for a free Black woman responsible for her sister, her team, and her business, being able to anticipate problems kept everyone fed and out of the stocks.

The road flattened out as they cleared the trees and rode into the farmland on the outskirts of Rio. Mateus smiled and tipped his hat to the slaves and their owners scattered amongst the coffee. The slaves returned the greeting. The owners and foremen did not. They never did. The owners preferred to act as though free Blacks didn't exist. Maria was content to be ignored and ignore in return, but Mateus greeted every person like an ambassador of the Almighty. It looked exhausting.

They dismounted at the customs outpost on the edge of the city, and Mateus greeted the customs officer and walked him through their cargo. The official made meticulous notes, counted, weighed, and counted again. Soldiers stood guard around the outpost ready to haul away anyone caught smuggling.

As far as customs knew, the train was run by Mateus. It was why he rode in the front on the last stretch into the city. No one would trust a woman, a young unmarried woman at that, to carry gold over the mountains, but Maria had been determined to carry on her father's legacy. Every merchant had trusted him as the best muleteer in Rio and wanted him to captain their train, and she'd ridden at his side for a decade. She could track, shoot, fight, and hold the profit from each trek for the last four years in her head, but she couldn't negotiate her way out of being young and female.

Mateus had been the solution. He'd known her family for years through the capoeira circles, a skinny boy learning the fluid martial art set to drum and song, and was one of the few men willing to play capoeira against her. She offered him the chance to escape apprenticeship to a shoemaker in exchange for being her second and public face of the train.

He'd agreed, with the addition of a five percent partnership. Maria felt only a twinge of resentment at losing the entirety of profits. Self-delusion was not a luxury she could afford, and openly running the train herself would result in no contracts and thus no income for her or her father's team. She'd rather eat than be called captain at her funeral. As long as her team knew whose orders to follow when on the trail, she was satisfied.

Mateus always followed her orders. Never questioned her in front of the team. He was an ideal partner. Until he fell in love with her.

She knew what she was giving up. *Who* she was giving up. There wasn't a line of men willing to marry a woman who tromped though the forest in pants. Mateus was honest, loyal, and would be a wonderful catch for someone, but she wasn't fishing. Maria had enough responsibilities without a husband.

She remembered the distracted silence her father succumbed to after her mother died. At eleven, with a single trek to her name, she could see that her father's grief put himself, his daughters, and the entire team in danger, and falling in love always led, one way or another, to grieving a love. Grief was a distraction Maria couldn't afford.

There was always some threat to assess, be it a washed-out trail, jaguar tracks, or two Bats rummaging through her team's cargo. The sight of the two men with their black coats flapping about their knees sent her hand to her whip and her eyes accounting for every member of her team.

They were members of the royal guard, the most brutal of the city's new security measures. They weren't soldiers, and there was nothing royal about them. These men answered to the superintendent of Rio and patrolled the city with the purpose of ridding it of vice and disorder. From what Maria had observed, they had a very long list of behaviors that qualified as vice, ranging from prostitution to whistling. The members of the royal guard slipped through the shadows in their long, dark coats and waited to swoop down on anyone with the bad luck to disrupt order within their earshot. The practice had earned them an appropriate nickname.

A customs post near midday was neither the time nor place for Bats. They would only mean trouble for her team. Maria needed to get her men rounded up and back on the road.

As if in reply to her thoughts, one of the Bats drew a knife and proceeded to jab the caiman, not caring that it was still draped over her horse.

She was at their side in two strides, fists clenched. "Can I help you, senhores?"

The men looked up, startled. The younger Bat glanced away embarrassed, clearly a new recruit if still capable of shame, but the older man puffed out his chest. "We're looking for any illegal goods. This animal wasn't declared."

"Because game shot on the trail belongs to the man who killed it, senhor."

The man turned the color of boiled lobster. "You think you can argue with a member of the royal guard?"

Maria winced and gritted her teeth. She'd played it wrong. She should have been more deferential. They were due at the bank, and her team always delivered on time. Although it would fetch a nice price, the caiman could be sacrificed to preserve her team's record.

"We have the right to search any cargo," the older Bat continued. "There might be contraband."

Maria drew a knife from her boot, slashed the rope holding the caiman, and let it plunge to the ground at the soldiers' feet. The younger Bat yelped. Maria hauled the animal to eye level. She strained under the weight but forced her back straight and shoulders square.

"Where do you want it cut? Down the belly? You can rummage around the intestines for any diamonds. Would you like me to cut open the stomach, too, in case someone shoved gold down its throat?"

Maria raised the blade but stopped with the point pressed against the animal's throat. She glanced at the new recruit. "You might want to step back, senhor. You'll never get the blood out of your pants."

"It's also going to stink worse than a piss pot in the noon sun," Isabel added, strolling up with a cheerful smile.

The young Bat blanched and backed away. He must have been recently arrived from Portugal to have such delicate sensitivities. In his hasty retreat, he stepped on his partner, who shoved him away directly into the army captain coming to investigate the commotion. The Bats snapped to attention as the officer proceeded to curse them both for incompetence. The entire outpost stopped to listen, and Maria stood with a knife in one hand and a six-foot caiman in the other, its head flopped over her arm. She bit back a smile.

Mateus appeared and interrupted, speaking to the captain, "Senhor, we were hoping to sell the carcass to a collector but will of course open the body if you wish to inspect it. We're loyal subjects of the Prince Regent and are happy to comply with any order from his esteemed representatives."

"That won't be necessary, Mateus. You and your team have an excellent reputation. There is no need to spill crocodile innards all over my outpost."

The senior Bat began to protest, but the officer cut him off with a glare. "This outpost is under my command, and my orders are enforced by Her Majesty's soldiers. You men have no authority and no place here. Go back to patrolling the streets and catching pickpockets. Leave the gold under the army's protection." The officer dismissed Mateus with a wave. "Mateus, you and your team may proceed to the bank."

The officer shot a final withering glare at the old Bat who passed it on to Maria. She dropped the caiman to the ground at his feet and smiled as he flinched. He stomped away with the younger Bat scurrying behind, and Maria hid her triumphant grin by tucking the knife back in her boot. Two cowed Bats were worth a slight delay. She couldn't remember ever leaving a customs inspection in a better mood than when she arrived.

The same wasn't true for her team.

They left the outpost with an escort of armed soldiers. One sergeant slapped a mosquito hard enough to leave his handprint across his neck. He cursed Brazil and drew a glare from Isabel, who spat at his back. With protesting mules and the ever-rising temperature, they rode into the bustle of Rio a collection of lit tempers with short fuses.

From the rear, she kept the train tight with an occasional crack of her whip. Fish vendors pushing wheelbarrows, quitandeiras balancing baskets of mangos atop their turbans, slaves carrying their mistresses in sweltering boxes, and soldiers suffering in their wool uniforms all jostled for space in the teeming street.

"Olá, Rio, I've missed you," Isabel announced, throwing her arms wide as if to embrace the street and all the people and animals using it. She inhaled. "Pineapples are in season."

"I didn't notice with all the manure," Maria commented drily.

"You have no romance in your soul, dear sister. Look around and take in the city."

"Romance doesn't keep thirty-five mules in a straight line."

"*Santa Matilde!*" Isabel jerked her horse to a stop and gaped in horror.

"What?" Maria drew her pistol and scanned the crowd for the threat she'd missed.

"The windows!" her sister cried. "What's happened to all the windows?"

White homes with clay-tiled roofs butted up against one another lining the thoroughfare. The first-story doors were open to the bustle of the street. Slaves hurried in and out with barrels of wine or sacks of flour on their backs. In the second-floor windows, ladies melted into settees while fanned by still more slaves.

"The trellises are gone," Maria murmured, holstering the pistol.

The green or red wooden trellises that had stood out against the white walls and given the street a perpetually festive air were gone. Half the homes in front of her had removed the trellises and were in the process of replacing them with glass panes.

"Why would they take them down? They were so beautiful." Isabel wrung her hands.

"They'll suffocate without the breeze."

"You, girl! Why have you stopped?" The older Bat from the outpost rode up to Isabel, and Maria's stomach clenched, her good mood gone. They hadn't been back in the city ten minutes, and she'd made a new enemy.

"Apologies, senhor," Maria started.

"I didn't ask you," he barked.

"The trellises are gone!" Isabel looked as though she'd lost a personal friend.

"It's by order of Superintendent Viana. All trellises in the city are to be removed and replaced with window panes."

"But why? They were so pretty."

"They're being taken down because His Highness wants to make this city fit for a European court," the Bat snapped. "Proper homes have glass windows. They were also a security risk. Anyone could be hiding behind them, plotting an attack against the royal family."

"Maybe if the court didn't show up at the dock, throw half the city out of their homes, use up all the food and water, then expect a kiss on the hand for it, people wouldn't want to shoot them," Isabel shouted.

The man's face changed from red to beet purple. "What's your name little Indian? I want to know the mongrel who thinks she can criticize the Prince Regent."

Maria drew a sharp breath as her hope of getting to the bank without incident evaporated. She dropped her hand below the saddle, letting her whip unfurl but keeping her anger coiled tight inside. Her new goal was to get to the bank without anyone getting arrested.

Isabel edged her horse forward and said in a low voice, "My mother was Guarani, and they were here long before the royal family."

Maria caught Isabel's wrist in an iron grip before it reached for any number of weapons stashed beneath her skirt. Her gaze bore into Isabel's, and Maria shook her head once. They could not afford to have their cargo confiscated. A more thorough search would make insulting a royal guardsman a mundane offense.

"With respect, senhor, she's my sister," Maria said. The man scoffed, and she felt Isabel tense. "My adopted sister. My parents took her in after her own mother died, and I can vouch for her. She's a loyal subject of Her Majesty and the Prince Regent. We'll deliver the cargo directly to the bank without attracting any more attention."

"Oi, Maria! What's the delay? If we don't get this gold out of the sun, we'll be delivering soup instead of bars," Mateus joked loudly, pushing his horse between Isabel and the Bat. His smile flashed in the sun, but Maria heard the tension in his voice.

Maria wasn't sure who would swing first, the Bat or Isabel, but she was certain they were one insult away from ending up in the stocks and losing their entire earnings for the trek. She'd put on a dress and go to Mass before she let this small man grasping at power rob her team of their rightful earnings.

"Captain, apologies," she said to Mateus. "The Guardsman was kind enough to explain the superintendent's latest improvements, and I'm afraid we've let a crowd gather. It's going to be hard to deliver the crates before noon and collect the bonus Dom Joaquim promised for delivering early."

Mateus and Isabel glanced sharply at her, but Maria locked eyes with the Bat. "I'm sure the captain'd be grateful for any help you could give getting the crowd to disperse. He'd probably split the bonus Dom Joaquim promised us. Seems only fair a man so loyal to His Highness get what he deserves."

Isabel relaxed instantly, and Maria let go of her sister's wrist. They understood each other. She raised her eyebrows at Mateus.

"I don't need to tell you, senhor, that Dom Joaquim rewards handsomely when a job's done well." Mateus played along with only the slightest furrow between his brow. "I'd be happy to split down the middle."

The Bat leaned across his saddle to Mateus. "All of it. And this one," he growled, pointing at Isabel, "doesn't say another word until I've been paid."

Mateus cut his eyes to Maria, and she gave the slightest nod. "Agreed," he said.

"Then move out," the officer snapped, galloping to the front of the train and ordering the crowd to disperse.

Mateus edged up next to her. "Well, I suppose I'm going to be stabling the horses and mules on my own. Again."

"Sorry," Maria said.

"It's fine. Someone needs to avoid arrest and be ready to break you out."

Isabel tossed her hair over a shoulder. "I'm insulted you think there's a chance we'd get arrested." She looked at Maria. "And what exactly are we not going to be caught doing?"

"Mateus, at the bank, pay him all my share."

"Your whole share?" he gasped.

Maria leaned back in her saddle enjoying his shock. She had a plan brewing, and her share was a small price to pay. "All of it. Isabel and I will meet you at Dom Antonio's house at ten."

He let out a low whistle. "You're the captain. If I don't see you at Antonio's, I'll swing by the stocks." Mateus tipped his hat and road to the front.

Isabel raised her eyebrows. "*Santa Ana,* you're really going to give your share to that overcooked beet?"

"Didn't you listen to Papa? Cheap solves a problem for a day. A permanent solution always requires an investment. I'm investing in the Bats."

Chapter Two

Isabel

I sabel paused to toss back a shot of cachaça and give her audience a chance to lean forward in anticipation, their attention more potent than any spirit behind the bar. Her face flushed. "So, the caiman lay there, mouth gaping open, flesh-tearing teeth glistening, enjoying the shade while I perched in the tree above, wondering where to put my knife. I drew my dagger without a sound. Then I dropped!" She slammed her hand on the table and her onlookers jumped, one spilling a tumbler in surprise. "I plunged my blade through its brain before it felt me on his back. Dinner was served for the rest of the trail."

Her audience reacted with a variety of cheers, guffaws, and laughter, mixing with the din of conversation and marimba music filling the courtyard. Isabel basked in the appreciation. She stepped up on the bench and bowed repeatedly until she felt a tug on her skirt. The owner of the inn frowned up at her.

"Boa noite, Dona Antonia! You just missed the end of my story. Want me to tell it again?"

The crossed arms and furrowed brow told Isabel that Antonia was not interested in hearing her story.

The woman pointed a finger to the dirt. "We need to talk, senhorita."

Isabel shrugged an apology to her audience, gave a final bow, and hopped to the ground. "How are you, Dona? How's Tio Miguel and Dito? Nossa Senhora, it's more crowded than I've seen in a while. Business must be good."

"It would be better if you weren't distracting the customers from drinking," Antonia said.

"I can't help it if I have a gift."

"And telling stories is more important than me? You're back in town, and the first thing you do is put on a show for strangers without even a hello for me? I should throw your ungrateful backside out of my inn."

Isabel threw her arms around Antonia's waist. "I'm sorry, Dona. Very, very sorry. Please, forgive me."

She was sorry but not worried. Antonia's anger disappeared faster than a bottle of cachaça among freshly docked sailors. The woman couldn't stay mad. Otherwise she'd have barred Isabel permanently after that incident with the port bottle, oil lamp, and handsy coffee farmer's coat. The table in the corner still had the scorch marks.

"Let me start over." Isabel planted a kiss on Antonia's cheek. "Boa noite, Dona Antonia. I missed you. Did you miss me?"

"You know I did. Mending is tedious work without your stories. Are you paying me a visit soon?"

"I'll come this Sunday. I promise."

"We can practice your Guarani," Antonia said in Guarani.

Isabel cringed. She was curious about Guarani, but Antonia made learning it seem like a moral obligation. The priests gave out enough of those. Isabel didn't care for more. "My first mother didn't speak Guarani. Her parents didn't even speak Guarani. Mama told me my grandparents were both born in Rio."

"I was born in Rio, and I speak Guarani."

"Because your parents came from a mission down south. Things are different there."

"My parents said things *were* different, but now I suspect they're the same."

A flicker of sorrow passed over Antonia's face, a shadow amongst the laughter and music, and Isabel felt a stab of guilt. Antonia's parents ended up in Rio after fleeing a war between Guarani and Portuguese in the south. Isabel never asked. She assumed the Portuguese won. They always won.

She needed to stop letting words fly out of her mouth. The habit left a trail of problems, one of which she and Maria were in the process of cleaning up.

"Sunday afternoon. I'll bring a basket of clothes in desperate need of repair and adventures from the trail." Isabel linked arms with Antonia. The lamplight caught the white streaks in Antonia's black hair, turning them silver, and Isabel thought she looked like a queen. She hoped Antonia wouldn't be too upset with Maria's plan. "I promise to tell all my stories in Guarani."

"You can tell them however you want to, querida."

"Do I have permission to stay and tell more of them to your esteemed patrons?"

"Because the person you're spying on is still upstairs."

Isabel pursed her lips, widening her eyes and blinking in confusion. "Spying? I'm here for the food and the company and to tell you how much I missed your fried sardines."

"That's why you're watching the stairs like a wolf." The woman clucked her tongue. "Does the poor man know what's in store for him when he's done?"

"Do you hear the wolf coming?"

"He better have paid before you drag him off."

"We'd never cheat anyone out of what she's owed. We'll cover everything."

Antonia arched a thick black eyebrow. "We?" Before Isabel could answer, she was waved off. "Fine. But if you girls put holes in my port barrels again, you owe me double with interest."

Isabel nodded and murmured a promise even though her attention had jumped to the tavern entrance. As she didn't know precisely what interest was, her undivided attention would have made little difference to her response. Maria handled the money. She'd never had the patience to focus and hold all those figures in her head. What need was there to count beyond the coins necessary to buy food, drink, and the occasional new pair of boots? There was so much in the world far more deserving of her attention.

Like the tall figure who'd entered, in a broad straw hat, that was almost out of place in the late summer sun. Without a word to anyone, Maria took a position in the corner opposite the bar.

Isabel smiled in anticipation and slipped through the crowd toward the bar. While squeezing between tables, she lifted a brilliant yellow shawl off the shoulders of a woman, laying a coin on the table in front of her.

"This is lovely. Is it for sale? Should be. Yellow isn't really your color."

She didn't wait for an answer and swept past the now speechless and well-compensated woman with the newly acquired shawl draped over her head. She plucked a red carnation from the lapel of a young man and tucked it behind her ear. This she paid for with a wink.

"Oi, amigo!" Isabel called to the barkeeper's rear end, the front end being busy with a wine barrel on the floor. She reached out over the bar, a small stone resting in her hand. In a thick Bahian accent, she said, "The fancy Bat upstairs sent this down and said to buy drinks for the house. But I think he must be mad. I don't know what he expects to get with a rock."

The barkeeper spun around and snatched the stone out of her palm. His eyes grew wide and darted around the courtyard. He shoved the rock in his apron's pocket and bellowed, "Next drink is on a very satisfied customer."

Isabel backed away into the grateful and apparently very thirsty crowd surging toward the bar. She dropped the shawl on the back of a random girl and the carnation on the ground as she found a spot in the corner of the courtyard, where Maria leaned against the wall. She accepted a red and black skirt from Maria and slipped it over her brown one, a small frown on her lips.

"*Santa Regina*, you've picked the worst spot in the room. We'll have a terrible view from here."

"Don't worry. You won't miss anything." Maria nodded toward the front door. "Here they come."

A regiment of soldiers burst into the courtyard. All movement and noise stopped as the soldiers leveled their rifles at the patrons. An officer stepped forward, and the amount of baubles decorating his coat announced his authority.

"Senhores e senhoras," the officer announced. He tipped his head to a group of younger women. "Senhoritas. I'm here on behalf of His Royal Highness the Prince Regent. If you all cooperate and demonstrate your loyalty to His Highness, there will be no cause for distress or any unpleasantness. We have reason to believe a smuggler is doing business out of this establishment. Turn him over and there will be no further repercussions. Make any attempt to conceal him, and we will arrest you."

Antonia stepped forward. "We don't want any trouble. We're all loyal subjects of His Highness here." She cut her eyes toward the corner, and Isabel felt the force of her gaze from across the room. "Smugglers know they're not welcome. I haven't seen any here. Bernardo?"

The woman turned to the barkeeper and fixed him with a pointed look. The man could not have looked more distraught if he'd been asked to hand over his own child. He pulled out the stone Isabel gave him.

"The royal guardsman in the second bedroom upstairs. He paid for his drinks with this."

"A Guardsman?" The officer accepted the stone and raised his eyebrows as he held the raw diamond up to the lamp light. He looked to the soldiers nearest the stairs. "Bring him down."

Four men charged up the stairs. A murmur ran through the crowd that was quickly silenced by the sound of a door being kicked in. Men shouted. A woman shrieked. One man cursed loud enough to be heard above the cannon fire in the bay. Isabel recognized the voice, delight pricking her skin at the protests.

A smile crept across her face as the soldiers dragged the beet-faced Bat down the stairs and into the courtyard. He was still sweating despite the evening breeze and still angry despite the amount of pleasure he'd purchased in the last hour. Some people just didn't want to be happy.

Isabel was not one of them and delighted in the spectacle of the growling and spitting Bat tossed at the feet of his superior. She looked around for a plate of fried sardines or casava to nibble. A show was always better with dinner.

"Senhor, you will conduct yourself as befitting a representative of the crown of Portugal."

"What the hell is this?"

The officer's face hardened. "Search him. Check his coat and boots."

The struggle that erupted reminded Isabel of a fat capybara taking a drink near a nest of caiman. The Bat bellowed and flailed as four soldiers peeled his coat off and attempted to search his pockets. In the flailing, a leather sack fell to the ground. The commanding officer picked it up.

"This feels like an excellent payday, senhor. Where did a Guardsman come by such wealth?"

"That's mine. I earned it. Get your goddamn hands off me."

Maria raised her eyebrows in surprise. "He didn't strike me as brave enough to curse a lieutenant."

"He's not." Isabel pulled a nearly empty canteen from the leather pouch on her hip. Her eyes twinkled. "But the cachaça is. I thought he deserved a little extra after such a trying afternoon. I was topping off his drinks all night."

"He'd thank you if he wasn't busy."

"No thanks necessary. I was happy to do it."

The officer emptied the contents of the bag. Maria's share of the payment for their delivery spilled onto the table, but the officer didn't glance at the coins. He fondled the sack in his hand frowning. With a flick of his wrist, the officer turned the sack inside out. He drew a knife and sliced the seam at the bottom of the bag.

Raw diamonds tumbled into the lamplight. The crowd gasped. The officer jerked away as if a pit viper had dropped out of the bag. The Bat gaped in horror at the incriminating evidence rolling across the table, and Isabel suppressed a laugh.

The Bat spluttered and spit, finally choking out, "That slut! She set me up. It's not mine."

"Did you not claim this as your earnings a mere moment ago?" The lieutenant looked at the Bat in disgust. "Now you're blaming some woman for the stolen diamonds in your coin purse?"

"She gave me the sack. I didn't know the diamonds were there. That bitch set me up!"

Antonia marched up, chest puffed out and arms waving. "How dare you try to blame some poor girl! What kind of a man sacrifices a girl to hide his own crime? Get him out! Get that lying bastard out of my inn!"

The crowd took up Antonia's cry, and curses rained down upon the Bat's head. Many were quite creative, and Isabel made a point of remembering them. The Bat screamed back at the rising tide of anger against him. He seemed unaware of the fact he'd been stripped of authority, and the crowd he insulted was no longer obliged to tolerate it. Isabel couldn't decide if the old Bat was willfully stubborn or delusional. He was certainly entertaining.

"There's no mercy for smugglers. You will forfeit all your property and be imprisoned for life." The Portuguese lieutenant assessed the mostly Brazilian and angry crowd. Based on his clenched jaw, he'd made the smart decision to worry. "Take this man to the jail. A wagon leaves for Tijuco prison at sunrise. He'll be on it. Let's go."

The soldiers dragged the Bat from the inn to the crowd's cheers. The marimba players resumed playing, and the plunk of their mallets on the wooden bars followed the last soldier out the door. Antonia walked over to the sisters and tossed Maria the empty leather bag. "I'd have gotten your diamonds back, but the good officer confiscated them. Coins, too. That's a high price to pay for revenge, girls."

"He was rude," Maria said.

"That looked like more than ten carats!"

"He was very rude," Isabel added.

"Nossa Senhora, you two are going to wind up in the stocks," Antonia laughed, shaking her head.

"Will you come visit us, Dona?" Isabel asked.

"Absolutely not. I can't risk my reputation by taking up with criminals. I have a business to run. You're on your own, girl."

"Speaking of business," Maria interrupted. She held out a small pouch. "For the door."

"Maria Azevedo, you can't afford all this."

"I told you we'd cover everything." Isabel reached for the pouch, linked arms with Antonia, and dropped it in her apron pocket. "Sister, we should give Dona Antonia something for the girl upstairs. I'm sure the boiled lobster didn't bother to pay before getting arrested. Don't worry about the money, Dona. We have all we need, and we'll get more. There's always another job."

"Not if we're late," Maria said. "We need to go. Mateus is waiting."

Through an open window, a clock chimed quarter to ten. Isabel quickened her pace as they crossed Largo do Paço. Mateus was probably waiting for them at Dom Antonio's home.

On the opposite side of the square, newly installed whale-oil lamps lit up the walls of the royal palace. The royal family commandeered the building from the viceroy upon their arrival. Prince João was renovating a manor in the hills, but for now the entire royal family lived in, worked in, and greatly disrupted the heart of Rio de Janeiro.

Still, Rio's elite seemed to support the court. In fact, most people adored the Prince Regent. After being nothing more than a name on every official decree, Prince João now strolled through the streets of Rio. Isabel supposed for some people the court's presence in Rio was just shy of having God show up for dinner. If God then asked to borrow your house indefinitely and ate all the chicken.

They were at the east edge of the square that ran along the beach and even with the front doors of the palace. Light eased out of the open second-floor windows and carriages were lined up along the front doors. The hand-kissing ceremony was still going on. The drivers and horses were ready to race away the second their lord or lady's rear hit the seat, exhausted from a long evening of standing in line waiting to kiss the Prince Regent.

"Isabel, are you listening? I want to talk about the farm," Maria said.

"Not the farm!" she groaned. "*Santa Angela,* I thought that was momentary madness from the heat. You will never convince me to move to a farm in Bahia. I will enlist in the Portuguese Army before that happens." She wasn't bluffing. How could Maria consider giving up what they had? For beans? For quiet? She shuddered.

"Isn't a farm what we've been saving for?"

"No, we've been saving for when the mines dry up, and we don't have any other choice. Which will be years from now."

"But we're having problems with soldiers and Bats today." Maria stopped and locked eyes with Isabel. "There'll be a time we won't be able to save ourselves with a trick. We were close to being in real trouble today."

Isabel clapped her hands together, rubbing them back and forth. "I can't wait for real trouble. Where is the real trouble? I want to meet it."

Maria ignored her. "Isabel, I'm tired. Rio's my home, but I don't want to be on guard every second waiting for the worst to happen. I've been running the train for five years and I. . . I don't think I love it as much as Papa did."

The confession stopped Isabel in her tracks. She'd never heard Maria even hint at being unhappy with their lives. How long had she been feeling this way? Why hadn't she said something?

Maria didn't acknowledge Isabel's surprise and barreled on ahead. "A farm. Outside a city. We still work for ourselves. We hire men. Give them jobs—"

A high-pitched cry rose over rolling waves.

"Shh!" Isabel ran up and grabbed Maria's arm, jerking her to stop.

"What is it?"

"Did you hear that?"

She went to the edge of the stone wall separating the square from the beach, the sand a five-foot drop down. Isabel held her breath and listened. The warm night air carried the sound of Guanabara Bay lapping at the sand. The shrill chirp of a bat. A cry for help.

She leapt onto the sand and glanced back at Maria. "What are you waiting for?"

Her sister hesitated. Isabel knew what Maria was thinking. They were supposed to meet Mateus. The voice cried out again, higher pitched and more desperate.

"He'll live," Isabel shouted over her shoulder already racing up the beach. A second later, Maria ran along-side her. They stopped in front of five hulking shadows looming over a girl in a pale dress.

Isabel drew her daggers. It was good to be home.

Chapter Three

Victoria

As the ninety-seventh petitioner brought his lips to the Prince Regent's sweaty hand, Victoria wondered if she wouldn't have been better off staying in Lisbon and taking her chances against Napoleon's army. It was a horrible and treasonous thought, which she shook from her head. It was the most she'd moved in two hours.

In front of her, Prince João VI and his wife, Princess Carlota Joaquina sat flanked by their four oldest children standing at attention. Victoria had a view of the most important backsides residing in South America, but her gaze never left the white-haired woman slumped in a seat at the far left. Her mistress stayed awake long enough to be announced as Queen Maria I of Portugal then promptly began snoring. It was not the dramatic display the court gossips hoped for from Mad Queen Maria, but the line of petitioners still stretched to the street.

The queen would wake at any moment. It was a miracle she'd remained asleep this long, and imagining Her Majesty's reaction to a sweltering room filled with strange faces gawking at her left Victoria feeling queasy. She clenched her jaw as a viscount denounced his neighbor to Prince João for stealing his guinea fowl.

Victoria tried not to be critical of others, but she didn't believe the viscount's missing guinea fowl required the crown's intervention and Her Majesty's presence. Neither did the colonel's dispute with his tailor nor the coffee farmer's plea for more rain. She considered weather to rest firmly in the hands of the Almighty, but the dozen plantation owners who'd knelt before the Prince Regent during that evening's hand-kissing ceremony clearly felt His Highness had some sway.

Victoria did not, otherwise her mistress would have been asleep in her own bed.

She'd been fortunate enough to avoid the hand-kissing ceremony since entering the queen's service seven years earlier. Due to her condition, Her Majesty had never been called upon to attend back in Lisbon and had been essentially forgotten in her convent rooms during the past year in Rio.

Until this evening.

When the Prince Regent's valet delivered the summons to the queen's chamber, Victoria had begged him to inform His Highness that his mother was ill. She tried to explain the queen's need for routine and familiar faces. She reminded him of the crossing from Lisbon and the weeks Her Majesty spent screaming for help thinking she was being kidnapped.

The valet's visit ended with the maids drawing straws to see who would attend the queen during the ceremony.

The ninety-eighth petitioner asked to be excused from military service on account of a limp. Her Majesty coughed, and Victoria clenched the front of her skirt. The ninety-ninth asked for his son's prison sentence to be reduced. Her Majesty rolled her head to the other shoulder, and Victoria's leg began to jiggle.

A rotund sugar cane farmer was announced. As he bowed deeply to the Prince Regent, the queen smacked her lips and swallowed. Dread flooded through her veins. Victoria looked around, at a loss for whose permission she needed to escort the queen from the room. The farmer made a second sweeping bow to Princess Carlota Joaquina, and Victoria stifled a whimper. She didn't dare interrupt the obviously wealthy petitioner and address the royal family directly. The soldiers weren't close enough to hear her whisper. There wasn't a regiment of ladies-in-waiting nearby waiting for a signal to assist their mistress. Since being removed from daily court life, the queen was attended by a handful of untitled servant girls.

Her Majesty sat up and surveyed the room blinking. Victoria slipped along the back wall toward the nearest soldier. As the sugar cane farmer made to leave, he noticed the queen was awake and diverted toward Her Majesty. Victoria froze against the wall.

The farmer bowed at the waist and grasped Her Majesty's hand, bringing it to his puckered lips. He didn't see the blow coming. Queen Maria of Portugal slammed her fan down on the farmer's head.

"Help!" the queen shrieked. "Save me! A demon boar is trying to drag me to hell. God, save me. I'm damned, and the devil has come for me."

Victoria rushed toward her mistress, her only concern getting the queen back to her chambers with no permanent damage to anyone. Unable to raise a hand against his sovereign, the farmer remained bowed, shielding his face from the blows raining down on his head, and trapped without protocol for taking leave of royalty in the midst of delusion.

In a low voice, Victoria pleaded, "Your Majesty, please allow me to escort you back to your room."

"The demon will not take me. I will not surrender to the devil."

"Your Majesty, it's Victoria. I can—" She caught the queen's fan in her eye on the backswing. Tears blinded her. She tried to blink them away and see to dodge the next swing.

"Ladies and Gentleman," a booming voice filled the room, startling the raving queen and whimpering farmer into silence. Princess Carlota Joaquina addressed the shocked petitioners. "Her Majesty is clearly exhausted from an evening with her devoted subjects. It is a great tragedy that the French dogs have forced Her Majesty to flee her beloved home and suffer the effects of a tropical climate to which she is unaccustomed."

"We're all damned!" Queen Maria shrieked, pointing at the princess. "The devil is here!"

The room stilled. No one dared exhale. Even the ocean seemed to hesitate.

Her Highness turned away from the petitioners and stepped toward the queen and Victoria. "Help Her Majesty to her chambers." Two soldiers moved in response to the princess's order. "And please inform Her Majesty once she has rested, that we are all honored she would risk her health in order to be with her subjects on this momentous evening."

The soldiers each gripped an elbow, easily lifting the queen off her feet and propelling her from the room. At the door, Victoria risked one glance back. The young princes and princesses all stared grim-faced in any direction but their grandmother's. The Prince Regent pulled a chicken breast out of his pocket and began nibbling nervously. Only Princess Carlota Joaquina watched their retreat with a rage that chilled Rio's summer air and sent a shiver through Victoria. She knew what the look meant. The evening's public outburst would not be forgotten or forgiven, and she would be held responsible.

As they cut through the palace, Her Majesty branded the soldiers servants of the devil and screamed for help. Victoria raced ahead and threw open the door to the queen's chambers. At the sight of familiar surroundings, the queen bolted from the soldiers straight into her bedroom. Victoria followed, ignoring the two maids gaping from the sitting area.

The queen paced the length of her bed and clawed at the neck of her dress. She scratched her scalp. The fits had gotten worse since arriving in Rio. A three-months Atlantic crossing had undone what little was left of Her Majesty's sanity.

The screaming now occurred with the same frequency and intensity as when her father was brought on as Her Majesty's surgeon. He'd supported the new medical philosophies coming out of Austria and believed the insane should be treated humanely. Even if they couldn't be cured, their condition could be greatly improved through compassion, and he'd been right. Her Majesty's fits decreased.

Her father believed much of the world's ills could be treated with a healthy dose of compassion.

But her father was gone. All Her Majesty had left was an orphan girl who had picked up some skills hovering at her father's elbow, but who's primary distinction in the palace was the ability to administer the queen's tonic without losing a finger. It was no wonder Her Majesty had deteriorated.

Victoria searched the room for something to break through the hysteria before the queen started tearing out her hair. She snatched up a blanket embroidered with two emerald green dragons clutching a golden crown over a ruby red shield.

"Look, Your Majesty. It's your coat of arms. The symbol of the House of Braganza. Isn't it beautifully done?"

"Where's João?" the queen demanded. Her eyes locked on the dragons. "Is he safe?"

"Yes, Your Majesty. The Prince Regent is in the receiving room for the hand-kissing ceremony." Victoria laid the blanket on the bed and risked moving closer to the queen. "He's well-guarded and surrounded by his devoted subjects and loving family."

"I have to help him. I have to protect him from the Spanish witch." The queen lunged and clutched the front of Victoria's dress. "That devil wants the throne!"

"Then you must protect him." Victoria saw her opening. Family was the one topic that could still reach the monarch buried under the madness. Usually. Hopefully. If she was lucky, which she had admittedly not been of late. "In order to protect His Highness, you will need your strength. You should rest in order to rise early tomorrow."

"Yes, I must be ready."

Victoria helped Her Majesty recline on the bed. She didn't attempt to change the queen into a sleeping gown when the refuge of sleep was so close. Dealing with delirium clarified priorities. Sufficient sleep and meals should be pursued at all costs regardless of the proper dress or serving utensils. Victoria was grateful to have learned that lesson and considered it a silver lining to an otherwise difficult situation.

Stubborn optimism was a crucial trait for dealing with crazed royalty. She fell back on it now, as she adjusted the pillow behind Her Majesty's head. "Tomorrow will be another beautiful day in Rio. Perhaps His Highness will come for a visit."

"I must protect my son from the Spanish whore."

"Don't worry, Your Majesty. I believe Her Highness intends go out on the bay tomorrow."

"Maybe she'll drown." The queen fell asleep with a smile on her lips.

Victoria sighed. The queen had hated her daughter-in-law for as long as she could remember, but the paranoia had grown since arriving in Rio. She blamed the heat. It was impossible to think clearly when a person perspired even in their sleep.

She desperately wanted a cool cloth against her face, and when Her Majesty's snores filled the room, Victoria slipped out in practiced silence. The maids in the sitting room pounced the moment the door clicked.

"You let her have a fit during the ceremony? In front of everyone?"

"What were you thinking? Why didn't you bring her back earlier?"

"Why didn't you give her one of those tonics you make?"

"Isn't that why you're here, *doctor's daughter*?"

The girls hurled their accusation in whispers. The queen's screams and Princess Carlota's booming voice came back, along with the furious hushed gossip of the court members as they fled the ceremony.

Victoria covered her ears and shook her head. "There was nothing I could do. I couldn't interrupt the ceremony."

"Thanks to you, Her Majesty is going to be difficult for a month."

"Two months!"

"Her Highness will be furious!"

Victoria's face burned. Sweat raced down her back. The air felt sticky and clogged her lungs. She couldn't catch her breath. She was suffocating. "I'm terribly sorry. I must excuse myself. I feel ill."

She turned and fled. Not only from the queen's chambers, but from the convent. She ran through the square, passing the royal palace where the lights still burned in the receiving room. She raced to the water's edge and would have commandeered a boat back to Lisbon if she knew how to sail. But she couldn't sail. She couldn't even swim. She was trapped.

How had she come to be standing in her best dress ankle-deep in the Atlantic on the coast of Brazil?

Napoleon.

The Prince Regent ordered the evacuation of Lisbon with three days warning. From the deck of the *Royal Prince*, Victoria watched men and women plead with stone-faced soldiers for permission to board. Carriages and trunks sat abandoned along the road. Paintings in gilded frames and Persian rugs lay soaking up the mud. She remembered the shards of a bed frame scattered across a dock. Families abandoned their luggage at the dock, grabbing whatever they could hold in their arms.

More than ten thousand people evacuated on that misty November morning. Her Majesty had sailed with the Prince Regent. Their ship carried more than a thousand passengers. People slept on the deck with barely room to roll over. There were no blankets. Although by the time they reached the equator, nobody wanted one. They'd passed ten listless days under the equatorial sun. The stench of evaporating vomit mixed with hundreds of sweat-soaked bodies, and in Her Majesty's cabin, the queen screamed for deliverance from her captors.

Victoria was most assuredly trapped in Brazil because she would never set foot on a ship again.

She reached down and splashed the bay's cool water on her face.

As she licked the salty drops from her lips, Victoria realized this was the first time she'd walked alone on the beach since arriving in Rio. She'd dreamed of studying the local botany and filling a book with sketches of the local medicinal plants, but the city proved overwhelming. In the year since the court's arrival, she'd not ventured beyond the square next to the palace except as part of the queen's entourage. Brazil was supposed to be part of the Portuguese empire, but it didn't feel very Portuguese to Victoria. Not that she had much experience on which to base that conclusion after spending the past year clinging to Her Majesty's skirts. Her father would have filled a dozen journals in that time. He wouldn't recognize the timid servant she'd become. Victoria didn't recognize herself.

Maybe if she had a friend to explore with, she wouldn't have felt so intimidated, but it had been years since she last had someone who fit the definition of friend. After her father died and she went from royal physician's daughter into the queen's service, her old friends didn't have time for a maid who changed chamber pots. The other maids didn't have time or trust for the physician's daughter.

She was stuck between two worlds and between was a surprisingly lonely place to be.

But it didn't have to be boring. She stood on a tropical beach under a clear sky and full moon. The sand shone silver in the moonlight, and the water of the bay a squid ink black. She couldn't imagine a more perfect time for a first walk in Rio.

She slipped her shoes and stockings off and wiggled her toes in the cool sand. A wave washed over her feet, and she let out a shocked giggle. The icy Atlantic water stung like a thousand needles against her bare skin. It was a delicious pain against the stifling summer heat. Victoria strolled along the beach away from the palace. The waves lapped the shore on her right, and bats chirped in the trees on her left.

Victoria was staring up at the stars, her nose filled with salt air and fish, when she heard a whistle. Five men strolled toward her. She didn't realize she was in trouble until they laughed.

Chapter Four

Isabel

I sabel clenched her jaw. Five hulking shadows loomed over a much smaller shadow scrambling in the sand. Five men against one girl. She spun the daggers in her hands and picked which stomach she'd pierce first.

"Get away from her," Maria ordered with her pistol drawn and whip free.

The five shadows stopped short. The man in the center barked a laugh. The others joined in. Isabel knew who the leader was and fixed her gaze on the wide belly in the middle.

"Maybe you didn't hear my sister over the waves. Get away from the girl. Now," Isabel growled.

"Are you giving us orders, girly?" The center man lurched a step forward. "It's a good thing you showed up. You need a lesson in manners."

In the moonlight, Isabel could make out the man's mustache and balding head. She caught a whiff of cachaça. Of course. Predictable. The leader raised a bottle to his mouth, the contents sloshing. Drops of cachaça sparkled in his mustache. She exchanged a look with Maria who put her pistol away.

"Do us all a favor and jump in the ocean." Isabel sniffed loudly. "I can smell you from here."

"Oh, girly." The man with the soggy mustache pulled another swig from his bottle. "I'm going to enjoy this."

There was a hiss in the darkness. Then a crack. The man raised his hand. In it he clutched the top of half of a broken bottle. The bottom half lay in shards, the remaining cachaça soaking into the sand.

Maria twitched the whip in her hand. "No. You're not."

The night exploded in a series of cracks. One drew a shout from the pig in the center, and the remainder of his cachaça bottle fell to the sand. Another crack and a pistol dropped. A third and the men collectively shrieked and scattered. Isabel grinned, her teeth gleaming white in the moonlight. She always enjoyed how quickly a drunk man's voice could climb from low curses to shrill yelps.

A whimper caught her attention.

The girl crawled up the beach toward the square. Isabel raced to her side and hauled her up. "Are you hurt?"

"No, no. They didn't hurt me. I'm fine." The girl's voice and body trembled.

"You're not. Let's get you up and away from the drunks." Isabel lead the shivering girl toward the road but noticed a shadow charging towards them. "Wait here. I'll be back."

Fortunately, some people didn't know when they were beaten. Otherwise Maria would get all the fun.

Gliding towards the oncoming shadow, Isabel spun her daggers. Anticipation for impact built in her chest, the need to charge, to strike. The shadow raised his own weapon, a stick of some sort. Too slow. Her knives flashing in the moonlight, she slashed his wrist, sending the stick to the ground, spun under his arm slashing the back of his knee, and brought the butt of her blade down on the drunk's head as he dropped to one knee. The man hit the sand face first and didn't move again.

"Sorry to leave you like that. He was a brute, wasn't he? Moved like a drunken sloth." She cocked her head, considering. "It would've been nice to have a little more of a challenge. I've only had capybaras to hunt for the last two weeks, and they put up more of a fight than he did." Isabel slipped her knives back in her skirt and reached out to take the girl's arm, but at her touch the girl leapt back against the stone wall.

She examined the girl for the first time and almost regretted slashing the man's knee. Not because she cared a whit for failed rapists, but because she'd clearly scared the girl. . . no, young woman. Up close she appeared older than her whimpering suggested. Based on her narrow skirt, the high waist, touch of lace at the collar, and the fact she was alone on the beach, Isabel guessed the girl was neither from Rio, nor from a class that saw street brawls on a regular basis. Her already wide eyes looked about to fall out of her head. The knee slashing might have been a bit much for her.

"I'm not going to hurt you. My sister and I came to help you." Isabel pointed down the beach. "See? She's finishing up with the last of them."

One man still stood. Climbed actually. He tried to get over the wall and onto the square. As he pushed himself up on his hands, Maria lashed her whip around one of his arms and jerked it out from under him. The man's face bounced off the stone ledge before he fell back on the sand. He hurled a curse at Maria and lunged.

"Oh dear, that wasn't smart of him." Isabel clucked her tongue and leaned against the wall next to the young woman. "Why do you think men have such a hard time surrendering to a woman? A better fighter is a better fighter, right? A whip is a better weapon than a fist. If he'd dropped to his knees, and begged Maria to spare him, she would have. My sister's much more forgiving than me."

"After everything, she would walk away?"

"Maria never attacks first. She only defends, which I think is a waste of talent and boring as hell. She says it's about control." Isabel rolled her eyes. "She told me the other day I should work at it, but if I'm going to work at something, I'd rather work at breaking a bastard's nose. It seems more likely to leave a lasting impression. I don't know a man who walked away from a fight admiring his enemy's control."

Isabel flashed a friendly smile, but the girl watched Maria as she spun the handle of the whip and clocked the last drunk under his chin. The man's head snapped back. He fell in stages, staggering down to the sand, and didn't get up. Maria turned and walked toward them without giving the men a second glance.

"Nossa Senhora," the probably Portuguese girl murmured.

"I know." Isabel grinned. "She's amazing." A surge of pride swelled her chest—Maria, her unstoppable sister.

"I was referring to both of you." The girl looked at her with eyes wide enough to reflect the moonlight. "Who are you? How did you learn to do…?" She pointed at the bodies scattered over the sand. "It was remarkable."

"Before we get to know each other, we should find a safer place to talk. Somewhere away from the unconscious drunks," Maria said, striding up.

"There's light around the palace. We could peek through the windows and maybe catch a glimpse of a prince or princess. Maybe the Mad Queen herself!" Isabel swung herself over the wall and onto the street. The girl coughed and looked down at the sand.

"I'm not sure the guards are any less dangerous. This time of night, they'll think we're prostitutes." Maria followed Isabel over the wall.

"The guards won't bother you," the girl wheezed. She was on her stomach attempting to hike a leg over the edge of the wall, but her foot tangled in her dress. She kicked in the air as though trying to swim then fell back down to the sand. Isabel choked back a laugh at the helpless display.

"For the love of *Santa Rita*, no wonder this girl got attacked. She won't last a month in Rio," she muttered.

She was now certain the girl was Portuguese based on her accent and general incompetence. The combination was rather adorable. Her curls bounced as she tried to kick over the wall. Isabel had never seen anyone look quite so cute while floundering like a beached fish. She and Maria each grabbed an arm and hauled her onto the street.

"Thank you, and not only for the wall. You saved my life. I'm indebted to you both." The girl curtsied.

Definitely Portuguese.

"It was our pleasure." Isabel matched the girl's formality, throwing in the semblance of a curtsy with a laugh. "That's a lot harder than it looks. How did you learn? Did you practice in front of a mirror? You must spend a lot of time in front of the mirror to get curls that perfect."

"We need to move," Maria interrupted, glancing back down the beach. "Miss, why won't the guards arrest three women alone in the middle of the night in front of the palace?"

"Because I work at the palace."

Isabel's eyebrows shot up. Not just Portuguese but a servant in the palace. God in his wisdom was clearly rewarding them for dispatching a corrupt Bat and five drunks in one afternoon. Her curiosity spiked. "You work in the palace? Doing what? Can you get me into the kitchen? The smells that drift out of there are to die for." She glanced at Maria. "This is turning into a better night than when we sent that groping merchant back to Portugal in a cask of cachaça."

"I'm afraid I don't work in the kitchen." The girl fidgeted with the ribbon at the waist of her dress. Finally, she answered, "I'm one of the queen's attendants."

"The queen!" Isabel shrieked, grabbing the girl's arm. "What does the Mad Queen look like? Is she really mad? I've been dying to see the royal family. I saw one of the great aunts. I think. She was in a litter, so it was hard to tell."

"Can we talk while walking?" Maria suggested.

"Yes. Yes. We're going." Isabel linked arms with her new friend and strolled back towards the palace.

"Who are you?" the maid asked. In the lamplight, she stared at Isabel as if watching a constrictor suffocate its prey, fascinated but also a little bit horrified. The expression left Isabel humming with satisfaction.

"I'm Isabel, and this is my sister, Maria." Anticipating the next question as the maid frowned, she added, "My adopted sister."

"Are you some kind of municipal guard? Are women allowed to be police in Rio?"

Maria snorted. "No. Do they let women be police in Portugal?"

"Goodness, no. How did you learn to fight? You both were fearless. It looked as though you've been training your whole lives," Victoria stated.

"We have," Isabel said. "You can't grow up alongside a mule train and not get comfortable fighting."

"Your parents allowed you to accompany mule trains?"

"My father was a muleteer. He learned the trail from his father," Maria explained. "After our mother died, he wasn't going to abandon us, so he brought us with him. Now I run the train with Isabel."

"I cook, clean, sew, and provide entertaining conversation. Basically, I do everything while Maria pets her horse and cracks her whip," Isabel added, tossing a grin at her sister's raised eyebrow.

Rather than annoy, this girl's continuous wide-eyed expression drew Isabel in. The maid seemed to be in awe of them. The Portuguese regularly stared at her but never in amazement and gratitude. This woman curtsied to Brazilians, walked alone at night, something most of the displaced court members seemed to avoid at all cost, and worked for the insane queen. Isabel decided this unusual person was worth knowing. "You still haven't told us your name."

"Oh, I'm terribly sorry. How rude of me." The girl placed a hand on her chest. "I'm Victoria Cruz from Lisbon. It is a pleasure to meet you both. I believe I owe you my life." She dropped another curtsy.

"That's the second time I've been curtsied to," Isabel laughed. "I love it."

"Victoria, why were you on the beach at night?" Maria asked. "It's a terrible idea."

"I realize that now," Victoria sighed. Her body sagged under a weight Isabel hadn't expected to be there. She served the queen. What could possibly cause a sigh that deep? Victoria twisted the ribbon of her dress. "There was an incident at the hand-kissing ceremony. Her Majesty. . . well, something upset her. I got blamed. I was about to suffocate and had to escape for a moment."

"From the palace?" Now Isabel was the one staring in open fascination. "Why would you want to escape the palace?"

"Sorry to interrupt," Maria said, shooting Isabel a look, which she pretended not to notice. This girl had a story worth a chest of gold, and Isabel was desperate to hear it. Then she felt Maria's hand on her arm. "We're late to meet a friend."

"Mateus! I completely forgot." She grabbed Victoria by the shoulders and planted a quick kiss on both cheeks, noting the maid smelled faintly of oranges. "It was nice to meet you, Victoria from Lisbon. Go straight inside the palace. No more midnight walks on the beach without a loaded pistol. A word of advice—you can stash an arsenal of weapons under a skirt like yours," she instructed. "Thanks again for the fun. I'm going to practice my curtsy." Isabel winked and turned to leave.

"Wait!" Victoria cried. "I meant what I said. I owe you. I'm only a servant, but if you ever think of a service I could offer you, please come find me. The Queen's chambers are in the convent behind the palace. You can ask for me at the kitchen door."

"We'll keep that in mind," Maria said.

"Tchau, Lisbon." Isabel waved as the girl dropped another curtsy and rushed into the palace through a servant's entrance.

They were very late.

Mateus had probably started negotiations without them. Dom Antonio reminded Isabel of a particularly ugly tapir. The animals disappeared into the under-brush at the slightest whiff of trouble, and for Dom Antonio trouble described almost everything except dinner. Mateus had been surprised the merchant wanted to work with them in the first place, but Isabel knew from years carting gold that the promise of wealth could rouse even the meekest man to bold acts of selfish-ness. It made them predictable and easy money. Since they started dealing with Dom Antonio, they doubled their savings.

And now Maria wanted to spend that savings on a farm.

They had years before the mines went dry. Once the gold ran out, then they could languish away on a porch, fanning themselves and watching coffee grow. Isabel wasn't opposed to a house with a feather bed and a separate kitchen. She simply assumed they'd be older when it happened and with knee problems that made swinging into a saddle more of a challenge.

She snuck a glance at Maria. Her sister's boots made almost no sounds on the stone, and her hand rested on the butt of her whip. Always on guard.

Maria's confession unsettled her, like a roach in your bed roll. Isabel agreed that the trail taxed the senses but had assumed Maria welcomed the challenges like she did. Living amongst predators, animal and human, Isabel woke every morning daring life to throw some-thing new at her.

What challenge would life throw at her on a farm? Locusts?

Maria's hand clamped around her arm, and she immediately drew her daggers.

The grand homes of the merchant class lined the street ahead, facing the bay. With buffers of palms and foliage between each house, the owners could wake up to the sound of the waves instead of the clatter of vendors and carts in the heart of the city. Civilization had only a tenuous grip here, and the forest stalked the edges of the manicured flora waiting to rush in.

Isabel scanned the dark for what had spooked Maria. Dom Antonio's house lay ahead, silent, still, and glowing as if hosting a party. Light spilled from every window. Dom Antonio had been expecting them. He wouldn't have lit the house like a beacon. In the sticky summer night, her hands were cold.

She followed Maria into the forest that lined the street opposite the mansions. They slipped through the shadows and stopped in the cover of a lush mango tree directly opposite Dom Antonio's home.

"Rapido! Vamos!" a man's voice commanded from inside the house.

"Bats!" Maria spit the word out like a curse.

Two men in long black coats stomped out of the very house where Mateus was supposed to be. There was no sign of him anywhere. Isabel hoped he was crouched behind his own tree. The darkness beneath the canopy was nearly absolute. He could be a few feet away, and they wouldn't know. Maybe he fell asleep waiting for them.

The breeze carried a low voice that brought to mind a coiled constrictor. Her hope vanished. She knew that voice. Her fists tightened, nails digging into the palms. Major Miguel Vidigal, commander of the royal guard, with a policy of beating first and arresting later, emerged from the house. The lamplight glinted off the silver handle of the whip at his hip. Two more Bats followed him out, Mateus suspended between them.

A wave of nausea rolled over Isabel at the sight of her friend's swollen eye and his wrists bound behind his back. Only minutes earlier she'd thought Maria ridiculous for wanting to leave Rio, overly cautious, even weak. Isabel had never regretted anything as much as dismissing her sister's fear. The scene playing out in the lamp light was exactly what Maria dreaded, and Isabel had waved away her concerns.

She also publicly provoked that Bat from the customs outpost. Had the royal guard followed Mateus from the bank looking for her and Maria? Was Mateus going to jail because she lost her temper? Guilt churned with regret, and Isabel fought to keep the sardines down. Mateus tripped and fell to the dirt, nearly pulling a Bat down with him. The Bat answered by slamming his fist into Mateus's stomach.

The world exploded into flame before Isabel's eyes. Her body moved without conscious command. She'd cut down every Bat that crossed her path. Mateus wouldn't suffer because of her mistake.

Isabel drew a deep breath to release a battle cry. As she stepped from behind the tree, a hand clamped over her mouth and a long arm pinned her arms to her sides. She struggled to breathe as she was dragged back into the forest.

Chapter Five

Maria

Maria tightened her grip on her sister. "Stop! We *can't* get arrested." She spun Isabel around so they were nose to nose and begged, "Please! Stay quiet! We can't help him if we're in jail or dead. We're his only chance."

Isabel nodded once, and Maria let go.

She stood rooted to the ground as her family was ripped apart, because whatever Mateus was today, he had always been family. She gripped Isabel's hand, who squeezed back, and together they watched until the last trace of Mateus was swallowed by the night.

"He's gone." Isabel's voice cracked.

Panic threatened to swamp Maria's thoughts. She forced herself to breathe, in and out, deep and slow. She'd imagined this scene a hundred times. It kept her awake and haunted her dreams. Now she watched it play out before her eyes and did nothing to stop it. Worse than that. Mateus was here at this place and this time on her orders. She left her partner alone. Shame lit a fire inside her.

She released Isabel's hand and moved silently across the street toward the house. No sign of life came from inside. The sounds of Vidigal and his men faded completely.

"What's the plan?" Isabel whispered. "Are we going to ambush them along the way or do you want to break him out of the jail later tonight?"

"Neither. We're checking the house."

"For what?" Isabel protested. "Are we going to lock up behind them? Turn down the lamps? We need to catch up to the Bats. They're taking Mateus to prison."

"I know where they're taking him and what they'll do to him!" Maria snapped. "But I *don't* know what the hell happened here. Where's Dom Antonio? What if they're taking him for questioning because of something Dom Antonio did? We need to know where we stand before we attack the commander of the royal guard and become criminals."

"We've been criminals for what is it…five years now."

"Vidigal doesn't know that. Do you want to announce it to him?"

Isabel twirled her knives, looking between the house and after the Bats. "Fine. I'll wait for now, but when we finally attack, I get to kill that snake Vidigal."

"Not if I get to him first," Maria said, her voice as sharp as her sister's blades. She pointed to a tree at the side of the house. "Up to the open window on the second floor."

"Race you."

Isabel took a few swift steps and leapt for the lowest limb, swinging easily into the branches. Maria followed and within moments swung through the window and landed silently on a thick imported carpet. Isabel dropped beside her. Maria raised an eyebrow at her sister.

"Your arms are twice as long. It's cheating," Isabel huffed.

Maria cracked a grin, despite the tension. "It's winning."

They were in a guest bedroom almost as large as their entire house. A four-poster bed dominated the space, awash with silk pillows embroidered with silver flowers. Lamp light gleamed off a rosewood vanity inlaid with ivory and mother of pearl that probably cost more than Maria would make in her lifetime. The extravagance baffled her. Did a hairbrush and mirror require their own table? How many pillows gave the best night's sleep? Only the mattress stirred envy. She'd spent her entire life sleeping in hammocks or pallets on the trail and secretly longed to flop on a bed after a long day.

They crept to the hall. Maria unfurled her whip and shook out her arm, the fight at the beach still in her muscles, but she didn't want to use the pistol. A single shot would bring the whole flock of Bats back on their heads. Surprise was one of the few advantages they had.

"If you were a rich Portuguese merchant with ties to the black market and your home was recently filled with royal guardsmen, where you would be?" Isabel asked.

"Checking on my money with a drink in hand," Maria muttered.

She slipped toward Dom Antonio's office at the end of the hall. In portraits lining the wall, martyrs and saints groaned in perpetual agony. Impaled by arrows, run through, throat slit, the wealthy couldn't get enough of other people's suffering. They displayed it in gilded frames throughout their homes. Maria wondered how far removed from pain a person had to be to consider it decorative.

The foyer chandelier glowed. Light spilled out the open front door, and the sounds of Guanabara Bay drifted in. Not a step echoed in the grand house. It stood lit up, open wide, and still as death.

"Where are the servants?" Maria mouthed. Isabel shrugged and raised her daggers higher.

They jerked to a stop at the door to Dom Antonio's office. The merchant lay face-down in the middle of the room.

"Oh shit," Isabel muttered. She rushed past Maria to the body and tried to roll him over, but it was like a mouse trying to flip a beached whale. She turned his face toward her and shrieked, dropping the head with a thunk. The Dom's eyes bugged out like a squished gecko. Isabel wiped her hands on her skirt. "That's going to give me nightmares."

"They arrested him for murder. Of a noble," Maria whispered from the doorway. Mateus would be executed for this. Without question. What really happened didn't matter. Justice didn't matter. The Court's focus would be sending a message, and Mateus would be their messenger. Because she wasn't there on time. He entered Dom Antonio's house alone. Maria had failed him as his captain and his friend.

"I don't understand," Isabel said. "Why would Mateus kill him?"

"You think Mateus did this?" Maria pointed at the corpse.

"To defend himself? Sure. I would."

Maria's eyes skipped around the room taking in the general disarray. Chairs were tipped over. A mirror lay in shards. The drawers from a cabinet were emptied and scattered across the floor, their polished teak and ebony shining in the lamp light. Embers smoldered in a dish on the desk. Maria sniffed. "Lemon grass. Lit not long ago and not for us. Antonio was expecting or had company. Something isn't right. It looks like a robbery but. . . Do you see a wound?"

Isabel glanced over the body. "No. No blood. No holes. Not a blemish. But he's definitely dead. Dammit, I was hoping we'd get to interrogate the pompous asshole." She shrugged. "Oh well, I'll settle for ambushing Bats instead."

"How did he die?"

"Who cares?" Isabel headed for the door.

Maria ignored her. She heaved the body onto its back, looking for a wound under the coats and cravats. "If there's no blood, how did he die?"

"For the love of *Santa Marina*, it doesn't matter. He's dead, and Mateus is getting blamed. It's time to go get our friend."

"Look!" Maria pointed at Antonio's neck. A brilliant red line encircled his throat. "He was choked. Thieves wouldn't choke a man. They'd stab him or shoot him."

"What does it matter? They've arrested Mateus for it, and they're going to kill him. Our friend, your partner, is going to be shot. We need to save him now."

"Look at this room! Do you really think this was a robbery?" Maria leapt to her feet and turned in a circle holding her arms out. Her sister didn't see it, but years in the forest had taught her that everything, jaguar, monkey, or man, *everything* leaves clues. A person can follow the clues if patient enough to notice the details. Maria saw the details, and they chilled her blood. "If this was a robbery, why is he still wearing his boots? What thief would leave behind a brand new pair of boots?"

"I don't care."

"It wasn't a robbery!" Maria struggled to keep her voice low. "Somebody *wanted* Antonio dead. They want it to look like a robbery, but this was an assassination."

Isabel shrugged, prompting an irritated huff from Maria. "Dom Antonio was greedy, arrogant, and bought favor with the Prince Regent. I bet a lot of people wanted to kill him. I've thought about it. How does this help Mateus?"

"I don't know!"

She paced the room. Maria knew the fate that awaited Mateus, but her instincts screamed caution. This wasn't random. Someone deliberately set Mateus up to cover their own tracks, and if the murderer was expecting Mateus, wouldn't he have expected the sisters, too?

Maria froze. "We have to leave."

"Thank you! That's what I've been trying to get you to do. We need to ambush Vidigal's men before they get to the prison."

"No, we need to find the murderer." She crossed to the door, careful not disturb a single sheet of paper.

"Why? To thank him? Forget about him, and let's save our friend."

"We'll get Mateus back. I swear it. But the murderer set Mateus up, Isabel. And *we* were supposed to be with Mateus."

Isabel's eyes widened. Maria could see the pieces clicking into place. *Finally.* "If he used Mateus, then he was trying to use us, too," she whispered.

"Maybe. The only way to know for sure is to find him. I know you're worried about Mateus but—"

"I'm in."

Maria frowned in surprise at Isabel. "I expected more of an argument."

"You thought I wouldn't want to track the murderer who dropped my friend in Vidigal's scaly hands and is possibly hoping to take us out, too?" Isabel flashed a sly smile, twirling her daggers. "Sister, you need a rest. You're not thinking clearly."

Floorboards creaked, and Maria darted to one side of the open door. Isabel took up position on the opposite side. She unfurled her whip at the sound of boots on the stairs. Maria counted two, no, three men's voices. They were coming towards the office. Her pulse thundered in her ears. She crouched slightly, balancing her weight, waiting.

"We load up the body and take it to the prison first," a deep voice ordered. "The commander wants to examine it."

"Did you hear that boy they brought in is free?" another voice snorted with laughter. "Claims to be a muleteer. And you know, I believe it. He smells like—"

Maria looped her whip around the man's neck and yanked his face straight into her knee. She felt the crunch of his nose through her pants. With the whip still around his neck, she spun him out of the doorway. Isabel moved in on the second. The sisters coordinated the attack with a combination of instinct, years of practice, and complete faith in the other.

Her sister slashed at the second man. Maria kicked her Bat's knee out and slammed his head into the wall. As he crumpled to the floor, she sent her whip hissing over Isabel's head. It caught the third man around his neck. Maria jerked him forward over the top of the two crumbled Bats. Isabel dealt a finishing blow with the butt of her knife to the back of his head.

Maria vaulted over the pile of broken men blocking the doorway, Isabel a step behind her. She got three steps down the hall and slammed to a halt. Major Vidigal watched from the top of the stairs, his hands resting on two pistols at his hips, the silver-handled whip coiled on his belt and a searching frown on his face.

"Good evening, ladies." He planted himself squarely in their path. "That was both surprising and impressive."

He spoke softly. This was not a man who needed to shout an order. Vidigal's actions spoke much louder than his words, and his whip was his most effective means of communication. Maria had seen it in action against a group of runaways.

He'd commanded the royal guard for less than a year, yet already cultivated a reputation most zealots needed decades to grow. He didn't look like a man to fear. His shoulders slumped forward hiding his height, and the perpetual stoop made him appear meek, even lazy. Maria knew better than to dismiss him.

The most dangerous animal on the trail wasn't the strong and sleek jaguar. It was the lumbering caiman, who basked unmoving in the sun. When the other animals let their guard down, the caiman slipped into the water unnoticed. It only appeared again directly under its prey, surging from the water and snapping its jaws closed around the animal's throat. Maria kept her eyes fixed on Vidigal as he moved deliberately down the hall.

"It is an amazing coincidence," he murmured. "I find two capable young ladies at a murder scene the same day I'm looking for a pair of colored girls who encountered one of my most experienced Bats at a customs post outside town." He drew his pistols but kept them pointed to the floor. "You wouldn't happen to be the girls I'm looking for?"

"No," Maria said. The man had taken Mateus. She would give him nothing else, not her words and not her time. If he wanted more, he had to fight for it.

Her whip hissed then cracked. Vidigal dropped one pistol. Before it hit the floor, Isabel's knives sliced through the air towards his head. The whip distracted him long enough that he barely noticed the flying blades in time.

Vidigal ducked the knives. Maria and Isabel leapt over the balcony and fell to the foyer. Maria landed, rolled to her feet, and charged for the open front door. The door frame exploded just as she passed by.

"Maria!" Isabel screamed.

"I'm fine. Go!"

Maria sprinted toward the forest. Isabel panted next to her. They plunged into the trees, leaping over some roots and stumbling over others. With the moonlight blocked by the trees, the ground disappeared in shadow. Memory, instincts, and luck kept Maria from slamming face first into a tree trunk.

After a minute of running, she recognized the silhouette of an amendoeira tree. Its low branches with dense, wide leaves created an impenetrable blackness. That was their chance. "Up!" she ordered Isabel.

Maria climbed until surrounded by thick leaves. The branches at that height barely supported her weight. Isabel hugged the trunk below her. They waited. Sweat dripped into her eyes, and she let it burn. Any movement, any rustle of leaves, and they'd be surrounded. The foliage muffled shouts from just below. Maria pressed her face into her arm to smother her own gasping breaths. She prayed the tree was snake-free. Her arms had no strength left to wrestle a boa constrictor.

Someone stomped under their tree. Their footsteps faded into the nocturnal chorus of frogs and insects. The sisters remained frozen. Two sloths wrapped around the trunk, still enough for moss to grow. Bats chirped and flitted through the branches around them. Time passed. An owl hooted. Maria's left foot went numb. Some animal snuffled in the brush below, and she decided it was safe to come down.

"Ewww!" Isabel moaned the moment her feet hit the ground. "My hair is full of bat shit."

"Please," Maria said.

"My hair isn't wrapped," her sister snapped.

"You'll have to wash it later. I need you to find the team. Tell them what happened and to disappear for a couple days. Vidigal knew about our run-in at the customs outpost. Mateus could say something. Either way, the Bats might be coming for them."

"I'm not running errands now. We're hunting a murderer and freeing Mateus."

Maria rounded on her. "Isabel! They won't shoot Mateus tonight, not before a trial. But they might round up my team." She grabbed her sister by the shoulders. They didn't have time to argue. There were too many loose ends to secure, too many people to keep safe. "I can't help Mateus and my team at the same time. I need your help."

Isabel shook her head. "I'm not letting you go to the jail by yourself."

"I'm not going to the jail. I swear. I need to see about our cargo, and I need you to take care of my team." Maria nudged her sister's foot, hating herself for playing on Isabel's loyalty but determined to keep at least her sister safe. "I can't hunt a murderer while carrying the cargo around. I'll drop it at the stable then meet you at home. Tell the team to hide, and I'll find them tomorrow at the capoeira circles. Please?"

"Fine. But Maria. . ." Isabel stepped close and went up on tip toe until her nose almost touched Maria's. "If you go to the jail without me, if you're sending me away to protect me from a mad rescue attempt, I will *never* forgive you."

"I know," she said. "Be silent. Stay in the shadows. On top of everything, we've got a Bat problem."

Maria waited until her sister's footsteps faded into the night. She whispered an apology then raced to the palace.

Chapter Six

Victoria

Victoria's hands stopped shaking by the time she helped a drowsy queen squat over the chamber pot, and she was able to hold Her Majesty steady, preventing any final mess for the evening. The night's events had left her feeling bruised and empty, like the scooped-out rind of a papaya, and she worried that even the tiniest accident would rip her in half. She pulled Her Majesty into a sleeping gown and read aloud from Psalms until the queen's eyes closed for the second and hopefully final time that night.

Victoria closed the door to the bedchamber and rested her forehead against the mahogany frame. She could still smell the cachaça on the men's breath. A shiver went down her back.

"Tired? I suppose it was an exhausting evening." The voice flipped her stomach and nearly brought up her dinner. Waiting in the light of a single lamp, a furious hurricane barely contained by her bodice, was Her Royal Highness the Crowned Princess of Portugal, the Duchess of Braganza, Carlota Joaquina.

Victoria dropped into a curtsey low enough to examine the nails in the floorboards. "Your Highness, Her Majesty has gone to sleep. If you'd like to see her—"

"I'm not here for that old cow," Carlota Joaquina snorted, rising from her chair. "I've seen enough of her for a hundred lifetimes. I pray every night for the hag to simply stay asleep."

Victoria continued to stare at the floor, withholding the retort crawling up her throat. She knew better than to react to Carlota Joaquina's treasonous words. They were only words after all. The queen wished for the princess's death on a regular basis, so the feeling was mutual. Betrothed to Prince João at the age of ten, Carlota Joaquina left Spain for the Portuguese court as a child, and Queen Maria should have been a second mother. To the great inconvenience of everyone, the two women wanted nothing more than to attend the other's funeral.

Victoria felt Carlota Joaquina's glower and reeled in her unspooling thoughts. "How may I be of service, Your Highness?"

"How may you be of service?" The princess's voice was as smooth as her silk gown. "An excellent question. Maybe one you should have asked yourself before you brought that raving lunatic to the ceremony tonight." Victoria dared to peek at Carlota Joaquina through her eyelashes. Rage twisted the heavy brow and pinched mouth into a face that would turn men to stone. "Do you have any idea the damage you've done?"

"Your Highness, I'm very sorry." Victoria's knees shook from holding the curtsey, but she stayed bent, head bowed. Apologizing was her only hope of placating the princess—even though Victoria advised the Prince Regent's messenger the queen should not attend the ceremony. She'd known two hours in a receiving line bidding good evening to hundreds of gawking strangers would overwhelm Her Majesty, and she'd been right.

But Victoria would apologize to Carlota Joaquina's feet because she had nowhere to go and no one to help her. If the incident on the beach proved anything, it was that she couldn't survive this city on her own. She needed her position at the palace, so she'd accept responsibility and beg forgiveness for the fact no one had listened to her. "I apologize for any inconvenience or embarrassment Her Majesty's outburst caused."

"Inconvenience!" Carlota Joaquina roared. "You stupid, sniveling girl! You have no idea what that cow's public display of madness has done. Tonight we announced the celebrations to commemorate the royal family's first year in Brazil. The most important members of Court were here. Every public official. These celebrations are crucial. Some of these ungrateful barbarians from this sweltering hell of a city still don't realize the honor the Court has bestowed on them by coming here. We needed to show that the House of Braganza is strong and thriving after the past year. But now…" Carlota Joaquina strode across the room slamming her feet directly under Victoria's face. "Stand up."

She rose but kept her gaze fixed on the floor. The princess exhaled in great gusts like the bulls her countrymen enjoyed stabbing for sport. She could easily imagine Carlota Joaquina staring down a bull and running it straight through the heart.

"Did you know before your father died, he was the only doctor the queen wouldn't attack on sight? It seemed fitting, a quack surgeon for a raving lunatic, and it was useful to have someone around who could administer her sleeping tonics. When he died, I gave you a position because I heard you had nowhere to go and because of your father's gift for charming lunatics.

Despite your complete lack of experience in service, I thought you could be useful. Are you still useful?"

"Yes, Your Highness. I will try harder." Victoria agreed out of self-preservation but remembered events differently from Her Highness.

The princess had respected her father. Victoria spent enough years assisting her father at the palace to be certain. Carlota Joaquina would never have allowed Victoria to tag along with the young princesses to their lessons if she hadn't valued her father and his service to the royal family. Then one day, after a decade of being a trusted confidant, everything changed. Carlota Joaquina loathed her father. Victoria still had no idea what happened or why that hatred seemed to have passed to her.

"I take full responsibility for the outburst tonight. The past year has been trying for Her Majesty, and her fits have been more unpredictable but—"

The backhand caught her on the right cheekbone. A ruby ring sliced her skin below the eye.

"I don't want excuses," Carlota Joaquina raged. "Do not waste my time with them. If the queen makes a spectacle of herself in public again, I will order you thrown out the kitchen door with nothing but the clothes you're wearing."

Through her tears, Victoria watched the future queen of Portugal stomp out of the room and slam the door behind her. The footmen outside the chamber could have closed the door, but Carlota Joaquina never missed an opportunity to display her displeasure. The palace doors received a regular beating.

She examined the cut in a hand mirror. This one wouldn't require stitches. Victoria took a deep breath and blinked back tears, refusing to let one fall. She found a clean piece of cotton in her medicine chest and pressed it against the cut.

Maybe Carlota Joaquina was right. Victoria served the queen. She had no family, no other work in the palace, no skill except remaining in Her Majesty's favor, which allowed her to minimize the fits. If Victoria couldn't keep the queen calm, she was of no use to anybody.

She had to do better.

With a single lamp burning, she pulled out her journal and arranged a pen and inkwell on the desk. She held the cloth to her cheek with her left hand and scribbled away with her right. In three columns, Victoria listed the queen's activities for the day, including meals and nap duration, the weather, and Her Majesty's behavior, noting any fits. One outburst during the hand-kissing ceremony.

It was her father's method. Observe and record. A compass he'd left behind to guide her. By the fire every evening, they sat in matching chairs and recorded their days. Her father detailed his patients' ailments, and she described the most interesting person seen that day. A flustered customer outside the bakery whose face was as pink as her dress. A sailor disembarking off a foreign ship with an arm carved from the blackest wood. A young woman whose lip trembled through the entire Mass.

When she was older and allowed to assist her father during exams, he reprimanded her for staring at Her Majesty. The scolding confused her because he watched patients every day. He explained there was a difference between staring and observing, so Victoria learned to watch out of the corner of her eye.

Her father came to value her observations, including them in his own notes. She felt proud, believing her contributions helped Her Majesty, but after watching the queen deteriorate since her father's death, Victoria knew he'd merely been placating a child. She was no physician. The best she could do is keep track of the queen's meals and ask for fish instead of beef.

A soft thud made Victoria jump, knocking the lamp. She caught the base before it crashed to the floor.

"Nice catch."

Victoria froze. Her throat closed in terror. Thieves. She'd been expecting to get robbed since arriving in Brazil. It was finally happening.

"I'm not going to hurt you. I wouldn't save you from a pack of drunkards only to rob you myself."

A tall, formidable young woman stood just inside the open window. The moonlight silhouetted her broad shoulders, the whip coiled at one hip, and a pistol on the other. Victoria eased to her feet and cautiously stepped from behind the desk.

"You saved me. You're. . ." Her brain groped for a name, but it was numb with fear at the prospect of a stranger inside the queen's chamber. If the other maids walked in, being tossed on the street would be the best she could hope for.

"Maria." The woman strode into the room, scanning the corners and shadows. "My sister Isabel and I fought off five drunkards for you."

Up close in the lamp light, Maria looked younger than Victoria first thought. In fact, they were probably close to the same age, around twenty and some. Maria's presence made her seem so much older. She walked with her head up and dark eyes fixed ahead as if challenging the world head on. Having spent a good portion of the past few years staring at floors, Victoria could confidently stare down a kitchen mouse and little else.

"How did you get in here?" Victoria tried not to gape.

"There's a tree at the north end of the convent. Climb it then jump onto the roof. From there it's a matter of swinging down into the right open window. Simple." Maria shrugged.

Simple. As though women climbed trees and jumped off roofs every day. "I'm afraid I must apologize. I know I said I would help you in any way, and I will, but it would be more convenient if we met somewhere tomorrow. It's my morning off. I can come see you then."

"You said you worked in the palace," Maria interrupted, frowning.

"I work for Her Majesty," Victoria stammered. She didn't want to be rude to her savior, but if Maria was discovered, Victoria would be held responsible. "It really would be better if we met tomorrow."

"Do you have access to the palace?" Maria demanded. She glared down with such intensity her soul seemed ready to explode from her body.

Victoria eased away from the urgency rolling off Maria. She thought of how the woman assessed the room right upon entering. Her gaze slid to the whip on Maria's hip. "Why are you here?"

"At this moment, a friend of mine is being beaten in a prison cell because I was late meeting him. I was late because of you. You owe me a favor."

"Your friend's a criminal?"

"He's not a criminal." Maria stepped forward, and Victoria cringed. The muleteer glanced at the cut on Victoria's cheek. Her expression softened, and Victoria knew Maria overheard at least some part of her confrontation with the princess. When she spoke again, Maria's voice was calm. "No, he's not a criminal. He's been arrested for a crime he didn't commit, and I need your help."

Victoria straightened at the softer tone. She looked Maria directly in the eyes and was shocked to see desperation on her face. Whatever situation could make someone who dispatched five men in seconds now desperate was beyond anything she could help with. "I'm so sorry, but I don't know how I could help you."

"Why are the queen's rooms in the convent and not across the street in the palace?"

"Her Majesty is more comfortable when she has her own space." Victoria picked each word carefully. "Until the new residence for the royal family is finished, the entire royal family is living here at the former governor's house. It's quite crowded, so the queen's rooms are in the convent. There's a passageway over the street connecting the buildings, and I go back and forth to the palace every day." Victoria lifted her chin and met Maria's eyes. The woman came right up and seized her arm.

"Do you know anyone in the royal guard? Do you know any of Vidigal's men?"

"Major Miguel Vidigal?"

"Yes, *Major* Vidigal," Maria sneered. "Do you know any of his men?"

"No, I'm sorry. The palace is guarded by soldiers, members of the Portuguese Army that came with us from Lisbon. The royal guard is mostly local and patrols the streets."

Maria deflated before her eyes. Her shoulders sagged. Desperation overwhelmed the terrifying confidence that filled the room a moment earlier. The muleteer turned to leave, murmuring an apology, and Victoria's heart broke.

"The palace connects to the prison," she blurted. The enormity of her betrayal—and sharing this information with someone who broke into the queen's chamber qualified as a gross betrayal of the royal family—gave her only a moment's hesitation. Maria's expression took Victoria back seven years to her father's bedside. She recognized the expression of a person desperate to save a loved one but without any idea how. "There's a passageway, like the one connecting the convent and palace. Before the royal family moved in, the palace was the seat of government in Rio, including the courts, so the prison and courtrooms are connected."

"Can you get me inside the prison?"

That question settled it. Maria was definitely mad. She'd charged into a fight against five armed men and was completely serious about being smuggled through the palace and into a prison. Only someone mad would think that was possible.

Fortunately, Victoria had experience with crazy.

She spoke slowly, never breaking eye contact with Maria. "The palace is full of soldiers, and the prison is full of soldiers and royal guardsmen. There's no way I could smuggle you in tonight, but I can probably get you information." Maria's eyebrows lifted in what Victoria assumed was doubt. She pulled her shoulders back and held Maria's unblinking gaze. This was something she could do. This mad, fearless, whip-wielding girl needed help that only she could provide. "I can talk to the servants and messengers going to and from the prison. I'll find out what's happened to your friend, what the plans are for him. What's his name?"

"Mateus," Maria said. "He works with me as a muleteer. When you have news of him, come to the third door down from the butchers on Rua do Ouvidor."

Maria stepped up on the railing of the window, a second from jumping or flying—Maria seemed capable of everything else, why not flying—and Victoria thought of one last question.

"Why did they arrest him?"

Maria hesitated then faced Victoria, feet planted apart on the railing. "Murder."

"Murder?" Victoria's voice leapt an octave. Clearly that should have been her first question.

"He didn't do it."

"Of course." Victoria gave a tight-lipped smile. She didn't even gasp when Maria sent her whip lashing out then leapt from the railing into the black night.

Victoria eased back to the desk and perched on the edge of the chair. She forced her hands to abandon the ribbon and clasped them in her lap. Her back was straight. Anyone stepping into the room would have looked for the man painting her portrait, but Victoria wasn't posing. She was thinking.

She reviewed the events that had led her to this improbable agreement. Rushing a raving and spitting monarch out of a hall filled with gawking court members. Escaping the palace and neglecting her duties for the first time in her life only to be attacked on the beach. Getting rescued from certain rape by two local girls, one armed with knives and the other with a whip. Being berated and slapped by the future queen of Portugal. Agreeing to spy on the prison in order to repay her debt to a whip-wielding Carioca who was in the process of rescuing her murderer friend.

February 12, 1809, would be the longest journal entry of her life.

Victoria knew she should report the meeting to the guards, but she stayed behind her desk. Her fingers brushed the still-throbbing cut on her cheek. She couldn't imagine Maria or her sister —what was her name—Isabel. Victoria couldn't imagine they'd let anyone, not even a crowned princess, backhand them across the face. At least not without giving one back. Maria warned Victoria about being out alone at night, but she climbed trees and leapt through palace windows without an escort. This woman wanted to sneak into a prison in the middle of the night to rescue a friend. Victoria broke out in a sweat haggling for a couple mangos and never complained when they were bruised.

A little voice from the depth of her memory spoke up. It reminded her of a different girl, sitting on her father's lap and flipping through an atlas. Excitement colored that girl's voice as she begged her father to tell about faraway countries. The girl imagined scouring the jungle, pressing leaves and creating her own text on medicinal plants that her father would use to treat patients. She was brave enough to have dreams.

Since arriving in Rio, Victoria woke every morning praying to avoid disaster in the many varieties it came in here—a public fit, an armed robbery, yellow fever. The only thing she looked forward to in Rio was sleep. She'd spent the past twelve months clinging to the queen's skirt. Doing nothing. Exploring nothing. Learning nothing.

Her father would have made the most of every minute. He'd be disappointed with her.

Victoria had wilted in the face of Rio's heat and chaos, while Maria and Isabel seemed fearless. She wanted to be fearless, too, and make the most of every minute. Maybe they could teach her.

Victoria picked up her pen and listed every servant she thought might have access to the prison, their position, and when she'd most likely be able to find them alone. She studied the list for several minutes then held it to the lamp's flame. Careful to leave no evidence behind, she tossed the still-warm ashes out the window. They drifted away on a warm breeze off the bay. The breeze smelled of pineapple.

Third door down from the butchers on Rua do Ouvidor.

Chapter Seven

Maria

The drums and twang of the berimbau reached Maria before she passed the first lookout. That was careless. Vidigal and his Bats could confirm the capoeira circles' location without revealing their presence.

It wasn't like Mestre Felipe to forget that detail. More likely, the most advanced lookout got bored or hot or both and deserted for a minute, convinced a moment to himself wouldn't hurt anything. That sloppy thinking got men dragged away to a cell. A conversation with Mestre Felipe about his lookouts became one more errand for the morning.

She stepped beyond the tree line and onto the beach, shading her eyes as she scanned the capoeira circles for members of her team. The sun broke the horizon only an hour ago, but the men and boys already glistened in the early light.

Capoeira had been outlawed for decades in Rio, and the men flipping and spinning on the white sand risked public beatings at a minimum. Simply whistling a capoeira song could get someone tossed in jail. The risk hadn't stopped her father from playing or Maria from sneaking along to this isolated stretch of beach.

It hadn't scared Mateus away either. They met on this beach.

Maria remembered which tree she'd been hiding in that morning. It wasn't the first time she followed her father, and she'd been certain she watched the circles undetected. When her father and another man came to stand in the shade of her tree, she grinned down on their oblivious heads and listened as her father's voice floated up through the branches.

"This is the most men I've seen at these circles," her father said.

"Word's gotten around. I suspect after your next trek, we'll have another dozen." Maria recognized the man's voice. He was a fisherman. Mama always got her shrimp from him. He muttered something she couldn't hear over the waves then said louder, "More mouths to talk mean more trouble."

"We're not turning anyone away?"

"No, but we all need to be careful."

"If we're not turning away, someone I know wants to play. A young one though."

"Can the child keep a secret?"

"Like a grave."

"Then bring him along next time."

"Her. My oldest girl."

Maria nearly fell out of the tree. She hadn't said a word to her father about wanting to learn capoeira. Even though it was true, she knew girls weren't allowed, so she kept quiet. There didn't seem to be any point in talking about an impossible dream.

The fisherman confirmed her suspicions. "Josué, have you lost your head? You can't bring your daughter."

"You said we're not turning anyone away."

"I meant…that was…it's not right, Josué. The other men won't like it. Who's she going to play against?"

"The boys."

"The boys all want to fight the mestre. They're not going to go up against a girl. There's no competition."

"She was clever enough to sneak past the lookouts five times. If she was in charge of the guard, we'd all be in the stocks."

"Sneak past the lookouts?" The fisherman laughed. "Did she tell you that? You believed her? And how did a girl sneak past ten grown men?"

"Ask her." Her father looked up into the tree and locked eyes with her through the leaves. Maria's heart leapt into her throat. "Maria, come down."

The fisherman whirled around and gaped up into the tree. His slack-jawed astonishment lit a fire in her gut, and she dropped to the ground an inch from his nose. She tried to look him in the eye but came up a few inches short and got a face full of his open mouth and sardine breath.

"Maria?"

"Yes, Papa." She turned to her father. Now that he'd called her down, there was no point in hiding or excuses. They both knew the truth. Her father would either discipline her for following him or offer her the chance she wanted so badly she couldn't bring herself to say aloud.

"Do you want to learn capoeira?"

"Yes, Papa." The words leapt from her mouth. She bit her lip to keep from begging. Desperation was a terrible place to negotiate from. He'd taught her that.

"Josué, you can't be serious?"

Her father put a hand on the man's shoulder but kept his eyes on her. "No man will let you have a space here. You'll have to take one and defend it over and over again, until they learn taking it back is hopeless. Do you understand, minha filha?"

"I understand, Papa."

"And you still want to play?"

"I want to be the best."

Her father smiled, and it was like a second sun broke the horizon. He turned to his friend, still holding the fisherman's shoulder. "No one gets turned away. She deserves a chance to try."

The man held up his hands in surrender. "She still has to find someone to play against."

They headed back to the beach where the two circles had merged to form one large ring of dozens of men. If Maria wanted to play, she had to step into that ring. Her heart sped up at the unexpectedly large audience. There would be no second chance. She proved herself here and now, or she never came back.

The singing and clapping died down as men noticed her until only the waves continued as usual.

The crowd parted for her father. Maria straightened under the weight of her father's hand on her shoulder. She was tall for her age but felt fragile compared to the ring of grown men with a lifetime of labor on their shoulders. Retreating flitted through her mind, but that would mean losing a bet to Isabel. She'd rather be humiliated in front of two dozen of her father's friends. They wouldn't remind her of it at every meal for the next year.

"My daughter would like to play."

Every head in the circle turned to a man seated on a gnarled tree trunk. His white hair matched the sun-bleached log. He stood, and the disgruntled rumblings stopped. "Why do you want to learn capoeira, child?"

"My father's a muleteer. He's away on the trail for weeks. Most of the time it's me, my mama, and younger sister at home. He worries about us. I don't want him to worry."

"You think you can protect your family?"

A couple of the boys in the circle laughed out loud. Maria clenched her fists. They knew nothing about her. The mere sight of her was enough to make them laugh. Anger flooded through her which she coiled in her belly. She held it there, saving it for the circle. "If you teach me mestre, I'll protect anyone who needs it."

"Well, you sound like your father." The mestre smiled and gestured toward the center of the circle. "Let's see if you move like him."

Maria glanced up at her father. He whispered in her ear, "How do you know when an animal will attack?"

"It tells you. With its eyes, ears, muscles."

"A man is another kind of animal."

She nodded. Her father squeezed her shoulder and smiled. Maria ginned back.

The grumbling returned as Maria stepped into the circle. She ignored it. After watching from a distance for months, she was *in* the circle. She was going to play. Her knee jiggled under her skirt as she scanned the faces of the boys in the crowd. Three or four looked about her age and size. She caught one's eyes, and he shook his head.

"I'm not playing with anyone in a skirt."

She pulled a string at her waist. Her skirt hit the sand and revealed her father's old pants. Isabel had hemmed them, but they were still wide in the leg. They bunched at the waist, the cloth was thread bare, the dark blue faded to nearly white at the knees, and she loved them more than any clothing she'd ever worn. They made her feel strong, like her father.

She kicked the skirt aside and raised her eyebrows at the boy. "Do you have another excuse?"

Laughter bubbled up around the circle drowning the few gasps.

"I'll play," a voice called. A boy with a smile that barely fit on his face stepped forward. He was laughing as he stepped into position opposite her. "You must have been hot in all those clothes. It'd be sad to suffer in this heat then not even get to play."

"That's kind of you," Maria said. "I won't be."

"I hope not," the boy said, still grinning. "It'll be a dull game if you are. You don't seem dull to me. Were you really hiding up a tree? For how long? How did you sneak past the lookouts?"

"Are we playing or talking?"

"Playing. We're playing." The boy bent his knees and raised his hands in front of face. The smile didn't falter. "I'm Mateus. In case you were curious. Probably not. But it feels rude to knock a girl into the sand without introducing myself first. So my name's Mateus."

"I plan on staying on my feet."

The musician started on the berimbau, tapping out a rhythm on the taught wire and shaking the caxixi. The drum and bell players took up the tempo set by the berimbau. The singers joined in. Maria and Mateus reached out their right hands and brushed finger tips. He swept her feet before the singers finished the first line.

The music stopped. Maria blinked up at Mateus's still grinning face. He'd made a fool of her. That boy dropped her on her backside without a second thought. Exactly as if she was any other player. He offered his hand. Maria ignored it, leaping to her feet, but a smile tugged at her mouth.

"I told you I wouldn't be kind," he said. "Do you want me to slow down?"

"No."

"Really? Want to bet on how many times in a row I can knock you down? I bet ten."

"Four. I'm a fast learner." The boy laughed, delighted by the challenge, and Maria didn't bother to hold her smile back.

The mestre nodded, and the music started up again. She touched his hand and hit the sand a second later. Maria fell four times before she finally noticed his weight shifting to one leg and spun away. While he applauded, she swiped his feet, her heart leaping at the thud of his body on earth. He accepted her hand, and she pulled him up.

"I'm Maria."

For months he was the only boy who would play against her. Mateus worked with her every Sunday until she wasn't the worst on the beach, until she beat him, until she beat another boy, until she beat every boy, until she wasn't playing against boys but men, until she came to the circles without her father, until Mateus joined her on the trail as a partner and ended up in a cell because of it.

After Isabel, Mateus was the most constant presence in her life. What she loved most about her life, her business and the independence it gave her, her ability to support Isabel and her team, the community she had at the capoeira circles—Mateus's support made it all possible.

She reminded herself of the fact during the nightlong vigil outside the prison. If her eyelids closed, she imagined riding the trail without him, and they snapped open. Maria stayed at the jail until she overheard some soldiers' gossip confirming Mateus was alive then raced the news home to Isabel. Together they mapped out a plan. To find a killer—who might be coming for them next—they needed a trail to follow. There had to be witnesses considering the number of slaves Dom Antonio had. They'd split up and question everyone until they caught wind of where his entire household had gone.

Before dawn, she visited the washerwomen in Catete, the fishermen heading out for the morning, and finally the women stirring boiling pots of cassava in the squares preparing their daily supply of angu. She made the same request at each stop. *I need to find Dom Antonio's household. Please let me know if you hear anything.* So far no one had any information.

Maria refused to believe an entire household could vanish without a trace. Someone knew what happened, either they helped the household escape or buried the bodies. There was a trail to follow, but she needed more eyes and ears to find it. Her team had some of the best trackers in Rio. They'd be anxious to help, if Vidigal hadn't already arrested them all.

"Maria!" A skinny boy about to be swallowed by a brilliant colored top hat charged toward her, flinging sand in his wake.

"Bom dia, Benedito. Have you seen Berto or Zé? Anyone from my team?" She kept her voice light and smiled at the boy.

He pointed to the next circle over. Maria sighed in relief at the sight of Berto bobbing and weaving in the center. The rest of her team was scattered amongst the spectators, clapping to the music.

Before she could thank him and move, Benedito burst into story. "Did you hear a Bat got arrested for smuggling last night at our inn? They found a whole sack of diamonds on him. I was at the square and missed the whole thing."

She feigned ignorance. "A Bat got caught smuggling? Did he arrest himself?"

"No, Mama said the whole Portuguese Army came to arrest him."

"The whole army fit in the courtyard?"

"Well, a lot of soldiers. I wish I'd been there."

"I bet your mama wasn't too happy about so many soldiers barging in. Was she very angry?" Bringing the soldiers to Dona Antonia's had been the one piece of her plan she regretted. Maria knew Antonia had regular customers who would get drinks somewhere else if they thought she was friendly with the army.

"She thought it was funny. She was still laughing about it at breakfast." He pushed the hat higher up on his brow. "Did you hunt any jaguars?"

"Not this trip." Maria smiled. "How about you? Kill any jaguars? Pumas?"

"Only a dozen. Just a few flicks of the wrist." Benedito flipped open his razor blade and slashed the air in front of him with the dexterity unique to barbers. "I also found time to trim some beards."

"You must be trimming quite a lot of beards to afford that eye-catching new addition to your wardrobe." Maria nodded at the yellow and green striped hat slipping back down his head. The hat combined with red shirt and striped linen pants made it impossible not to notice the boy.

"Isn't it perfect? I found it and painted it myself. I thought yellow and green for the royal family. Maybe I can snag a few patriotic customers near Largo do Palacio." The boy spun the hat in his hands. "Every free boy who hasn't hooked up with a mule train is a barber now. There are so many walking around the square compared to last year. Most have no idea how to cut the Africans' hair in the patterns they like, let alone the skill to shave the Portuguese!"

"Well, I'll be sure to recommend you to anyone who needs his haircut."

"What about you? I bet you need a trim to keep that ugly short hair you like so much."

Maria gave him a gentle shove in the shoulder. "It's practical. And why does it matter what my hair looks like if it's always wrapped up?"

Benedito shook his head with all the gravity his twelve years could muster. "It will be a miracle if you find a husband."

The words caught Maria like a kick from a mule. Mateus wasn't her husband. Not that she wanted him to be. What they had was solid, dependable. But he was a miracle. It was a hell of a lot harder for a woman to find an honest business partner than a husband, and she'd watched her miracle get dragged off to prison. There wouldn't be any more divine intervention. It was all on her. Maria preferred it that way. She regularly disagreed with God's sense of justice.

"I'm sorry, Dito. I don't have time for a haircut today. I need to speak with my team."

He frowned at Maria. "What's wrong?"

She considered lying and telling him everything was fine, but he'd hear about Mateus eventually. Maria decided the truth was better than rumors. "Mateus is in trouble. Last night he was arrested by Vidigal."

Benedito's eyes widened. "The Bats got Mateus?"

She nodded. "They took him in for murder. He didn't do it. But the man who died was rich, and they've got to arrest someone. Isabel and I are trying to find out what happened. We're looking for anyone who may have seen something."

"I can help. I can ask around."

"No," she snapped. Dito flinched, and Maria realized she'd used her captain's voice on him. She put a hand on his shoulder. "I know you want to help, but you can't go around asking about a murder."

"But barbers walk all over the city. We gossip with everyone. Most of the time I don't even say anything. I just listen to them talk. I can find out anything."

Normally, she'd never let Benedito risk himself on her behalf, but she couldn't think of a better source of gossip than a chatty barber. She also thought giving him a specific task would be safer than letting him follow his imagination. "Fine. The man killed was Dom Antonio. He lived in the big house on the beach in Catete. I need to find his servants, his slaves, anyone who was at his house last night and might have seen what happened. If you hear anything, will you tell me or Isabel?"

The boy nodded with the confidence of someone who made a living based on charm. "I'll find them, Maria." He started charging up the sand back toward the city, but Maria caught him by the collar.

"You just listen. The Bats can't know anyone is looking, so no questions. No asking about Dom Antonio. Just listen. Promise?"

"Promise."

"Good. And don't run off without telling your Papa first."

Dito scampered off to find his father amongst the players, his barber's basin and razors clinking at his hip. The men sang and clapped with strong voices and broad smiles. The Atlantic sparkled under a blue sky. The breeze cooled the sweat on everyone's brow. Maria trudged up to the circle to end her teams' fun. She caught Berto's eye and jerked her head toward the tree line. The team gathered with frowns and murmured concern.

She hated herself for putting more people at risk, but she would become indebted to every person in Rio de Janeiro if it saved Mateus. Maria squared her shoulders and looked her team in the eye. "Isabel told you what happened. Here's what I need: I have to find a murderer."

Chapter Eight

Isabel

The city buzzed with activity as everyone attempted to finish their errands before the heat became unbearable. The basket of sweets stayed perfectly balanced atop her head as Isabel rushed to hit another two squares before heading home. It looked as though every door in Rio was thrown open to accommodate deliveries and gossip. Isabel hoped some of that gossip would be about the murder of Dom Antonio.

With her basket of sweets, she dodged people, mules, horses, the occasional dog, and concluded that hunting a murderer was, in fact, incredibly tedious. Hunting an animal for dinner required an hour or two of silent stalking. Hunting a man for revenge required talking with dozens of indifferent people, and she'd promised Maria not to punch any of them in the face.

According to her sister, they needed a witness. Someone who saw something at some time last night. Any one of the twenty people Dom Antonio always seemed to have running around his house would do, but after selling sweets on nearly every square in the city, Isabel hadn't found a single member of Dom Antonio's household or a person who had seen one.

Chasing ghosts all over Rio was exhausting, especially when they had a very real friend in a very real prison with very few guards a ten-minute walk from their home.

The sun rose across an unbroken sheet of blue, and the waves of the bay lapped lazily at the shore. A constant breeze rippled her skirt. It was a gorgeous day for a jail break.

But Maria made it very clear, she didn't want to do anything that would draw the attention of the authorities.

Isabel hadn't gotten much say in developing the plan of attack. By the time she arrived home after warning the team, Maria had worn circles into the floor and laid out her plan before Isabel pulled her boots off. They needed a witness. They were going to split up. Isabel would make and sell sweets on the squares. They would meet back home at noon, and before she could make a case for burning the prison down, her sister marched out the door.

It wasn't what Isabel would have planned, but from the speed of Maria's pacing and the way her hand never left her whip, she knew her sister was scared. She also knew that nervous Maria was the most determined, focused, and terrifying person in the entire colony, so Isabel trusted that Maria would take care of Mateus.

A gnawing sensation in the pit of her stomach told her everything was her fault. If she hadn't lost her temper in the middle of the street. If they hadn't split off from the team to clean up her mess with the Bat. If Mateus hadn't been alone. There was a person guilty of murder running around Rio, but Isabel couldn't shake the sense she owed Maria for what happened to Mateus.

She would start making it up to her sister by keeping her promises.

If Maria said don't attack the prison, she would not attack the prison. If Maria said find a witness, then she would find a witness. If Maria said don't start fights, then she would merely catch an ankle while passing and accidently send the deserving person face first into a pile of dung.

"Look out!" a man's voice barked.

She hurried past a man with a basket of gobbling turkeys on his head and ducked to avoid a slave holding a long rod of bamboo on his shoulder. Several feet behind him another slave supported the opposite end of the pole and between them a white man in a forest green jacket and straw hat relaxed in the hammock suspended on the pole.

"Pay attention, girl!" the man in the hammock scolded. Isabel didn't respond. She ground her teeth as the man swayed on by.

"Why do rich people even bother learning to walk?" she muttered.

Isabel entered the next plaza in a swirl of skirt. Her gaze landed on the figures in the center of the square, and she leapt back into the alley, crashing into a woman with strings of garlic around her shoulders. The woman cursed, but Isabel didn't bother to apologize. She flattened against the wall and clutched the basket to her chest, letting the crowds trample her remaining sweets. When no one came charging around the corner to arrest her, she peeked into the square.

Vidigal and a group of Bats surrounded a man on his knees with his hands tied behind his back.

Isabel swore. "For the love of *Santa Catarina*, hasn't the bastard arrested enough men in one day?"

The Bat commander was like horse shit, foul and always in the most inconvenient places.

"I promised Maria," she murmured. "Walk past. Don't stop."

From the shadow of the building, she surveyed the square. Families of churchgoers gossiped and preened before heading to morning prayers. Vendors moved among them offering sweets and fresh water. Sailors staggered towards the beach after a night ashore. None acknowledged the Bats in the center of square except to give them a wide birth.

Isabel lifted the shawl from around her shoulders over her head, pulling it out around her face, and strolled out of the alley with her basket balanced like any other quitandeira. She glided past the Guardsmen amongst the morning crowd. Halfway across the square, a sharp crack stopped her. Another made her turn back.

Vidigal paced without his jacket, whip in hand. His stood over the bound and now half-naked man. Where the whip struck the man's back, blood ran down mixing with sweat and dirt. Vidigal snapped his arm, and the whip cracked again. More blood. Isabel noticed the man had no shoes. A slave. After the next blow, he dropped his head, and she noticed the half-moon scar on the side of his face. He came from Mozambique.

Her feet stuck to the dirt. She told herself to keep walking. Maria waited for her to come back with information. She expected Isabel to keep her promise. They were in the middle of a plan to save someone else. Vidigal's whip cracked again, and her feet refused to move.

A small cluster of street vendors watched, but the vast majority of people crossing the square never glanced over. Isabel didn't realize she was moving forward until she'd closed half the distance between them. She was close enough to hear Vidigal.

"Where did you learn that song? They sing it at the capoeira circles. Capoeira is practiced by criminals," Vidigal spat. "Who taught you the song?"

Isabel's breath caught. If the man practiced capoeira, Maria and Mateus probably knew him or had at least seen him in the circles. Why was Vidigal looking for the circles? Had Mateus said something?

She became aware of the pressure of her daggers against her thighs. Vidigal's back loomed large in front of her. Her promise to Maria echoed in her head. She could not make a scene. She was one person against four Bats.

She crept another step forward.

Another crack. Where were the soldiers? Rumor said the royal guard had been ordered to stop public beatings. Maybe a soldier would intervene.

"A disgrace," Vidigal hissed. His voice dripped with disgust. Isabel stepped closer, making sure to pull her shawl further over her face. "A disgrace on my city. Bringing disease, crime, and disorder, they drag my city into their filth."

The Bat's commander muttered to himself as he shook out his arm. The whip coiled on the ground like a snake. He shook his head at the ground. "No respect. No vision. You're a stain on my city."

Vidigal suddenly rushed at the man. He jerked the man's chin up and cupped his face. "Don't you want to be better? Don't you want to live better? Help me create a city to rival any European capital. Help me make Rio as great as any city in the world. Tell me where the capoeira circles are."

Isabel held her breath, straining to hear the man's response. There were four Bats in the square. She had two daggers. Her fingers twitched toward the slit in her skirt.

The sea breeze whispered a warning. It spoke in a voice she knew, always sharper depending on the amount of trouble she considered causing. Her mother's voice swept Isabel back to a different square at a different time under the same burning sun.

"Isabel Azevedo, what are you doing? Have you gone mad?" Isabel heard the fear in her mother's voice, as sharp in her memory as that day in the square.

They'd been selling coconut sweets and cups of water near the viceroy's mansion. The royal family was still an ocean away and eating their own chickens. She drifted away from her mother toward a small group of young men, shouting up at the Viceroy's mansion. Isabel was curious why the men were so angry when they clearly had enough to eat and shoes on both feet. Maybe it was all the heavy coats. She'd be cranky, too, if constantly sweating like a pig.

The men didn't seem to be arguing about fashion. One brandished a newspaper over his head, and curiosity drove Isabel forward. He must have recently returned from Portugal or some other foreign land because Rio didn't have any newspapers.

She couldn't read, but once she passed a man sitting along the sea wall with a paper that had a drawing of a person with wings and swirling clothes, a large flag waving above her head. Or his head. She hadn't been close enough to tell. She only remembered the beautiful image of a swirling, godlike figure.

Isabel grasped the water pitcher and tin cup in one hand, freeing the other to snatch the paper the moment the man's grip slackened.

He waved the paper over his head and bellowed, "Why is slavery outlawed in Portugal but allowed to flourish here? What is moral and righteous in the mother country should be moral for her children! Slavery must be outlawed in Brazil!"

Isabel straightened, the paper forgotten as the other men in his group cheered. Was it true? Were there places without slaves? Not just any place, but Portugal. Where the queen lived. Did the *queen* not have slaves? The most modest homes in Rio had one or two slaves. Isabel couldn't imagine a palace without slaves.

She had to know the truth.

Isabel darted through the families who stopped to gawk at the group of abolitionists. A white-haired man branded the group traitors and madmen. An official with a ruby sash stretched over a well-served belly appeared on the mansion steps and threatened to summon the police if the group didn't disband. Voices rose in support of the threat.

But the men refused to leave. The crowd got larger, and the shouting grew louder. Isabel grinned.

She used the tension as cover to slip right next to the man with the newspaper and outrageous claims which rang truer than any Mass she'd been forced to sit through. She realized the group was only seven men strong. Their faces young and red. Their fists clenched, and Isabel fell in love with each and every one of them. They didn't blink at the viceroy's threats. They shouted the truth. They could explain the world. She reached out to tug on the nearest sleeve and ask about the queen's slaves.

A hand snatched the back of her shirt and jerked her away.

"Isabel Azevedo, what are you doing? Have you gone mad?"

She felt the fury in her mother's grip as she was pulled away from the crowd to the far side of the square. Her mother rounded on her and glared down from under the shadow of her wide straw basket. "Running off right into a pack of trouble. Do you want to end up locked in the stocks?"

"But they're not trouble. They're right. Those men are asking the viceroy to end slavery."

Her mother crossed arms. "They're playing at being important."

"They're not playing, Mama. They're angry."

"Well they can afford to be. We have to sell all these sweets if we want supper, and angry doesn't sell anything but guns and rum. Come away," her mother said. She turned on her heel, her basket steady and full skirt swaying around her ankles.

"But we should help them. Someone needs to tell the viceroy to change the laws. We should be shouting at him, too."

"I'm not wasting my breath on a person who doesn't care if I have any. I said come away."

"Can I ask them one question?"

"No. We're leaving."

"But I want to know if the queen owns slaves."

Her mother's body stilled, like an animal that senses a predator nearby. "Isabel Azevedo, do not ask that question of any Portuguese. Ever. Do you understand?"

The force behind her mother's words rose like waves before a storm, so Isabel decided to let the question about slaves go. If she got her hands on the newspaper, maybe it would have answers. "All right, I won't ask about the queen. Can I get his newspaper?"

"No, you cannot steal his newspaper."

"I'm not gonna steal it, Mama. I'm gonna ask for it. I'm good at getting people to give me—"

"No. You cannot go back there. We're leaving."

"Why don't you want to help? Slavery is evil. That's what you always say. Grandmama ran from a coffee farm."

"Hush." Her mother whipped around and grabbed Isabel's shoulder giving her a shake. Isabel yelped in surprise. Her mother never raised a hand against her or Maria.

Her mother lowered her head until they were close enough to share the basket's shade. The fear in her eyes stole the protest from Isabel's lips. "Never speak of my mama outside our home. Promise me."

"I promise," Isabel murmured, staring in wonder at the change in her mother. Normally, her mother was like the bay on a windless day, smooth and calm, flowing around the chaos of the city. Now, her mother's eyes darted from side to side. She licked her lips. Isabel stroked her mother's face, hoping to smooth the fear out of it. "Don't worry, Mama. I understand."

Her mother smiled. She set her basket of coconut sweets on the stones and Isabel's jug beside it. Then she drew Isabel in a fierce hug.

"Mama," Isabel murmured into her mother's waist. "Can they take you back to your mama's farm?"

She felt her mother stiffen. Her hand paused on the back of Isabel's head, and she knelt down so they were eye to eye. "I was born free here in Rio. The church wrote it down. They have a birth record for me, for Papa. We made sure to get one for Maria."

"Do I have one?"

"I don't know, sweet girl. But don't worry. You're Guarani and Portuguese, and the Guarani can't be held as slaves anymore."

"So, we're all safe? They can't take you away?"

Her mother pursed her lips, and Isabel knew she wouldn't like what came next. "The law says we're free, but there are always men who don't respect the law. People aren't supposed to kill, but some men do. We have to be ready if we ever meet one of these men who doesn't care about the law."

Isabel threw her arms around her mother's shoulder. "I won't let anyone take you or Papa or Maria. I'll kill them."

She felt the rage burn through her body at the idea of a stranger dragging her mother away. She imagined clawing his eyes out. If anyone wanted her mother, they'd have to kill her first.

"Isabel, we've talked about this." Her mother's voice was low and urgent. "You cannot say things like that. If a soldier or Portuguese hears you, they'll get upset, and you could end up in the stocks or dead. Make the wrong person angry, and they will kill you."

Isabel clenched her fists around her mother's shawl. "But I'm angry. Why doesn't anyone worry about making me angry?"

"People don't believe your anger can hurt them, minha filha."

"So if I hurt people, they'll care what I think?"

Her mother gripped her by the shoulders and gently pulled away. Mother and daughter stared at each other. Her mother seemed to be looking for something in her eyes, and whatever she found made her sigh. She reached through a slit in her skirt and drew a bone-handled dagger. "Your father gave this to me before he left on his first trek after we were married. It's for protection against being hurt, Isabel. You can get people to listen to you by saving others from hurt. Protect yourself and your sister. Protect this family, and people will learn to respect you."

"Only our family? Lots of people need protection."

"Protect family first, always. Then whoever you think deserves your life. Because that's what your risking if you draw this against anyone."

Isabel accepted the dagger from her mother. She tossed it from hand to hand. The blade caught the sunlight, and Isabel fell in love. With her fingers curled around the smooth handle, she felt stronger. Her mother was wrong about one thing. She wouldn't be risking her life if she was a better fighter than her enemy.

Smack.

The sound of Vidigal's backhand against the man's face snapped Isabel out of her memory.

"I expect an answer," he growled. "I know you play capoeira. Have you seen a woman at the circles? One in pants, skin almost as dark as yours?"

Isabel's heart stopped. Since watching him get dragged away, she'd thought only of Mateus. She hadn't considered the possibility Vidigal would be hunting them—hunting Maria—but she should have known he'd want revenge. They sent one of his men to prison for life then escaped from under his nose.

None of this would be happening if she'd kept her temper with that lobster-faced Bat. Maria wouldn't have intervened on her behalf, and the royal guard wouldn't have any reason to remember her. They would have gone with Mateus from the bank to Dom Antonio's. He wouldn't have been alone. Isabel hadn't only failed to protect her family, she invited their enemies to dinner and served Mateus and Maria to them.

Using her basket to hide her movements, she slid one hand through the slit in her skirt. She'd promised not to draw any attention, but if the man gave up the location of the capoeira circles, she'd have more than one family member in a cell. Vidigal couldn't walk away with that information. It was her fault the Bats hunted them, and she wouldn't let them take away anyone else she loved.

"Have you seen her? Answer me, and I'll let you go," Vidigal growled in the man's ear.

Isabel wrapped her fingers around the familiar bone handle.

The man from Mozambique stayed silent.

Vidigal stalked back to his previous position and turned his back to Isabel. Her eyes fixed on a point below his ribs.

Isabel cocked her arm back. Vidigal raised the whip.

A whistle pierced the din of the square.

A Bat on the opposite side of the square waved. Soldiers. Vidigal slunk away, his black coat flapping behind him. His men followed, dragging the prisoner along.

Isabel remained rooted in place, still gripping the dagger. She dropped her basket to the ground, snatched the shawl off her head and faced into the breeze. That was the second time in less than a day she'd watched that caiman drag a man off. Her skin burned from the inside.

The hum of the square returned to normal. Vendors flooded into the space left in the Bats' wake. The drops of blood on the ground disappeared under the dust of people in a hurry. Isabel replaced the basket on her head, straightened her shoulders, and made another promise. She would kill Vidigal. Not today, but there would be other days. Right now, her sister waited for her.

Chapter Nine

Maria

Maria dragged herself through the heat of the day back home and collapsed in her hammock, whip, boots, and most of the dust in Rio still on her.

Not for the first time, she wished her body responded to orders as reliably as her team. Time was her most precious resource and using it on sleep was a monumental waste, but her eyelids sagged, indifferent to the chaos engulfing her life. She surrendered rather than pass out in the street.

She kicked off her boots and coiled her whip on top of her stomach. The familiar scents of smoke and over-ripe jaca fruit, remnants of Isabel's sweet making the night before, eased the crease from between her brows. One hour. She'd concede one hour to sleep and then continue the search.

The hammock rocked gently as church bells rang and cannon fire announced the arrival of a ship. Mules and their drivers complained about each other. A vendor stopped right outside her window to proclaim the sturdiness of his baskets. Another sold chickens, which by the clucking must have numbered in the hundreds. Maria could have stuck her head out the window and bought the sweetest coconut candy in Rio, the most sturdy hat, most flavorful coffee, but sleep, the only thing she wanted, was the one thing not on offer.

Maria wrapped her arms around her head in an attempt to stifle the city bustle. She resented the vendors. She resented the crowds. She resented the world for going on as normal while she lived her worst nightmare.

What events played out so that Bats found Mateus with Dom Antonio's body? They were always so careful, and Mateus could read a negotiation as well as she could. It was one of the reasons they worked so well together. He instinctively understood people. The light pouring out of Dom Antonio's house should have been a warning.

Why didn't he walk away?

The question haunted her, and the response was always the same.

Why wasn't I there?

Guilt clawed at her. She'd arranged the deal under Mateus's name and told him when and where to be. As the captain of the mule train, he was her responsibility. Then she'd failed to show.

And he loved her, which made it worse. For some reason, she felt she owed him for not returning his affections, despite only signing on for a business relationship.

Bastard. How dare he make her doubt herself this way. What if she left him in jail? A deserved punishment for violating their agreement with his romantic inclinations. He broke his word.

But he wasn't the captain. Maria's resolve to free him hardened. The one thing she would never allow herself to be was a disappointment. When it came to Mateus's feelings for her, the question would sure as hell not be if she deserved his love, but whether or not she wanted it.

"You're sleeping?" Isabel's voice cut through her thoughts. "I've worn the soles off my shoes walking down every street in Rio. Your little sister has been combing the city basically barefoot to save your partner, and you're taking a nap."

"There's a man with the most durable shoes ever made right outside the window so that's one problem solved." Maria cracked an eye open. Her sister stood silhouetted in the doorway, hands on hips and woven basket balanced atop her head. "You sold everything?"

"Of course I sold everything. Dom Antonio got himself killed before paying us, and you spent your share of the last trek on a prison sentence for a Bat, so we need the money."

"It's a good thing your sweets are the best in the city."

Isabel smiled at the compliment then her expression softened with worry. "Weren't you on watch the last night of the trek? When *was* the last time you slept?"

"Some time before framing a Bat for smuggling, saving a Portuguese girl, watching my best friend get dragged away for murder, being chased through the forest by the commander of the royal guard, interviewing half the city, and convincing the team to sleep away from their homes in case Mateus gives their names to Vidigal."

"He'd never do that."

"None of us know what we'd say while being beaten," Maria said quietly. The truth hung in the humid air.

"Well, you can't give up sleeping and eating. I'll get lunch started." Isabel tossed the basket on the floor, ripped off her boots, and went outside to build a fire in the oven.

Maria stored her hammock in their mother's trunk and unrolled a woven straw mat across the dirt floor.

She passed Isabel strips of dried beef to mix in with the cassava flour and water before heading out for a bucket of water to rinse the bowls and spoons. The sisters prepared lunch in practiced silence. The distribution of tasks set over a lifetime together.

They sat opposite each other on the mat. Maria stirred the thick, steaming angu and felt her throat close up. She forced down two bites. "Did you find a witness?"

Isabel's silence answered the question.

"Neither did I."

"Then it's settled. There's only one thing to do. We break him out."

Maria sighed. Her sister always opted for plans that risked extensive property damage and long prison sentences, and while usually a great deal of fun, she had no interest in playing with the life of her oldest friend as the prize.

"It's too much of a risk. The two of us cannot storm the prison unless our goal is to end up there."

Isabel set aside her bowl and leaned forward, grinning. "Not just the two of us. We gather the team. We go to the capoeira circles—"

"No!"

"We get every one of Mateus's friends behind us, and we burn the place to the ground."

"Isabel, we're not starting a war!" Maria stared at her sister in horror. "Mateus would never forgive us."

"We can take out a few guards."

"And then what? After we break Mateus out, we run away to Bahia while every one of our friends is hunted down and slaughtered?" Maria stood and glared down at her sister. She never used her height or age to shoot Isabel down, but this idea needed to be stamped out for good. "Our friends don't have the money to pack up their families and flee the city with us. So when the soldiers come—and if a mob of free Blacks and Indigenous attack the prison, the entire *army* will come—our friends will be the ones stuck in front of the cannons."

Her sister leapt to her feet indignant. "But we have to do something. I *have* to do something. I can't sell any more damn candy and whisper pleas for help in people's ears. I can't let that snake take my friend and threaten my family. I won't let him win!"

Isabel's eyes glistened, hinting at something more, something deeper.

Maria frowned. "Isabel, this isn't your fault."

"I should have listened to you," she said. "I didn't think anything bad would actually happen…"

A knock at the open door ended the argument. Maria snatched up her whip, and Isabel drew a dagger.

"My apologies for startling you." Victoria fidgeted with a parasol, wearing a pained expression as if she'd hurt the door by knocking on it. "I didn't want to interrupt, but I felt the situation demands expediency."

"I remember you," Isabel declared. "You're the girl we saved last night. Victoria from Lisbon. How did you find us?"

"I have news about your friend," Victoria said to Maria. "I talked to some servants this morning, and your friend's alive."

The relief Maria felt lasted a second. Isabel glanced between Maria and Victoria, and her eyes widened in understanding. Maria braced for the onslaught.

"You snuck into the palace."

"And nearly frightened me to death," Victoria answered. "Your friend. . . or sister, yes? She is completely mad."

"You snuck into the palace without me?" Isabel bellowed, rounding on Maria. Any hint of tears in her sister's eyes burned away in an indignant rage. "You can't break into palaces without me!"

"It wasn't the palace. It was the convent across the street," Maria said.

"Oh, so breaking and entering is something you two do together?" Victoria smiled, but her voice had jumped an octave.

"No, it's not something we do," Maria assured her.

"At least not together," Isabel retorted.

Maria glared at Isabel. Her sister's jokes could scare Victoria away before they got the girl's information. Isabel caught the look and held her hands up. "I'm joking. We're not thieves. She's a muleteer, and when we're back home in Rio, I make and sell sweets." Isabel pointed to the basket on the floor.

"Do you make guava sweets? I love guava."

Maria admired the girl's heroic effort at polite conversation while clearly trying not to faint from nerves.

"I make every kind of sweet there is. I'm an amazing cook. In fact, I've just made lunch. Come in and join us. There's plenty of food and space on the floor," Isabel gestured to the mat.

"That's very kind of you, but I don't want to intrude."

"You're here. Lunch is ready. We're not letting you leave without a meal. It's too hot to be walking around now anyway."

Annoyance flared in Maria. She wanted to get Victoria's information and send the girl on her way, but now Isabel had offered lunch. Hopefully, the girl would refuse. Victoria looked from Isabel's bare feet to her own slippered and stockinged feet to the mat on the dirt floor. Their one-room home had little in common with the queen's chambers and its velvet chairs, polished floors, and gold candlesticks. She waited for the Portuguese girl's polite refusal.

Victoria cleared her throat. "If it truly is not an imposition, then I would be honored to accept. Thank you. Although I feel after rescuing me and now feeding me, I will never cease to be in your debt."

Isabel waved Victoria's words away. "You can pay us back with palace gossip."

The queen's maid stepped warily into the house, placing each foot gingerly as if expecting to find a sink hole. At the mat she slipped off her shoes, then hesitated, frowning at her stockings, kept them on, and folded her legs beneath her, sitting on her heels. Having gotten herself seated, Victoria searched for a place to put her white parasol. First in the middle of the mat, along the edge, then her lap where it rolled off. At the fourth attempt, Maria rescued the girl before she attempted to swallow it.

"Let me put that on the table for you."

"You took your shoes off!" Isabel laughed delightedly, setting a fresh bowl of angu in front of the maid. "Maria, look! We have a real Portuguese lady at our house. Fine, I'm not angry you went to the palace without me. I'm glad you found her. She's so fancy."

Maria noticed Victoria's face turn pink. "Sorry, Isabel's honesty can take a little getting used to."

"It's fine. I appreciate the compliment," Victoria said, the blush deepening.

"Before my sister tries to force-feed you, can you tell me what you heard about our friend?"

"Of course, my apologies for not saying straight away." Victoria glanced over her shoulder at the open door. She lowered her voice. "A free Black man, a young muleteer, was brought into the prison last night. He's being held for the murder of Dom Antonio de Sousa, and—I'm very sorry—he's been scheduled for execution."

The girl's words dropped in her stomach like a stone, but Maria didn't flinch. She swallowed and forced her face to remain blank. "I'd like you to tell me everything you heard."

"Dom Antonio was important. He recently made a significant donation to the crown, and the Prince Regent made him a viscount. I didn't need to inquire about your friend. Dom Antonio's murder is all anyone at the palace is talking about. I heard the magistrate visited the prison first thing this morning. Someone has to be held accountable." Victoria clasped her hands. "I'm so very sorry. I believe you. That your friend didn't do it. But they're going to execute someone."

Maria expected a death sentence, but hearing it confirmed straight from the palace made her numb. She met Isabel's gaze.

"I should have been there."

Her sister grabbed her shoulders and jerked her close till they were nose to nose. "*We* should have been there. Now *we're* going to get him out. We'll storm the prison. We'll tear down the goddamn walls. It's the only way."

"Unless you find the real murderer," Victoria said.

Maria frowned at the maid. Finding the real killer had been the plan when Maria thought she and Isabel might be targets, but saving herself was her lowest priority now. "What does the real murderer matter if Mateus is being shot today?"

"He's not. They've determined he'll be executed but not until after the anniversary celebrations." Victoria smiled, her words spilling out. "An acquaintance was attending His Highness during the meeting with the magistrate. Prince João doesn't want any executions happening while the city is celebrating the royal family's first year in Brazil. I thought about it on the way here. They're going to hang someone, but if they have the actual murderer, then they won't need your friend."

"He'd be free and wouldn't be a fugitive," Maria murmured as she examined the plan from every angle in her mind. Any escape plan would have them fleeing Rio as fugitives. By handing over the real murderer, Mateus could walk out of his cell and resume his life. She'd tracked capybaras, tapirs, and even pumas, but finding one murderer in Rio de Janeiro would be the most challenging hunt of her life. Challenging but not impossible. Not for her. She could save Mateus. Hope beat back exhaustion. "Do you know when they plan to execute him?"

"The anniversary celebrations will last a week. So eight days from now at the earliest."

It wasn't much, but it was enough.

Maria's shoulders sagged in relief. "Thank you," she said to Victoria.

"No thanks, please. I owe you both my life. Listening to palace gossip is nothing compared to confronting a group of armed assailants."

Maria assumed after saving Victoria on the beach that they were rescuing another Portuguese immigrant from her own naïveté. Then she overhead Victoria's conversation with Carlota Joaquina and the slap. Even from the roof, Maria cringed at the sound of the blow. She expected to find a girl crumpled on the floor, tears running down her face, but instead a clear-eyed Victoria staunched blood flow with one hand and made notes with the other. The girl kept her promises and secrets. Two traits more rare than diamonds.

She reassessed the foreigner in front of her. The curls framing her face, the ribbons, and the dress were all perfectly arranged with deliberate indifference to the gash on her cheek. Picking the right team was essential for a muleteer. On the trail, lives depended on courage and calm heads, and Maria was beginning to think the same might be true of the palace.

"Victoria, you've been a great help. And you kept my visit secret. I won't forget that," Maria said. She turned to her sister, the thrill of a challenging hunt replacing the worry. Mateus was in prison, but death wasn't imminent. She'd thought he had hours. Days felt like an eternity. "Can we catch a murderer in eight days?"

"What can't we do in eight days?" Isabel slipped a knife out from her skirt and twirled it.

"We need to organize our search of the city based on where Dom Antonio's servants would be most likely to go. Tonight we'll split up. You take the river. I'll check north on the way to the quilombo."

"We'll have to avoid the Bats' patrols," Isabel cut in. "I forgot to tell you. I saw Vidigal and some Bats interrogating a man this morning. He's looking for a Black woman in breeches. You're hard to forget."

A small cough caught Maria's attention. Victoria still perched on the mat with a full bowl of angu. "I'd like to help, but I need to return to Her Majesty."

"Of course. Thank you again for the help," Maria said.

"I knew I'd love having a friend inside the palace." Isabel threw her arms around the maid, knocking her bowl and sloshing angu into one of Victoria slippers. "Shit! I'm sorry."

"It's all right. I can clean it later."

"*Santa Ines*, you are *not* cleaning it. I am." Isabel snatched the slipper away and marched to the wash bucket. "Mama will come back to life to kill me if I let a guest walk out of our home with stains on her clothes because of me."

"I appreciate your kindness, but it's really unnecessary." Victoria slipped the clean shoe on and hopped after Isabel.

"You don't have a choice. Sit back down, and while I clean, you can tell me if the queen really is stark raving mad. I want all the details."

Maria stood and patted Victoria on the shoulder. "It's best not to argue with her."

"At least allow me to help with the dishes." Victoria reached for the clay pot with the leftover angu. Maria's stomach flipped. Isabel dropped the slipper. They both rushed for Victoria at the same time.

"I'll take it."

"You don't need to—"

"It's nothing, really."

Maria and Isabel reached Victoria as she turned with the pot in hand. The three collided. The clay pot slipped from Victoria's grip. Maria's heart leapt into her throat as the pot cracked against the floor, and the bottom split apart.

The false bottom.

Diamonds spilled out of the broken pot and across Victoria's bare foot.

Chapter Ten

Victoria

Victoria had enough time to wonder why a person would hide rocks in a cooking pot before Isabel slammed her against the wall and put a knife at her throat.

"Isabel, stop!" Maria shouted.

She thought it was Maria. The world had gone fuzzy, and her heart seemed to be pounding from between her ears, making it difficult to be sure of any detail other than the narrowed black eyes an inch from her nose.

"I'm sorry, Victoria, but we have a problem now." Isabel's voice was so matter-of-fact Victoria knew she'd do it. The girl would stab her in the throat and then go back to relating the morning's gossip. How could a person go from so pleasant to so deadly in a matter of seconds?

"I'm sorry. Please. It was an accident."

"Nossa Senhora, Isabel! You're not slitting anyone's throat in this house," Maria ordered.

"I'll clean up the mess. She can't have more guts in her then a male capybara," Isabel countered. Victoria's knees buckled and blackness crept into the edge of her vision.

"Let her go!"

"Are you serious? Since when do you put our lives in the hands of a Portuguese stranger? A servant of the royal family at that. The same royal family you wish had drowned in the Atlantic before reaching Rio."

"She's not going to tell."

"Have you forgotten what Papa said? Let the jaguar go, and it will thank you by eating you."

"Does she look like she's about to eat anyone?" Maria pointed out.

There was a long moment of silence. Victoria couldn't say what happened because her eyes had been squeezed shut since being compared to a large rodent.

"She looks like she's about to be sick."

The pressure of the blade lessened and hope flooded through her. Maybe she would walk out of here. Victoria didn't want to die and certainly not at the hands of someone she'd hoped to at least be better acquainted with, if not friends.

The problem was she had nothing to offer in exchange for her life. She'd given them all the information she had so that left the clothes on her back, which she knew at least Maria wouldn't care for. She couldn't even threaten that someone would come looking for her. Her Majesty didn't remember her name most days. The other maids would miss her only when trying to administer the queen's tonics. Her solitude was absolute, and the weight of that realization pulled any fight from her. If not one person in the world expected her, what reason did she have to walk away from that house?

"Hello! Lisbon, are you still conscious? Do not get sick on me. If you toss up your lunch on my toes, I will definitely stab you."

"If you put the knife away, she'd be able to relax."

"How can you be so calm? She knows! All she has to do is walk into the street and yell 'smuggler' and we're as good as dead."

The pieces shifted together in her mind, and shock freed her voice. "You're smugglers!" Victoria opened her eyes and looked at the rocks scattered about the dirt fl oor. "Those are diamonds!"

"What did you think they were?" Isabel asked in amazement.

"I thought they were rocks. I've never seen a recently mined diamond."

Maria's laugh filled the room, bright and clear as the diamonds set in the queen's best necklace. "She didn't know. We held her at knife point in order to confess our crimes." She wiped her eyes. "Confessing to the one Portuguese who didn't assume we're all smugglers. Nossa Senhora, if she turns us in we deserve it."

"Is this the exhaustion? Have you fi nally lost your mind?" Isabel released Victoria and stomped to her sister in a frustrated swirl of skirt. "This girl could get you hanged. As the captain, they'll hold you responsible and you'll be executed. I will not let this stranger destroy my family."

Maria put a hand on Isabel's shoulder. "Nothing is going to happen to me. She isn't going to tell anyone."

The sisters stared at each other, seemingly communicating without words, and Victoria knew she should speak in her defense. She wanted to tell them how she'd never betray someone who had saved her life. She thought they made Rio better, safer, diamond smugglers or not. The women helped people who couldn't help themselves. According to her father, that was the highest calling a person could have. A grand speech formed in her mind, arguing the value of life above all things and thus those that protect it, but when Victoria opened her mouth, the words didn't come. Her fingertips brushed the cut on her cheek, and she murmured, "I wouldn't mind if the royal family had fewer gems."

Maria gave her a sad smile. Victoria smiled back and knew she'd make it back to the convent. Somehow, she'd reached an understanding with the muleteer. If not total trust, then at least an understanding they would keep each other's secrets.

"What was that?" Isabel demanded. She jabbed a blade in the air back and forth between Maria and Victoria. "Since when are you sharing secret smiles with the Mad Queen's maid? Does this have something to do with your trip to the queen's bedroom last night? The one you didn't invite me to."

Maria sighed. "Can we argue while picking up the stolen diamonds from the middle of the floor?" She knelt and gathered diamonds into her shirt.

"I'm not doing a damn thing until I know exactly what happened last night," Isabel declared.

"Fine. You stand there in a rage, and I'll keep us from going to prison. As usual."

"As *usual*, you made a plan without me. With some Portuguese girl we've known for a second! I want to know why. I want to know what happened."

"What *you* want is not always the most important thing!" Maria yelled.

The words landed like a blow against Isabel. She staggered back from Maria. The girl spun towards Victoria with a shriek and snapped her arm. A flash of silver. Victoria dropped into a crouch with her arms around her head. The blade landed deep in the window frame. Maria didn't even glance up from the diamonds.

Victoria gave the knife an experimental tug. It didn't budge. The surrounding gouges and chips suggested years of arguments and weapons lobbed in frustration.

Emotions played out across Isabel's face. Victoria could have read her from across a ball room in lamplight. Anger. Hurt. Guilt. Finally, shame. Then Isabel held out a palm basket to Maria, who dumped out the diamonds nestled in her shirt. The sisters knelt together and cleaned up the remaining contraband. The tension faded as the sisters cleaned in silence. Without a single word being spoken, the fight ended. Maria gave Isabel a nudge, and they exchanged a smile.

This was what a family looked like. Having the same fight for the hundredth time. Unspoken apologies. Shared secrets. Trust. Victoria ached with longing. She no longer wanted to escape the sisters. She wanted to be one of them.

She remembered the last time she promised to keep a secret. The weight of her father's book made her arms burn, but she'd carried it all the way to him in his high-back chair by the fire where he spent every night during Lisbon's winter, reading aloud with Victoria in her nightdress at his feet.

He raised his eyebrows at her choice. Not the epic poems of Camoes but his medical text.

"This isn't a book for young girls," he said gently.

"I'm not young," she protested.

"And why do you want to read about guts and bones when we can read beautiful words about great adventures at sea?"

"Because I can't help you if I don't know how the body works. I want to help people feel better like you do."

Her father put the book on the side table and scooped her into his lap. "It is a very noble thing to want to help others, but there are many ways to do that besides being a surgeon. You can sew clothes for the poor. They also need bread."

"Why don't you bake bread?"

Her father laughed. "Because other work is expected of men. All of it necessary."

"Who assigns people their work?"

"Society. Tradition. It's how people have lived for centuries."

Victoria thought about this. She twirled her hair around a fi nger as she dissected her father's argument. He waited patiently. He'd taught her to consider her words before speaking them and as she thought, there seemed to be a contradiction in using tradition as an argument for keeping things a certain way.

"But Papa, traditions change. We don't wear robes like the Romans. Sailors today don't sail in the same ships as Camoes's sailors. Portugal even has a queen now instead of a king, and you always say she's a better ruler than her father. Or she was before she went mad." She glanced at her father to gauge his reaction. Was he pleased or not with her argument? The tiniest hint of a smile gave her the confi dence to continue. "If Portugal can have a queen, then I can study medicine."

Her father beamed and pride filled her tiny chest. "You make a persuasive argument. But…" He paused and raised an eyebrow, a challenge. Victoria squirmed in anticipation. "Many say that a woman's brain and constitution are too delicate to handle crude subjects such as medicine. Examining a man's body, or even another woman's, would overcome them. That is why medicine is the purview of men."

Victoria chewed her lip and twisted her hair even tighter. She stared into the flames, letting her mind pick apart the argument. "I think we should do an experiment."

"Oh really? What experiment?"

"You should read to me about the human heart and see if I am overcome. After we finish the material on the heart, we record my reaction. If I don't faint or present as flushed, then you can move on to reading about the lungs. We repeat until I am overcome or we finish the book."

She wouldn't have known her father was laughing if she hadn't been in his lap. He laughed with almost no sound. His shoulders shook as if the laughter were trying to escape, but he wanted to hold it inside. He kissed the top of her head. "I cannot refuse after you have courageously volunteered to be the subject of this experiment."

Victoria planted a kiss on his cheek. He pulled her away gently and held up a finger. His face turned serious. "But you must understand. There are many people who would not agree to this experiment. You are right that traditions change, but it takes many, many years. Even today there are still many people who would prefer Portugal had only kings. That is why our experiment has to be our secret. You can't tell your friends what I'm teaching you. Do you understand?"

Victoria nodded gravely. "I understand, Papa. I won't tell a soul. It's our secret."

Her father took the secret to his grave, and she hadn't shared another secret with anyone until Maria dropped in through the window.

Victoria cleared her throat and detached herself from the wall. The sisters glanced over. "I want to apologize for breaking your…storage compartment. I'd also like to apologize for causing strife between the two of you. Isabel, I believe your sister's reticence in speaking of last night's events stems from the fact she overheard a rather embarrassing exchange between myself and a member of the royal family. It was a kindness to me, but I'd like to tell you what happened."

"Your words are as fancy as your hair, Lisbon." Isabel waved her hand as though shooing a fly. "Don't worry. I'm going to let you live."

"Please, I'd like to explain," Victoria cut in. Face burning, she smoothed the front of her dress and continued. "The queen suffered a fit last night during the hand-kissing ceremony. Because I was attending Her Majesty during the ceremony, Her Royal Highness held me responsible. I believe Maria overheard the reprimand I received which included this." Victoria touched the cut on her cheek. "Later Maria and I reached an agreement. I will repay my debt to you by providing information about your friend. You don't know me well, but I assure you, I will honor my debt and keep my promise. I believe keeping your secret is part of honoring that debt. I won't tell a soul."

Isabel shrieked with laughter, prompting Victoria to take a step back in surprise. "I understood maybe half of what you said. *Santa Nicole*, you're one of the most surprising people I've ever met. Since you asked so nicely, I'll forgive my sister. As long as she promises to take me along the next time she sneaks into the palace."

"I won't be sneaking into the palace again. Too much perfume. I could barely breathe," Maria said.

"See, the adventure was wasted on her. Next time there's a meeting in the queen's bedroom, I'll go," Isabel said.

Church bells rang out midday, and Victoria snapped into action. "I must go. I need to give the queen her sleeping tonic for her afternoon nap." She snatched her half-cleaned and soaking wet shoe from the bucket and headed for the door.

At the threshold, she turned and found the sisters a step behind her. "Are you heading out?"

"We have eight days to catch a murderer, and we've yet to pick up a trail," Maria said from beneath a wide, straw hat. "There's no time to waste."

"Eight days is more than enough time." Isabel flipped a dagger before stashing it under her skirt. "I'll bet a month of laundry, I have the trail before you."

"I accept. You always overestimate your tracking skills."

Victoria hesitated, twisting the ribbons of her dress. She imagined Maria turning to ask for her opinion, where they should search first, who they should speak with. Not that she had any invaluable advice on how to track a murderer through a crowded city. It was best they didn't care to ask her. Having to give an opinion would only be another chance for her to demonstrate her incompetence at anything beyond changing the queen's bedpans. Still, being asked might make the ache in her chest go away, but she'd already been forgotten.

"Well, I wish you both the best of luck. I'll continue to gather information about your friend and return if I have anything new to report." Victoria dropped a curtsy.

Isabel grinned. "All those curtseys are going to go to my head. I'll start to think I deserve them."

"Can you get back to the palace? Do you need an escort?" Maria asked.

"I'll be fine, thank you. Please don't worry about me," Victoria answered and Maria, taking the request seriously, tipped her hat and headed off in the direction of the bay. Isabel gave a wave and hurried after her.

Victoria watched them disappear into the crowd. They didn't look back. The last thing she heard was Isabel's voice carried on the breeze.

"If she does tell, I'll get to say I told you so, and that will almost be worth the trouble."

Chapter Eleven

Isabel

Isabel's eyes snapped open as the first hint of morning slipped through the trellis. She sprung from her hammock and dressed before the distant call of bugles at the barracks announced dawn. Even the roosters still slept.

They'd spent the entire afternoon after Victoria's visit combing every street in Rio for the faintest suggestion of what might have happened—a witness, a conspirator, a disgruntled neighbor— and returned home with nothing but blisters on their feet. A new day demanded a new plan. Isabel had one, but it required ignoring every rule Maria set the day before, hence the early morning departure.

She scooped leftover angu from the pot, mixing it with mushed bananas, and ate it cold. Going outside to the oven and building a fi re would wake Maria for certain. As she ate, Isabel spied on her neighbors through the slits in the trellis. They had fi sh to catch, shirts to sew, ships to unload, chickens to feed. They all had normal days ahead while she hunted a murderer. She wouldn't have traded places with them for all the diamonds in the world.

Not that she wasn't sick with worry for Mateus. Not that she didn't have a voice in her head whispering everything was her fault. Not that she didn't feel a blinding desire to stab something every time her gaze landed on a Bat. But fueling all the worry and guilt and anger was a thirst for more. Isabel woke up without any idea how the day would go, and it sent a thrill through her that left her giddy.

Maria continued to snore despite the growing commotion outside. Isabel eyed their mother's trunk warily. She stored her extra knives inside, and it was definitely a six-blade day. She lifted the lid enough to slip her hand under. The hinge creaked, and she froze. Maria didn't move. She slid the knives out and strapped them on over her breeches, adding a cotton skirt over the entire ensemble.

Even without the need to hide a half dozen knives strapped to her legs, Isabel would have worn the skirt. She understood why Maria shunned them. The only things made easier by a skirt were pissing and hiding weapons, but Isabel loved how a skirt rippled in the sea breeze. How it flared out when she spun to stab an attacker's belly. And the sound of a swishing skirt brought back her mother.

She belted a leather pouch around her waist with a few coins and dried pineapple then crept to the door barefoot, boots in hands. A rooster crowed.

"Isabel?"

Isabel cursed the bird and vowed to find it, pluck it, roast it, and have it for dinner. "Everything's fine. I'm just getting an early start."

"And you didn't wake me? We don't have time for sleeping." Even half-asleep, Maria's voice was commanding.

"There's not time for you to collapse from exhaustion in the middle of the street either. Besides I'm already heading out. I'll cover the distance of two people for the next hour while you have a hot breakfast."

"I do not need an hour for breakfast."

"Fine. Five minutes. Or none. I'm heading out now. Meet you at São Bento square at noon. Happy hunting."

"You remember the plan?"

Isabel turned back to her sister, flashing a brilliant smile. "You mean the plan for you to go back to the capoeira circles and for me to sneak around Dom Antonio's street and interview his neighbors' kitchen staff? Yes, I remember the plan. Don't worry. I'll have a trail by lunch."

With a wave, she rushed out the door and down the street in the opposite direction of Dom Antonio's house. Maria's plan wasn't bad. Hers was simply better and one Maria would never approve. To find a criminal, they should talk to other criminals, not kitchen maids scrubbing pots.

Dona Antonia's inn sat on the edge of the city and attracted a lot of customers looking to enjoy themselves away from the center of authority. Many of them came for breakfast after a night of hard work. Isabel planned to take advantage of their full bellies and drowsy thinking.

Maria advised her explicitly to stay away from Antonia's. They'd brought more than a dozen soldiers storming into her courtyard, kicking in doors, arresting a patron, and her sister thought they should avoid the inn for a while. Even if Antonia wasn't angry with them now, they shouldn't take advantage of her forgiveness. A person can only forgive having her property invaded so many times.

Isabel agreed, but as she had no intention of breaking anything or alerting any authorities, the reasoning didn't apply to her. Also, she knew Antonia better than Maria. While Maria went to the capoeira circles with their father, their mother took Isabel to Dona Antonia's. Every Sunday afternoon, the three of them sat under the amendoeira tree mending stockings, pants, and frayed hammocks. Well her mother and Dona Antonia mended. Isabel spent most of the time climbing the tree.

Only two blocks from the house, sweat beaded her brow. Isabel walked barefoot, relishing the cool, compacted dirt beneath her feet. The Portuguese obsession with shoes mystified her. She'd watched Victoria struggle with the idea of removing hers even inside on the straw mat. They insisted on wearing them at all times regardless of the heat or if they were even walking. If someone carried her around in a litter all the time, she certainly wouldn't waste money on shoes. She only tied on her boots to protect her toes before wading into the flood of vendors and church goers on the boulevard.

Isabel took a shortcut down an alley between houses and found herself blocked by a family on their daily parade to morning mass. The patriarch with his wide hat and even wider belly strolled in front of the alley a second before Isabel could slip out. The golden head of his walking stick glinted, and his cravat flapped like a limp sail. Isabel groaned. The more ostentatious the accessories, the larger audience they wanted to draw, and the slower they walked. She had criminals and morally flexible businessmen to interrogate before they went home for a good day's sleep. She jiggled her leg, ready to dart through a gap between family members.

The father was followed by a young daughter, with a lace shawl draped over her long-sleeve dress, who was in turn followed by an older sister on the verge of being swallowed by the enormous ruffled collar on her dress. A third daughter strolled by and finally the mother in fifth position.

Behind the matriarch came her personal maid, a woman with golden-beige skin who could have passed for a family member if her hair had been straighter. The maid wore almost as fine a dress as her mistress with stockings and slippers, declaring her higher rank in the household in comparison to the rest of the entourage who followed barefoot. A wet nurse with a fourth child. Two women. One footman. Isabel bit back a scream of frustration as two house boys passed by, and the procession reached fifteen people.

When the final member of the household passed, Isabel bolted across the boulevard and headed for the farms on the outskirts of the city. It was a longer route, but she'd make up time by avoiding the crowds in town. If she got caught behind another parade of piety someone would lose an eye.

The clatter of the city and ring of church bells faded as Isabel entered the hills surrounding Rio. Coffee covered the nearest hillside, and she paused to watch men and women picking the beans. This was what Maria wanted. A piece of land with neat rows of the same bush repeating over and over, and endless hours spent bent over them picking beans. Years of stooping and picking on the same piece of land until she died. Isabel shuddered and hurried past.

As tedious as farm life appeared, Isabel could admit it did smell better than the city. The city smelled of dead fish, sun-cooked horse dung, and overheated bodies. In the hills, she inhaled the scent of earth and the color green. A person could definitely breathe easier on a farm, but Isabel dreaded any way of life where inhaling was an activity worthy of note.

Isabel intended to prove they didn't have to give up their lives in Rio. She'd find the murderer, knock him out, and drag him unconscious to the prison. Mateus would be free, and Maria would realize there was no problem they couldn't solve, because what could be worse than having a lifelong friend wrongly imprisoned and set for execution? Been there and handled that. Vidigal did seem to have a personal vendetta against them, but she could take care of that problem with a single blade and trip to a caiman nest.

The Bat's commander wouldn't be her first kill. Isabel started hunting game with her father at ten, and she killed the first man who attacked her when she was eleven. Any animal that couldn't fight back got eaten. It was how nature worked. Everything's born. Everything dies, and in the time between you eat or get eaten. These were obvious truths she'd accepted as a child. She didn't go looking for reasons to kill, but it became necessary from time to time. Vidigal was one of those times.

First, she had to save Mateus, so her sister could sleep again.

Isabel hurried past the farms and grand estates, keeping an eye out for soldiers. They patrolled the roads coming into the city searching for smugglers and runaway slaves. There were also Bats to look out for. She didn't normally worry about them this far out of town, but after the customs outpost, she kept one hand near the slit in her skirt.

The road curved back toward the bay, and the farms gave way to dotted forest. A few homes lined the road, small buildings of clay with only three sides or simply hammocks strung between trees under a roof of palm fronds. Closer to the beach, the houses became bigger and more numerous. A group of chained prisoners, under the guard of mounted soldiers, cleared a section of trees to build still more. None of those houses existed when she was a girl. With the arrival of the Court, the population of Rio exploded. The flood of new arrivals still continued a year later, and Isabel wondered if there'd be any forest left in Rio by the end of her life.

For now, the forest pushed back against the city, filling any empty space. The gleaming white walls of Dona Antonia's inn stood out against the emerald canopy on either side. Trees in every hue of green shaded the inn while blossoms of yellow, pink, and white bobbed on the breeze. The inn faced the waves of Guanabara Bay washing up lazily along the sand, and Sugar Loaf Mountain towered over the forest to the south, a sentinel guarding the city. Isabel fervently prayed heaven looked like Rio de Janeiro. She couldn't imagine anything more beautiful.

The man sitting alone in the back corner of Antonia's courtyard came close. He had the brim of his hat pulled low, but it didn't hide the fact she could sharpen her blades on his chin.

If the man hoped to blend in, he'd gone about it the wrong way. Keeping his hat on while sitting in a shady corner only piqued her interest. He held himself carefully, shoulders deliberately hunched and head down, but glanced at Isabel as she crossed the threshold. The beautiful stranger was looking for someone, to meet or to avoid, that was the question.

"Bom dia, Isabel." Benedito popped up next to her with a mouthful of corn cake.

"Bom dia, Dito."

"I heard about Mateus. That he got arrested by Bats. Maria told me. She asked me to help look for someone who saw the murder."

"Maria asked you to help?" Her sister must be desperate if enlisting children. She needed to find a trail before Maria petitioned the Prince Regent during the hand-kissing ceremony.

"Yup, I haven't told Mama. She wouldn't like."

"Good thinking. Parents never like the exciting stuff. Dito, that man in the corner." Isabel cut her eyes in the stranger's direction. "Has he been here before?"

"Yeah, he started coming here a few weeks ago," the boy mumbled through another bite of cake.

"Does he have a room?"

"No, a couple times he rented a room for the night, but usually he comes only for a meal. I started—"

"Can you do me a favor?" Isabel cut Benedito off before he could change the subject.

"No. I've got to get to Rua Quitanda before any other barbers. But will you come over Sunday? I've been practicing knife throwing. I'm really good now."

"I can't wait to see, but I might be a little busy this Sunday helping Mateus escape prison."

"Oh right. Tell Maria I'm still listening for gossip about Dom Antonio." He shoved the rest of the cake in his mouth and wiped his hands on his shirt. "Tchau."

Benedito loped out the door, and Isabel turned her attention back to the man in shadow. On the edge of forest and civilization, Antonia's inn wasn't a place visitors stumbled across. People found it by word of mouth or desperation, then came back for the discretion and sardines. The stranger's table was empty except for a tin cup of Antonia's swamp-thick coffee. She recognized a fellow connoisseur of discretion.

Antonia's voice floated out of the kitchen. She should go straight to Antonia and ask about Dom Antonio, but the sun had barely cleared the horizon. Mateus wasn't going anywhere for seven days. She could spare a minute on a handsome stranger.

"Bom dia, senhor." Isabel perched on a stool opposite the man, tilting her head so her hair fell across one cheek. "Are you having breakfast? I was about to and thought we could keep each other company."

"Oh. . . uh, no. . . no, thank you. I mean. . ." The man stuttered, caught off guard, before recovering enough to remember his manners. "Bom dia, senhorita."

He lifted his hat, revealing sapphire-blue eyes. The eyes and the accent betrayed him as foreign, but he wore the loose linen pants and shirt of a Carioca. Although the clothes had clearly never been used for work harder than lifting a fork.

"Bom dia again, senhor." Isabel smiled and held the man's gaze until his face turned pink. It reminded her of Victoria.

"I didn't mean to imply your company was unwelcome, senhorita. I meant to say that unfortunately I've finished my business and will be leaving shortly."

"You're not staying here at the inn?"

"No, I come to get away from the bustle of the city."

Isabel recognized a lie when she heard one, and the man was a liar as sure as he was foreign. "And Antonia serves the best fried sardines in Rio de Janeiro."

"Agreed. The company one finds here is also exemplary." He raised his cup to Isabel. His eyes widened in recognition. "Goodness, are you Dona Antonia's daughter?"

"No, just a devout patron of her breakfast." Isabel propped her chin in her hand and openly studied the man. "Your Portuguese is excellent, Senhor. . .?"

"Please, call me Thomas."

"Your Portuguese is excellent, Senhor Thomas."

"Thank you. I studied for years in anticipation of making a voyage to Brazil. I was going to compliment your Portuguese as well."

"Excuse me?" Isabel frowned.

"Your Portuguese is excellent."

"I'm from Rio."

"But your people don't traditionally speak Portuguese."

"My people?" Isabel pursed her lips.

"The Tupi?" He seemed to notice the clouds gathering in her gaze, and his voice turned uncertain.

This foreigner was complimenting her Portuguese and talking about her people.

Isabel could tell him the truth and explain she was born in Rio like her birth mother and her maternal grandparents. Her ancestors were Guarani, who'd been enslaved by the Portuguese, brought to Rio, and forced to adapt to the city more than a century earlier. By the time native slaves were freed by royal decree more than fifty years ago, *her people* had been Cariocas for generations.

Her grandfather eased the troubles of the entire city with the pews he built and the marimba he played, and her grandmother's baskets, sturdy enough for coconuts, were sought after by every quitandeira. Her birth mother washed the city's clothes and kept it smelling of lemon grass instead of sweat. Her adopted mother cooked sweets for all the viceroy's parties. Rio de Janeiro was their legacy, and she'd inherited it from them.

Not that she expected the handsome stranger to recognize her claim. After a lifetime of explaining herself, Isabel had crafted a dozen origin stories, complete with crowd-tested winks and asides. She deployed them according to the mood of her audience and what she hoped to get from them—admiration, sympathy, a round of drinks. The truth she kept for herself.

Her story was more precious than any of the gold or diamonds they carted back from Minas. She gave it only to those she trusted with her life because it required opening her heart, and any knife fighter worth a damn knew leaving the chest exposed was a good way to die. Tomasinho would not get *her* story, but Isabel had one that included a lesson he clearly needed.

"It's true; Portuguese is not my people's native tongue." Isabel dropped her eyes as if in embarrassment. "My people are more comfortable in the forest, but we come into Rio to trade. It's actually my first time here alone."

"You came alone? This city is much too dangerous for a young woman to wander alone."

"My family didn't have a choice. My mother is taking care of my eight younger brothers and sisters, and my father was attacked by a pack of wolves. He needs medicine. I was sent to the city to trade for it."

The moment she said it, Isabel realized a wolf attack might have been a bit much on top of eight siblings, but the man nodded along, wide-eyed. He seemed genuinely concerned, and she felt a tiny prick of guilt on her conscience.

"You're very brave to come into the city on your own. Rio is dangerous even for someone who knows it well. Allow me to assist you."

"Would you?" Isabel pouted and wrung her hands. "I came to Dona Antonia's because I wanted to ask one of my own people first, but she's had a hard month and doesn't have cash on hand to give in return."

"What is it you brought to trade?"

"Topaz."

Thomas sucked in a breath. "Topaz? You have gems?"

"Our village is near a river, and we find gems from time to time. The people in the city seem to like them." From the leather pouch at her waist, Isabel pulled out three dusty stones.

"They're beautiful," the man said, lifting one to catch the light.

They were, which was why Isabel collected them in the first place. They were also worthless crystals, but the man seemed happy with his assumptions.

"I'll take them."

"No senhor, I don't need your pity. I want to make a fair trade."

"That's what I'm offering. I'll buy the stones."

He pulled a small, drawstring bag from inside his shirt then reached for her hand. He put the bag in it and closed her fingers around it. Gold dust. She recognized the feel, and the weight felt like enough to buy Maria a new saddle.

"It's gold dust. Don't give it all to the doctor. Give him half and save the rest to buy some supplies for your family." He deftly swept the crystals off the table and into a pocket inside his shirt collar.

Isabel suddenly wondered if she was the one being conned. Nothing about the man made sense. He had secret pockets like a smuggler and frequented a place known for attracting people who followed laws by accident, but he couldn't spot a counterfeit topaz and naïvely helped strangers with sacks of gold dust.

"I wish very much that I could stay and assist you further, senhorita but I must return home before——" The man stilled. His eyes locked on the entrance.

Two Bats dragged themselves to a table with barely a glance around the courtyard, probably at the end of a night patrolling. Far more interesting than the Bats, Thomas's smile disappeared, and he scanned the corners of the courtyard. He was a man looking for an exit.

"Not friends with the guardsmen?" Isabel asked cheerfully.

"I find their application of the law questionable." He grimaced in annoyance. "This is what I get for expecting a rich man to show up somewhere before sunrise."

"Would you like to leave without being seen?"

"I admit it would be preferable if authorities didn't see me here, but you don't need to trouble yourself."

"Leave it to me," Isabel said. "You helped me, so I'll help you. Give me your hat and bandana."

"I'm sorry?"

"Give me your hat and bandana. I'll distract them. Then you slip out through the kitchen. Tell Antonia you need the back door."

Now that she'd taught him a lesson, Isabel felt compelled to keep him out of jail. He was ignorant and as street savvy as a nun straight from a Portuguese convent, but those weren't faults that deserved Vidigal's claws.

She twisted her hair into a bun and wrapped it up in the bandana. She donned the hat and cut off his protest. "Tomasinho, I'm helping you out today. In the future, don't be so trusting."

Isabel winked and strolled over to the Bats' table.

"Bom dia, senhores? What can I bring you?" She used a Paulista accent, changing her *R* and *S* to match the southern residents of São Paulo.

"Where's Roberta? She always serves us."

"Apologies, senhor. I don't know Roberta. I'm new. Maybe she's the girl not feeling well? I heard a girl was up all night attending one poor guest. She's been running to his bedside the last two days, the fool. You wouldn't catch me at the bedside of a man with a raging fever unless he was paying me in gold. Maybe if he was my husband, and even then, I'd have to think before doing it for free. Especially if he was the same awful color as that poor man upstairs. I swear his face is yellow as a banana."

The men were on their feet faster than a viper strike. "We have to leave."

"What about your breakfast?" Isabel asked, frowning in concern. "Don't you at least want coffee? Bowl of beans? Fried bananas?"

One hesitated, but his partner jerked him away. "No, thank you. We're late. Good day."

Isabel waved at their retreating backs. "Tchau senhores. Don't come back."

"Isabel Azevedo."

Antonia marched out of the kitchen. "Are you telling royal guards there's a yellow fever outbreak at my inn?"

"Maybe."

"And did you tell that gringo to sneak out through my kitchen after telling him you live in the forest and your father was recently attacked by a wolf?"

"If I did, would you be angry with me?"

"For lying to that young man. He's good business and has a trusting heart."

"I know. That's why I didn't ask for more for those fake topaz," Isabel said.

"You sold him counterfeit gems? What would your mother say?" Antonia rolled her eyes to the heavens as if asking for support and retreated to the kitchen.

Isabel scrambled after her. "Don't be mad, Dona. It was only three. He needed a lesson in humility."

"You can teach people without stealing from them."

"Fine. Next time I'll give him a lecture on not getting conned out of your gold by being a fool, but today I don't have time to be some foreign boy's nanny." Isabel pointed back to the empty courtyard in dismay. "Where is everyone? When we were here two nights ago the yard was full."

"A full house has become a rare event," Antonia said, swinging a pot of beans away from the fire. She gave instructions in Spanish to a kitchen girl stirring a pot of cassava and spoke in Guarani to another peeling potatoes. Then Antonia grabbed a knife and set to work on a fresh pile of sardines before picking up her conversation with Isabel in Portuguese.

"We haven't had as many early customers lately. The Bats have been cracking down at night. More arrests. More beatings. I think people are afraid to go out at night, so fewer people wanting breakfast in the morning. Meanwhile, more inns are opening while meat costs its weight in gold, and if any more homeless Portuguese nobles show up in Rio, there won't be a fish left in the bay."

Doubt slithered up from Isabel's stomach. Her plan required a bustling courtyard of bleary-eyed, hungover miscreants. Isabel forced her thoughts away from failure. She could sell sweets to a fasting nun. When she wanted something, she found a way to get it.

"There have to be customers I can talk to," Isabel pleaded. "What about at lunch? And dinner? People still come for dinner. I could come back at dinner. Everyone has to eat. Even murderers. How many guests do you have? Can I deliver the coffee to their rooms?"

Antonia stopped scraping scales from a sardine and frowned at her. "Is this about Mateus? Dito told me everything. I'm very sorry. I know he's like a brother to you girls."

"He's innocent, Dona."

"I know, sweetheart."

Antonia laid a hand on her shoulder and something inside snapped. Isabel whirled around, knocking the hand off. "He's innocent, and the Bats don't care. The superintendent doesn't care. The Prince Regent doesn't care because he doesn't even know Mateus exists. His life is in the hands of people who don't give a damn about it. All it would take is one conversation with him, a minute, and you'd know Mateus could never strangle anyone. But a rich man died, and someone has to pay."

"Dom Antonio was strangled?" Antonia stopped breathing.

"He had this awful red line all around his throat, no other wound, and he was dead."

The innkeeper took Isabel's arm and steered her out the back door, past the men unloading barrels of port, beyond the garden, to the edge of the forest. Far from any eavesdroppers. "Tell me what you found that night."

"We found him in his office. The room was torn apart, like a storm had blown through."

"But nothing was missing," Antonia finished.

They stared at each other. Isabel's pulse quickened. "How did you know that?"

Antonia searched Isabel's face, a deep crease between her brows. Whatever internal struggle happened didn't last long. "You've already lost too much family. I won't let you lose more. I didn't know Antonio was strangled, or I would have found you yesterday. Two weeks ago a guest was strangled in one of the rooms. A red line around his neck. The room was made to look like a robbery, but his coat, boots, even a ring were left."

"We've asked the entire city about Antonio's murder. Why hasn't anyone said anything about your guest?"

"Nobody knows. I promised the family I'd keep it quiet. They thought being strangled in a cheap inn wasn't an honorable end, and silence worked for me, too. A murder isn't going to bring more business."

"Who was killed?" Isabel held her breath.

"Dom Afonso. The one in the big house on—"

"Thank you, Dona!" Isabel shouted over her shoulder, already running to the street. She didn't need to hear any more because she knew Dom Afonso. They'd sold him black market diamonds. Just like they sold to Dom Antonio.

It was about the diamonds.

Isabel didn't stop running until she found Maria in São Bento square. She relayed Antonia's story without taking a breath.

"We have to interview any man we've sold to," Maria said. "No matter the station."

Isabel let out a whoop. "We haven't needed to interrogate anyone in months. Not since Tio Miguel tried to poach our clients. We should use knives. Blades are nice and quiet." She twirled, sending her skirts flaring wide. "I knew I'd need six blades today."

"Before you pull out the daggers, we need to see if the royal guard has made the connection between Dom

Antonio and Dom Afonso, and if not, we point them in the right direction."

"How are we going to do that? Walk into the jail and ask to meet with the officer in charge?"

"We know someone who works next to the prison and has proved she can find out what the royal guard knows."

"Victoria!" Isabel smiled at the prospect of seeing Victoria curtsy again. "Are we sneaking into the queen's room?"

"No. We're asking for her at the kitchen door."

Isabel felt a flash of disappointment, but it disappeared in her excitement. They had a trail. They were going to interrogate some very wealthy men, and she had a sack of gold dust for all her troubles.

"By the way, sister, you're doing laundry for the next month."

Chapter Twelve

Victoria

Prince João pulled a chicken leg out of his coat pocket, tore a bite off, and continued speaking without bothering to swallow first. From inside the queen's litter, Victoria cringed. A sovereign needed to keep his strength up, but the Prince Regent's regular stash of chicken parts seemed indulgent. And untidy. She pitied His Highness's grooms.

The queen dozed off before they got out of the city, and Victoria sat across from her fanning the heat and flies away. Princess Carlota Joaquina tromped through the nearby jungle with a rifle hoping to spot some game. The nobles hovered around the prince swatting mosquitos and probably regretting choosing this particular outing to gain favor. Oblivious to them all, the Prince Regent continued to pontificate about the grand palace that would soon exist on this hilltop overlooking Rio.

A family outing. That's what the prince's valet told Victoria to prepare the queen for. A family outing to visit the future royal residence and see the renovations. The Prince Regent wanted to show off the additions he was making to the grand manor. Now they were all surrounded by forest with the tension thicker than the humidity, while Prince João droned on between bites of chicken. From the looks Princess Carlota Joaquina kept shooting her husband, Her Highness clearly hoped for a tragic accident involving a jaguar to befall him.

The heat, undeterred by the litter's shade, smothered thought and feeling. Victoria sat on the velvet cushions counting the beads of sweat as they trailed down her back. The queen snored like a boar. The Prince Regent droned on. The princess glared, and the lords stifled yawns. When Victoria thought about how long it could take to renovate the house and how many of these family outings through the jungle to the hilltop might lie in front of her, she wanted to cry. Of course, if they kept dragging the queen on these absurd excursions for public display, Her Majesty wouldn't last the year. Then what would happen to her?

Victoria reached to adjust the queen's head which had fallen into a decidedly unregal position, drool trickling down her chin. At her touch, the queen started awake, and Victoria snapped back to her side of the litter. The queen frowned at the view out the window as if trying to remember why she'd been carted to a hilltop in the middle of nowhere.

"I need to relieve myself," Queen Maria announced, flinging the curtain aside and plunging out of the litter.

Victoria grabbed the chamber pot and scrambled after Her Majesty. She informed the guards they'd be stepping into the woods for privacy. Neither the Prince Regent nor princess looked in their direction.

She caught up to the queen and clasped her elbow, guiding her around roots and patches of slippery, rotting leaves. When she found a relatively clear space with enough foliage to shield them from sight, Victoria set the pot down and helped Her Majesty lift her skirts and position herself. She looked away as she heard liquid ping against metal.

"I always thought being royal should exempt one from pissing and other vulgar necessities," the queen commented. It was one of her good mornings. She'd slept well and had kept up a string of enlightening if somewhat embarrassing observations all morning.

"It would certainly give Your Majesty and His Highness more time to spend on important matters of state," Victoria said.

Her Majesty snorted. "João would use the extra time to eat."

"His Highness has to run an empire. He needs to keep up his strength."

"The empire is an easy task compared to that Spanish boar at his side. Boars are notoriously hard to kill, but I'll find a way. I see her."

Victoria held back a sigh. She hated whenever the conversation turned to Princess Carlota Joaquina. She didn't disagree with the queen about the princess's faults, but agreeing with a comparison of the crowned princess to a boar could have severe consequences if the wrong ears overheard. It was a constant balancing act. At least the queen and princess were honest. She didn't have to waste energy parsing every sentence and interpreting every frown like servants for other family members. A small but appreciated blessing.

"The empire is fortunate to have such a strong and dedicated monarch looking out for it, Your Majesty."

"You should be a diplomat," a voice said from the trees.

Victoria leapt in front of the queen. Her scream died in her throat as Maria and Isabel dropped into the clearing.

"What are you doing here?" she whispered. Her mind raced. If the queen screamed, they'd be arrested and probably executed. She had to keep the queen from panicking and get Maria and Isabel to leave. She needed a lie. An explanation for the girls' presence that didn't involve murder or diamond smuggling.

"Your Majesty, these are Cariocas who have been teaching me about the local flora and fauna in hopes I might be able to use some for medicinal purposes. I asked them to meet us here to point out the abundance of medicinal flora in this jungle."

"Your Majesty," Isabel said. She dropped an awkward but respectfully low curtsey. Victoria was relieved until Isabel winked on her way back up. "Told you I would practice."

"Do all Brazilians live in trees?" the queen asked, looking between the girls and into the tree they'd been hiding in. Her Majesty was still squatting over the pot and Victoria hauled her to her feet. This meeting needed to conclude immediately.

"We don't live in trees, Your Majesty," Maria said in an even voice.

"We just spy in them," Isabel added, grinning.

"Oh, are you spies? Excellent." The queen stepped forward heedless of the chamber pot she knocked over. "Spying seems an odd profession for two colored girls but as my options are limited, I would like to engage your services."

"Who do you want us to spy on?" Isabel's eyes glowed with interest.

"What do you pay?" Maria asked.

"No!" Victoria jumped between the queen and the muleteers. "Your Majesty, they don't mean spying on people. They mean birds and wildlife. My friends are muleteers. They lead mule trains from Minas Gerais and have developed an extensive knowledge of the jungle." She turned her back to the queen and clasped her hands at her breast begging Maria and Isabel. "They're going to tell us which plants can be used to clean wounds and help with headaches."

"Girl, I don't care about trees. Not unless one of them produces a glass of wine. I'm parched. Let us return."

"Would Your Majesty care for some pitangas?" Isabel held out a handkerchief filled with shiny, red berries the size of her thumbnail. The bumps encircling the berry reminded Victoria of tiny pumpkins. "They're ripe and sweet."

"Thank you, Isabel, but I don't think Her Majesty. . ."

"What a delightful color." The queen accepted the handkerchief, all the berries, and plopped down at the base of a tree. The three women stared in silence for a moment as the queen tossed a few ruby berries into her mouth, chewed, and spit the pits into the dirt.

"She isn't what I expected," Maria said.

Victoria whirled on Maria. Not what she expected? What on earth gave her the right? "What are you doing here? You're going to get me fired at best, shot for treason at worst!"

"Why would talking to us get you killed?" Isabel asked.

"For helping you assassinate the queen!" Victoria waved her arms around at the thick forest surrounding them. "We've got the queen of Portugal alone in the jungle. What would any soldier think if he walked up on us? You have to leave!"

"We have new information," Maria whispered. "The murderer killed someone else. Dom Afonso."

"How do you know it's the same killer? With all due respect, people are killed frequently in this city. I overheard a British diplomat talking about a man being stabbed to death and left on his doorstep!"

"Dom Afonso was strangled and the scene made to look like a robbery like at Dom Antonio's, and they were both smugglers," Isabel said.

Victoria fell silent. That was too many similarities to be coincidence. If they'd been in her room at the convent, she could have them relate the details of both crimes and come up with a list of similarities that could help them narrow down…but they weren't at the palace. They were hiding a few feet away from the royal family's military escort. This was madness.

"I'm sorry. I can't help you now. I can come to your home tomorrow after midday."

"We want you to tell someone about the new murder and the connection to the diamonds." Maria stepped up to her. "Dom Afonso was killed two weeks ago. We were in Minas, so Mateus can't be the murderer. Once the royal guard knows about the new murder, they'll let him go."

"Who do you think I am?" Victoria's face grew hot. She saw hope in Maria's eyes and couldn't bear being responsible for destroying it. They asked too much, expected too much from her. She could only disappoint them. "You can't come charging up to me in front of the queen talking about murder and smuggling! Are you mad?"

"No, but she seems to be, so we didn't think it mattered what we talked about," Isabel said with a shrug.

"It does matter. She hears everything and will repeat at random. She might tell her next visitor about the mystery man murdering diamond smugglers."

"Good. Then someone will listen," Maria said.

"No! No one is going to listen! To me or to her," Victoria snapped. She glanced at the queen still gleefully eating pitangas. They needed to leave, so she unleashed the truth on Maria and Isabel. "Her Majesty's mad, and I'm a servant. Neither of us have any power or influence. They aren't going to release a man who Major Vidigal himself put in prison because the Mad Queen's maid said he caught the wrong person."

She stopped, realizing that neither Maria nor Isabel were looking at her. They stared into the tree over her head. "I'm sorry. You came all the way up here to ignore me?"

"Victoria, don't move," Maria ordered in a tone that froze her in place. "Isabel?"

"I see her."

"See who? What's happening?" Victoria choked out through growing panic.

Isabel drew a dagger from her skirt, her eyes never leaving the tree. Victoria's gut clenched. Before she could protest, Isabel's arm snapped. A blur flew into the tree branches. She heard a thud on the ground behind and something solid smacked against her ankle nearly sweeping her off her feet. Victoria spun to find an enormous snake with a dagger through its middle writhing on the ground. She staggered backward and would have screamed if her voice hadn't abandoned her in terror.

"Excuse me." Isabel stepped around Victoria. She pinned the snake to the ground with another dagger before bringing a third down below the head. The snake stopped moving. Isabel withdrew one dagger from the body and stabbed the snake through the head. "Always good to be thorough." She winked at Victoria's wide-eyed expression.

As Isabel collected and cleaned her daggers, Victoria took in the full size of the snake. It was a constrictor type and could have stretched the length of her bed and dangled its tail off the end, probably twitching it while pondering how tasty she would be. Isabel staggered under the weight of the snake as she hauled half of it onto her shoulders. "A little help, dear sister."

Maria shouldered the back half of the snake.

"What are you doing?" Victoria gaped at the girls grappling with the monster's carcass.

"Taking it home for dinner." Maria adjusted the constrictor higher on her back.

The queen's cackle turned their heads. "My dear, you were right. These girls are quite the naturalists. Bravo!" She applauded then spit out two pitanga pits.

"She really likes pitangas," Isabel observed. "I'll bring her some more next time we visit the convent."

"No, there's not going to be a next visit!" Victoria felt as though her chest was being squeezed by one of those horrid snakes. Her chemise clung to her legs and a bead of sweat ran down the back of her knee. "You need to take your dinner and go. Leave! I'm going to be dismissed because of you. I said I would pass you any information about your friend, and I will keep my promise, but that's it. You can't drop into my room or out of the trees anytime you want! You're crazy. This country is crazy!"

"Victoria, everything's fine. We'll go. You don't need to panic," Maria said slowly.

"Yes, I do because I'm in hell. Rio is hell. It's burning hot and filled with murderers and giant snakes. It's hell."

"I can't really argue with that description, but I always imagined hell as more red and less green." Isabel glanced around the surrounding jungle.

"A green hell then!" Victoria stomped over to the queen. "Your Majesty, we've been gone too long. It's time to return to the escort." She helped the queen to her feet, pitanga pits spilling from her skirt. Isabel and Maria said nothing as Victoria led Her Majesty through the jungle.

"Enjoy your dinner, girls." Queen Maria of the House Braganza gave the dead snake a pat then glanced back at the chamber pot still on the ground. "Victoria, don't forget my piss pot."

Victoria rested her head against the cushioned seat in the litter. They were finally on the outskirts of the city. The queen snored again. By some miracle, Her Majesty hadn't said anything about the two Brazilian girls jumping out of a tree and killing a giant snake. Hopefully, the queen would assume it was a dream.

Carlota Joaquina came storming over the moment Victoria and the queen cleared the forest and announced they were returning to the city. Prince João would stay on to discuss plans with the architect, but he wanted the queen to return to the palace and had asked Carlota Joaquina to escort her. The princess reeked of indignation. Victoria wondered if she hated playing escort to Her Majesty or being ordered around. Most likely both.

Her Royal Highness's silhouette rode past the curtained window heading to the front of the party. Despite a limp, the princess was an excellent rider. Better than most men. She was a good shot, too. Victoria had to admit that what the princess lacked in kindness and decency, she made up for in skills.

"Halt, in the name of Her Majesty Queen Maria I," a soldier's voice rang out.

Victoria peeked out. A lone rider moved off to the side of the road to let the train pass. He touched his hat and tipped his head to Carlota Joaquina.

"Good day, Your Highness." The man had an accent Victoria couldn't place. He wasn't Portuguese or Brazilian.

"Is that how you address Her Majesty the queen of Portugal and your princess?" Carlota Joaquina snarled. Victoria pursed her lips. This was the first time she'd ever heard the princess demand respect for the queen. "You will dismount, and show the proper respect."

"I'm sorry, Your Highness, but Americans have no princess. I wish you well and a safe journey." He bowed his head again but made no move to dismount.

American! Victoria stuck her head further out the window to get a better look. She'd never seen an American before and was a little disappointed he looked so similar to the English she'd seen. He had dark blond hair pulled back from a young, clean-shaven face. Nothing distinctly different from the British. She'd over-heard that American delegates recently arrived in Rio and wondered if this man was part of that delegation.

"How dare you flaunt such disrespect," the princess snapped. "You will dismount and kneel!"

"No, I will not."

Victoria nearly fell out of the window in shock. She'd never seen anyone refuse Princess Carlota Joaquina and certainly never while making eye contact. If someone had to say no, they gripped their hat in their hands, lowered their nose to the floor, and prayed she was in a forgiving mood. Victoria was certain this poor man had moments to live.

Carlota Joaquina shouted to the guards. "Pull this man from his saddle, and force him to his knees."

Four soldiers surrounded the American, who remained upright on his horse. The officer reached for his whip. "Sir, you will dismount or you will be whipped."

Without batting an eyelid, the American reached under his coat and drew a pistol in each hand. The man leveled the pistols at two of the guards, including the officer holding the whip.

"If you raise that whip, sir, I will shoot you dead."

Victoria gasped. The man's eyes flicked to her, and she ducked back inside the litter, closing the curtain. She couldn't watch a man die.

Silence.

She risked a glance at the scene. The American still had the pistols pointed at the soldiers, and his expression left no doubt he would pull the trigger. Victoria held her breath, twisting the ribbon around her finger so tightly the tip turned white. Everyone waited for the princess.

"Leave this republican," Carlota Joaquina sneered the word as if referring to the most wretched type of people imaginable. She spurred her horse ahead. The party immediately moved to keep up with her.

As the litter passed the American, he caught Victoria's gaze and tipped his hat. She collapsed against her seat. She couldn't decide if she'd glimpsed the bravest or dumbest man of her life. Nobody stood up to Carlota Joaquina and won. Generals and diplomats, even the Prince Regent, went silent in her presence.

Not this American. He'd held his ground and for what? So he wouldn't have to kneel? It seemed a ridiculous thing to be shot for, but at the same time, Victoria envied him for having a cause he was willing to die for.

What was she willing to die for?

Her books.

Sometimes, Victoria envisioned and planned for various crises, a fire, an outbreak of plague, an earthquake, and in every imagined disaster she grabbed her books. If a spur-of-the-moment transoceanic ship voyage had taught her anything, it was that having some sort of mental diversion was far more important than hair combs or stockings.

Although books seemed like silly things to die for.

Maria and Isabel had something to die for. They had family and a friend they loved enough to surprise the queen during a privy break with an armed escort through the trees. They were insane, determined, and most likely right about the murderer.

The truth was, and Victoria cringed to admit, that she hadn't completely believed in Mateus's innocence, but the story of another diamond smuggler dying in exactly the same circumstances wasn't a coincidence. Her father taught her to consider illnesses by looking at the entire body. How was each organ affected? What was every symptom? If two people had exactly the same symptoms manifesting in the same order, they more than likely had the same disease.

If two people with the same profession were killed in exactly the same manner within days of each other, they had the same murderer.

"Hold!" Princess Carlota Joaquina's command brought the train to a halt.

The queen continued to snore, so Victoria had leave to observe Carlota Joaquina through the back window. Perhaps an indifferent Dutchman had upset her this time.

They'd stopped in the shadow of two large buildings, maybe storehouses, and creeping out of an alley between the buildings, Major Vidigal appeared with two of his guardsmen wearing the telltale dark coats of the royal guard. Carlota Joaquina extended a hand which Vidigal kissed. With a jerk of her head, the princess sent the nearby soldiers away and remained alone with the major. She murmured to Vidigal. He gestured, and one of the Bats came towards the queen's litter. Instinct told Victoria to feign sleep, so she slumped in her seat and drooled along with the queen. She sensed a man peering through the curtain.

"Both sleeping," the man called walking away.

Carlota Joaquina then ordered the slaves to put down the litter and get water. The princess never acknowledged a slave's presence let alone gave them breaks. Being careful not to disturb them, Victoria peeked through the gap in the curtains. Carlota Joaquina and Vidigal spoke for several minutes, while the Bats kept watch. Finally, Carlota Joaquina pulled a note from her riding jacket and slipped it to Vidigal as he kissed her hand in parting. Then the Princess smiled.

Victoria had never seen Carlota Joaquina look happy. It was chilling.

The intimate conversation, the secret note, the kiss, that smile. Victoria grimaced. Vidigal had to be sixty, and Carlota Joaquina…She had less warmth than the snake Maria and Isabel carried home for dinner.

Maria and Isabel.

They were trying to prove their friend was innocent which meant they were simultaneously proving Vidigal wrong. The major was a trusted advisor to Prince João and a trusted something to Princess Carlota Joaquina. That didn't bode well for Mateus. The Crown Prince and Princess didn't agree on anything except apparently the trustworthiness of Vidigal. Victoria couldn't think of anything that would make Vidigal release Mateus, short of having the real murderer confess and then kill someone in the middle of the hand-kissing ceremony.

Victoria regretted losing her temper with Maria and Isabel. When they'd appeared, she'd been hot, anxious, and afraid their appearance would trigger one of the queen's fits. Victoria worked so hard to keep the queen calm and surrounded by the familiar, and her meticulously crafted routine didn't include a giant snake falling out of tree. Thank God, Her Majesty was having a good day.

She owed Maria and Isabel her life. More than that, she believed an innocent man was on the verge of being executed, but what could she do? She spent all her time with books and an aging monarch. She knew about some tonics and medicine from her father and could name the genus and species of all the native birds of Lisbon.

Maybe she could pick up bits and pieces of information for them about their friend's trial dates and condition, but those scraps of information couldn't get Mateus out of jail. The mere act of asking for them put Maria, Isabel, and Mateus at risk, and Victoria could lose her position. Was the help she could offer worth the risks?

The American man risked death for his beliefs. Maria and Isabel were risking death to help a friend. Her father had risked his reputation by treating the queen when every other physician wrote her off as lost.

She asked him once why he kept attending the queen when everyone else, including the Prince Regent, wanted to send her away. Her father said everyone needs someone who will fight for them, and the queen then improved under his care. Her screaming fits tapered off.

She started sleeping through the night again. He wasn't able to cure her, but he helped ease her mind.

Maybe that's what she could do for Maria and Isabel, keep them informed regarding Mateus so they at least didn't have to search for that information. For what it was worth, she could tell them she believed he was innocent. But first, she'd apologize for losing her temper and calling their country a green hell. Even if it was true, it was impolite to point it out.

Chapter Thirteen

Maria

From the matching glares, Maria knew her team finally agreed on something. They hated her latest order.

"Captain, I trust your instincts. They've saved us before. But I can't do this." Zé kept his voice low, hidden under the morning din of street vendors, but his passion was loud and clear.

"I'm not asking. Stop inquiring about Dom Antonio's household. Leave it alone."

"We're not going to abandon Mateus to the Bats," Zé countered. Berto and the rest of the team nodded in agreement.

"No one is abandoning him."

"With respect, captain, you and Isabel can't search the whole city."

"We're not searching the city. We have a lead, and it's better if Isabel and I handle it. We draw less suspicion."

"We're not afraid, captain," Berto said.

"Then you're a fool because people are dying," Maria snapped back.

The team went quiet. Berto stepped back in surprise or disappointment or insult. Maria wasn't sure, and the second guessing bothered her more than any questioning of her orders.

She took a deep breath. As she spoke, Maria looked each member of her team in the eye. "People are dying. Each of you have family that depends on you. They depend on you to stay alive, out of jail, and working. Asking about Antonio's murder puts you and your families at risk. Zé, you're about to be a father. Do you want to be in a cell when your wife has the baby?"

Zé kicked at the dirt in frustration, but he didn't argue.

"Dom Antonio was not a random murder. This is something bigger than one rich merchant." Maria paused, debating how much to tell them. "I don't think we'll ever find anyone who worked in Dom Antonio's house. I don't think there's anyone to find."

The team's silence shifted from angry to somber.

The stakes of their investigation escalated quickly after Isabel's discovery of Dom Afonso's murder. They changed their focus from Antonio's household to buyers of black market diamonds, and Maria uncovered a third murder, a Portuguese baron who arrived with the court and took to the black market like an eel to water. He was found strangled behind his stables. His family blamed thieves and bemoaned the violence of this savage city, but thieves didn't take the time to strangle men.

A suspicion slithered into her gut and hardened into a cold certainty. Dom Antonio's household was dead. Murdered. Loose ends tied off. Anyone willing to murder high-ranking nobles would think nothing of making a household of slaves disappear. A mule team would be even easier. Tragic accidents happened on the trail all the time.

"I know you want to help. Trust me that you *are* helping by not asking questions. I think the murderer has money and if he hears people are looking for him, he might fl ee. Isabel and I can be subtle, and if in trouble, we can disappear more easily than any of you."

Isabel appeared at the end of the ally and waved. Time to end this discussion. "Go home. Take care of your families. Look into picking up some extra work because I honestly don't know if we'll head out in two weeks."

She stalked away without giving her men a chance to protest. They couldn't change her mind. She wouldn't have them add to the body count.

Maria emerged from the alley into the bustle of Monday shopping. Pantries needed to be restocked after Sunday lunches, and every kitchen maid seemed to be out on the streets. Isabel sat on a wine barrel, eating an orange and sharing bits with a street dog. Her feet dangled in the air, and her loose hair caught the sun. She didn't look twenty-three. Maria felt keenly that by including Isabel in the search for a murderer, she might be failing in her promise to watch out for her little sister, but she trusted no one more. Also, the only way to stop Isabel from helping would be to tie her up and put her on a ship bound for Great Britain, and even then she'd probably charm the captain into turning around.

"Do you think they'll listen?" Isabel asked.

"Would you?"

"I'd have snuck off before you finished your speech."

"That's why I'd never hire you for my team. I only let you cook to keep my promise to Papa." Maria dodged the orange peel Isabel threw at her. "I see you found a snack. Did you also find the bakery?"

"Dom Tiago's bakery is the last building on the left next to the cobbler. This morning there are three slaves, the baker, and as of two minutes ago, four customers inside. There's the street door and an interior door almost directly opposite that leads into the kitchen. So yes, I found the bakery."

"Then let's get this over with."

Her boots left prints in the fine layer of flour coating the wooden floor of the bakery. Maria stepped in line behind a woman whose wide red skirt and even wider woven basket atop her head filled most of her view. The woman waited behind two boys with equally black skin but one wore a crisply tailored jacket with large brass buttons and the other tattered, dusty pants.

The boy with brass buttons stashed the warm rolls he purchased in a leather sack slung across his chest. He waited for the other boy who came away with one partly burnt roll tucked into a pocket. Maria guessed the boy in the coat was the son of free Blacks and the other the family's slave. They acted like friends. She wondered for how much longer.

The woman in front of her bargained fiercely over a dozen rolls. Maria caught Isabel rolling her eyes. There were only five bakeries in the city, and their prices never changed.

She took stock of the bakery while waiting. Freshly delivered wheat in cracked leather sacks lay on the floor near her feet. To her right a small mill stood silent early in the morning when most of the day's customers came through. On the wall opposite the mill, floor to ceiling shelves held baskets full of steaming baked goods. Her stomach growled, but she ignored it. They weren't here for the bread.

With a huff, the woman finally passed over some coins and filled the basket atop her head with bread. She marched out the door, her arms swinging at her sides.

Maria stepped up to the counter, while Isabel stayed by the door as lookout. A round man who bore more than a passing resemblance to the rolls he sold had his back to her.

"Be right with you," he called.

She did a final survey of the people. Behind the counter seated in front of the kitchen door were three men hunched over a table separating the newly delivered wheat. Isabel kept watch behind her on the left. Finally, the baker **stood** behind the counter.

He stepped down from the stool and brushed his hands against his apron. "Good morning, what can I get…" He froze mid brush when he saw Maria. "What do you want?"

"Bom dia, senhor. The bread smells delicious."

"I said 'what do you want.'" The man crossed his arms across his chest. She thought he was going for menacing, but with his sleeves rolled up tightly, it looked more like he was squishing uncooked lumps of dough.

Maria leaned closer and lowered her voice. If he wanted her to get to the point, she had no problem with that. "I know that you and the owner here, Dom Tiago, are in a special export business. My family and I are in the same business. We worked with Dom Antonio before he got killed, and I need to speak with Dom Tiago."

"Get out," the man pointed to the door. Pink splotches spread across his face. "I have nothing to say to you."

That was the second time he'd interrupted her. Maria rubbed her thumb against the leather grip of her whip. He wouldn't get away with a third. "Three people in our business have been murdered in the last two weeks. I need to know if Dom Tiago has been approached by anyone new to the business or to Rio. His life might be at stake."

"I'm not talking to prostitutes." The baker glared across the counter.

"Excuse me?" Maria pursed her lips. She always ran into pigs at the most inconvenient times.

"Running around in pants like a man. It's disgusting. Can't expect better from you people. But Dom Tiago is a respectable man. The Prince Regent made him a viscount."

Isabel laughed from her spot against the wall. "Everyone is these days. Did Tiago buy *his* title with the diamonds he's been stealing from under the Prince's nose?"

"Get out!" the man bellowed in Maria's face. "And take your mutt with you."

"Are you referring to my sister?" Maria's tone froze the room. The three men separating the wheat stared at her. She heard Isabel's boots on the wooden floor coming closer but kept her glare fixed on the baker's face. "I'd apologize if I were you."

The man guffawed, slapping his hand down on the counter. "This is my business. I give the orders here."

Silver flashed in the corner of her eye. A thud and the counter shook. The pink drained from the baker's round face. Isabel gripped two daggers planted deep into the counter in the narrow slits between his fingers.

"No apology necessary." Isabel batted her eyelashes at the man's horrified expression.

The men sorting wheat had disappeared. Probably for her and Isabel's sake. If they weren't around, the men wouldn't be able to act as witnesses against them. Good. Since they were alone, it was time for brutal honesty.

"Someone is killing diamond smugglers. Your boss is a diamond smuggler. He should talk to us. We might be able to help him not die." She gestured to Isabel's daggers. "You can work with us, or you can deal with the consequences of ignoring us."

"Goodness, you two must get the best prices in Rio." Victoria stood in the doorway smiling.

Maria instinctively gripped her whip and looked beyond the Portuguese girl for soldiers. "This is a surprise."

"Now you know how it feels," Victoria responded, and for a second Maria's gut clenched. Then Victoria smiled. Isabel burst out laughing, and Maria relaxed her grip on the whip. Victoria hadn't brought a platoon with her, and if dropping in on the queen pissing amongst the trees didn't get her to turn them in, nothing would.

"Personally, I love surprises." Isabel plucked her knives up and slipped them back into her skirt. "I can't say the same for my sister."

"How did you find us?" Maria asked.

"When I didn't find you at home, I began asking some of the nearby vendors. You two are quite famous. Finally, a boy in a very colorful and tall hat said you were visiting bakeries near Praia de Manuel."

"Benedito," Isabel said to Maria.

"He said I looked like an honest person and could be trusted."

Maria shook her head. "I have to talk to him about what information he gives out and explain that pretty Portuguese girls can lie as well as anyone. Even the ones who work in the palace."

"Especially the ones who work in the palace," Victoria said. "It's a survival skill."

"One you're surprisingly good at. Has the queen asked for another trip to the forest with your local guides?" Maria asked.

Victoria cleared her throat. "About yesterday, I wanted to apologize."

"You're apologizing to us?" Isabel's eyebrows shot to her hairline. "We scared you half to death and risked your job. I would have stabbed me on the spot."

"But I compared Brazil, your home, to hell. That was thoughtless, unkind, and horribly crude. I should have been more understanding of why you were there. You're doing everything you can to help a man you love—"

"We're not in love," Maria interrupted forcefully. Victoria's mouth snapped shut, and she rushed to explain. "Mateus is my business partner and a family friend. Nothing more." Things were complicated enough without rumors getting started and expectations trickling through the city.

"Oh, no! Of course, I didn't mean to imply you were romantically involved. I meant that you are trying to help someone you obviously care about, and you are willing to do whatever it takes. As I would have done for my father. I didn't. . . I wouldn't assume. . . I'm sorry if I offended you." Victoria bit her lip.

"You didn't," Maria assured her. "Mateus is an old friend, and we *would* do anything for a friend. But that's all he is."

Isabel barked a laugh. "You should say it again. I don't think she understands that Mateus is simply a friend."

Annoyance flared in Maria's chest. Isabel looked at her with an expression of amused pity. She wasn't going to waste time debating whether or not she knew her own feelings.

Maria looked pointedly away from her sister to Victoria. "Now that you've offered two apologies, we need to offer one. I'm sorry we risked your job yesterday. We don't have time to spare."

"Don't be mad at Maria," Isabel interjected. "I insisted on finding you once we saw the queen wasn't in her rooms. I didn't want to miss a chance of seeing royalty up close. It's all my fault." She threw an arm around Victoria's shoulders. "Forgive me?"

"Forgiven." Victoria gave Isabel a small smile. "What are you doing here, if I may inquire?"

"We're trying to meet with the owner, who happens to be a still-breathing diamond smuggler. His employee is being difficult." Maria forced the last word through gritted teeth.

"Perhaps I should threaten to take the palace's business elsewhere?" Victoria offered.

"That might be more effective than Isabel chopping off a finger." Maria looked around the bakery. "Except the cowardly baker has run away."

"Then I'm going to help myself." Isabel reached across the counter and plucked a roll off the shelf. Before Maria could protest, Isabel held up a coin. "Relax. I'm paying for it. Anyone want a piece?"

The sound of boots charging toward the door silenced them. Four soldiers rushed into the bakery with the sweaty baker panting behind them.

"That's them! The Black and the Indian! They held a knife to my throat and tried to rob me!" the baker wheezed in a shrill voice.

"That's a lie!" Isabel shrieked.

Maria didn't bother to protest. She assessed the soldiers crowding through the door. One officer armed with a pistol and a sword accompanied by three infantry, each with a rifle. That was four shots, one sword, and three bayonets between them and escape. They probably had a few knives stashed in boots, too. The small space wasn't ideal for whips or knife throwing. She licked her lips. They were in trouble.

"Her!" The baker barked, stabbing the air in front of Isabel with his finger. "She never paid for that roll!"

"The money's on the counter, you bloated rodent." Isabel turned to pick up the coin.

"Don't move, girl!" the officer bellowed. In unison, the soldiers raised their rifles. Isabel froze. Maria's pulse pounded. Her eyes flicked from side to side taking note of every detail. "You both need to come with us. Lay your weapons on the floor."

"Sir, she's telling the truth." Victoria, who was being ignored by the soldiers, stepped toward the officer. "Her money for the bread is on the counter. These women have been keeping me company while I waited for the baker to return."

"She's lying! She's their friend. They were talking when I managed to escape." The baker grabbed the sleeve of a soldier.

"Why the hell would we be talking with a friend if we were in the middle of robbing you?" Isabel threw her hands in the air.

"Miss, for your safety please step outside," the officer said to Victoria.

"Lieutenant, I speak for these women. They are *not* criminals!"

"Then you're another victim of their lies and deceit."

Major Vidigal slipped into the bakery with two of his Bats, forcing the soldiers to shift apart. The officer pulled Victoria aside, so that a semicircle of armed authority now surrounded Maria and Isabel. The baker's boiled-shrimp face peeked out from between the black jackets of the guardsmen.

The situation had gone to shit quickly, even by a muleteer's standards.

She caught Isabel's eyes and tipped her head back to the kitchen door. Isabel nodded once. If they managed to make a break for it, out the back was their only option. Then Maria met Vidigal's unblinking glare. A smile crept across his face, and all hope of escape evaporated. He remembered her.

"Thank you, lieutenant, but my men and I will take it from here. We've been looking for these two. The African's man is already in custody for the recent murder of Dom Antonio."

"I was born free in Rio de Janeiro, and my partner is innocent," Maria growled.

"And that freedom has deluded you into thinking you have the right to address your superiors." Vidigal's voice was barely more than a whisper. His stance suggested he was bored with the whole exchange, but Maria saw a twitch of disgust in his lip. "A visit to the post at the nearest square will remind you of your place. It's almost nine. What fortuitous timing."

Maria's body jerked as if punched in the stomach. The posts erected in every major public square were why she never walked the streets between nine and ten in the morning.

"You can't do that!" Victoria cried out. She clutched the lieutenant's sleeve. "The post is for slaves. She's not a slave. And there's no crime. They haven't stolen anything! Lieutenant, the major can't beat anyone he pulls off the street."

Maria wanted to tell Victoria not to bother. That nothing she said would help. That Vidigal was famous for enacting the sentence before the arrest. But Maria's tongue stuck to the roof of her mouth, and her eyes fixed on Vidigal's face. *Take care of the family.* Her mother asked it of her. Then her father. Now Isabel was going to jail, and Mateus would be executed. Maria couldn't see a way out. She'd failed at the one request her parents made of her.

The lieutenant frowned at Vidigal. "Major, I'm not aware of women being subjected to public beatings, and the law clearly states the punishment of whipping is only carried out at the request of the owner after receiving approval from—"

"The superintendent," Vidigal finished. He turned his reptilian eyes on the soldier. "And I speak for him. I am investigating the murder of one of Rio's most illustrious citizens. These girls are intimately acquainted with the suspect and may have even been accomplices. I'd hate to have to inform the Prince Regent his soldiers were impeding my guards' pursuit of justice."

With a single sentence, he sealed their fate. Vidigal made it a choice between the Prince Regent of Portugal and two local girls from Rio de Janeiro. No soldier alive would pick her and Isabel.

"This isn't justice!" Victoria pleaded, disbelief in her eyes as she looked into the faces of soldiers and guardsmen. "This isn't the law."

The lieutenant gripped Victoria's elbow and pulled her gently to the door. "Miss, it's best you leave now. I'll escort you home." At the officer's touch, Victoria's pleading eyes disappeared under a furrowed brow.

She looked Maria dead in the eye and nodded. The haze of panic in Maria's mind cleared instantly. She tensed, waiting.

As the officer led Victoria in front of the soldiers toward the door, she dropped into a dead faint, falling toward the middle soldier who dropped his rifle to catch her. The lieutenant moved to help hold Victoria, effectively shielding Maria and Isabel. Another soldier turned to watch the commotion. Maria took a second to admire the chaos caused by one unconscious Portuguese girl. Then she struck.

Crack.

Her whip ripped open bags of flour atop the mill sending a massive white cloud cascading down on their heads. Her second strike dropped the rifle from one soldier's hands. Isabel slashed out at a Bat. The last soldier holding a gun spit flour and sneezed. Maria wrapped her whip around his ankle. With a jerk of her arm, Maria sent the snorting soldier flat on his back. Isabel's skirt flared out as she spun out of the way.

Shouts and faces were muffled as soldiers, police, and smugglers swung away in the cramped space. The flour made everyone look like painted actors playing out some epic battle. A rifle barrel aimed at her through the white cloud. She knocked it aside. The rifle fired into the floor and set her ears ringing.

A thud to her right told Maria that Isabel had dropped one of the Bats. A soldier charged at her with his bayonet. Maria looped her whip and swatted the rifle to the side. She spun, catching the soldier's head in the loop as his momentum carried his legs past her, and smashed his head to the floor.

Maria landed on one knee and looked up in time to see the third soldier raising his rifle to bludgeon her. She planted a hand on the floor and kicked her feet straight up into the soldier's stomach. He doubled over, eyes bugged out. Maria spun on the ball of one foot slamming the other into the side of the soldier's head as her leg traced a complete circle in the air.

"Guess you're going to have to thank Mateus for all those capoeira lessons?" Isabel shouted. She used a fallen Bat as a stool to face the second eye to eye.

Maria grinned at Isabel. "What are you talking about? I've been giving the lessons since we were ten."

She turned back toward the soldiers and found a pistol in her face. Vidigal loomed in front of her, his black coat stark against the cloud of flour.

"You will not run from me again," he growled. "Your people will not continue plaguing my city."

Maria straightened and held his gaze. She would not cower from this man who lurked in the shadows. Isabel screamed her name. Vidigal cocked the hammer.

A surge of movement from the corner caught Maria's eye. Vidigal hesitated.

Victoria pulled free from the lieutenant shielding her. She planted her foot in his thigh and kicked. As he fell, Victoria drew his sword. A flick of her wrist brought the blade across Vidigal's hand. He dropped the gun, and Victoria placed the tip of the sword at his throat.

It was like watching a deer attack a pack of maned wolves. And win. How did a maid learn to fight, lie, and spy while in service to the queen? The shock consumed all her senses, and Maria lost track of the last guardsman on his feet.

The flash of a knife snapped her back to the fight. The Bat swung for Victoria. She dropped her guard of Vidigal and leapt back. Vidigal reached for his fallen pistol. Maria spun her whip handle into the side of his head, and he dropped to the floor.

"Lisbon!" Isabel shouted.

The guardsman lunged for Victoria. The Portuguese maid parried the knife, spun, and planted a kick in the middle of his back. He tripped over the fallen lieutenant and crashed face first against the side of the mill. The wall shuttered, and the remaining sacks of flour tumbled onto his head. They exploded, sending a fresh cloud into the air.

"Time to go!" Maria called.

She sprinted for the back of the store, snagging Victoria's arm as she passed. Isabel vaulted over the counter and landed next to her. They charged out the back door onto the street. A dozen people going about their day stopped and gawked at the three girls covered with flour and brandishing a variety of weapons.

"Wait, I have the lieutenant's sword," Victoria panted. She started back toward the bakery, and Maria grabbed her arm. "Keep it. You might still need it."

"Since you can use a sword. *Santa Francisca*! Where the hell did you learn to do that?" Isabel shoved Victoria's shoulder, grinning from ear to ear. "Never turn your back on the quiet ones."

Maria glanced up and down the street ignoring the gawkers. "This way. The street along the beach will be crowded with fi shermen unloading their catch. We can disappear there."

"It might be diffi cult to disappear. We are quite memorable in our current state," Victoria observed, struggling to keep up in her long and narrow dress.

"Head for Catete," Isabel said. "We can use the river, and the laundry women will keep a look out for us."

They bolted toward the crowded beach. Maria wove through the crates and wagons, taking care not to lose Isabel and Victoria. They made it to the river without encountering any more Bats. Isabel explained their plight to the women washing clothes, who offered them refuge within their ranks and added their flour covered clothing to the pile of undergarments waiting to be scrubbed.

After scrubbing her face, Maria rolled up her pants and dangled her bare legs in the river. She relished the icy prick of the water on her feet and the burn of the sun on her back. She'd made a mistake today. They had to be more careful who they approached and what questions they asked. She'd assumed that other smugglers wouldn't go to the authorities out of fear of being caught themselves, a terrible assumption in hindsight. She needed to be more discreet which was, she could admit, not one of her strengths.

But she did know someone who slipped through the palace unnoticed. The unassuming Portuguese maid basked under the sun like a lizard in nothing but her petticoat and stockings with a stolen sword in the grass next to her. It was time to hear the full story of Victoria Cruz from Lisbon.

Chapter Fourteen

Isabel

I sabel had the wash women in thrall. Stockings lay sopping on scrub boards. Shirts dripped into the river, half clean and forgotten, as the women waited for the conclusion of her morning escapade. She ended the story with an exaggerated reenactment of passersby staring slack-jawed as they fled the bakery and was rewarded with a chorus of laughter.

"Bats *and* soldiers after you today, Isabel? The list keeps growing," one woman teased.

"I'm very popular, Dona Lucia," Isabel countered with a grin.

"Isabel, go see my husband across the street." The woman waved at a man fanning himself next to a pile of coconuts. "Tell him to open a coconut for you and each of your friends."

"No, we can't accept."

"Hush!" She waved Isabel away. "It's my thanks for the best story I've heard all week."

Isabel collected the promised coconuts with the bright smile and light step of someone who'd impressed herself. They'd crossed off Dom Tiago as a potential ally, confirmed that Vidigal was still hunting for them, fought soldiers and won, fought Bats and won, humiliated

Vidigal, escaped, and gotten three fresh coconuts. It wasn't even midday yet.

She strolled back to Maria and Victoria, taking care not to spill from any of the coconuts balanced in her arms, and arrived as her sister said, "Victoria, I'm curious. How did a maid learn to fight, lie, and spy while in service to the queen?"

"Wait," she ordered. "*Santa Patricia,* this is going to be a hell of a story. And a good story needs refreshment!" Isabel lifted her armload of coconuts and offered the batch to Maria. "For the woman who almost got shot in the head an hour ago."

Maria took the closest, running a hand over the shiny green husk. "You paid for these, right?"

"Of course, but I had to sneak the money into his pocket."

"What is that man doing?" Victoria sat up and squinted at the coconut man down the street. "Is that an ice skate? Is he using an ice skate to open coconuts?"

"What's an ice skate?" Maria frowned.

"You mean the boot ax?" Isabel asked at the same time.

"A boot ax?" Victoria brought her hand up to hide a smile. "It's called an ice skate."

"You know what it's used for?" Isabel shoved a coconut into Victoria's hands and dropped to the ground beside her. She wiggled right up next to Victoria, thrilled to have the mystery of the boot ax solved. Those shoes had baffled her since they came off a British merchant ship months ago. She considered herself an expert in knives but could not for the life of her think of a reason why a person would wear a knife on the bottom of his shoe.

"You wear them to skate on ice." Victoria looked back and forth between the sisters. "In winter when the lakes and ponds freeze."

"People in Portugal wear shoes with knives?" Isabel tried to imagine how someone could possibly walk in them.

"Those aren't knives on the bottom."

"That sharp metal thing that cuts isn't a knife?" Maria raised her eyebrows.

"I suppose it is a blade of a sort, but we don't use it for cutting."

"But you wear the blades on your feet?"

"Not all the time. Only in winter. We wear them to move smoothly and quickly across ice."

"And ice is water? A sailor from Porto once told me about it," Maria said.

"Yes. Exactly. Ice is frozen water."

"Portuguese wear shoes with blades to walk on water?" Isabel asked.

"Well, yes but—"

"Of course the Portuguese think they can walk on water," Maria muttered.

"Not on water. On ice. In the winter, the temperature gets so cold the water in lakes becomes hard enough to walk on."

"Why would people send shoes that require cold to Rio de Janeiro?" Maria asked.

"That man seems to have found use for one," Victoria said with a smile.

Isabel watched the river rippling and tumbling toward the bay and tried to imagine the water still. She pictured people running up and down on a river as though it were dirt. The image was absurd and wonderful. "Before I die, I'm going to walk on water," she announced. She leaned forward and grabbed Victoria's knee. "Will you come with me? And teach me how to use those shoes?"

Victoria's smile lit her face. "I'd love to show you Lisbon in winter! It gets much colder than here. Also, I have to confess I've never gone ice skating myself."

"Then we'll learn together."

"You're both mad. The coldest night in Rio is as cold as I ever plan to be," Maria said.

"You can go off to your farm in Bahia, and I'll explore the world with Victoria."

"Bring me back a nice present, and I'll promise not to rent your room out."

"Deal." Isabel and Maria touched coconuts then gulped the remaining water from inside. Isabel's coconut was particularly sweet. She smacked her lips and tossed the empty husk aside. She stifled a laugh as Victoria experimented with different angles and tilts of her head in what appeared to be a pointless effort to avoid coconut water dribbling down her chin.

"Just drink!" Isabel urged. "No one cares if you spill coconut water down your chemise. It's a hot day. You need to drink in order to keep outrunning Bats."

"Oh, I don't plan on running for my life again. Once was enough."

"Then you probably shouldn't spend time with us because it's a regular event." Isabel winked. "Now, back to Maria's question. How does a maid know how to use a sword?"

Victoria plucked a leaf from the ground and began twisting it between her fingers. Isabel got the feeling this wasn't a story her friend often told, so she laid back against the dirt, content to wait. After a few seconds, Victoria took a shuddering breath.

"Princess Carlota Joaquina allowed me to fence alongside her daughters."

Isabel bolted upright. "The future queen of Portugal let you fence with the princesses?"

"The bitch who slapped you in the face had you entertain her children?" Maria rephrased.

Victoria nodded. "She even oversaw our lessons. My father was the queen's surgeon. He was one of dozens of doctors brought in after she started having fits. No one could cure her. Not even my father, but he at least helped control her fits. He was able to reduce their frequency, end them faster when they did come. He made life more bearable for her. For everyone in the royal family. Prince João and Princess Carlota Joaquina respected him. They gave him rooms in the palace, and I went with him. I'm the same age as Princess Maria Teresa, so Her Highness allowed me to join many of her lessons. Not only fencing, but also riding, languages, dancing. Her Highness consulted my father regularly. Even then she was blunt and stubborn and had a tendency to throw things at people...but she helped my father gain respect among the court. Until four years ago."

Victoria fell silent, and Isabel leaned forward, clenching her skirts to keep from shaking the rest of the story out. Confiding clearly didn't come easily to Victoria. If Isabel startled, she'd probably never hear the end, so she waited in painful silence for Victoria to collect her thoughts.

"My father died suddenly. When he died, I became an orphan with nowhere to go. At first, I thought the princess was being kind when she placed me in service to Her Majesty. I was able to stay in the palace and earn a living, but she was merely helping herself. I had helped as my father's assistant and after he died, I became the one person Her Majesty would allow to administer her medicine and tonics. She attacked everyone else. So when I was fifteen, Carlota Joaquina assigned me to the queen, and I became responsible for everything Her Majesty did. I was never invited to another lesson. Now Her Highness hates me and only acknowledges me to yell at me."

Isabel's burst of applause startled both Victoria and Maria.

Isabel was a connoisseur of stories. She'd spent her life rewriting her own, tweaking her first mother's last words and trying out various deaths on whatever man had fathered her. Not constrained by any memories of the actual events, Isabel had learned through trial and error that the right combination of tragedy and triumph could secure anything from free drinks to declarations of love, and Victoria's story could keep a person fed and watered for a lifetime. A life in the court. A crazy queen. An orphaned daughter and hateful princess. The story and its teller were as good as gold.

"That is one of the greatest stories I've ever heard. It's amazing! Not your father dying, of course. Losing your parents is tragic. I know. I've lost two sets. And Carlota Joaquina sounds truly horrible. But all the best stories have loss. It's the only way a person can triumph, and that's what makes your story gold!" She threw an arm around Victoria's shoulders. "You survived loss, the wrath of a princess, an ocean voyage with a mad queen, all to befriend two brave Cariocas who take you under their wings and teach you to survive by your sword and your wits in a new world."

"I suppose I'm teaching the wits," Maria cut in.

Isabel stuck her tongue out at her sister before continuing. "You looked a monster in the eyes today and not only stood your ground, you drew a sword on him. A sword you stole off an officer! Lisbon, you're a warrior."

"I appreciate the compliment, but I'm not a warrior. I think my night on the beach proved that."

"It was five against one, and you were unarmed." Isabel waved Victoria's denial away. "Then you still went out alone the next day and found two complete strangers in a strange city. You didn't know anything abouts us except we were trying to help a man in jail for murder."

"You had saved my life."

"So you knew we're good at leaving men unconscious on the beach. Nossa Senhora, the more I think about it, that was a completely mad and brave thing you did seeking us out." Isabel squeezed the maid's shoulders. "You really are one of us."

"Victoria," Maria interrupted. "Why did the princess start hating *you* after your father died?"

"I don't know." Victoria pursed her lips. "I've made lists trying remember everything that I or my father might have done to displease the princess, but nothing I can remember explains her hatred."

"You made lists? 'All the Reasons the Crown Princess Might Hate Me' lists?" Isabel asked.

"Of course. My father taught me you can only solve a problem once you understand what is causing it. Whenever I have a problem, whether it's the queen suddenly having more fits or trouble falling asleep, I make a list of potential causes," Victoria explained.

"Isabel prefers to burn problems down," Maria laughed.

"Not all of them. Not everything catches fire," she retorted.

"Well, I make lists. In fact, I made a list of ways I could help you save your friend. That's why I came to find you…Oh no, I hope it's not ruined." Victoria reached frantically into her dress pocket and pulled out a damp sheet of folded paper. "Oh dear, this was the list. I think I can remember most of it. It was all the reasons Mateus could be released from prison and how each might be achieved."

Isabel accepted the soggy paper with a sense of wonder. Since seeing the queen in the forest and watching Victoria scurry behind the old woman, used piss pot in hand, she no longer imagined the Portuguese girl eating grapes while reciting poetry at Her Majesty's pleasure. She understood now what Victoria's days entailed and what she risked by helping them. The maid didn't have to seek them out at the bakery, and she certainly didn't have to stay with them when army officers could escort her home. Yet, here she was air drying on the banks of the Catete River with a stolen sword and flour-dusted hair, offering a dripping list of not one but a dozen ideas to help them.

She couldn't read the list, but in Isabel's world actions spoke louder than words. She yanked Victoria into a fierce embrace. At first her friend stiffened, but after a moment she returned the hug.

"I'm glad I didn't kill you that day you found the diamonds." Isabel laughed as Victoria's eyes widened. "I'm kidding. I wouldn't have killed you."

"Probably," Maria added. "Either way, it's good she didn't, because we need all the help we can get. Anything you can offer Victoria, thank you."

"I first thought about what you need to get your friend not merely out of jail but declared innocent. With Vidigal against Mateus, and Princess Carlota Joaquina supporting Vidigal—"

"Why is she supporting Vidigal?" Maria interrupted.

"They're having an affair."

"That's a problem," Maria sighed.

"That's disgusting," Isabel exclaimed. "Can you imagine kissing him? His face looks like an iguana desperate to shed. She's not exactly beautiful, but surely a future queen has higher standards."

"I can't explain why, but it's true. I've seen them meeting in secret and exchanging notes. He even made her smile." Victoria shuddered and shook her head as if to remove the memory. "And with Vidigal in her favor, you'll have to find the real murderer and substantial proof against him. Do you have any idea who it might be?"

Maria shook her head. "We found out about a third murder this morning. Another wealthy man strangled who bought black market diamonds. That's why we rushed to the bakery. I shouldn't have been so public, but these smugglers are our only hope of finding the real killer. I have to talk to one before they all end up dead."

"Which at this rate is going to be in days," Isabel interjected. Her sister was always too hard on herself. "You were right to confront the baker. Smugglers are getting killed off faster than pigs at Christmas. We can't afford to wait around for the ideal moment."

Victoria raised a hand shyly. "Well, I did have an idea that might get you in the presence of every major smuggler in Rio. Not that I know who the smugglers are, of course, but based on what you told me about the first two—"

"What's the plan?" Isabel interrupted before Victoria could list all her criteria for determining likely smugglers.

"As part of the anniversary celebrations, there's going to be a ball at the palace on Friday. Every prominent member of Rio's society will be there. I can sneak you in."

"Yes!" Isabel cried.

"No," Maria said at the same time. "Isabel, we're not crashing a party at the palace if there's another way to get what we need."

Isabel recognized Maria's tone. It was her sister's guilty voice, the one she used whenever she blamed herself for a recent disaster and was now preparing to shoulder the responsibility for it on her own. Whenever Maria used that voice, it meant she'd rethink every decision ten times and be an insufferable bore for the next month.

"I have other ideas, but they don't get you close to as many potential smugglers as quickly," Victoria offered.

"Let's hear them," Maria said.

"*Santa Elisa* save me!" Isabel buried her face in her hands. "I'm surrounded by planners! And now there's one who can write. I'm going to spend the rest of my life listening to lists get dictated." She leapt to her feet and glared down at her sister and newest friend.

"We're not going to sit here coming up with more plans when we have a good one. A crazy one, definitely, but one that gets us everything we need in one night." She drew up to her full height, which wasn't much, but she had their attention. "Mateus could be hung in a week! Maria, I know you feel guilty about us almost ending up in jail and Victoria becoming a fugitive. You almost got shot, but that was hardly the first time. . ."

"Which reminds me…" Isabel turned to the maid. It was best she heard the truth now before they plotted to crash a ball together. "Lisbon, you should probably know that if you're working with us, between jaguars and thieves and royal guardsmen, there's usually something trying to kill us."

She turned back to Maria who looked up at her from the ground, and for a heartbeat, Isabel's confidence faltered. Her sister was the captain of their family. She gave the orders. Isabel carried them out. The sudden role reversal felt unnatural, but guilt was making Maria doubt herself. Someone needed to drive their train forward into the darkest part of the forest. "Do I want to wind up dead or in jail? No. Both seem boring. But am I willing to risk both to save the closest thing to a brother I'll ever get? Yes. We're going to the ball because we've saved plenty of strangers in our lives, and now we're going to save Mateus. And I want to see inside the palace."

Victoria spoke up timidly. "They're borrowing extra help from families all over Rio. There are going to be dozens of new faces. Many from Rio who won't be known by the staff from Lisbon. I can get you inside."

"Then count me in," Isabel declared. She could tell from Maria's creased brow her sister wasn't convinced. "Sister?"

Maria held her gaze. "They won't arrest us for this. They'll execute us."

"You think after Vidigal's speech this morning we don't know that?" Isabel bent down and grabbed her sister's shoulders. "This is not on you. I'm volunteering."

"So am I," Victoria chimed in.

"That settles it. Me and Victoria will be attending a royal ball. Want to join us?"

Isabel held her hand out to help her sister up. Maria hesitated for a moment then grasped it, hauling herself off the ground.

"Fine," Maria said. "But I don't want to be stuck in a damn dress."

"About that. . ." Victoria bit her lip and pulled out another sheet of folded paper. "I wrote down what you both would need to blend in. New dresses are the first things on the list."

Chapter Fifteen

Victoria

For two days Victoria jumped every time someone knocked at the queen's chamber door. She expected to open the door and find soldiers there with her arrest warrant. Surely the officer from the bakery would remember her face. One of the guardsman would spot her escorting the queen to morning prayers, but as the days passed and no one came, Victoria realized just how invisible she'd become.

A week earlier the realization would have weighed heavily, but Victoria embraced her invisibility as she adopted a second life. She read from Psalms to Her Majesty before lunch and helped Isabel buy fabric for new dresses during the queen's afternoon nap. She updated Maria about Mateus while the royal family attended Mass then hurried back to dress Her Majesty for dinner. By the time guests started arriving at the anniversary ball, Victoria simply wanted to sneak the sisters in, commit the crime, and be done with it so she could get a full night's sleep.

Fires burned in all four enormous stone ovens. Sweat beaded on the roast pigs and kitchen staff . Twenty people, four whole pigs, two dozen pheasants, and a shipload of candied fruits and cakes claimed every open space in the kitchen. Victoria hugged the wall near the door to the courtyard and tried to gulp a breath of fresh air.

From her carefully selected spot, she could see the doors leading out to the square and into the inner court-yard through the main entrance where carriages, horses, and servants on foot were spilling through. Victoria fid-dled with the buttons on her gloves. They should have been here. She was supposed to be supervising the queen during the party and slipped away at this pre-cise moment on the excuse she had to relieve herself. She needed to return before Her Majesty caused a fuss.

A tall woman in a pale green dress with gold trim around the neck and hem stepped into the kitchen from the square. Her hair was wrapped in gold fabric that matched the trim. She yanked at the empire waist of her dress as if to punish it. *Maria*. Victoria exhaled. Isabel stepped through the door next and almost got knocked in the head with a tray of stuffed crab. Isabel's dress was all white except for three wide stripes of ocean blue at the bottom. Her hair was pinned in a ball high on her head with a matching blue ribbon. She rushed over before anyone noticed her friends and assigned them a job.

"It's about time. With two maids sick the day of the ball, Her Majesty has been in a state." She grabbed Maria and Isabel by the elbows and steered them out of the kitchen. "Her Highness informed Her Majesty that Dona Teresa had generously offered to send two of her girls one hour *before* the ball. I'm sure your late arrival does not reflect Dona Teresa's level of respect for Her Majesty." She stopped when they got to a quiet corner in the courtyard behind a parked carriage.

"I hope I don't need to know what you were talking about because I didn't understand a word," Isabel said. She went up on tiptoe and peeked inside the carriage. "*Santa Larissa*, do you ever sneak inside one of these and take a nap?"

"No," Victoria gasped. "When would I have time for a nap?"

"I don't know how any woman works in all this fabric." Maria plucked at her long skirt as if pulling leeches off. "And these ridiculous slippers. Do more than shuffle your feet and they fall off. Why the hell do we have to dress up to play the part of slave?"

"A poorly dressed attendant means the master cannot afford to clothe him," Victoria explained. "If you can buy your personal slaves fancy clothes, then you must be very rich, and everyone here wants to at least look very rich." Maria scoffed and rolled her eyes. Victoria hoped Maria could keep her disdain to a minimum, at least while walking through the ballroom.

"Let's go over etiquette one more time before we go up," she said. "No scoffing or eye rolling at the royal family or guests. No dumping wine glasses or decanters on the royal family or guests. No drawing weapons on the royal family or guests."

"Is there anything we *can* do?" Isabel asked.

"Smile and curtsey," Victoria replied, demonstrating her own quick curtsey.

"Is there anything fun we can do?" Isabel retorted.

"We're not here for fun," Maria said. "We question Dom Tiago or any other smuggler we see. We ask if they've been approached by any new buyers, then we leave. Understand?"

Isabel linked arms with her sister. "Don't worry, dear sister. We'll find out what we need and still have time to try the wine. Besides, you need to do a few laps around the room in that dress. You look beautiful!"

Maria pursed her lips, but the corners twitched up. "Fine. But no sampling the wine until after you've talked to at least two smugglers."

"Yes, Dona," Isabel cooed with a smile while dropping a curtsey. She caught Victoria's eye. "See? We know how to behave, and I've nearly mastered that curtsy. Now which way to the party?"

"Second floor. All the rooms along the north side of the palace are open for the ball. Servers take these stairs here." Victoria led the group to the back stairs, taking two pitchers of wine as they passed through the kitchen and handing one to each of her friends. "Don't try to carry a food tray. The men do that. We poor wine or water or fetch chairs if someone asks. If anyone—"

"We understand," Maria cut her off. "You should go back to the queen. We'll be quiet, and if anything does go wrong, we won't know you."

Victoria frowned as Maria swept around a corner and disappeared. "Is she all right?"

"She's nervous," Isabel answered. "It wasn't easy for her to do nothing for two days while Mateus sat in jail. She also called off our team from trying to find any of the murdered smugglers' slaves. She thinks it's too dangerous. We haven't found a witness to any of the murders, which is mysterious since the men all had more slaves than shoes. Maria won't talk about it, but I know she thinks their workers were killed. So she doesn't want the men from our mule team getting caught asking questions. She's right, but it means it's all on us to learn something that can help Mateus. Wish us luck!" Isabel raised her wine pitcher. "And you look stunning. Red is definitely your color!" Isabel winked then glided up the stairs, hopefully before she noticed the flattered flush warming Victoria's cheeks.

She took a few deep breaths after Isabel disappeared. There were so many ways this plan could fail, and Maria and Isabel had pinned all their hopes onto her plan. She'd been nervous before but was now on the verge of losing what little dinner she'd forced down.

She hid her nerves under a bland smile before stepping onto the freshly buffed wooden floors. The floor and guests sparkled in the lamp light. The length of the palace stretched before her, room after room filled with Rio's most illustrious residents, the wealthy, the respected, and on the rare occasion both.

The royal family's dais commanded the center room. Every few feet along the north wall, a floor-to-ceiling window opened to a small balcony which overlooked the square. The balconies were more decorative than functional with barely room for two people to stand, but the heat was driving people to test the sturdiness of the iron railings. Windows along the opposite wall looked out on a second interior courtyard used as a garden by the royal family. The space was closed to guests, but lamps and candelabras burned throughout, causing the courtyard to glow an emerald green.

Victoria squeezed past the well-wishers and hand kissers to take her place against the wall behind the queen. Her Majesty sat in a velvet chair on the dais behind her son and daughter-in-law who stood at the edge to receive an endless stream of admiration.

She relieved the girl holding the queen's cup and frowned at the dark liquid inside. She sniffed. *Wine.* Victoria stamped her foot. She'd been gone less than ten minutes, and Her Majesty had talked someone into giving her wine. The last thing she needed was a drunk, mad queen causing a spectacle. Although, Isabel would probably enjoy the display.

Victoria scanned the crowd for Maria's golden headwrap or a flash of Isabel's white dress, but wasn't high enough to peer over the crowd gathered around the royal family. Feathers and fans blocked her view. She looked for a gap between bodies, and her eyes snagged on a black jacket. It stood out against the jewel tones of silk and velvet. Major Vidigal waited in line to greet the royal family.

His slouch and half-closed eyes made him the most subdued guest in the room. Amidst the puffed chests and craning necks, Vidigal looked meek in compar-ison, but Victoria's skin crawled at the sight of him. The walls pushed in around her as the commander of the royal guard stepped closer to the dais. Her mouth went dry. He would recognize her from the bakery, and if by some miracle he didn't recognize her, Maria and Isabel were wandering the rooms. Victoria had never pointed a gun at someone's face but was certain if she did, she wouldn't forget it.

As Vidigal stepped up to Prince João, Victoria offered the queen her cup, turning away from the crowd. "Would Your Majesty like more wine?"

"Ugh, no! I told that other girl it tastes like monkey piss." Queen Maria's lip curled in disgust, and with a flick of her hand, she sent the cup flying over her chair onto the dais. The queen blinked at the wine spreading at her feet. "Where did this mess come from?"

"I'm sorry, Your Majesty. I'll clean it up." Victoria signaled to another maid to get a new cup before kneeling to sop up the wine as best she could.

For a moment she lost herself blotting wine and forgot about Vidigal, until she glanced up to find herself eye level with his lips against Carlota Joaquina's hand. She froze. Not from the sight of the old Bat's cracked lips in a display of aff ection, but from the note passed from Her Highness's hand to Vidigal's. Neither offi cer nor princess gave any indication they knew each other beyond formal court courtesies. Only her vantage point from the fl oor allowed Victoria to see the exchange.

While she had no aff ection left for the princess, Victoria didn't blame her for wanting an aff air. Prince João seemed kind but was decidedly frog-like. He'd also banished Carlota Joaquina to her own palace outside the city during their last few years in Lisbon, and it was probably diffi cult to rekindle romance after banishment. She suspected the princess was lonely. A lover might do wonders for her temperament and save Victoria from a slap or two.

But Vidigal? The man slunk around in his charcoal coat like a demon waiting to drag someone to hell with him. He was old and sullen, while the princess seemed barely contained in her skin, bursting in and out of rooms and speaking in bellows. He was from Brazil. She was from Spain. What could they possible have in common beyond Catholicism?

Whatever reason drew the two of them together, Vidigal's presence at the ball turned her precarious plan into an almost guaranteed disaster. She had to fi nd Maria and Isabel and get them out. The maid returned with a fresh cup of water, and Victoria asked her to watch the queen while she stepped out for air to relieve a headache.

"Your Majesty, I'm not feeling well. Luiza will attend you. I'll be back…"

"Fine. Go. Abandon me like your father." The queen waved her off. It was only a twitch of two fingers, but reverberated through her like a punch.

Victoria absorbed the queen's words and buried them under purpose. Find Isabel and Maria. Get them out of the palace. Don't let Vidigal see you.

She pushed to the middle of the room where the temperature seemed to double. The sea of faces offered no clue as to which direction her friends might be in. She had once felt comfortable at court, never a member of it but always surrounded by it. Now she looked at the well-groomed guests and wondered who was a smuggler, a liar, a murderer? The palace was infested with enemies. Vidigal was only the most obvious.

She should never have brought Maria and Isabel here.

Chapter Sixteen

Maria

Maria stepped over the unconscious soldiers at her feet and continued toward the prison. She paused before an open window and let the salty night air whisk away the stench of overheated bodies.

She hoped the guards would wake with nothing more than a headache but didn't have time to worry. She needed to talk to Mateus and get back to the ball before Isabel or Victoria noticed she was gone, because without doubt they'd come racing through the palace to find her. Victoria would be convinced Maria was seconds away from getting tossed in a cell, and Isabel would be furious she wasn't invited.

She hated to hide her plans, but she couldn't bring them. Even though Victoria's knowledge of the palace would have been very useful, and Isabel could watch her back while providing a joke to lighten the mood. Even though she would have welcomed their company, she would take the risk alone because she was the captain. It was her responsibility to assume the most risk and avoid stupid things like walking into rich men's houses lit like the sun with the doors wide open but no hint of life.

If that's how it happened. She still had a hard time believing Mateus would have walked straight into such obvious danger. She needed to talk to him. She'd scoured Rio for witnesses when the most important one was locked up right off the main square. While Isabel had been hunched over needle and thread making dresses, Maria gathered information about the palace, the jail, and how to go between. Victoria was the most well-connected palace servant Maria knew but not the only one.

She moved as quickly as her dress allowed across the passageway over the street connecting the palace to the chamber headquarters and public jail. If anyone walking from the beach toward Rua Direita looked up at that precise moment, they saw a woman with a golden headwrap and dressed in the imperial colors race past the windows along the overpass. Fortunately, anyone who would have cared to stop an unknown woman from running toward the jail was focused on the ball, and anyone not focused on the ball didn't care to stop her.

The prison cells were on the ground floor. At the top of the stairs, she unwound her whip from around her leg. She'd had a hell of a time wrapping it in a way the handle's bulge didn't show under her skirt. Isabel's daggers were much more discreet. Maria might consider training with them if she kept having to sneak into government buildings.

Maria stopped at the bottom of the stairs and listened.

"I showed up late to duty twice this month. What did you do to get stuck here?" one man said.

"Stuck here? You wanted to be on duty at the palace? Standing for hours and staring at food and drink you can't have?" another retorted.

"It's an honor to serve in the throne room," the first voice replied shocked.

"Personally, I'd rather have less honor and more drink."

That was her chance. Maria stepped into the room, hands clasped behind her back holding the whip, and eyes fixed on the boots of the two startled soldiers. "I was sent from the palace to see if you would like any food or drink."

"Who sent you?" the first voice demanded. Maria peered through her lashes. Both were frowning at her, but they didn't raise their rifles. Their mistake.

Maria wrapped her whip around one's ankles and snatched his feet out from under him. His head thudded against the ground. Her whip sliced open the remaining soldier's hand. He dropped the rifle. She sprung forward, looped her whip over his head and brought it smashing down on her knee. Both soldiers lay unmoving at her feet, bringing the total unconscious soldiers count to five. Maria wondered how many soldiers she could leave lying around before someone noticed.

She hurried past offices to a room that stretched the length of the building. Cells lined both sides all the way down and a long stock ran down the middle of the hall.

Maria stopped when she saw the two slaves laying on woven mats with their feet locked in the stock. The men looked at her in surprised silence. One propped himself up on his elbows and craned his neck to see around her.

"The guards aren't coming," she reassured them.

"Maria?" a voice called from the last cell.

"Mateus!" She started toward him but looked back at the men. She hesitated for one breath then grabbed the keys from their hook. She heaved the long wooden bar off their ankles and helped the men to their feet.

"Run. Leave the city. Go northeast. There's a quilombo three days from here. Ask any Black face you find once you're a day out of the city," Maria urged, pushing them to the door. The street was clear, and the men fled into the darkness without a word or glance behind.

"It'll be worse for them now if they're caught." Mateus's voice drifted through the dark.

"They at least have a chance now." Maria watched the men disappear then turned toward the cells. The dread she'd been ignoring felt like iron in her gut. In response she lengthened her stride, grinding the fear under her boots as she marched to the door of his cell. Maria vowed that no matter what she saw, she would not flinch from her friend.

"Boa noite, amiga. You look magnificent," he said. She could just make out his silhouette, crouched in the back corner blending into the shadows. "If I'd known you were coming, I'd have cleaned up a little."

"Why? You never bothered cleaning up for me before," Maria countered managing a small smile. She draped her whip around her shoulders and forced a casual tone. "Are you going to come say hello?"

He stepped carefully as he came into the glow of the lamps. His right eye was swollen shut, his bottom lip split open, and he wore nothing but a tattered pair of pants. Maria clenched her jaw, grinding her teeth together, but otherwise showed no hint of the fury that exploded in her breast.

"You look lovely. The whip is nice. All the ladies will have one by next season." Mateus smiled, and it nearly broke her. He looked her over from head to toe. "Maria Azevedo dressed for a ball. And now that I've seen everything, I can die happy."

"Shut up!" she hissed. The words dug inside her, knife blades slicing closer and closer to her heart. He couldn't say that. Not to her. "No one is dying."

"We're all dying. I'm thankful I got to see this miracle before I go."

"Stop saying that! Dammit, Mateus, you're not dying. The only reason I put this thing on is to stop that from happening."

"I'm not running, Maria." His smile vanished, and his voice became hard as stone. "You can tear the bars off the wall, I'm not leaving this cell. They'll hunt me and whoever helped me. I won't give them a reason to come after you and Isabel."

"I'm not here to break you out," Maria interrupted.

"Then why are you breaking into the jail in the middle of night and attacking guards?"

"I need information. You're going to be released free of charges because I'm tracking the real murderer." She'd do it. She'd save him. He had to help her, be her second, like always. They couldn't let something like a murder conviction stand in the way.

Mateus dropped his head and muttered to the floor, "No, Maria. No. No."

"Finding him is the only way you don't get executed."

"Maria, it's impossible. One murderer in all of Rio."

"There've been three identical murders. All buyers on the black market," she whispered, leaning toward the bars. "Mateus, it's about the diamonds. I need to know everything you saw that night." She noticed his eyebrows twitch together before he shook his head. He knew something. "What did you see?"

"Maria, you can't. It's too dangerous."

"Stop there." She held up a hand. There was no time or point in arguing about this. Stalling any longer could get them both killed, and she couldn't bear to hear him ask her to give him up one more time. "First, you're my partner, but I'm the captain. Second, do you think there is a man I can't drag to the prison doorstep? Especially with Isabel at my back. We even have a friend inside the palace now."

"You have a man in the palace?"

"A maid, Victoria. She works for the queen."

"The mad queen?"

"The very mad queen. I met her peeing in the forest."

Mateus chuckled softly. "You always make the most interesting friends."

Maria waved away his attempt to change the subject. "And third, you shouldn't have been there alone. I set the place and time, and I was late. I could have stopped you from going inside. At least we could have fought them off together. I should never—" Maria's throat closed. She squeezed the bars until her fingernails dug into her palms and forced the words out. "Mateus, I'm sorry. I'm so sorry."

Mateus's hands over hers stopped her apology. "This is not your fault. It's a miracle you were late. If you'd been with me, you'd be in here, too."

"You don't know that."

"Vidigal was already there waiting."

"What?"

"I knew something was wrong as soon as I saw the house. Every lamp in the house lit. The door wide open. I watched from the trees and when the house seemed empty, I went straight to Antonio's office. He was sprawled on the floor, dead but warm. I was still checking for breath when Vidigal and his Bats stormed into the house. They hadn't even seen the body, but they knew something was wrong."

"Someone tipped them off."

"Someone Vidigal listens to." Mateus pressed his head against the bars. His unblinking gaze sent a chill down her back. How had it come to this? How could they fight these odds? He gripped her fingers, and behind his urgency, Maria sensed fear. "Maria, the commander of the royal guard doesn't move on the word of anyone. Whoever had Dom Antonio killed has the Bats in his pocket. You have to stop."

"Mateus, I swear to god, if you tell me to stop one more time, I will leave you in this cell," Maria hissed. His insistence on ignoring her was using up the little time she had.

"I wish you would."

"Goddammit. Do you want to die?"

"No, but I'm ready to if it means you're safe. Making sure you weren't in trouble is the only reason I went into Antonio's house in the first place."

The confession landed like a kick from a mule, and she pulled away from the bars. Away from him. Her gut churned with guilt. She couldn't meet his eyes. "It is my fault. If I'd been there with you—"

"That is *not* what I'm saying! I went into the house to make sure you weren't in danger. Because that's what I do. You lead the team, and I watch your back. It's what I've been doing since the first day you showed up at the capoeira circles."

His voice grew soft, and the emotions roiling inside Maria stilled. Her body tensed to receive a blow. She knew what declaration was coming. He didn't need to tear himself apart—tear them both apart. These wouldn't be his last words. "Mateus, you don't need to explain."

"Sorry, captain, but a dying man gets a final confession."

The protests died on her lips.

"So you do respect some traditions," he teased. His smile was back, and it banished the shadows from his face. "I never told you my mother was born a slave. Bought her freedom with money she earned moonlighting as a seamstress. As a boy, I woke up to her singing every morning. Didn't matter if Papa's shoes weren't selling and money was low. Didn't matter that her eyes were ruined from all the late nights sewing. She sang every morning. I asked her once how she could be happy all the time. She told me she wasn't. She got sad and angry, but she chose not to carry it with her. She didn't want to waste a second of her freedom on anything but joy. And that's what she taught me. It's my choice to leave behind the anger and sorrow but keep the joy close."

Maria's eyes burned. They'd been best friends for nearly twenty years, and he'd never told her this. How many stories were left untold? How many unspoken thoughts and memories had he kept to himself? How much of a stranger would he always be to her if she failed him now?

"I remember the first time your papa brought you to the capoeira circles. You were all legs, and you used them to march right into the middle of a circle of men and boys. Watching you, I could tell you were right where you wanted to be, doing exactly what you wanted to do, and loving it. Everybody else be damned. You were the freest person I had ever seen, and I knew I had to keep you close."

Mateus's voice was so low, but he drowned out the music and laughter from the ball. She stopped tracking how long the soldiers had been unconscious. She forgot about the soldiers completely. Her senses filled with Mateus.

He sighed and shrugged as if in apology. "At first it was as a friend. We were kids. And later after your papa died, I knew you needed a business partner and wanted a friend." He gritted his teeth. "I tried to leave it there. I swear I tried. I'm sorry, Maria, but I'm going to stay in this cell and go to my execution because I pick your life over mine. So please, stop looking for the murderer. Stay away from the Bats. Take care of Isabel and the team and Dito, and let me take care of *you* one last time."

Maria held his gaze. Her pounding heart filled the silence.

He'd felt like this for months. They'd ridden side by side, hunted side by side, and slept side by side under the stars, but Mateus had never breathed a word of his feelings. She knew what this confession meant. He believed he was going to die. He'd given up. That realization drowned out all other thoughts and left her filled with a cold fury.

"You're giving up?" Maria charged up to the cell with such force Mateus stepped back in surprise. Her eyes burned into his. "No. We don't give up. We don't get that luxury. The team looks to us, Mateus. Me and you. They expect us to get them home every time. I have never lost a man. *We* have never lost a man. I am not your confessor, and I don't need your protection. I'm your captain, and what I need is my *friend*!"

A groan from the next room sent Maria spinning away from the cell and reaching for her whip. She shifted to the balls of her feet, arm tensed, ready. She listened. Silence followed.

Maria cursed herself. She'd let herself get distracted and lost track of her surroundings. Where was Isabel now? How long had she been in the jail? She couldn't think while looking at the resignation on Mateus's face. She couldn't breathe. Maria edged a step away from the cell, hands shaking. She couldn't give him what he wanted.

"I'm going to find the murderer. Then you're going to walk out of here. There's nothing else to say." Of course, there was so much more to say. But not now. Not here.

Mateus's eyes widened as she took another step back from the bars. "Maria, please—"

She cut him off with a gesture. "Whatever else you want to say to me can wait until after you've walked out of this prison. I told you I've never lost a man. Not to any disease or animal the trail could throw at me. I will not lose you to those goddamn Bats."

If he said anything else, she didn't hear it. Maria sprinted past the two guards still sprawled on the ground. She leapt up the stairs to the connecting passage and stopped in the shadows to stash her whip.

A glance out the window revealed a deserted street except for some carriage drivers and footmen milling around the front of the palace. The trot of a lone horse echoed across the square. Music and conversation drifted out of the throne room. Maria assumed there would be a little more fuss if the unconscious soldiers had been found, so she picked up her dress and ran the length of the passage.

The only good thing about the ridiculous leather slippers on her feet was their silence. Maria crossed back to the palace as if a ghost. Between heavy cur-tains, she glimpsed the jail where Mateus sat half naked in the dark while whoever put him there was most likely dancing and drinking across the street.

She turned away from the prison before her fury slipped out of her control and gazed out at the mountains around Rio. Their forest blanket was black and silver in the moonlight, and not for the first time, Maria wondered why people chose to pile on top of each other in one room when so much world stretched out around them.

A burst of laughter floated by on the breeze, and Maria remembered she had a sister and friend amongst very dangerous people. There wasn't time to wonder or worry. She had to act.

Maria glided through the shadows giving almost no trace of her presence. She turned a corner and slammed into a man hurrying in the opposite direction.

Maria sprang back and raised her hands in defense as the man raised his in apology.

"I'm terribly sorry, miss. I didn't realize this shadow was taken."

The man's accent stopped Maria before she swiped his legs. He wasn't Brazilian or Portuguese, but he seemed to speak Portuguese well enough to call the guards. Still she hesitated. It seemed unlikely a foreigner hugging the wall in a deserted hallway of the palace would want the guards around.

In a heartbeat, Maria weighed her options. The less commotion she caused, the faster she'd get back to Isabel and out of this suffocating building, so she straightened and smoothed her dress, dropping her gaze to the floor. "I should apologize, sir. It's my first time serving in the palace, and I got lost. Could you tell me how to get back to the ballroom?"

"Lost?" His tone told her he didn't believe the lie, so she dropped the servant act to get a good look at the threat. She raised her eyes and met his gaze.

Young and rich. Even in the dark hallway his wealth was obvious from his perfectly tailored breeches and the fashionable cut of his coat, but he lacked the gem-studded accessories that indicated a noble. Then he bowed. To her. And Maria no longer knew the color of the sky or if water was wet.

"It seems we are both turned around in a strange place. I'm sure you're as eager to return to your errand as I am to mine. I wish you good evening, miss. I'd advise you not to take the second left. I left a rather drunk viscount in that direction."

He bowed again in parting before slipping back into the shadows. Maria spent one second to wonder what would drive a wealthy foreigner to sneak around a palace and concluded she didn't care. She had enough mysteries in her life. Maria left the man to his own crimes while she resumed hers.

Chapter Seventeen

Isabel

Isabel swiped another crab ball off a tray and popped it in her mouth. It melted on her tongue, the crab as soft as butter on a summer afternoon. She'd decided while lacing up her dress there was no point in stalking Dom Tiago at a ball if she wasn't going to enjoy herself at the same time. If it was simply a question of getting information, she'd sneak into his bedroom and hold a knife to his throat. Crashing the royal family's anniversary ball, that was a once-in-a-lifetime opportunity. Isabel intended to make the most of it.

She'd not forgotten Mateus in the midst of her snacking. Her eyes scanned every face she passed. Dom Tiago was somewhere in this very crowded room. She'd find him if she had to pour wine for every person at the palace.

In retrospect, she shouldn't have chosen white, but she hadn't known she would be serving red wine. Isabel's elegant dress might never recover from the effort. A few ill-timed bumps and elbows had left several stains around her hem. She consoled herself with the hope she'd be able to scrub the wine out.

She'd made the gown in twenty-four hours of frantic sewing, and it was the most gorgeous thing she owned.

The white glowed like moonlight. The fabric brushed her skin, as smooth as the lazy waves of Guanabara. Admiring her reflection on the way to the ball, she wondered how party goers would tell slave from guest, but now that she was among them, Isabel's dress was a table cloth compared to the brilliant plumes of feathers in the women's hair and the jeweled medallions hanging from the men's coats. Her illusion of peacock wilted to farm bird as she surveyed the wealth dripping from each chest. Staying upright in full party regalia had to be the most strenuous exercise the wealthy got.

A booming laugh close by stopped Isabel in her tracks. She'd heard it before, at an initial price Maria had requested for their diamonds. She'd never forget its disdain.

Dom Tiago eyed a young woman who looked barely old enough to attend the ball. Isabel couldn't tell if he was leering at the woman's ample chest or the diamond necklace resting on it. He held an almost empty wine glass. The evening couldn't be going better.

"Excuse me, *senhor*." Isabel dropped a quick curtsy. "More wine?"

Dom Tiago held his glass out. "To the brim."

As she poured, Isabel went straight for the man's jugular. "Of course, sir. Who wouldn't celebrate when all his competition is being eliminated. That relief must be worth its weight in gold. Or diamonds."

He gave such a violent jerk wine sloshed out of his cup onto Isabel's dress. She bit back a curse and merely held Tiago's startled gaze. He glared down at her, and she knew he would have tried to kill her on the spot had there not been a few hundred witnesses.

The smuggler turned to the girl and waved her off. "My dear, I believe the heat is getting to me. Please, don't let me keep you from the party. Enjoy yourself, and I'll find you to claim a dance after a breath of air."

The girl snapped open a fan with enough force to make clear she did not appreciate being dismissed. She stalked off, and Dom Tiago turned his attention back to Isabel.

"I'm sure she'll forgive you for a reasonable price on earrings to match her necklace. What are you selling your black market diamonds for?"

Dom Tiago's face turned a brilliant scarlet. He shoved his way to a window and up against the iron railing around it. Isabel almost moaned in delight at the touch of breeze against her skin.

"Who are you? And why shouldn't I pitch you over this railing?" he growled.

"Because the fall won't kill me, and when I don't die, I will definitely tell everyone you smuggle diamonds." Isabel shrugged and grinned. "And to answer your first question, I'm a friend of Maria and Mateus. Some of your suppliers."

"Mateus. The boy who killed Dom Antonio."

"He didn't do it."

"Then he chose a very foolish place to spend his evening, next to the corpse of a murder victim."

"He didn't do it, and you know he didn't." Isabel went up on tiptoe to meet Tiago's face. "You know diamond smugglers are being targeted or you wouldn't have your baker handling all your business. You're in hiding, senhor."

For a second, Isabel thought he might actually toss her over the rail, then Dom Tiago took a long drink from his cup. "What do you want?"

"Answers. Have you been contacted about the trade by anyone out of the ordinary? Are there any new names or faces in the market in Rio?" Isabel twitched in anticipation. She couldn't believe she'd found Dom Tiago before Maria and was imagining her triumphant reunion with Maria and Victoria. They'd catch the murderer, and Mateus would walk out of prison in a day, two at most.

"You're trying to find the killer?" He barked a laugh. "I'm afraid I can't be of any help. I've retired. I'll stick to slave trading. It's nearly as profitable and perfectly legal."

Isabel's temper lit deep in her gut. She pushed a finger against his chest, not caring what people saw or thought. "You're lying. You wouldn't walk away from that much money without a reason. Tell me what you know, and I'll go away and forget your name. Refuse to talk and I march right up to Prince João, fall to his feet sobbing about how I can't bear to live with myself knowing I've helped steal from such a gentle and good sovereign, and then I give him your name. Now, you don't know me. You have no reason to believe I'm mad enough to clutch the Prince Regent's feet in the middle of a party and lie to his face, but trust me, I am."

Dom Tiago tugged his jacket down and rolled his shoulders back, as if looking his best might help him forget the fact he was confessing to a serving girl half his size. "I spoke with Dom Afonso a day before he was killed. He asked me if I'd heard about a meeting to consolidate our efforts in…exports. I hadn't. He said he'd received a request for a meeting with a new exporter. The request came with raw product. I told him he was a fool for agreeing to see an unknown person, but he merely laughed, saying the man wasn't unknown. Merely new to export."

"So Afonso knew the man who killed him?" Isabel's heart picked up speed.

"I said Afonso knew the man who requested a meeting. I never said that was the man who killed him. All I know is that Dom Afonso had a meeting arranged one night, and the next morning, he was found dead." Dom Tiago suddenly snatched her arm and jerked her within a breath of his face. "I told you what I know. Now, you're going to walk away and forget about me."

"Happily." She flashed him a brilliant smile before plunging into the crowded ballroom.

The rush of success made her dizzy and a giggle escaped her lips. She hurried from the window, ignoring some noble's call for wine. The mysterious new player meeting the smugglers had to be the murderer. She needed to find Maria, so they could plan how to put a name and face to this new smuggler. Lost in thought, she absentmindedly snatched a stuffed date from a passing server.

"Are you eating from the trays?" Victoria stood in front of her with eyes wide and round as the crab puffs.

"You don't?" She popped the date in her mouth.

Victoria took her elbow and dragged her to the wall at the back of the dais. "Vidigal is here!"

Isabel almost dropped the pitcher to draw her daggers. She turned to search the crowd, but Victoria tugged her back around. "Don't look! I saw him in the receiving line. He could still be close by. You and Maria have to leave now!"

She nodded. "I found Dom Tiago. I have what we need. Let's find Maria."

They pushed through the crowd around the dais. A sickly sweet stench with a slight metallic tang assaulted her nose.

"*Santa Karina*, what is that?" Isabel scrunched her nose in disgust.

"That's His Royal Highness. He doesn't like to bathe. Or change clothes. And he keeps chicken legs in his pockets to eat between meals."

Isabel searched Victoria's face for a joke, but there was no humor to find. "Meeting you has destroyed all my fantasies about palace life."

"Imagine smelling that for almost a decade," Victoria said.

"Five minutes is enough for me. Let's get the hell out of here."

They crept through the crowds, keeping their heads down. It was difficult to search for someone while simultaneously trying not to be found by someone else. After making their way from one end of the throne room and back down, neither had glimpsed Maria. Isabel's delight began to give way to nerves. With her height and gold head wrap, her sister should have been easy to spot.

"Where could she be? Would she leave without telling you for any reason?" Victoria chewed her lower lip.

The last of Isabel's excitement evaporated. Maria would leave in secret, and she knew exactly where Maria would go. "Dammit! She went to find Mateus. Without me!"

Isabel began shoving guests aside like underbrush in the forest, indifferent to how many titles belonged to the owners of all the toes she stepped on. Angry heat built up within her, further inflamed by the number of bodies between her and the door. She glanced over her shoulder at Victoria.

"I need you to show me the fastest way to the jail. You said the palace connects with it, right?"

"Yes, but the passage is guarded by soldiers. How would Maria even get across?" Victoria dropped a curtsy to a rotund man in burgundy that Isabel elbowed in the stomach. "Our apologies, senhor. Very sorry."

"If you keep apologizing to everyone, we'll never get out of here," Isabel complained.

"The same applies if you keep elbowing members of court," Victoria countered.

"Good point," she conceded and made a little more effort to look for toes before stepping.

They made it out of the ballroom and into a quiet hall. Victoria hurried past Isabel taking the lead. "Follow me. The fastest way is to cut through some private sections of the palace. If we run into anyone, let me talk."

Despite her certainty that Maria had crossed into imminent danger, curiosity fl ared as they moved past the personal quarters of the royal family. Isabel fought the urge to open one of the closed doors. She was dying to see the bedroom of a princess, but Victoria kept moving without pause. Maids must learn to move fast while still walking. Isabel had to jog every few steps to catch up.

Her dress did not allow for speed. Normally, Isabel wore a much fuller skirt that stopped above her ankle with breeches and boots underneath. It was an unusual combination, pants and skirt, but she could reach full stride in it. This formal dress was narrow and best suited for holding still or shuffl ing. The hem brushed the fl oor, and Isabel took care with every step not to trip on it. By the time Victoria stopped in a random interior hallway, she no longer loved her new dress. She planned on turning it into a pillow case.

"What are we doing?" she glanced around the hall.

"I need to change. Wait here, please." Victoria opened a door and rushed inside.

"Why do you need to change?" she whispered, but Victoria had already shut the door behind her.

Isabel wondered what to do. The hallway was deserted. The only light came from two lamps on small side tables. She had no idea how to get to the prison and reluctantly decided there was no choice but to wait.

A man staggered out of a room down the hall cursing. From the jeweled medallions catching the light, she guessed he was important. He was also drunk.

When the man noticed Isabel, he changed direction and came lurching toward her. She sighed. It was inevitable given the number of men and the amount of alcohol, but it didn't annoy her any less.

"I'm apparently not the only one who is lost," he slurred.

"Yes, you are," Isabel said. She slipped a hand around one of the half-dozen daggers strapped to her legs.

"Come here. Let's explore together." The man leered at her.

She had no patience left for bejeweled pigs after Dom Tiago. In two steps, Isabel closed the remaining distance between them. "I could ask you to leave me alone and go back to the ball, but we both know you won't. So…"

She slammed the butt of her dagger into the man's groin. The man's eyes bulged out of his head, in both shock and pain. He dropped to his knees. She smashed the side of his head into the railing that encircled the interior courtyard. The man slid to the ground, his diamond decorations glittering in the lamplight.

She plucked a smaller, ruby-encrusted medallion from his chest. A door opened behind her.

Victoria gasped. "Why is the viscount on the floor?"

"He was going to attack, so I knocked him out and am taking a memento." Isabel slipped the souvenir into her pocket. She looked at Victoria and couldn't contain her laugh.

The maid tugged at too-long sleeves of a man's coat. The coattails hit below the knees of baggy breeches pulled on over her stockings. The shirt ballooned out at the waist, full of hiked-up undergarments. The only piece of her ball attire that remained were the slippers.

"What are you wearing?"

"I needed a disguise," Victoria said, her voice muffled by the scarf hiding her face. "Anyone at the palace could recognize me, so I borrowed from the men's laundry. What did *you* do to the viscount? I was only gone a moment!"

"Oh, it didn't take more than a second. I can teach you."

"I'm not referring to your speed. How did you find someone to fight in the time needed to grab a coat and breeches?"

Isabel looked down at the man and shrugged. "*He* found *me*. They always find me. Ask Maria. Speaking of. . . are we going to the prison?"

"This way." Victoria hurried down the hall, moving even faster, and Isabel stared longingly at Victoria's ill-fitting breeches.

"How much further?" she whispered.

"The passage over the street is to the left at the end of the hall."

Maria bolted around the corner and slammed into Isabel. Relief flooded through her. She hadn't even realized how worried she'd been until her arms wrapped themselves around her sister's neck. Maria gave her a quick squeeze in return.

"Why aren't you at the ball?" Maria asked, frowning at Victoria's extreme change of attire.

"Are you joking? You're why we're not at the ball!" Isabel's relief was quickly consumed by annoyance. Once again, Maria left her behind. A jail break would have been the greatest story—except there didn't seem to have been a jail break. "Where's Mateus? I know you went to the jail."

"I went to get information from him," Maria said.

"You risked your life and left me out of all the fun, to have a nice chat?" She wanted to punch her sister. "He'd better have given you the address of the murderer. What the hell were you thinking?"

"I'm terribly sorry to interrupt, but does anyone hope to be alive tomorrow?" Victoria interrupted. "If so, you both need to leave the palace."

"Fine. I'll finish yelling at you at home." Isabel stomped past her sister, but Maria snagged her elbow.

"We can't go that way. Unconscious soldiers," Maria warned.

"Can't go back that way. An unconscious viscount." She jabbed a blade in the direction they'd come. They turned in unison to Victoria.

Victoria chewed her lip, brow furrowed, then gave a curt nod. "Through the convent. You'll avoid the carriages and footmen around the square, but the passage is at the back of the palace and now I look like…" Victoria gestured to her outfit.

"What are you wearing?" Maria asked.

"I thought we were sneaking into the prison, so I needed a disguise. I have to work here tomorrow."

"We'll stay in front and hide you," Maria said. "If we see anyone, Isabel and I can say we're getting something for the queen."

As they moved through the halls to the convent, Victoria whispering directions, a thought popped into

Isabel's head. "If the queen's in the convent, what happened to the monks and nuns who used to live there?"

"They moved to a seminary in Lapa once Her Majesty moved in," Victoria explained.

"You mean they were ordered to leave?" Maria rephrased.

"Probably," Victoria admitted quietly. "But the royal family is very pious. I'm sure they made a very large donation to the church in return."

"*Santa Ludmilla*, we must be the only ones who haven't been thrown out of our home by the court. I'm beginning to feel insulted," Isabel muttered.

She tried to imagine what the world would be like if she could have anything that caught her eye, to be able to point at a horse or a house and claim it, but she couldn't summon any feelings of joy or satisfaction. Isabel could more easily imagine life as a parrot than a life where people gave you their own homes.

"Halt!" The command came from behind on the palace side of the passage. "Who goes there?"

Isabel's pulse quickened, the thrill of the chase, the promise of action. "Finally!" she said. "I thought the evening had been too easy."

"What about this has been easy?" Victoria squeaked.

"It's a narrow space." Maria eyed the passageway from top to bottom. "Let me strike first, but I need a distraction to find my whip under this damn dress."

"Done." Isabel stepped in front of Maria.

"In the name of His Royal Highness Prince João, state your business here." An officer and two soldiers strode down the passage. The soldiers raised their rifles, and indignation set Isabel's face aflame. The ballroom was currently packed with smugglers, murderers, and cheats, yet the soldiers were about to arrest them for the crime of attending a party without an invitation. She planted her feet in the middle of the passage and stared the soldiers down.

"I said state your business."

"Of course," Isabel answered, smiling. "We're sneaking out of the palace after pretending to be servants so we could get information from the diamond smugglers on the guest list about the murderer currently strangling rich men around Rio. All so we can catch the murderer and get our innocent friend out of jail."

The soldiers glanced at each other. The officer opened then closed his mouth like a beached fish.

"Well since there doesn't seem to be a problem, we'll be leaving," Isabel chirped.

"Don't move!" the officer stammered, drawing his sword. "You're all under arrest."

"My turn," Maria said.

She stepped aside as Maria raised her arm. The whip cracked, and the officer dropped his sword. Before the sword hit the floor, Isabel flew down the passage to the open window on the left of the soldiers. A second crack. The soldier closest to her dropped his rifle. Isabel planted her foot on the iron banister across the window and pushed off toward the center of the passage. She reached up, a dagger in each hand, and drove them into the ceiling.

The impact jarred her spine. She tightened her grip and swung from the daggers. Isabel slammed her feet into a soldier, knocking him out the opposite window onto the roof of a carriage as it passed underneath. She dropped to the floor and whirled back to the second soldier. Isabel drew two more daggers, but Victoria stepped in front of her, holding the fallen officer's sword.

The maid brought the sword down against the rifle, so the soldier fired into the floor. She pivoted into him, drove her elbow into his nose, and shrieked as blood spurted into her face. Isabel barked a laugh. Victoria's combination of fierce and dainty was absurd, charming and unlike any person Isabel had ever met.

"Victoria, bend over," she called. She launched herself off Victoria's back. She grabbed the daggers still embedded in the ceiling and knocked the bloodied soldier out the window. She patted Victoria on the shoulder after landing. "Thanks for the boost."

Victoria smiled. "I'm happy to help."

Isabel looked around for the officer and found him lying on the floor at Maria's feet. Her sister stood over him in a still-spotless dress, her head wrap perfectly centered. There was not a trace of effort on her. It was a skill Isabel envied. Even on the trail, Maria always managed to appear in control of everything, including her clothes. The clothes were most likely afraid to make her sister look bad by wrinkling. Her own dress was askew, torn at the hem, and stained with wine. Then she looked at Victoria and doubled-over laughing.

In addition to the improvised and ill-fitting disguise, Victoria's face and hair were now splattered with blood. Her hair had been through a hurricane. She was the exact opposite of the refined Portuguese girl they had rescued on the beach a week earlier.

"I don't think we've been a good influence on you, Victoria," Maria said, grinning. "Is this what being friends with us does to a person?"

"Nossa Senhora, do I look so awful?" Victoria patted her hair and face trying to assess the damage.

"Relax, it suits you." Isabel reached out and wiped a few blood droplets off Victoria's cheek with her thumb.

The skin was smooth, flushed. She showed the smear to Victoria and winked. "Like I said, red is your color."

Isabel waited for a gasp or frown, but Victoria smiled at her. "This has been, by far, the most enjoyable ball I've ever attended."

The words sent a shiver of delight down her spine. She slung an arm around Victoria. "We should do this more often. The food was excellent."

The sound of boots charging reminded her that a gun had gone off only moments earlier, and someone would need to be held accountable for gunfire in the palace. Isabel had no intention of being that person. "But I guess that's enough excitement for one night. My sister needs her beauty sleep."

Maria snorted a laugh as they ran down the passageway. Victoria led them to a servants' entrance on the back side of the convent away from the palace.

"To the right, this road will lead you back towards the square." Victoria pointed.

"So, we'll be going the opposite way." Isabel tussled Victoria's hair as she passed, taking an extra second to appreciate the silky texture. "Warrior looks good on you."

Maria squeezed Victoria's shoulder then pushed her back through the door. "But go change your clothes before the soldiers find you."

Victoria waved, then disappeared into the shadows of the convent. Isabel felt a tug of disappointment that the surprising and blood-splattered Portuguese maid wasn't coming home with them. A shout from Maria sent the thought racing away, and she hurried to catch up with her sister. Isabel reveled in the sea breeze against her skin. The night air was hot and thick, but at least it smelled like the ocean and not sweaty nobles.

The party had been a raging success, and she had captured the prize. Dom Tiago's words remained crystal clear in her memory. Whoever requested the meeting with Dom Afonso the day of his death was the murderer. Isabel knew it. She felt it in her bones the same way she felt a storm coming.

As a rule, smugglers didn't discuss their trade with strangers, which meant Afonso knew and trusted the man who requested the meeting. Afonso was murdered by someone from his circle. They were hunting among the elite. Isabel doubted a pompous Portuguese would be much of a challenge, but she was dying to find out.

Chapter Eighteen

Maria

The midday heat clouded Maria's judgement, making it difficult not to pitch the indifferent captain off the dock. She woke at dawn despite the late night at the ball, and a morning wading through the self-importance of ship captains quickly consumed what little patience she could muster. Sail through one hurricane and a man became a god in his own mind.

"Sorry, Maria. I can't help you." Captain Silva, a veteran of Rio's port and black market, wiped the sweat from his brow with a brown rag. "It's a damn shame about Mateus. I know it'll be tough to keep your father's train running now that you're on your own."

"The mule train will be heading out on schedule next week. Mateus will be with us," she said. Maria tried to marshal her thoughts, but the stench of baking fish guts nearly broke her composure. Hell was undoubtedly a fish market near midday in summer.

Seeing the glittering gulf between herself and Rio's elite made clear no member of court would help her due to a common enemy. A rather naïve assumption she now realized and scolded herself for making it, so rather than talking to the people buying the diamonds, she'd talk to the people moving them. Her people. Well, closer to her people.

There were two ways diamonds got out of Rio, by sea or by river south to Argentina. She'd gone to Catete at dawn to speak with the river smugglers. The crews were smaller, Brazilian born and raised, and when Maria asked about their most recent shipments, she trusted their answers. No new faces. No new names.

The sea captains were a different story. When the Prince Regent arrived in Rio, he immediately opened the port to British merchants as recompense for British protection during their Atlantic crossing, and now Maria knew only a fraction of the captains personally. Her frustration grew as one captain after another either waved her off, claiming he knew nothing, or refused to speak with her at all.

Victoria's presence at her side didn't make the captains more forthcoming.

Maria hadn't intended to interrogate smugglers in the company of a freshly-pressed Portuguese maid, but Isabel showed up at the wharf with Victoria in tow. They arrived fresh from the palace with news that they were free of any suspicion from the previous night's escapade. The now recovered prison guards were telling everyone about the half dozen men who'd attacked them after sneaking into the ball dressed as women.

Victoria delivered the news with a pride that Maria had never seen in the girl. Her head held high, radiating joy, Maria couldn't bear to send her away when she asked to help. Isabel offered to take Victoria along to interview crewmen, but Maria knew her sister's methods for procuring information had a tendency to get out of hand. She assumed Victoria had not stashed a weapon under her skirt before leaving the palace and would be better off talking to the captains with her.

Refusing to be brushed off yet again, she pressed Captain Silva. "What about another ship? Have you heard of any captain working with a new buyer? A rumor? A whisper?"

"I told you, I got out of the business last year and haven't heard anything." Silva's brow furrowed under his hat, and his mouth clamped tight in a thin line.

Maria felt a scream of frustration building in her chest. She closed her eyes. Mateus's bruised and broken face came back to her. His body hunched in the back corner of his cell. The resignation in his voice. *A dying man gets a final confession.* No. Mateus was not dying. Captain Silva would talk to her. One stubborn mule couldn't be allowed to put the rest of the team in danger. She reached for her whip, but Victoria touched her sleeve and stepped forward.

"Captain," she said, dropping a curtsy, "your desire to protect your clients and ship is admirable. We've spoken to a dozen captains this morning, and not one has shown your discretion. The last thing we want is to cause you any trouble. We're simply desperate to save a friend from a great injustice, and we apologize for any inconvenience we may have caused."

Maria narrowed her eyes at the completely unde-served apology but kept silent. Victoria hadn't inter-rupted all morning, so Maria waited, curious to see what compelled the maid to finally speak up.

"Thank you for speaking with us. I hope that the real killer is apprehended soon before even more busi-ness disappears into the hands of a murderer or worse… moves to São Paulo. We will continue our search. Good day, Captain." Victoria dropped another curtsy and turned to walk back down the dock. Maria hesitated, cutting her eyes between Victoria and the captain.

"One minute, miss," the captain called. "You're right about business disappearing. It's getting harder. . ." he continued, his voice trailing off as he stared out at the bay. He sighed and smiled at Victoria. "A nice girl shouldn't be here asking these questions. The work is more dangerous with the Prince Regent hiding here in Rio. It's true I'm out of the business, but not by choice. There's no product to move. No one's asked me to take anything in a fortnight." He leaned forward and dropped his voice. "From what I hear, no ship has been asked to move anything in weeks."

"But at least nine trains have returned to Rio in the last month," Maria interjected. She ran through the names in her head: Zé, Little João, Rodrigo, Joaquim. They were all back in the city, and their trains always arrived with extra heavy papayas.

The captain shrugged and wiped his face again. "All I know is that nothing's getting out by sea. Not for weeks now. And you ladies would do well to stop asking questions nobody wants to answer." Turning to leave, he met Maria's gaze. "And I am sorry for you."

A final tip of the hat was the last thing they got out of him. Maria stalked back toward the street. Victoria caught up, chewing on her bottom lip.

"I hope you're not angry I interrupted your interview."

"Angry? I should've had you do all the questioning. He took one look at you and started talking," Maria said, impressed. "Is that some sort of Portuguese girl witchcraft?"

"Groveling gets you a lot of favors at the palace. I thought it might work on the captain, too. Apologize.

Flatter. Ask for help. People will say almost anything in front of someone they think is helpless."

Maria stopped walking and eyed Victoria from under the wide brim of her straw hat. "I think the girl from Lisbon is learning to survive in Rio."

"It is surprising how well the skills acquired in court life are useful in the world of smugglers."

"We're all stealing from someone," Maria muttered. She swiped away a bead of sweat running down her face. "Right. I'm roasting alive. Let's get in the shade then find Isabel. Maybe she can add to what Silva told us."

Maria marched down the street dodging the crates, carts, and general chaos of the docks. Victoria struggled to catch up, and she slowed her pace. Too fast. She was moving too fast. Another mistake. Rushed caused as many as accidents as distracted. She knew better. Just like she knew better than to lose her temper with Silva. She was off her stride today. Her thoughts darted around her head, and she couldn't hold on to any one long enough to tell if it was a good idea or likely to get them arrested.

"Sorry," she said. "I didn't mean to leave you behind."

"Please, don't worry about me. I'll keep up." Victoria hiked her skirts up and navigated through a fresh catch of haddock spilling out of their net across the dock.

This was not the same timid, servant girl she'd rescued off the beach a week ago. That girl scurried after them, practically clinging to their boots, but this Victoria tricked a Rio smuggler out of his secrets. A small knot of worry loosened in her chest. The girl needed to be able to take care of herself because the moment Mateus was free, she was packing her train and her family and getting out of this damned city.

Mateus.

His name swept her back to the prison, staring at his face through the iron bars. He appeared before her, clutching the iron bars of his cell, beaten yet smiling. She pushed the memory away. She'd sworn to get him out, and she couldn't dwell on him if she wanted to free him.

"Maria?"

She startled from the dark thoughts. "Sorry, I was thinking."

"I was as well. About what the captain said." Victoria tilted her head. "Where are the diamonds if they're not being smuggled out by ship? Has the black market died out?"

"No. I know the muleteers who've arrived in the last few weeks. They always have some hidden cargo, and they would have unloaded it as quickly as possible. No one wants contraband diamonds in their home."

"But if the local buyers are dead or dying and the diamonds aren't getting smuggled by sea…"

"Where are the diamonds?" Maria finished the thought. Her hand gripped and ungripped the butt of her whip. The diamonds were the answer. If she found the diamonds, then she'd find the murderer, and Mateus would be free. She sensed an answer in her tangle of thoughts. "It doesn't make sense. Why kill the competition but not move the diamonds?"

"There you are! *Santa Agueda,* I've been looking everywhere for you." Isabel popped up between Maria and Victoria. "It's hotter than midsummer in hell. Who wants a mango? Or mango juice? Juice would be perfect. Let's head home. I've got a basket of mangos at home ripe and ready to eat." Without waiting for an answer, Isabel slipped her arm through Victoria's and pulled her away from the beach, quickly weaving through the crowd. Too quickly.

Maria narrowed her eyes at her sister. "Isabel? What did you do?"

"Why do you think—" Isabel's indignant protest was cut off by shouts coming from the end of the wharf. Three uniformed soldiers shoved through fishermen as they hurried up the beach toward the street.

"Those are British marines." Victoria frowned as one of the soldiers pointed at them. "Are they...are they yelling at us?"

"Isabel, why are British marines yelling at us?" Maria snapped.

"You said chat with the crews."

Her jaw dropped. "Of the merchant ships! Not the British navy!" she shouted. Of all the things that could get them arrested.

"Oh. . ." Isabel puckered her lips and shot a glance over her shoulder at the oncoming soldiers. "Next time be more specifi c."

"Stop! You there, halt!" a heavily accented command rang out.

Isabel propelled Victoria down the street. Maria took the rear, and the soldiers picked up their pace.

"Faster!" she urged. They couldn't be caught. Any questioning they'd be subjected to would last for days, if not indefi nitely. No one would know to petition the British navy for their release. Mateus could be executed in two days. She did not have time for this.

They ducked under baskets gleaming with sugared fruit rinds and hopped over streams of fish blood and salt water pooling between the granite stones. She hoped they could slip away among the crowd at the fish market, but a glance back dashed that hope. The soldiers had closed in and increased in number.

"Stop! You are ordered to stop in the name of His Majesty's navy."

"Run!" Maria ordered.

Isabel broke into a sprint, dragging along Victoria, who tried to look back.

"Go!" She pushed Victoria ahead. A rifle cracked, and they dropped to a crouch. A crate burst into splinters over Isabel's head.

Clearly the soldiers weren't interested in questioning them. Maria scrambled to her feet pulling Victoria up with her. Isabel charged ahead, clearing a path through people and animals. A second shot thudded into a stack of papaya on her left.

She scanned the stalls and crates lining the street ahead. Her hand flew and without breaking her stride, she wrapped her whip around the leg of a stall. With a quick jerk as she raced by, Maria sent mountains of passion fruit rolling across the street.

"I'm sorry," she called to the man standing aghast behind the now collapsed table.

The obstacle sent one soldier sprawling to the ground. The other four leapt over and kept coming. With a flick of her arm, Maria brought a crate of squid toppling into the soldiers. One marine caught six purple tentacles square in the face. He let out a shriek, dropped his rifle, and flailed into another marine, sending them both into a squishy pile of squid. She smiled and committed to memory the effect of catching a squid full in the face.

The crowd hurled curses at the runners. Understandably, considering the amount of product their chase was ruining. Vendors and merchants took up arms to defend their goods, broom sticks, hammers, one even wielded a massive piece of salted cod. Anything to beat the runners back from their stalls. They had to get off the market street and find a place to hide.

Victoria slipped on a slick stone. Isabel and Maria both reached for her. A shot hit a stone a foot away sending sparks in the air.

"In less than one day, we've had soldiers from two countries trying to shoot us," Victoria gasped, gathering her skirts higher to gain speed.

"It makes you feel important, doesn't it?" Isabel shouted, grinning.

"It does beat emptying chamber pots." Victoria smiled, and Isabel let out a whoop.

Maria glanced back. Three red coats were still shoving through the crowd. "This way!" She yanked the others through an open door as another shot smacked a hole in the wall.

"Excuse us." Maria nodded to the cook and girls who gaped as they charged through the kitchen toward an interior courtyard. On the opposite side, a door opened into what she hoped was an alley behind the house.

"It smells wonderful," Victoria called, rushing past two bubbling pots on the stove.

Isabel snorted. "Only you would offer a compliment in the middle of running for our lives."

"Why are we running for our lives, Isabel?" Maria huffed.

"It's not my fault. They're overreacting."

They flew out of the kitchen, crossed the courtyard, and raced through the door before they skidded to a stop in front of a massive stallion. The horse reared up, startled by the commotion.

"Stables," Isabel groaned, holding her palms up to calm the horse.

Maria sprinted to the carriage entrance blocked by a black iron gate. She shook the heavy chain around the bars.

"We need a key." Victoria turned in circles scanning the stable.

"I can open it. Give me one of your hair pins." Maria knelt down and attacked the lock with the pins Victoria offered. For the first time since the ball, her mind cleared as she focused on the lock.

A deep voice stumbled through Portuguese in the kitchen. "We're looking for three young women. Did they come through here?"

"Hurry," Victoria urged.

"Almost there." Maria glared at the lock willing it to open.

"Don't worry. Take your time," Isabel called.

A horse snorted, and Maria glanced back at her sister. Isabel led the horse into the courtyard they had barreled through. She lined the massive animal up with the kitchen door, drew a knife, and frowned at the horse.

"I'm really sorry about this." Isabel pricked the stallion's side with the knife and jumped back. The enormous animal reared up, shrieking in protest, and charged directly into the kitchen. Screams, bellows, and whinnies filled the air.

"Nossa Senhora," Victoria gasped.

Maria focused on the lock, ignoring the mayhem from the kitchen. "Got it!"

She yanked the chain off. Together they pushed the gate open and fled onto a back street. They turned north away from beach. Dishes crashed and English curses rang out from the kitchen. Maria didn't look back.

The alley opened up onto a busy thoroughfare. Slaves carried litters and mules pulled carts through every available space. Maria led the way, gliding among the chaos with a sixth sense. Compared to a team of mules, leading Isabel and Victoria around was easy. Except Victoria was limping. She hadn't so much as whimpered, but Maria noticed the hobbled gait.

If you couldn't outrun a predator, the only option was to put up a hell of a fight.

"You two go ahead. I'll delay the soldiers and meet up with you," she ordered.

Isabel snorted. "I'll invite Vidigal for dinner first."

"Victoria knows all the information we learned today. If I get caught, at least you two can still work to get Mateus out. Go!"

"She's right. It's smarter to split up," Victoria added.

"You can handle them?" Isabel's black eyes bore into her own.

Maria nodded once. When they'd disappeared into the crowd, she faced the armed soldiers emerging onto the boulevard one block down. She shook out her arm. Six marines caught sight of her. Their bayonets glinted under the noon sun.

She planted herself in the center of the street. Guilt twisted her stomach as she considered the amount of produce she was about ruin. Again. She'd robbed dozens of people of a day's income with the mess left in her wake. These were not people with time or money to spare. The knowledge sat heavy in her gut, but she locked the guilt away with the promise she'd come back and repay them.

First, she had to protect her family.

The soldiers' shouts and bayonets cleared a trail through the center of the street. Her whip cracked against the flank of a horse and sent it tearing off toward the soldiers along with its cart. The soldiers yelped and dove to the side. She brought the whip around her head. Leather hissed through the air, and she sliced the rope holding a banner over a door. The banner, hung to celebrate the anniversary festivities, plummeted onto the soldiers, forcing them to drop their rifles and grope their way out from under. A scattering of applause broke out among some of the onlookers.

"Drop the whip and surrender!"

Two soldiers managed to avoid the banner and aimed their rifles as best they could through the crowd. Maria turned and ran up the street toward an ornate litter held up by four slaves. Her timing had to be perfect.

With the last two soldiers on her heels, she sent her whip tearing into a basket of mangos. The rose and green fruits spilled onto the street and rolled around the feet of the slaves forcing them to stop. Maria sprinted at the litter. In the last second before the collision, she dove feet first rolling under the litter across the mangos. She slid out the other side leaving the soldiers behind crashing into each other and the litter.

Four hands gripped Maria by the arms and hauled her up to her feet. The familiar faces sent a shock of exasperation through her.

"Goddammit! I told you both to go."

"That was never going to happen." Isabel rolled her eyes then pointed at Victoria. "Besides, she was the first to say turn around." Maria fixed her glare on Victoria.

The girl shrugged her lace-trimmed shoulders. "It's Isabel's influence."

"Aw, thank you." Isabel linked her arm through Victoria's.

The soldiers were caught up in a hail of insults and accusation by whoever was in the litter. The woman's shrill accusations carried over the din of the street. They used the distraction to slip up the street. Victoria hobbled as best she could. They needed to end this. Maria had more important things to do than evading soldiers.

"Good morning, ladies. Do you need a ride?"

Maria looked up at the driver of a nearby wagon and recognized the man from the palace hallway. He held up his hands in surrender.

"Please, don't put a knife in my stomach. I want to help," he said, eyeing the blades Isabel held.

"Tomasinho," Isabel said, lowering her daggers and grinning. "I'd recognize that jaw anywhere. I see you've gotten a new hat."

"I lost my last one to a worthy cause." He tipped his head to Isabel. "Unlike my gold, which was lost because of my own gullibility."

"Gold? Isabel, how do you know him?" Maria demanded.

"I helped him sneak past some Bats."

Victoria let out a gasp. "You're that American who threatened to shoot Her Highness's guards."

The man coughed, embarrassed. "Yes, that was me. I was regrettably short on patience that day. My name's Thomas, and I'm happy to tell you my life story, but I think you should hide now." He looked pointedly to where the soldiers had righted the litter and were helping the woman back in. He flipped back part of the tarp covering his cart. "Your coach, senhoritas."

A warning hummed in Maria's head. There was too much information and too many questions to sift through. Victoria started to climb in the cart, but Maria pulled her back down. "We don't know this man!"

"He won't turn us in. Americans aren't allies with the British," Victoria argued.

"That doesn't make him our friend."

"I can't run anymore," Victoria whispered, "and I trust him."

"So do I." Isabel hopped in the cart and offered a hand to Victoria.

"Why in god's name would you trust this man?"

"He's got a pretty smile." Isabel's answer made the man's grin even wider. "And he owes me a rescue." Isabel hauled Victoria up, and they settled in under the tarp. She raised her eyebrows at Maria. "Coming?"

In two long strides she was up in the driver's bench, the butt of her whip under the man's chin. She spoke low and clear. "I know it was you I ran into at the palace. If you tip the soldiers off, I will use my last seconds of freedom to denounce you and take out both your eyes. Understand?" The man nodded, his smile gone. "Take us to Largo do Paço."

She jumped down and settled in the cart between Isabel and Victoria. When they were completely covered, Thomas whistled, and the cart lurched forward.

They were silent, straining to hear a command to halt. Maria sucked in her breath as the voices of the soldiers, still apologizing, came through the tarp. She only exhaled when the cart turned off the main road in the direction of the palace. As the cart picked up speed, frantic whispering broke out.

"Why does this American owe you a *rescue*?" Maria asked Isabel.

"He actually pulled a pistol on the princess?" Isabel demanded.

"Maria, why are you so nervous?" Victoria said with wide eyes.

The onslaught bore down on her. Too many loose ends, too few clues, too close a call. It was too much to carry. She risked breaking.

"One question at a time," Maria snapped. "Isabel, go. Keep it short and true."

Isabel stuck her chin in the air. "My stories are always true." Maria raised an eyebrow, and her sister held her hands up in surrender. "Fine, I'll give the boring version."

She explained how she met Thomas after ignoring Maria's instructions about Antonia's, selling counter-feit gems, and lying to Bats. "So he snuck out through the kitchen while I distracted the guardsmen. Don't be mad, sister. I had control."

Maria wasn't mad. She had only one question. "What did you do with the gold dust?"

Isabel pulled the sack of dust from the pouch on her hip. "I haven't been able to do anything. Turns out taking advantage of someone's ignorance isn't as satis-fying as taking advantage of someone's greed. All right, now I want to hear about Thomas almost shooting the princess."

Victoria finished her story in a breathless rush. "He had a pistol in each hand pointed directly at the prin-cess's guards! And would have shot. I saw his face."

"I think I'm in love with him," Isabel declared. She grinned at Maria. "I hope you're not feeling left out without a Thomas story of your own."

Maria rolled her eyes. "Actually, I met him yes-terday." Isabel and Victoria sat up in surprise. "Last night while sneaking back into the palace from the jail. I ran into him creeping through the shadows of a deserted hallway."

"Goodness that sounds decidedly nefarious," Victoria said.

"Decidedly," Isabel added with a giggle. She elbowed Victoria, and Maria thought she saw a blush creep up Victoria's cheeks.

Maria silently cursed herself for ignoring her instincts and climbing into that cart. They were completely at the mercy of a man who snuck through palaces, hid from Bats, and didn't give a damn for royal authority. The warning in her head grew shrill. Her instincts bristled as if they were being stalked by an unseen threat.

A thought snapped Maria upright, her head smacking against the tarp. "Isabel, did Dito say why Thomas rents the rooms at the inn? Or anything about his profession?"

"No, but Thomas mentioned meeting with a rich man there."

"Rich enough to buy smuggled diamonds?" Maria dropped her voice and leaned forward. "When I saw him last night, he was wearing perfectly cut silk. He was not at the ball as a servant."

"You think he was a guest?" Victoria frowned. "Why would he be sneaking if he was invited?"

"Because he wasn't there for dancing and drinking. I bet a lot of deals were struck last night without royal approval."

"You think he's a smuggler," Victoria said, her eyes widening in understanding.

"No." Isabel shook her head. "A smuggler would know a crystal from a topaz."

"Not if he's a recently arrived gringo new to the game." Maria locked eyes with Isabel. "It's him."

Maria's heart raced as she laid the pieces out. "We know there's a killer targeting wealthy buyers of black market diamonds. The killer is able to meet with these men alone in private locations, so it must be someone the victims trust. A wealthy, handsome gringo? The killings started recently. Dom Tiago said there's a new player in the smuggling game meeting with buyers. We thought it was someone new to the trade, but what about new to Rio? All three victims were strangled. So, the killer is not afraid of violence or the consequences of killing powerful people. Like a man who draws a pistol on the crowned princess of Portugal."

For a long moment the only sounds came from out-side the tarp, then Isabel drew her daggers and shifted to a crouch. "I'll take him from behind. Maria, you take over driving. Victoria, just hang on to something."

Victoria grabbed Isabel's arm. "We can't attack him while he's driving the cart. We'll crash and die. And we have no proof. If you were seeking revenge, you could kill this man and be done, but you're not." She let go of Isabel and focused on Maria. "If you want your friend released then listen, please. I hear the talk at the palace. I've seen Major Vidigal coming and going from the Prince Regent's quarters. You're not going to overrule the commander of the royal guard and free your friend with a string of coincidences. You need proof. Which you won't get if you kill him now."

"Fine. We track him." The certainty in Maria's stomach hardened and turned cold as river water. Now that she had her prey in sight, she could be patient. She would stalk him and wait for the right moment to attack. "We stay on him day and night until we have something to lock him away forever."

A jolt sent them all into the crates at their backs. A second later, the tarp was ripped away, and Rio's midday sun slammed into her face.

Chapter Nineteen

Isabel

I sabel threw her hand up against the onslaught of sunlight.

"O Largo do Paço, as requested," Thomas announced. "I hope you ladies had a pleasant trip. Allow me to help you down."

Her eyes adjusted, and the face of the dashing murderer came into focus. For Isabel there was little doubt the man was a criminal. Nobody who spent that much time sneaking around and avoiding Bats was innocent. She knew from experience.

"We made it," Victoria exclaimed, "without getting arrested."

"I'm a man of my word." Thomas swept his hat to the ground and bowed before holding out a hand to Victoria. "May I help you down, miss?"

Victoria recoiled as if the man's hand was covered in festering boils. The girl would be the world's worst card player. Isabel stretched her arms and gave a loud yawn, drawing Thomas's attention before Victoria gave their suspicions away.

"Oh, are we there? It was so warm and cozy under that tarp, I fell asleep." She stretched and hopped to her feet. "Don't mind Victoria. She's a little shy when meeting beautiful people. She still barely looks me in the eye."

Thomas barked a laugh. "I believe most people are dazzled to distraction by your beauty. I speak as the owner of some rather lovely rocks." He extended his hand to Isabel. She hesitated a second and assessed his face, expecting anger or understandable mortification at being so thoroughly duped, but Thomas held her gaze with a smile and tipped his head in respectful surrender.

A man who respected a good con and threatened to kill royalty. If he weren't a murderer, she could have been great friends with this American. And it wasn't the murder of a criminal noble that upset her so much as him letting a poor man get executed in his place. A man with honor doesn't make victims of people who already have nothing.

Isabel reached passed Thomas's hand and gripped his shoulder as she jumped down. "I'm so glad you love the stones. I was sure you'd think you overpaid."

"On the contrary. They came with an important lesson. And the possibility of an alliance."

"With whom?" Isabel asked.

"You. I've been hoping to meet you again because I think we can do business together."

"You're talking to the wrong person." Isabel waved his suggestion away. "My sister handles all the business dealings."

"Sister?" Thomas looked up at Maria who jumped to the ground ignoring his hand. He raised an eyebrow. "One of your eight siblings?"

"Her only sister. Isabel likes telling stories to gullible foreigners," Maria said, and deliberately eyed Thomas from riding boots to blond hair. Isabel grinned when

Thomas glanced away first. She loved watching her sister the muleteer in action.

A small cough interrupted the tension. "I'm terribly sorry but would you mind?"

"Oh miss, forgive my manners. Allow me." Thomas hurriedly offered his hand to Victoria. Isabel marveled at her still perfect curls. She had to ask Victoria what the secret was to a hair style that held after being chased by marines through the fish market.

"Thank you, sir."

"My pleasure, miss. . .?"

"Cruz. Victoria Cruz from Lisbon," Victoria answered automatically then froze halfway through her curtsy. She glanced up with the wide-eyed fear of someone who had without thinking given her full name to an agreed upon murderer. From behind Thomas, Isabel frantically motioned for her to rise from the curtsy.

"Miss Cruz, it's a pleasure to meet you formally. I remember your face from the unfortunate incident with the princess."

"Your Portuguese is impeccable, senhor," Maria said.

"Please, call me Thomas. Thomas Sumpter from Philadelphia at your service," he said, tipping his wide straw hat to Maria.

"You could have gotten arrested for helping us. Why would you risk prison for strangers?" Maria kept him pinned beneath her gaze.

"If the soldiers had arrested me, I wouldn't have stayed in jail for long. Perks of being part of a diplomatic envoy. Well, the son of the envoy. My father is a successful merchant and part of the diplomatic mission from the United States." Thomas gave a wry smile. "Please, don't think I'm boasting. I simply don't wish to give the impression I'm braver than I truly am. I was far more concerned for you ladies than myself. Jail is not the place for such impressive women."

Maria scoffed, Victoria blushed, and Isabel laughed until she had tears in her eyes. Wealthy, young, American, and handsome. Catching this man was going to be fun.

"A diplomat? Have you met Prince João?" Isabel said.

"I've been received by the Prince Regent and attended a few dinners at the palace, but I've never had an official audience. As I said, my father is the envoy."

"And you sail around on his coattails and ships?" Maria asked.

"I am fortunate to have a couple ships of my own that I hope to use for trade between Rio and Philadelphia."

"Ships your father gave you?"

The tone of voice reeked of suspicion, and Isabel jumped in. "Oh, sister, go easy on Tomasinho." She draped a hand protectively on his shoulder. "He hasn't done anything you haven't. He accepted a job from his father. The only difference between you and him is that our Papa had mules to give and his had ships. I think he's proven himself to be quite noble."

"We don't know that he's noble," Maria said. "Just rash and well connected."

"I can see you don't trust me, miss. Normally, I'd tip my hat and be on my way, but based on the look in your eyes," he nodded to Maria, "I think you'll stop me from leaving. What is it you'd like from me?"

"To know for sure you won't betray us to the royal guard."

"I won't. Just as I didn't turn you in last night at the palace. I remember you, and I hope keeping your secrets twice in less than a day at least earns me a favor in return."

"What do you want?" Maria said.

"I'd like your trust." The diplomat and the muleteer eyed each other in a silent standoff.

"Enough!" Isabel announced. God, she'd never seen two people so stubborn they'd rather be roasted alive by Rio's sun than concede. "It's too damn hot for a battle of wills, and my stomach's complaining about delaying lunch. We need to decide. Do we knock the man out and dump him on a ship headed for Angola or do we give him a chance?"

Thomas gave a disbelieving chuckle but grew quiet after observing the silent conversation between Isabel and Maria. His smile vanished, and when he looked significantly concerned for his safety, Isabel patted his shoulder.

"Don't worry, Tomasinho. I'm on your side. I vote we give him a chance. He did save our lives."

"We could have saved ourselves. We didn't need his help," Maria countered.

"Of course we could have," Isabel said, "but he offered his help and saved us from more work."

"And more blisters," Victoria added. They all turned in surprise at her sudden appearance in the conversation. She seemed to regret chiming in. The blush sweeping across her cheeks made the Portuguese girl even more adorable, and to her credit, Victoria smoothed her dress and stated her mind despite being obviously mortified. "I agree with Isabel. I do not believe Senhor Thomas deserves banishment."

"That sounded like a royal decree to me." Thomas's smile returned.

"Victoria is the forgiving one." Isabel winked at her friend before pointing to Maria. "My sister is the skeptical one."

"And which one are you?"

"I'm the honest one. And honestly, sister, we know you're too honorable not to accept the request of someone who helped you."

"Fine," Maria conceded. "Thomas Sumpter of Philadelphia I don't trust you, but in return for helping us, I'll give you a chance to earn my trust."

"I'll take it," Thomas agreed and held out his hand. Isabel grabbed it and gave a hearty shake. Thomas's eyebrows lifted as he shook Isabel's hand. "Your hand tells me you have a story, Miss...Wait, I still haven't gotten your name."

Isabel flashed a smile that left the American stunned. "Don't take it the wrong way, but if I gave my name to every handsome American diplomat who asked I'd never get a moment's peace." She slipped her arm around Victoria's waist and steered her away. "Tchau, Tomasinho! Thanks again for the rescue." Maria tipped her hat, and they left the American alone in the middle of the square.

"Wait," Thomas shouted after them. "How am I going to earn your trust if I don't know your names? And what about my business proposal?"

"I'm sure we'll meet again," Isabel called back.

They walked in silence until they turned off the square and Maria said, "He has ships."

"Two of them. Lucky boy."

"If he uses his own ships it would explain why the local captains haven't moved any diamonds recently," Victoria said.

"New to the city. Not intimidated by authority. Willing to take risks. The clout of a diplomatic envoy. Absolutely sure of his immunity to consequences. And has two ships sailing to another country." Maria nodded. "It's him."

"The whole conversation back at the square was a kind of interrogation?" Victoria asked. "You were trying to get him to talk about himself."

"Don't be so impressed. It's easy to get rich men talking about themselves," Isabel said. She gave Victoria a nudge. "You helped a lot. Blisters?"

"Please don't remind me," Victoria moaned, burying her face in her hands.

"What happened to the girl who pulled information out of a hardened sea captain?" Maria asked.

"The captain wasn't a murderer. I don't know how to make polite conversation with murderers."

Maria stopped walking and stared at Victoria. "Why in God's name would you assume that captain hasn't killed anyone?"

"Well, I thought. . ." Victoria looked slightly stunned. "Because he's a captain. Of a ship. Captains aren't. . . He's responsible for so many people. . ."

Isabel laughed and tugged one of Victoria's curls. "You are so sweet. I hope you assume the best about me, too." Victoria's cheeks turned pink again. The girl changed color faster than a chameleon. "Lisbon, it's been a lovely morning. We must do it again sometime."

"You're leaving?" Victoria said.

"I have to trail a diamond-thieving murderer to find proof of his crimes."

"While you trail Thomas, I want to follow Dom Tiago. We should follow the buyer and the seller. Tiago said he was out of the business. I don't believe it," Maria added. "Victoria, since Sumpter knows your name, you should get back to the convent and stay there until one of us comes to you," she ordered. "Isabel, meet at Catete at eleven?"

"If I'm not there, you'll find me dragging a handsome American to the prison doorstep."

Maria pointed a finger at her sister, her voice sharp enough to cut diamonds. "Do not attack him. We need proof. They're not going to arrest the son of a diplomat without proof."

"Don't worry. He'll never know I'm there. I'll see you at eleven. Take care of those blisters, Victoria." Isabel heard her friend groan as she raced away, skirt and hair streaming behind her.

She hadn't taken Thomas Sumpter for a hermit.

After his daring rescue, he returned home for lunch and stayed there. Her opinion of Thomas Sumpter fell considerably over the course of the afternoon. A strong breeze cut through the heat and made glorious conditions for sailing or promenading or whatever diplomatic offspring enjoyed, but Sumpter stayed in his rooms. Which meant Isabel spent an afternoon of blue skies in the shadow of empty coffee crates.

"I'm spying on the most boring scoundrel in the history of smuggling," she muttered, sharpening a dagger to pass the time. "He's young, rich, handsome, and spends the entire afternoon holed up in his room napping? I thought a diplomat's son would have engagements all over Rio."

Around early evening a storm crept up over the Atlantic. The wind gusted through the alley. Isabel had no intention of spying in a downpour and decided to start a fire at the back of the house and smoke the man out. Before she could find any kindling, Thomas slipped out the kitchen door and headed down an alley running along the back of the house.

Isabel gave a silent prayer of thanks and fell in step behind him.

He wore the loose pants and shirt of a Carioca from the first time they met. His stride was long and firm, the assured walk of someone who assumed he had an absolute right to be wherever he was, and at a speed that made every errand seem urgent. No one would mistake the American for a local.

The clouds rolled closer, darkening the sky, and the streets bustled with preparation for the storm. Grooms stabled horses, and maids scrambled to collect the laundry. Fruits left to dry in the sun were scooped up. Windows shuttered. Isabel's hair whipped across her face, but her eyes never left the broad brim of Sumpter's hat.

He barreled through the city, head down, clearly following a familiar path, a path Isabel knew well. Her skin tingled as Dona Antonia's came into view, and Thomas ducked inside.

She thought about running for Maria or sending Benedito to find her, but dismissed both ideas immediately. She couldn't send Dito out with a storm brewing, and Sumpter was probably meeting with a smuggler at that moment. There wasn't time to fetch her sister. If she wanted to catch him in the act, she had to act now.

The courtyard was already full, and the crowd in high spirits despite the impending storm. Anything that brought the temperature down from hellish to pleasant was a cause for celebration, and the cachaça flowed freely. Sumpter's hat stood out along the edge of the crowd.

"Isabel Azevedo!" Antonia's sharp voice pulled Isabel's attention from Thomas. "I'm losing business because of your story about a yellow fever outbreak here."

Isabel flinched. "Things look busy tonight, Dona."

"At the bar, but I've only got two rooms rented."

"I can order something. Is there bacalhau tonight?"

"Isabel, I love you, but this inn is my family's livelihood. Whatever you and your sister are planning, put a stop to it right now. I can't have you girls bringing soldiers and Bats and stories about yellow fever here anymore. You need to find somewhere else to take revenge on whatever poor soul has wronged you today."

"We aren't planning anything," Isabel said. "I swear. I'm scouting a new buyer. Maria's not with me tonight."

"So that young woman by the stairs wearing pants, brandishing a whip, and trying to disappear into the shadows isn't your sister?"

Isabel looked where Antonia pointed, frowning, and locked eyes with Maria. The sisters stared at each other in disbelief for a moment, then Isabel tossed an apology to Dona Antonia and darted across the courtyard to Maria.

"Dom Tiago?" she asked.

"He headed upstairs two minutes ago."

A wide brimmed hat disappeared up to the second floor. "There goes Thomas!"

"Isabel, wait!" Maria called.

But Isabel was already halfway up the stairs.

They had him. They had the murderer. They'd catch him meeting with a smuggler, get the proof they needed, then hand him over to the royal guard. Mateus wouldn't be executed. Maria's nightmare wouldn't come true. Her family wouldn't suffer anymore because of her temper, and they could go back to their lives in Rio.

Isabel reached the hall in time to hear the last door on the left click shut. She moved lightly down hall, drawing a dagger in each hand. The familiar feel of her mother's dagger gave a surge of confidence. She banged the bone handle against the door.

"Drinks," she called in a cheerful voice.

Silence descended inside the room. Maria stepped into the hall behind her. She spun her knives and dropped into a crouch, tensing for the initial strike.

The door cracked open.

She kicked it wide and sent Dom Tiago flying backwards. Blood streamed from his nose. Sumpter leapt up from a small table. He reached for a pistol at his hip but hesitated when he recognized her. His mistake. She threw a knife at his head. He dropped below the table, and the knife buried into the wall.

"You bitch," Dom Tiago bellowed. He spat blood and drew his gun.

Maria looped her whip around Tiago's neck and jerked his head into the iron bedpost. He crumpled to the fl oor, a mess of blood and oily hair.

"Stop," Thomas cried. He peeked above the table. "I don't want to—"

Isabel threw another dagger. He ducked and the blade lodged into the table, missing the American's hand by a second.

"Isabel, we need him alive!"

She didn't answer. There was no chance of killing Sumpter. She wasn't aiming for a vital organ, only to inflict pain, so he could have some idea of how she'd felt imagining her friend, a brother, locked and beaten in a prison cell for days, unable to help him. All the fury and hopelessness she'd kept locked away since Mateus was taken broke free, and Isabel let it consume her.

She drew two fresh blades, searching the gaps between chair and table legs for a glimpse of flesh to bury one in.

"Please, I want to explain myself."

"I don't care what you want," Isabel growled. "I want you in jail. I want you to pay for your crimes. Toss your pistol on the bed, and you sleep tonight with all your fingers still attached." It was a lie. He'd be lucky if he left with seven.

"What crimes—"

A third dagger landed in the floor at the tip of his boot. "I'll also let you keep that lovely shirt clean. Your supplier didn't get off so easy."

"Isabel," Maria murmured.

"He's not my buyer! What are you talking about? I saved your lives today!" Thomas's voice rose in indignation.

Isabel snorted a laugh. Did he really believe that? Did he consider them so helpless? "From the soldiers getting berated by an old lady? You gave us a ride. Do you expect us to fawn over you and forgive all your crimes over a ride?"

"Isabel," Maria repeated.

"I thought you'd support what I'm trying to do."

"Our friend is going to be executed because of you!" The man's arrogance fueled her rage. With a shriek she leapt on a chair then the table. She stared down at Sumpter who gaped up at her. He fumbled with his pistol as she snapped her arm back.

Crack!

Maria's whip shattered the bedside lamp.

"Everyone stop!" Maria bellowed.

Her sister's command froze the room. In the silence, Isabel realized the storm had arrived. Rain poured down and splattered the floor through the gaps in the trellis. Between the tension and humidity, Isabel could barely breathe, but she didn't lower her arm. Sumpter gripped his pistol.

"All right, I'm going to ask some questions and you're going to answer them." Maria held her whip ready, but her voice was calm. "Isabel, if he twitches the hand holding a pistol, put a knife through his chest. Senhor Sumpter, why do you think we'd support you?"

"I didn't think you were monarchists. I thought you'd support the people."

Isabel's certainty cracked. She glanced at Maria, who frowned back.

"How does murdering diamond smugglers support the people?" Maria asked.

Judging by his blank stare, Thomas had to be an excellent actor, or they'd truly blindsided him. "I haven't murdered anyone. I don't know what you heard, but I'm not a killer, and I don't smuggle diamonds."

"If you're innocent, why are you avoiding the royal guard and sneaking around Rio?" Isabel demanded.

"I never said I was innocent. I said I wasn't a murderer or diamond smuggler."

"Then what the hell are you guilty of?" Isabel shouted, her patience exhausted.

"Printing."

"Printing?" Maria repeated. She dropped the whip and looked slightly dizzy. Despite the confusion overtaking her anger, Isabel refused to lower her blades.

Thomas slowly raised his hands above his head, letting the pistol hang lose in his grip. "May I retrieve my hat without having my guts spilled over the floor?"

Isabel grinned. "Let's find out."

Keeping his eyes on Isabel, he stood slowly and placed his pistol on the table. He reached for the wide-brimmed hat which had an unusual inner lining. With a jerk, Thomas tore away the lining. Pamphlets spilled across the table and Isabel's feet. She stared down in horror at the proof of his innocence. "I'm trying to smuggle a printing press into Rio to make pro-democracy pamphlets. That's why I wanted to work with you," he insisted. "I'm not a murderer or a diamond smuggler. I'm a republican."

Maria sifted through the papers. "Isabel," she whispered.

"No," Isabel snapped. She jumped to the floor, scattering the papers everywhere. "It's him Maria. We have the murderer. Mateus is coming home tonight."

Her sister slowly met her gaze, and Isabel felt Maria's desperation like a blade between her ribs. Maria shook her head. "It's not him."

"But it has to be. The papers are a cover. He's the murderer." She jabbed a blade in his direction, and Thomas flinched back.

"It's not him, Isabel."

"All afternoon," Isabel murmured. "We've been chasing a politician?"

"Republican," Thomas interjected.

"But how many days. . ." Isabel trailed off.

She'd lost count of the days since Victoria had first shown up at their house. They blurred into one another.

"Six days," Maria said. "We've used up six days."

"He only has two days left."

"I know."

"It's not enough time," Isabel whispered. She felt numb. She never doubted they'd find the murderer.

The idea that Mateus might actually die never entered her mind. They always caught their prey, but two days might not be enough. What if they were wrong again? There had to be another way to free Mateus.

"Him!' Isabel pointed her blade at Thomas. "We trade him to the Bats for Mateus."

"Trade me?" Thomas looked offended.

Isabel ignored him. "He's working against the monarchy. I'm sure the Prince Regent would rather have an American preaching rebellion than a muleteer from Rio."

"Mateus was charged with murder. They're not going to trade him for a man printing paper that'll just stock the outhouses," Maria argued.

Isabel's hands shook. They couldn't lose this chance. They were out of clues and trails and time. "Nobody liked Dom Antonio. I bet even the Prince Regent is glad to be rid of him, and João definitely cares more about his throne than justice for a dead man. We take Thomas in," she said.

"You owe me," Thomas protested, all decorum gone.

"We owe you nothing," Isabel growled. "A ride in your cart is nothing compared to our *family*."

Footsteps pounded down the hall and stopped the conversation. Everyone raised their weapon. Benedito burst into the room.

"Hi, Maria. Hi, Isabel. Mama told me you came up here. I'm supposed to keep you from breaking. . . is that blood?" Benedito gasped staring at Dom Tiago. "Is he dead? My mama's going to be mad if you have a dead man in here."

"He's not dead," Maria said.

"Not for lack of trying," Thomas muttered.

"Hi, Tio Thomas. I didn't see you there," Benedito said.

"Tio Thomas?" Isabel gaped at the term of affection. "You know him?"

"Sure, he's in here a lot. He's teaching me English. That's what they speak in the United States. I tried to tell you the other morning but you interrupted."

"Benedito is a bright young man. You wouldn't take a boy's teacher away from him would you?" Thomas pleaded.

"We're not taking anyone away. We're going home." Maria's face was calm, but Isabel heard the uncertainty in her voice. Her sister wasn't sure what to do next.

"Why do you want to take Tio Thomas away?" Benedito asked.

"Your friends seem to think I am a murderer." Thomas gathered papers from under the table.

Benedito burst out laughing. "Tio Thomas couldn't kill a man. He won't even kill a rat under his chair. I had to do it."

"But you pulled pistols on the princess," Isabel said.

"I was bluffing I'm afraid. I excel at intrigue," Thomas said. "Intrigue is quite different from violence. We Quakers do not believe in violence."

Isabel blinked. Gibberish. Every word. "We need Victoria here to translate rich-person talk."

"I'm wasting time here. This whole day was wasted." Maria turned on her heel and left the room. Isabel rushed after, surprised her sister would leave Dom Tiago sprawled on the floor.

"Are you going to simply leave an unconscious man lying here?" Thomas called, voicing her own doubts.

"He'll live. And he's not going to tell anyone where he was if you're telling the truth. He'll slink home and

make up a story. Dom Tiago is the least of my problems," Maria muttered darkly.

Isabel agreed about Tiago, but it was still unusual
for her sister to leave without paying for the broken door,
lamp, and various other damage. They pushed through
the crowded courtyard and out into the street.

The rain had stopped, leaving the air thick and
heavy. Water dripped from the palms, rippling in pud-
dles below. The only light came from the candles set out
on window sills, and Isabel stepped carefully through
the dark, unsure where they were headed. A boot
squished in the mud behind them.

"Go home, Tomasinho," Isabel growled without
turning around.

"I'm terribly sorry to frighten you," he said.

"You didn't," she said.

He hurried to catch up with the sisters. "And I don't
wish to appear forward, particularly given our unusual
introductions and the events of this evening, but I see
that you ladies are in distress."

"You're observant, senhor," Maria said from several
paces ahead.

"I'd like to offer my assistance. I believe I'm responsible for adding to your distress by not being entirely
honest with you, and I want to help you."

"We don't need your help," Isabel snapped.

"But I'd like to help."

She rounded on him. "What I'd like is for my friend
to be home instead of in a cell. I want him surrounded
by his friends instead of bloodsucking Bats. I want to
sleep well knowing everyone I care about is safe. But
none of that's going to happen tonight because you're
not a murderer, and no one cares that an innocent man

is in jail. Now me and my sister are going home to make a new plan to find Dom Antonio's killer."

"What if you can't find him in time?"

"Of course we'll find him. My sister always finds a way." Isabel waited for Maria to chime in, explain a new plan or at least offer a reassurance, but her sister said nothing. She walked ahead, shoulders rigid, and didn't acknowledge Isabel's vote of confidence. More so than any words, her sister's silence drove home the hopelessness of their situation. The anniversary celebrations ended tomorrow, and they had no idea who the killer was.

Chapter Twenty

Victoria

The Queen woke from her nap convinced Satan had taken rooms across the hall, and Victoria didn't have the heart to say otherwise. She'd spent the morning interviewing diamond smugglers and evading capture by British marines. Maybe the devil had moved in while she was out. Life had infinitely more possibilities than she'd been led to believe. Her morning was proof of that. She wouldn't judge Her Majesty's reality, only convince her they didn't need to flee out the window.

The smell of supper—chicken roasted with oranges—restored peace to Her Majesty, and she allowed Victoria to serve her a slender piece of breast with a spoonful of black beans and boiled greens on the side.

"Are you trying to starve me, girl?" The queen barked. "I can't fight the devil on an empty stomach."

Victoria hid her surprise and added a piece of fish.

"Come on, girl. I need my strength for the battle to come."

She didn't ask who Her Majesty planned on fighting and simply piled the plate with more chicken, fish, and mussels then covered the beans with dried cassava flour.

Her Majesty finished the meal with glistening slices of mango and guava.

Victoria's stomach growled at the sight of the rose-colored guava. She hadn't eaten since breakfast, but her own supper was a low priority. Her Majesty yawned through dessert and had to be supported during a very undignified stagger to the bedroom. Fortunately for her servants, the seventy-five-year-old monarch was little more than bones and skirts. Victoria didn't need tonic or Psalms to coax the queen to sleep. The day's hysterics had proved exhausting enough, and Her Majesty was snoring before the summer sun set.

With the queen tucked in, Victoria collapsed at the writing desk. She dropped her head in her hands and for the first time noticed the state of her hem. Wrestling snakes in a swamp would probably have the same effect on her clothes as a morning with Maria and Isabel. She peeled off her shoe. The small toe on her left foot peeked out from a hole in her stocking and sported an enormous blister. She wrapped the toe in cotton. New stockings. New dress. A pair of boots. Time with the sisters was wearing out her savings as well as her feet.

No one had commented on her limp or her hem. Nobody asked where she'd been. For the first year after entering the queen's service, Victoria resented her obscurity. She'd gone from being the respected daughter of the queen's even more respected surgeon to a nameless servant. Eventually, she realized it had been her father who was impressive. The respect she'd felt entitled to had trickled down from that given to her father. She'd never done anything worthwhile.

Only after meeting Maria and Isabel did she realize her nameless position could be an asset. The flurry of anniversary events and their preparations over the past week hid her extended absences. After the disastrous hand-kissing ceremony, the queen hadn't been summoned to any official function, save the anniversary ball. While other members of the royal family were out christening ships, Queen Maria and her retinue were left to themselves in the convent.

Her stomach protested again, and Victoria pushed up from her seat. She started to put her slipper back on but hesitated at the sight of her bandaged toe. Why should she keep her shoes on with no one around? Isabel wouldn't. In fact, Isabel would probably kick both boots off, prop her feet on the table, and put the entire plate of chicken in her lap. With a defiant grin, she yanked her other slipper off and wiggled her toes in the plush carpet.

A small cough made Victoria turn. A mortified blush swept over her face. "Ana Maria, what do you need?"

The morning maid wrung her hands. "Victoria, I'm sorry, but. . ."

"What's wrong?" Victoria asked.

"While you were out this morning a message came," the girl whispered. "From Her Highness."

Victoria's stomach flipped. "What did she want?"

"She wants to see you in her chambers. The messenger asked for the queen's tonic girl. You're supposed to go as soon as Her Majesty has settled for the evening."

Her heart pounded for the hundredth time that day. Her ribcage had to be bruised on the inside by this point. She calmly set her plate down and smoothed her dress. "Thank you. I'll go now, if you can watch over Her Majesty."

The girl answered with a curtsy and regretful look.

Victoria forgot about dinner. She hurried to her room and changed into a fresh dress. She tried to imagine why Carlota Joaquina would summon her. Any official request regarding the queen or royal family would be handled in the parlor. If it had something to do with the prisoner escape during the ball, surely Prince João would be present or the superintendent of police, and neither of them would meet with her in Carlota Joaquina's chambers.

Maybe Her Highness had personal suspicions she didn't want to share with the police. A shudder ran through her. The princess sought power the way other people sought air to breathe, and she'd been looking for power over the queen for years. Blackmail was entirely within her nature. The queen was entirely dependent on her servants, and if Carlota Joaquina could get one of them under her thumb, it would be devastating for Her Majesty.

By the time she reached Carlota Joaquina's quarters, Victoria's stomach threatened to toss out what little was in there. She sank to the ground just outside her door and put her head between her knees. The door opened, and almost swung into Victoria crouched against the wall. A man stepped out. From behind the door, she could only see his shadow across the hall.

"Your Highness, I promise when I see you again I'll have an even greater treasure to present you." The man's shadow gave a low bow. He closed the door, and the first thing Victoria saw were the tails of his long, black coat. She looked up into the black eyes of Major Vidigal.

"What are you doing down there?" he demanded in a near whisper.

"I serve Her Majesty, and Her Highness summoned me," Victoria stammered.

He glared down his nose. "I would never deign to meet my sovereign in such a state. Pick yourself up girl. Stop sniveling. Show Her Highness the respect she deserves."

He sniffed in disdain then slunk down the hall, a shadow in search of a corner.

Victoria wondered how long to wait before knocking in order to pretend she hadn't witnessed the parting. She counted to thirty.

A lady ushered her into a small piece of Spain. The Melendez and Velaquez paintings on the wall, the mantillas of the ladies in waiting, even the guitarist quietly strumming in the corner. All Spanish. Globes and books covered the tables, and sheets of music spilled off a stand and lay scattered in a corner. The colors and music were a shock coming from the queen's chambers which had been pious and spartan even before her sanity slipped beyond recovery. Victoria hadn't realized that a privilege of being royal was the ability to take your home with you to any part of the world.

All she had left of Portugal was her accent, and the shoes she'd worn when they evacuated Lisbon. The clothes she wore reeked of sweat and sick after months at sea and were burned within days of arriving in Rio. Her constant vigilance over the queen kept the nostalgia at bay during the day and left her too exhausted at night to dream. Most nights. When she did dream, she didn't return to the streets of Lisbon but to her father's study. She woke longing to feel at home.

The lady announced her, and Victoria dropped a low curtsey. Carlota Joaquina said nothing. Through her lashes, she watched the princess relax into her chair and peel an orange with a dagger from her boot. Her Highness hummed along to the guitar. Victoria held the curtsy. The peel spiraled to the floor in a single strand, and the princess cut a slice.

"I wanted to inquire after Her Majesty's health. I hope the excitement of the ball last night was not too much for her."

Victoria was grateful to be staring at the floor, so Carlota Joaquina didn't see the flash of surprise at the princess's consideration for the queen. "She's well, Your Highness. There were a few moments of hysterics today, but I believe they were brought on by the heat, not the lovely ball you and His Highness threw. Thankfully, Her Majesty calmed down and ate well. She was able to sleep without tonics, and her body seems in good health." Victoria dropped another curtsy. "It is very considerate and kind of Your Highness to be concerned."

"Why would I not be concerned? Her Majesty is a second mother to me." Carlota Joaquina gestured for Victoria to rise. She held the orange to her nose and inhaled. "The smell of oranges still reminds me of home. I came to the Portuguese court as a child. I was ten when I married the Prince Regent. He was eighteen. Even then I was the stronger one. Have you heard the story of when I bit João on the ear and bashed him over the head with a candlestick? I'd known him two months."

Victoria knew the story of the candlestick. It was legendary among the servants, but in all her years at the palace, she'd never heard Carlota Joaquina acknowledge the truth behind it. The princess was in a nostalgic mood, and Victoria had no desire to be her confessor. At any moment, Carlota Joaquina would wake from this blissful delirium and lash out at whoever happened to have overheard her moment of weakness. Victoria did not care to be the latest victim of Her Highness's candlestick.

"At the time I thought João was merely immature." Carlota Joaquina frowned at her orange. "Now I know he's a fool and a coward."

Victoria flinched. The audience would not end well for her.

"I was very unhappy my first years in Lisbon," the princess continued. "I gave up all my music and dance and libraries to sit in the gloom of a crumbling palace, where everyone prayed morning, noon, and night. And for what? João wasn't the heir when we married. When I said my vows, I accepted my fate to remain a princess for life. Princess. A worthless title without the power to name a bridge. Then the crowned prince died of small pox, and now I'm in line to be queen."

She hated the way Carlota Joaquina smiled at the mention of Prince José's death. The queen still called out for her eldest son when seized by a fit, her grief undiminished by time. Victoria couldn't stomach any more of the princess's reminiscing and risked a glance around the room for help to escape. All the servants had vanished. Only the Spanish guitarist remained, and he was lost in his music.

"I would have preferred to be queen of my own country, but since I was never supposed to be queen of anything, I'll take Portugal. It was once a great nation." Carlota Joaquina flipped the pages of a book of nautical charts on the side table next to her. "Centuries ago the Portuguese ruled the sea. They conquered the globe with their ships and sextants. That kind of greatness never dies out completely. It may go dormant, but it can be resurrected. I intend to resurrect Portugal's greatness when I am queen." Carlota Joaquina looked at her, and Victoria knew a response was expected.

"The people of Portugal will be in your debt. You'll be remembered as one of our greatest queens."

Victoria decided she much preferred the queen's screaming to Carlota Joaquina's quiet reflections. She shivered as the princess sliced off sections of orange without glancing at the knife.

"Yes, I will be great. It's in my blood." Her Highness sucked a piece of orange off the blade. She chewed slowly. "It's pathetic how many people think they can become great from nothing. Pathetic but useful. Their enthusiasm is highly entertaining. I've learned that if greatness pays their ambition the slightest bit of attention, the great can reap the reward tenfold."

Carlota Joaquina set the knife down and pulled a pale brown rock from her dress. She rolled the dull surface between her fingers. "This was a gift from a pointlessly ambitious man. He will never be of consequence, though he desperately wants to be."

"It's natural Your Highness has many admirers. You are heir to the throne of Portugal. You deserve nothing less than all Brazil has to offer." The words were hollow, bitter on her tongue.

Carlota Joaquina snorted. "Brazil! The only thing worthwhile here lies buried deep in the earth and even that is drying up." She slipped the rock back into her dress and tossed the rest of the orange out the window. She marched to a chest of drawers, returning with a delicate glass bottle painted with the green and yellow dragons of the Braganza family.

"A gift for Her Majesty." Carlota Joaquina held the bottle out to Victoria. "I know the queen and I have had our differences, but the more time I spend in this hellish country full of mongrels, the more I've come to respect and value true greatness. Her Majesty was the first queen to rule Portugal in her own right. I have not given her the deference that feat deserves."

Carlota Joaquina pushed the bottle into Victoria's hands. "It's a tonic for aches in the bones. I noticed Her Majesty had some difficulty walking when we visited Tijuca forest the other day. I asked my physician to prepare something. It should be administered three times a day. A gift from one queen to another."

Victoria smothered the urge to point out Carlota Joaquina was not a queen yet. Instead, she clasped the bottle to her chest and dropped another curtsy. "I will pass along your concern to Her Majesty. I'm sure she will be grateful. Your Highness is very generous."

Carlota Joaquina waved her hand and turned toward the window. Victoria didn't hesitate. She dropped a final curtsy and fled from the princess's disconcerting kindness.

An empty table waited for her in the queen's chamber, a bowl of fruit all that remained of dinner. Tears threatened to spill over. After all she'd been through—chased all over Rio, hiding in a crazy American's wagon, keeping the queen alive, and a surprise summons from the princess—she didn't require anything, except a warm meal.

The maid left in charge snored from a highbacked chair in the corner. Victoria glared at her and plucked a banana from the bowl. The girl could have asked the staff to clear dinner later or leave a plate, but apparently she couldn't stay awake long enough to spare Victoria a thought.

Or maybe the girl didn't think she was coming back. Carlota Joaquina fired staff almost daily. Slavery was illegal in Portugal but not in Brazil. Over the course of the year, Victoria noticed more and more staff brought from Portugal replaced by slaves. She reminded herself that she still had a job that paid a wage, which was more than many people in Rio could claim. The job was thankless and exhausting, but she ate well (most days) and had rooms in the safest place in the city.

She opened the shutters and leaned against the window sill, listening to the rain and nibbling on the banana. The downpour cooled the air. Victoria closed her eyes and relished the spray of rain on her skin. Her temper cooled, and she let her mind wander.

She had considered the palace the safest place in Rio, but befriending Maria and Isabel had opened her eyes and taught her even the ballroom was crawling with snakes, summoned there by engraved invitation. Victoria remembered Isabel's laugh when she said ship captains weren't murderers. Worse than the laugh, Maria looked at her with pity. The muleteer felt sorry for the foolish, ignorant girl from Lisbon unable to take care of herself. Shame burned her cheeks. She'd been raised by a man of science, but the sisters seemed to know more truths about the world than she did.

Why did she assume someone was honest and law-abiding because he wore fancy clothes or had an impressive title? *Major* Miguel Vidigal was hardly honest or law-abiding. What would the Prince Regent say if he knew the commander of the royal guard was meeting in the princess's private chambers and leaving her gifts? Victoria doubted any staff would inform on Carlota Joaquina. They feared her far more than Prince João.

Vidigal was undoubtedly the pointlessly ambitious man who gave Carlota Joaquina the rock. Surely he knew her disdain for Brazil. After a year in Rio, the princess still refused to let anything made from cassava touch her plate. She scorned everything native to Brazil, which included the major. Diamonds were the only exception.

A memory flashed in Victoria's mind, and she nearly choked on a bite of banana. Her hands trembled as her mind sifted through all the facts and observations over the past week. They pointed to a single, heart-stopping conclusion.

"Ana Maria," Victoria snapped. The girl stirred and blinked in confusion. "I have to go. Please attend Her Majesty should she wake."

The rain had stopped, and street lamps lit the square. She realized this was her first time out alone after dark since that fateful walk on the beach when she met Maria and Isabel.

They saved her from a terrible mistake, and now she had to do the same for them. She didn't notice the pain of a blistered foot. Victoria had one thought in mind as she ran to Maria and Isabel's house. The memory of Carlota Joaquina holding a pale brown rock given to her by a pointlessly ambitious man. A rock that looked exactly like the ones that tumbled across the floor her first day at Maria and Isabel's.

Her friends had the wrong man. The American didn't kill Dom Antonio. The truth was much worse.

Chapter Twenty-One

Isabel

Isabel pleaded with Maria for the hundredth time. "We have to storm the prison tonight. We're out of time. *Santa Brigida*, they're executing him in two days."

And again Maria shook her again. "No. We have two days. We're going to use them."

"To do what? We have no other suspects. Half the city is involved in the black market. We can't trail them all in two days." Isabel wanted to tear her hair out. Her body twitched, and she felt on the verge of exploding.

"You were willing to keep following the trail this morning," Maria said.

"When I trusted it, but now we know this trail can lead us to fifty innocent men before we find the murderer. We have to get Mateus tonight." Why wasn't she listening? Why hesitate now, with no other options open to them?

"Then we'll all be fugitives. Our lives as we knew them will be destroyed."

"At least we'll all be alive. They're going to kill him."

"I know!" Maria shouted.

Isabel froze. The shadows of the alley couldn't hide the fear on her sister's face. She didn't understand why Maria wanted to suffer. They could have Mateus back before sunrise.

"Perhaps I could assist you in your search."

Isabel gritted her teeth at Thomas's voice. After her scolding, he'd gone silent but continued following them. When confronted, he said it was a public street, and he happened to be going the same way they were. She'd almost managed to forget him.

"Would it not be easier to search with more people? Especially given your limited time," he said.

"What are you doing here?" Maria snapped.

"I know you don't want my help."

"I wasn't talking to you." Maria waved Thomas away. "Benedito, I know you're there."

The boy slipped out from the shadow of a doorway, hanging his head.

"Dito, your mother is going to die of fright, and then her ghost is going to kill you and probably us, too," Isabel scolded.

"You're trying to save Mateus. He's my friend, too, and I want to help," he insisted. "The more people helping the better. Thomas makes three, and I make four."

"Nossa Senhora." Maria ran a hand down her face. "All right, you want to help us?" She pointed at Thomas. "Take Dito back home. My sister and I will be fine from here."

Maria turned and barreled down the alley. The sisters burst onto the main road. Thomas stayed right on their heels. Dito followed behind him. Isabel clenched her jaw to keep from screaming. No one was listening to her. Not Maria. Not Thomas. Not Dito. She loved the boy, but this was not the night to try being a man.

"Dito," she snapped. "Do what Maria said. Go home. You, too, Tomasinho."

"Isabel! Maria!"

"Lisbon?" Isabel turned in disbelief. The Portuguese girl hurtled toward them. The panic on her face made Isabel's stomach clench.

Victoria doubled over, gasping for breath. "I found you."

Isabel supported her friend, glancing at Maria. Her sister unfurled her whip and tensed for an attack, scanning the alleys and shadows. "What are you doing here?" she asked.

"How many times tonight are we going to have to ask that?" Maria muttered.

Thomas stepped up, and Victoria's eyes grew wide. She jerked Isabel away from him.

Isabel laid a hand on her friend's arm. "It's all right. He's not—"

"It's not him," Victoria said between gasps. "He's not the murderer."

"How do *you* know that?"

"Don't answer," Maria ordered. "We have to get off the street. You two go back to the inn."

Thomas frowned. "But I can—"

"Go home!" Maria's voice cracked like her whip.

Benedito tugged on the man's sleeve. "Tio Thomas, we should go."

"Fine. I'll take Benedito home. But if you need me, you can find me at my home. I suspect you already know where it is." He tipped his hat then led Benedito away.

As soon as they disappeared, Victoria opened her mouth, but Maria held up a hand. She headed across the street to an alley barely visible behind a cart filled with port barrels. "Isabel?"

"We're alone."

Victoria took a deep breath. "Vidigal killed them."

The words landed on Isabel like a bucket of frigid sea water. A story tumbled out of Victoria. A story about a lonely princess, an ambitious man with more power than conscience, and diamonds. "And the stone looked exactly like the ones I saw at your home. It was a raw diamond. And a royal guardsman could never afford to buy a diamond. Not even the commander. It's him. Vidigal is the murderer."

Certainty hit Isabel between the eyes. She should have guessed Vidigal from the beginning. The man tortured people for whistling. He probably considered getting murdered a merciful fate for a man dealing on the black market, and he wouldn't give a second thought to consequences because he was the one who delivered them. The only people in the city who could arrest the commander of the royal guard were the superintendent or the Prince Regent.

Even as the hopelessness of the situation dawned on her, a lightness filled her as another realization came. "So the night Mateus was taken, Vidigal wasn't there because he was following us."

"He was already there because he killed Dom Antonio," Maria finished.

"So it's not my fault," Isabel whispered. "The Bats weren't following us because I lost my temper. I didn't get Mateus arrested."

Isabel's voice trembled. She fought for control. They didn't have a second to spare on tears, but the wave of relief that tore through her couldn't be stopped.

"I thought everything was my fault. Because I didn't listen to you."

Maria gathered her into an embrace. "I never blamed you. Not for a second. None of this is your fault."

Maria hugged like their father, leaving no space between them and holding tight. Isabel pressed her face into her sister's shoulder and squeezed back. Guilt flooded out of her. The relief left her dizzy, but Maria held her up.

A sniff caught her attention. Victoria stood off to the side, dabbing her eyes. Isabel yanked her into the hug. "You're the reason we know who the murderer is."

After a few deep breaths, Isabel stepped back. "Right, Vidigal."

Victoria gave her an apologetic look. "I'm sorry I couldn't give you another name."

"Don't be sorry," Isabel said. "I've wanted to kill that man for a while."

"Vidigal is not the most powerful man in Rio," Maria declared. "We can go over his head to the super-intendent or the Prince Regent himself. It's possible to bring him down, but we need to move carefully. We need proof."

"I think he lives at the north end of the city," Victoria offered. "After I saw them meeting secretly, I asked Carlota Joaquina's servants about him. She sends him crates of oranges. I have the address. We could go there tomorrow."

"We should go now," Maria countered. "Vidigal and the Bats usually patrol at night."

"What are we waiting for?" The hour didn't matter. Sleep was a waste of time. She had a chance to take down Vidigal. Isabel wanted to dance down the street and invite the entire city to join her. Freed from guilt, her steps became effortless. She said as she flipped the daggers in the air, "It's a good thing I wore six knives today. So where are we going?"

"North. At the beginning of Rua do Valongo."

"Valongo!" Her breath caught, and dread gripped her heart. "You want us to go to Valongo?"

"Yes," Victoria said. "That's where a groom delivered the oranges. Why? What's wrong?"

"You've never been there have you?" Isabel said softly.

"Of course she hasn't," Maria answered.

Her sister stood rigid and unmoving. Isabel put a hand on her shoulder. She'd fight the devil to protect her sister, but daggers couldn't spare her the horrors of Valongo. "We don't have to do this. *You* don't have to do this. I'll go."

"Mateus would do it for me. He'd go through hell for me."

"Well that's exactly where we're going, but you don't…" She let the thought die as Maria walked down the alley and turned north without glancing back. "To hell it is then."

"What's at Valongo? Why don't you want Maria to go?" Victoria whispered.

She sighed. "Valongo is the slave port."

"I didn't know…I'm sorry. Is Maria upset with me?" Victoria stammered.

Isabel bit back her reply. Victoria's lace-trimmed sleeves and satin hair ribbon sparked a flash of indignation, but the maid didn't deserve her anger. Probably no one in Victoria's circle ever mentioned Valongo. The rich Portuguese acted as though the port didn't exist. That's what she hated. A world that not only caused so much pain but also allowed those who benefited from it to live in ignorance. The wealthy of Rio killed with torture and neglect every day then wrung their hands about the smell of corpses. When Isabel cleaned her blade she knew whose blood was on it. She owned her actions.

"Come on. Maria's about to leave us behind."

She hurried after her sister with Victoria on her heels. Isabel could still remember the smell of her first and only visit to Valongo two years ago. One of their diamond buyers insisted on meeting them at the port. It was one of their first deals after Maria inherited the train. With both parents gone, her sister lay awake every night worrying about money and didn't think they could afford to refuse.

For the first time in her life, Isabel wanted to run away. Maria's unwavering presence at her side kept her standing. They finished the deal, Isabel breathing through her mouth, and walked home in silence. Maria gripped her whip so hard her arm trembled. Finally she said, "We are never working with that man again."

"We can't stop working with slave owners," Isabel argued. "We'll starve."

Maria shook her head. "It's not about Dom José's slaves. He insisted on making us meet him there. He was sending a message to me and to Mateus. And I won't listen to it again." They never spoke of it after that.

It was impossible to run a mule train and avoid the labor of slaves. Slaves dug the diamonds and gold out of the ground. They built the roads the teams traveled. They unloaded the cargo at custom houses then reloaded it onto ships. They tended the mules and horses at the stable in the city. It seemed as though half the people in Rio were enslaved.

Maria always slipped something to the boys working at the stables or whoever unloaded their cargo at the docks. Two of the men on their team had escaped from sugarcane plantations. When making sweets for sale, Isabel always hired a moonlighter, a slave who'd finished her master's work and was allowed to earn money outside the home. She paid more than the girl's mistress expected, so the moonlighter could add to her savings and hopefully buy her freedom more quickly. It wasn't much. She knew the gesture was as much for herself as the girls she hired, but those small gestures were how Isabel got through each day living free in a city where so many were not.

But Valongo was different. It wasn't like passing people in the streets with no shoes and sacks of coffee on their heads. Not even the whipping Vidigal gave the man from Angola compared. Valongo was something you experienced when there was no other choice, like death.

And her sister marched straight to it.

They moved in silence. Households prepared to turn in and, through the open windows, families gathered around the matriarchs for the nightly Bible reading. Isabel caught snippets of Job and The Great Flood. Another window revealed children seated on the floor at their mother's feet as she brushed and searched their hair for lice before bed. On every street, people slept in hammocks by open windows dreaming of a cool breeze, but the air that slipped through Isabel's hair was hot as a jaguar's breath. Rio's summer didn't take nights off.

Maria signaled to stop. They pressed into the shadows along the building as three men trudged past towards the sea. Each man carried a reeking barrel balanced on his back. Isabel could smell them from across the street. The men's bare backs were streaked with white stripes to the waist.

"Who are they?" Victoria whispered.

"The tigers," Maria answered.

"Because of the stripes?" Victoria watched the men until they disappeared. "Why do they paint stripes on their backs?"

"It's not paint. That's what piss does to black skin," Isabel said. "Can't you smell it? They're collecting waste to dump in the sea. It leaks out of the barrels and drips down their back. Carry piss on your back every night for years and you end up permanently marked."

"It's later than I thought if the tigers are already headed to the bay," Maria warned. "We need to hurry."

The stench was Valongo's warning shot. It hit visitors still blocks away and warned those with weak stomachs to turn back. Victoria gagged. Isabel undid the shawl from her waist and passed it to her.

"Tie it over your face. You'll be hot as hell, but it might dull the smell enough to keep you from getting sick." She pursed her lips. "It gets worse."

Another block and the narrow street opened up to a view of Guanabara Bay and Valongo Port. The night masked the full extent of Valongo's horror. No ships unloaded the first of thousands of slaves to arrive that day. No silk and lace-clad shoppers browsed through the warehouses scrutinizing naked men, women, and children. But Isabel remembered. She knew what the darkness hid. It was seared into her memory, and even the dead of night couldn't hide everything. The mountain of bodies was plainly visible, silhouetted against the glistening bay.

Starvation. Disease. Beating. Shot as an example. The causes of death varied. Some people died en route. Some lived just long enough to die in Rio. They burned the bodies every night and every day ships arrived and added their dead to those who'd died in the warehouses overnight. The pile of bodies never got any smaller.

Isabel covered her nose against the smell of charred flesh drifting on the breeze. She tasted bile.

"They couldn't at least bury them?" Victoria held her stomach. She looked on the verge of being ill.

"They're worried about disease. The dead are burned as fast as they're piled up," Isabel explained. Her own throat closed up as she inhaled. She spat viciously, sure she'd felt ash hit her tongue.

"They'd be burned no matter what. Black people aren't allowed church burials." Maria's voice was hard as diamond. It broke Isabel's heart.

"You can't be buried?" Victoria whispered.

"Some are, if their skin is light enough, and they make a generous enough donation to the church. A lot of people work their whole lives to get buried," Maria answered.

In the silence that followed, muffled sobs escaped from a nearby warehouse. Isabel's chest squeezed as she looked at the similar warehouses lining the street and stretching into the dark.

Victoria's voice barely carried over the waves. "I'm so sorry. I didn't know...I'm so, so sorry, Maria."

"Don't apologize to me. My parents were born free. I'm not the one who needs your prayers." Maria turned to Victoria and pointed toward the office buildings running along Rua Valongo behind the warehouses. "What I need is help saving my friend from execution. Can you help me, Victoria? There is one life we can save."

She nodded, and in a shaky voice said, "The third door on the left is where the servant delivered the oranges. He said Vidigal himself accepted them."

"If you wanted to be left the hell alone, this is the place to be," Isabel muttered.

They crept down the side of the building away from any passersby on the main road and crouched below a shuttered window. No light shone through the slats. They heard only silence from inside.

"I'm going first," Maria whispered. "Wait until I call for you. If I don't whistle, know not to come in after me," she said this staring at Isabel. "If we're all arrested, there's no one left to get any of us out. This time, you have to leave me and run."

"Fine. We'll run." The idea of running away while Maria stayed behind was almost physically painful, but this time Isabel agreed one of them needed to escape in order to save everyone.

She slipped a dagger between the shutters and flipped open the latch on the inside. As she sank back down, Maria eased the shutters open and silently vaulted into the room. Isabel held her breath, listening. Finally, a low whistle signaled the all clear, and Isabel and Victoria climbed through the window.

A match flared to life revealing a room of contradictions. A bed in the corner boasted no blankets and only the thinnest of straw mattresses, while an intricately patterned rug hid the dirt floor. A bookshelf held dozens of leather-bound volumes, but the spines were pristine, uncracked. Isabel fingered the threadbare velvet curtains framing the window and left a trail through a thick layer of dust.

"Why hang curtains and never use them?" Isabel wondered.

"Because it's too damn hot to close them," Maria answered.

"So they're for decoration? Like a painting?"

"That's what the books are. I don't think they've ever been opened." Victoria pulled a volume off the shelf. "Maps and nautical charts of Africa."

Isabel snorted. "Who is he trying to impress?"

"Himself," Maria said. She set down a candle on a chair in the center of the room and turned to Victoria. "Other than the diamonds themselves, what would prove Vidigal's the murderer?"

"My father was a physician, not a lawyer," Victoria protested.

"But you know how nobility thinks. What would convince the Prince Regent?" Maria pressed.

"Maybe correspondence between Vidigal and any of the dead smugglers. A ledger or list of names. Although, I doubt he would keep anything written down if he were working in secret."

They scattered about the room. Victoria continued examining the books, squinting at their titles. Maria searched under the bed and the rug. Isabel stood in the center of the room, thinking.

The whipping she'd witnessed in the square came back to mind. She heard Vidigal plead, *"Help me! Don't you want to be better?"* The man believed he was doing the right thing. And if a man believed his actions moral and had the future queen's support, why would he hide?

Isabel sat down at Vidigal's desk. The top left drawer was locked, but a knife and a little force popped it open. She smiled, imagining the look on his face when he found the lock broken. She pulled out a leather-bound book, fl ipped through. A bunch of squiggles and lines. She waved it in the air. "I think I found a journal. Would that help?"

"He left his journal out on the desk?" Victoria sounded incredulous.

"Mostly."

Isabel gave Victoria the chair, and Maria held the candle close as she flipped through the pages looking for recent dates.

Victoria paused, frowning. "He's complaining about Rio here. It's a little. . . odd."

"Is odd courtly speak for evil?" Isabel said.

Victoria continued. "It's from last July, not long after the court arrived. He writes, 'The crime and filth teeming in this city are an insult to decency. We Brazilians are disgracing ourselves on a daily basis. The begging, thieving, whoring, gambling, murdering, and brawling have only increased since the Royal Family's arrival. We don't deserve them. The city must be cleansed to be worthy.'"

"So much for love of country," Maria muttered.

Victoria flipped a few more pages. "Listen to this! 'His Highness the Frog Prince'—"

"No!" Isabel gasped. "He wrote that down?" Victoria nodded, and she clapped her hands. "This is better than stories around a campfire. Keep going."

"'His Highness the Frog Prince has allowed the savages to start a newspaper. Why is he encouraging them?' . . .He's underlined why three times. . . 'The people don't need newspapers. They need a moral compass. More slaves and runaways are flooding the city every day, and he gives them a newspaper to print lies and sedition."

"What's sedition?" Isabel asked.

"A call for rebellion," Victoria answered then pointed to another entry. "The Frog Prince has proven himself once again. I've heard his plans to open a university here and allow the printing of books. As if a population of weak-minded mongrels can be educated. The grovelers at court praise his kindness and generosity.

Don't they know giving handouts teaches a dog to beg? Discipline and purity are the keys to advancement."

Isabel scoffed and placed a hand over her heart in feigned dismay. "Weak-minded mongrels! Maria, I think he's referring to us!"

"He should look in the mirror. That hair didn't come from France," Maria muttered. The furrow between her brow deepened. "What about the murders? Is there anything about why he'd go after the diamond smugglers?" she pressed. Victoria skimmed through the pages, muttering to herself.

Isabel looked around at the worn-out and dust-covered furnishings. "If he has the diamonds, he's not using them to decorate."

"I understand why he'd go after people in the black market. He's clearly disgusted by all criminals, but why kill them? Why not arrest them?" Maria asked.

"And why hoard the diamonds?" Isabel twirled a dagger between her fingers as she thought. "What can a Bat buy with a chest full of black market diamonds?"

"A coup," Victoria whispered.

The dagger froze between her fingers. "A coup?"

Victoria pointed to the middle of a passage that used more ink underlining than writing. "'The Frog Prince is not what Brazil thought he was. When we saluted his portrait, we imagined a strong ruler, not the sniveling, stinking child who fled his enemies in Europe to cower in Brazil. Now he sits in Rio, filthy and selling ancient titles of nobility to any half-breed with money, while the city consumes itself in vice. But I am sworn to protect the city of Rio de Janeiro from any threat, whether it be herself or a frog prince. I will not betray my oath.'" Victoria stopped reading and looked up at Maria and Isabel. "When he left Carlota Joaquina's chamber he said 'When I see you again, I will have an even greater present to give you.' He means a crown. He's planning to overthrow Prince João."

A week ago, Isabel was arguing with her sister about moving to a coffee farm. Two days ago, she crashed a ball on the trail of a murderer. Two hours ago, she nearly killed an American envoy. Now, they'd uncovered Major Vidigal's plot to overthrow the Prince Regent.

Only in Rio could a single night out save a friend, destroy an enemy, and maybe earn the good graces of a future king. Her chest swelled. This was her home. She would never leave Rio de Janeiro.

"By killing the smugglers no one knows he's gathering up diamonds," Victoria muttered, still piecing Vidigal's plan together. "But why does he want the diamonds in the first place?"

"To pay his team. Like I do." Maria paced the room. "He's rounded up men, loyal Bats of course, and now he's got to pay them. What better than diamonds that are already off the books? You don't have to steal from any banks. Smugglers aren't going to report you, and if you have to kill one, there's one less criminal in the city. It's a decent plan."

"It's brilliant," Victoria murmured.

"Please," Isabel snorted. "Snakes are always good at being snakes. They don't deserve a medal for it."

"That settles it." Maria stopped pacing. Her hand found her whip. "We break Mateus out tonight, and run for it."

"Run for it? *You* want to run?" Isabel couldn't believe the words came from her sister.

Victoria leapt to her feet. "You can't! We have to stop him. We have to save Prince João. Vidigal said it would be done by the next time he sees Carlota Joaquina. It's going to happen soon!"

Maria shook her head. "I'm sorry, Victoria. I know you have a history with that family, but I'm not putting *my* family in the middle of a fight between a bunch of nobles who don't give a damn about us."

"But João is the rightful ruler." Victoria charged out from behind the desk with surprising ferocity. Her curls bounced as her gestures grew more emphatic, and the restraint she normally maintained succumbed to indignation. "I know the Prince Regent is completely ridiculous and afraid of thunder and crabs and never takes a bath, but he's not malicious. And if João's gone, Carlota Joaquina will serve as regent, and she is cruel. Or perhaps Vidigal intends to kill her, too. Maybe he has a plan to be acting viceroy. Imagine what he would do if put in charge. You heard what he wrote!"

"You can have the journal and go to the superintendent like we planned, but I'm getting my family out. I won't let them be pawns in some European power struggle," Maria said, then turned to Isabel. "You've wanted to break Mateus out from the beginning. What did you have in mind?"

Isabel had followed Maria's lead since they snuck out the back window as kids to pick mangos from the church's garden. They were a team, but when multiple paths appeared, Maria had the final say. Always. Tonight, with their friend's life and the fate of the monarchy on the line, her sister finally turned to her for a plan. Maria had clearly gone mad.

Fortunately, Isabel had a plan, and it didn't include running away.

"We're not breaking Mateus out. We're going to destroy Vidigal."

Chapter
Twenty-Two

Maria

Isabel's announcement silenced the room. Maria recognized the tone in her sister's voice. It was the tone of voice that set buildings alight.

"Isabel, no," Maria ordered. "You can't murder the commander of the royal guard."

"But I can murder a murderer to save the Prince Regent."

"We save the Prince Regent by presenting the journal and our story to His Highness," Victoria countered.

Isabel barked a laugh. "He's as likely to arrest us as Vidigal. We're smugglers who broke into the office of Major Vidigal. I don't trust anyone in the palace to decide who's guilty. That's why we need to cut the head off the snake ourselves. Vidigal has to die."

"Killing Vidigal doesn't get Mateus out of jail!" Maria snapped in frustration. They'd lost focus. Mateus was the goal.

"Killing him gets rid of the only person who recognizes us and would want to chase across Brazil. He's already tried to shoot you twice. He knows your face!" Isabel's hand flew around, gesturing in every direction.

"Killing Vidigal doesn't stop the coup if he's already paid off his men. What if they still go through with it after Vidigal's dead?" Victoria pleaded.

"Then there's one less fat noble eating all the chicken," Isabel declared.

"If the Prince Regent dies, Carlota Joaquina will rule as regent. Please, listen. Whatever you think about Vidigal, the princess is worse."

Their arguments were useless. She'd thought Isabel would have an idea, but the discovery of the journal made them lose sight of the objective. "None of this matters if we free Mateus, take our diamonds, and get the hell out of Rio."

"You and Mateus will be on the run until Vidigal is dead." Isabel pointed out the window to the city. "And what about all our friends left here in Rio with Vidigal in charge? What will happen to Dito and his friends? That's why you didn't want to break Mateus out. What's changed?"

Maria gripped her sister's shoulder, willing her to understand. "If we try to kill Vidigal and fail, we'll all be executed. Then no one is saved, and we add to the body count. I won't take that risk. I swore to Mateus I would get him his life back. I promised our parents that I would protect you."

"Not from things worth dying for!"

"No one is dying," Maria bellowed.

"It's my choice!"

"I'm not losing anyone else I love! Not you! Not Mateus!" Maria fell silent. Words deserted her as if they'd fulfilled their purpose in her revelation and ceased to exist. Only three stayed behind. "I love him."

"Finally!" Isabel cried. She clapped her hands and embraced her sister. "I've been dying to tell you what a handsome couple you'd make, but I didn't want to scare you. Because you truly believed he was only a brother to you. You even had me fooled for a long time but then you snuck into the queen's chambers in the middle of the night, and I knew only love would make a person that crazy."

"Isabel, please…I…give me a moment." Maria held up a hand to stop her sister's verbal onslaught while she struggled to get her bearings.

A quiet fell on the office, the kind of silence that only happened in Rio during the last moments before dawn when even the bats had gone to sleep. In the stillness, Maria realized the truth. She wasn't protecting Isabel or Mateus or her team. Everything she'd done in the last week was to protect herself.

She loved Mateus. The feeling had been there like a heartbeat, ever present but taken for granted until under threat, and like a heartbeat, Maria couldn't acknowledge it without considering its inevitable end. Whether by death or heartbreak, love stories always ended with goodbye. Her parents taught her that, and she wanted as few goodbyes as possible in her life. That was why she ran away from his confession in the jail. She could fail him, and it was easier to fail a business partner than the man she loved. Easier for her.

But a captain didn't choose a path because it made things easier for her. So, what now? What path did she take, now that she'd accepted the truth? Rescuing Mateus and running would spare her the pain of his death and the guilt of failing, but she wouldn't be able to live with herself if she sacrificed her team and Dito and Tia Antonia, all their friends, to save her own happiness. Vidigal threatened the safety of her home. She needed to eliminate the threat.

The silence shifted from stifling to calming. The anguish that clouded her mind since the moment Mateus got dragged out of Dom Antonio's house disappeared. She made a decision, chose a path, and would face whatever came next.

"Victoria, you're right. Letting Vidigal succeed would leave Rio worse off and more dangerous for our friends. Isabel, you're right. None of us will be safe with Vidigal free. So we're going to stop him."

"Thank you, Maria," Victoria gushed.

"Wait, we're not going to talk about Maria being in love?" Isabel complained. "But I have so many questions. And jokes. Only half of them about your whip."

Maria pulled her sister into a hug. "I swear you can make fun of me later as long as you promise me one thing."

"And what is that?" Isabel narrowed her eyes in suspicion.

"Do not kill Vidigal." She held up a hand to cut off Isabel's protest. They were not animals, no matter what the Portuguese nobles and self-hating guard commanders believed. Vidigal's beatings and arrests could never be seen as necessary. "If we murder Vidigal, we prove him right. The snake will become a martyr. That can't happen. We're going to the palace. We'll present the journal to the Prince Regent and tell him everything we know about all the murders, the diamonds, and Vidigal. If he arrests us instead of or along with Vidigal, that's a risk I'm willing to take."

"Fine. I'm in. But 'let's go get a Bat arrested and justly charged with his crimes' is not a very inspiring rallying cry," Isabel muttered.

Maria laughed, and it felt so wonderful tears pooled in her eyes. "I'm sorry about that. Maybe you'll still get to attend his execution."

"We should take the journal straight to the soldiers guarding the palace. Not the army barracks. The palace guards are the most loyal to the royal family," Victoria said, clutching the journal to her chest.

"Then let's go. The sooner we get Vidigal in chains, the sooner we get Mateus out of them." Maria threw open the front door. Since they planned to confess everything, there wasn't any point hiding their presence in Vidigal's office.

As they ran, kitchen doors swung open along the streets. The clang of pots dropped on stoves for morning coffee rang out through the city even before the church bells. Maids trekked to the river for water, and fishermen pushed out to sea, anxious to haul in what they could before the sun drove them back ashore. Finally, the roosters began stirring.

Isabel, Maria, and Victoria burst onto Largo do Paço as the bells signaled six. Victoria leaned against a lamppost, one hand to her chest.

"One moment, please," she gasped. "I'm sorry. I can't run for extended periods."

"All the running we've done this week, I'm surprised you're not used to it," Isabel teased.

"At least you've got proper boots on this time," Maria said. Maybe they'd taught the little servant girl some good habits after all.

A shout rang out from across the square cutting off Victoria's response. The stable gates at the palace swung open, and four soldiers rode out followed by a gilded carriage. Two more soldiers on horseback followed the carriage along with a man in a long dark coat hunched over his saddle.

"That's Prince João's carriage and Vidigal is leaving with him," Victoria said.

Maria scanned the entourage. She couldn't see inside the carriage. "How do you know it's not some other family member?"

"The man next to the carriage driver is the prince's attendant. He'd never leave the palace in a royal carriage with anyone other than Prince João."

As the entourage swept around a corner, two Bats stepped out of the thickening crowd and followed behind on foot.

"Nossa Senhora," Victoria whispered.

She picked up her skirts to run, but Maria grabbed her arm. "We can't run after them screaming accusations at Vidigal. Remember the bakery? He knows us. He'll have us arrested before we finish a sentence."

"But we can't let them get away! This is it! Why else are the Bats following on foot?" Victoria strained against Maria's grip.

"She's right. Those Bats aren't there to protect the Prince Regent," Isabel said.

Maria's instincts hummed, telling her Victoria was right. They needed help that outranked the Bat commander, but detouring for help meant losing the Prince Regent and Bats in the morning crowds. It was time to see how much the maid from Lisbon had learned.

"New plan. Isabel and I follow Vidigal," Maria announced. "Victoria, you go explain the situation to the highest ranking soldiers you can find. Do NOT talk to any Bats. Portuguese soldiers only. They'll know where the Prince has gone and can send troops. Isabel and I will keep a watch and step in if things go bad."

"Bad meaning Vidigal and his Bats start killing people?" Isabel asked.

"Exactly." Maria let go of Victoria. "I don't know how long we can hold off a group of Bats if things do go badly. You need to hurry."

"I'll tell the officer on duty at the jail and get him to send help. I promise!" Victoria raced across the square kicking up a cloud of dirt behind her.

"Good thing she wore better shoes," Maria observed.

Isabel turned to her and smiled. "I have to be honest with you, sister. Concerning Vidigal, I hope things go badly."

Chapter
Twenty-Three

Victoria

With her skirts hitched high and boots on her feet, Victoria dodged the carts and mules moving goods through the square. She swerved around a woman with a basket of eggs and cut through a line of men waiting to buy a steaming bowl of angu for breakfast. Women with pitchers of water and tin cups. Quitandeiras balancing baskets wider than their skirts. A wagon hauling lumber. She slipped between them with ease and sure feet.

She charged through the prison door convinced she was invincible.

"His Highness is in danger! Major Vidigal is planning a coup. You have to send a regimen to his aid immediately." Victoria held Vidigal's diary high in the air.

In the silence that followed, she assessed the scene before her. One soldier held a half-polished saber and cloth, a stack of unpolished swords on the table in front of him. Another soldier's lips were puckered to blow on a tin cup of steaming coffee. A third wiped drool off his chin acquired during a nap he'd been startled from.

The three stared at her with wide and unblinking eyes. It was the perfect illustration of a group struck dumb.

Victoria's confidence shriveled to an empty husk. She lowered the diary and clutched it to her chest.

The coffee drinker, who had distractingly uneven sideburns, recovered first. "What in the name of Saint Mary is this?"

Victoria bobbed a curtsey. "Sir, my name is Victoria, and I'm one of the —"

"You said the Prince Regent is in danger?" he barked.

"Yes sir, I believe he is." Victoria's mouth went dry. She stepped towards the group holding out the journal. "This is the personal journal of Major Vidigal, and it contains evidence that the major is planning a coup against His Highness. They rode out together a moment ago, and I believe the major intends to stage the coup today. Troops must be sent to protect the Prince—"

The two soldiers howled with laughter. Dumbfounded, she stared at them. The coffee drinker heaved a sigh. He muttered under his breath as he stomped over and snatched the journal, fanned the pages, then glared at her. Victoria assumed he was the officer in charge.

"Who the hell are you?"

"Victoria Cruz. I'm one of Her Majesty's servants."

"Now she's got her maids running around crying coup." The officer chucked the journal on the table. "Go back to Her Majesty and tell her His Highness is perfectly safe."

"But sir, the journal is from Vidigal. He's going to kill the Prince Regent!" Her voice sounded shrill and thin.

The officer pointed a tobacco-stained finger at her chest. "Next time Her Majesty tells you someone's about to kill His Highness, leave the room for a few minutes, go get something to eat, change your stockings, make a young man's day." This elicited a cheer from the other soldiers. "Then go back and tell Her Majesty the Prince Regent is safe. I don't give a damn what you do, but do not come down here to waste my time and insult prominent members of this city with her delusions."

Victoria hadn't considered the possibility they wouldn't believe her, a gross lack of foresight on her part. Of course they didn't believe her. She heard her own voice explaining that truth to Maria under the jungle canopy. *Who do you think I am? No one is going to listen. To me or to her. She's mad, and I'm a servant.*

Victoria twisted the ribbons on her dress, tighter and tighter until the tips of her fingers turned white. Her face burned in shame. She was useless. Unimportant. The soldiers' jeering faces blurred before she scurried out the door to the square. She knocked into a man with a basket of chickens on his head. His curses and the chickens' angry clucking prompted a fresh round of laughter from the soldiers.

Without a plan, panic hovered at the edge of her thoughts. Maria and Isabel risked their lives trailing Vidigal. Prince João was in the company of a man who hoped to overthrow him. The anniversary celebrations ended today, and Mateus could be executed as soon as tomorrow. Everyone's survival depended on her sending reinforcements, but she couldn't even convince one officer to read a page in the journal. No help was coming. Maria and Isabel had been wrong to trust her. She'd failed.

No. She wouldn't accept that.

She spent seven years alone, without family or friends, in service to a woman who couldn't remember her name. In that time, she'd been beaten, forgotten, assaulted, chased by guardsmen, Portuguese soldiers, and British marines, and she survived. Against relentless waves of despair and loneliness, she held her ground. She stayed on her feet. She made friends, and those friends were counting on her.

A wave of determination straightened her spine. She was her father's daughter. He'd taught her to trust herself, and there was always more than one way to solve a problem. These were not the only soldiers in Rio.

Victoria marched back into the jail to retrieve Vidigal's journal, laying forgotten on the table.

"Don't cry," said the sword polisher. "I'll read your book for a little favor in return."

At the soldier's touch on her back, the store of anger from years of abuse and humiliation exploded.

Victoria reached past the journal and grabbed the hilt of a saber. She spun and slammed the hilt against the polisher's head. She stomped on the sword still in his hand, breaking it in two, and held the point of her blade against his throat.

"Listen to me! Your sovereign is in danger. Do your duty. Read the journal, and save his life." She glared at the offi cer while pressing the tip of the sword into the soldier's throat.

The offi cer held his hands up as he came towards her. "I'll read it, but no matter what it says, you're under arrest."

"I don't care. Just read the journal. I'm telling the tr—"

The officer's neck tensed. She jumped back in time to avoid the saber swipe meant to disarm her. She parried his second attack. Freed from her blade, the polisher reached for the remaining sword on the table. With her left hand Victoria pulled a chair between herself and the polisher. He turned and toppled over it.

The officer and Victoria jumped apart to avoid getting dragged down by the soldier now sprawled on the floor and bleeding from the head.

"I'm so sorry!" Victoria yelped, jittery from the sudden violent turn. "I simply want someone to listen to me. Why is that so hard?"

The officer's response was a vicious lunge aimed at Victoria's chest, which she parried and instinctively countered with a lunge to his right shoulder. She didn't intend to hurt anyone, but the officer was terrible with a sword. He fumbled his footwork and poorly defended against her attack. Victoria's blade sliced across his upper arm. He paused to take in the gash.

Victoria gasped at the officer's wound but adjusted her stance, readying for the next attack. She wasn't running. "I truly am sorry. This is not why I've come. I came here to get your help with the prince."

The officer met her gaze. His eyes blazed with the embarrassed fury of a man bested by someone he considered inferior. He hated her and wanted to kill her.

With a growl, he threw himself into a full battle. Victoria stopped thinking and let her body react. Her muscles remembered what to do. As she deflected his attacks, her anger grew. This man's wounded pride was using up precious time. How long ago had she left Maria and Isabel? Had Vidigal made his move?

Victoria held her own. She was faster, and he was careless, which wasn't a surprise given the state of his sideburns. She backed towards the cells, letting the officer continually lunge and exhaust himself. Back during her lessons, Victoria had been consistently complemented on her excellent footwork. Now she used it to circle the officer, until his back was to the row of cells. She parried twice, before exploding forward with such ferocity the offi cer stepped back. He tripped over the stocks along the fl oor and fell backwards dropping his sword. Victoria kicked it away and brought her saber to his throat. The offi cer held up his hands in surrender.

Panting, Victoria glanced around for the other soldiers. The polisher was still sprawled on the fl oor. She cringed. Apparently he'd hit his head harder than she thought. The third soldier she'd seen earlier—the drooler—never appeared. He probably went for reinforcements against the queen's maid.

Victoria addressed the offi cer pinned under her blade. "I want you to know, I truly am sorry about all this." She kicked him in the head, and he dropped to the dirt fl oor.

She quickly found the keys and locked the unconscious officer's legs in the stocks he'd fallen over. She stood over the restrained offi cer. She won. Against two soldiers. A giggle bubbled out. The fencing instructor had complimented her during lessons, but she always assumed he was being generous out of pity. The strange commoner amongst royalty must feel out of place. Maybe he'd been sincere.

A noise from the last cell caught her attention. She picked up her sword and hurried down the rows of iron bars. A young man with a week's worth of beard and no shirt leaned against the bars of his cell. As Victoria approached, he backed away with his hands up in surrender.

"I won't make his mistake. I promise to listen if you ask." He smiled, amused despite his surroundings.

She took a chance. "Mateus?"

"Do I know you?"

She unlocked the door without hesitation. Victoria had exhausted her patience for asking and being ignored. "We've never met but I know who you are."

Recognition lit the man's eyes. "You're Maria's new friend. The maid."

"She told you about me?" Pride filled her chest. Maria referred to her as a friend.

"Yes, but she definitely left some things out." He peered out from his cell at the unconscious soldiers.

"I need your help."

Mateus shook his head. "I heard what you said about the Prince Regent, but I can't help you. I already told Maria I'm not leaving this cell and putting anyone else at risk."

"Maria and Isabel are in danger."

The effect was instant and exactly what she hoped for. Mateus strode out of the cell and hurried around the jail collecting clothes, boots, and a soldier's pistol that he hid under his freshly acquired shirt. Victoria grabbed Vidigal's journal, and they met at the door to the street.

"Where's Maria?"

"We were trying to rescue you. I was helping them find the real murderer to save you but things. . . got out of hand."

He nodded, a wistful smile on his face. "That happens a lot when Maria and Isabel are involved." A piercing whistle and shouts interrupted him. "Maybe you should explain while we walk."

"Yes, of course," she agreed.

They turned up the street away from the palace. For a moment, neither spoke and they concentrated on putting distance between them and the soon-to-be very active assembly headquarters. Victoria led the way around the corner at the end of the street and was suddenly knocked backward by a blow to her legs. Mateus steadied her and stepped in front.

"Mateus!" A boy with a memorable hat engulfed Mateus in a hug.

"I know you!" Victoria exclaimed. "You told me Maria and Isabel were at the bakery."

"Dito, you're in this, too?" Mateus said.

"Yes, Maria asked for my help." Dito puffed up his chest. "I have to hurry. I'm supposed to go to the jail and find Victoria and tell her to bring the soldiers to Botafogo. The Prince Regent is going to Botafogo."

"Mission accomplished," she said smiling.

"You're Victoria?" The boy swiveled his head around under the hat looking left and right. "But Maria said you would be with soldiers."

She grimaced, wishing she had better news. "There was a small misunderstanding."

"There won't be any soldiers," Mateus interrupted. "And if we do see some, they're trying to arrest us. We need to get far away from here."

He steered the boy down the street. Benedito cut his eyes up at Mateus and said, "You could use a good barber."

"They don't give razors to prisoners."

"How'd you escape? I thought they were going to execute you."

Mateus glanced back at her, and Victoria tried to look calm despite realizing the full magnitude of her crimes. She freed Mateus on impulse because she knew he'd care what happened to Maria and Isabel, but now in addition to assaulting two soldiers, she'd also freed a convicted murderer just before his execution. No judge would care about the fact Mateus was actually innocent.

She abandoned all hope of retaining her job with the queen, but maybe she'd be able to keep her freedom at the end of all this. The only chance of that happening was an official pardon from His Highness Prince João, and the only way to procure a pardon was to save his life.

"When we save Prince João, we'll all get pardons. Mateus won't be executed," she said to Benedito with far more hope than certainty.

"Save Prince João? You said you needed help to save Maria and Isabel." Mateus dropped Benedito's arm and faced her. So many emotions played out across his face, she couldn't guess what he was feeling.

Benedito glanced between them. "Since I know the story, I'm going to leave now."

"You're not going to help us?" Victoria was devastated to lose help in any form, even a reed-thin, child barber dressed as a traveling player.

"I did help. I told you they're in Botafogo. Now, I've got another job for Isabel."

Before Victoria could ask what errand Isabel deemed more important than preventing a coup, Benedito tipped his hat and scampered off into the crowd. With a growing sense of panic at their dwindling options and time, she steeled herself to explain how deeply involved she'd gotten Maria and Isabel.

Twisting the ribbon on her dress around her finger until it was purple, Victoria began, "I didn't mean for any—"

Mateus held his hand up. He gently took Victoria by the elbow and guided her inside the closest doorway, a small shop selling straw hats, then pointed to the stoop saying loudly, "Here, Dona. Rest in the shade."

Victoria frowned as Mateus bent low fanning her with a hat. He whispered, "A Portuguese girl cannot conspire with a Black man in the middle of the street without attracting attention. Pretend you're weak from the heat."

Mateus asked the store owner for a cup of water, effectively clearing him out of earshot. Victoria marveled at how much Mateus and Maria had in common. They pulled brilliant ideas out of their head on demand. Maybe they learned the skill carting gold through the jungle. Isabel was the same. She didn't blink at killing and then cooking the enormous constrictor. A life in the forests of Rio made people quick thinkers. The Portuguese way was to let problems age like fine wines and then pray about them.

"Where is Maria?"

Mateus spoke the name with such reverence, Victoria knew there was no place he wouldn't go for her, so she told him the truth. "Like your young friend said, Maria and Isabel followed the Prince Regent to Botafogo. They're protecting him from Vidigal. We were looking for Dom Antonio's murderer in order to save you and discovered that Vidigal has been killing your buyers and collecting the diamonds in order to pay for a coup."

"Anything else?"

"I was supposed to alert the army and bring reinforcements."

"And now Maria and Isabel are alone with no reinforcements and a group of Bats about to stage a coup."

"They won't be alone. I found you!" she protested. While she appreciated Mateus's ability for succinct summary, Victoria couldn't bear to hear the severity of the situation spelled out so clearly.

"I'm flattered you think I can substitute for a platoon of soldiers, but I can only aim in one direction at a time. We need more men to fight off a group of royal guards."

"But we don't need to fight them. If we get the prince back to the palace, we win. I can show him the journal, and Vidigal will be finished. We only need cover for our retreat, a spectacular diversion." Victoria clutched the journal to her chest wishing Maria and Isabel were with her. What did they do when cornered? They'd escaped imminent danger together enough times to have a long list of examples. The drunks on the beach, the Bats at the bakery, the palace guards, British marines. What would Maria and Isabel do to cause a distraction?

"I've got an idea. But it's madness," she murmured.

"What do you think my friends called me when I agreed to work for a pant-wearing, whip-wielding, capoeira-playing girl muleteer?" Mateus grinned.

Victoria smiled back. "In that case, I hope you won't be offended if I ask to borrow a pair of pants."

Chapter
Twenty-Four

Maria

S weat burned Maria's eyes and forced her to look away from the two Bats hidden amongst the trees. She'd barely blinked since Vidigal's agents discreetly fell in behind the Prince Regent's entourage. Now she was down to one set of eyes while Isabel scouted the surrounding forest for other Bats, and Maria's tracking instincts took over.

Prince João's entourage included Vidigal, six soldiers, the carriage driver, and the servant Victoria had recognized. Three royal guards followed the procession in secret. Despite the Bats, Maria hadn't been completely convinced Vidigal's attack was imminent until the train left the busy downtown for the forest of Botafogo. When the Prince Regent abandoned his carriage due to an enormous tree across the road, Maria's instinct screamed danger like a hoard of cicadas in her head.

A muleteer knew how to spot an ambush, and the half-built mansion the Prince Regent now examined on a deserted beach surrounded by forest could not have been a more perfect place.

But she couldn't guess from which direction or what form Vidigal's attack would take.

Vidigal was outnumbered six soldiers to three Bats. If he planned to attack, he'd need at least an even number to stand a chance, so Maria sent Isabel in search of the Bats that had to be in hiding.

She caught enough scraps of conversation to piece together the Prince Regent and Vidigal were inspecting an estate under construction for Princess Carlota Joaquina. Vidigal claimed there were security matters regarding the location he wanted to discuss with the Prince Regent. How convenient for the commander, the problems required Prince João's presence at this isolated location on the outskirts of the city.

To mark the end of the anniversary celebrations, the royal family declared an official holiday, and the construction site was deserted. Several rowboats and tents sat abandoned on the beach, each offering cover to a potential threat. She couldn't have planned a more perfect ambush.

Maria crouched in the branches of a cambuca tree inside the tree line bordering the white sands of Botafogo beach. She licked beads of sweat from her upper lip and risked shifting her weight further out on the branch. She wasn't worried about being spotted. Not having a lot of experience with jaguars, the soldiers and Guardsmen never looked up for potential threats.

From her perch, Maria could take in all the players. Vidigal led the Prince Regent toward the mansion apparently in deep discussion. Three soldiers formed a loose line facing the water, and the others stood at attention spaced along the tree line not far from where she hid.

The soldiers were not at peak performance. In their dark blue coats buttoned to the neck and tall black hats, they suffered in the humidity and rising temperature. They bore it stoically, but rolled their shoulders and shifted weight to discreetly unstick a sweaty shirt. The soldiers were hot and distracted. She recognized the symptoms from her own team.

The thought of her team triggered a wave of guilt. She hadn't been in contact with them for days. She'd abandoned her responsibilities as a muleteer and focused entirely on saving Mateus.

Because she was in love with him.

She'd avoided thinking about her revelation by focusing on the task at hand, but in the deep breath before action, quiet and still in the treetop, she thought of Mateus. She knew now she didn't long for the trail and life in the jungle. What she loved about the treks was Mateus's presence at her side, his joy to temper her worry, his loyalty, his smile. Growing up, she thought her dream was to be a muleteer like her father and keep his legacy alive, but maybe she could honor him in other ways. She could fi nd her passion and support her family with it as he had done.

Raised voices focused her attention. Her instincts hummed.

The Prince Regent stood in the shade of a tree near the mansion. Vidigal pointed to the beams and half-finished roof of the second floor. The commander gestured for the prince to join him at the wall, but Prince João toed the edge of the shade dubiously. He frowned at the sun as if its strength was a personal insult against him.

João ordered Vidigal to return to the shade. The police major stilled, eyes narrowing at the Prince Regent. The buzzing in Maria's head became a shrill screech.

She dropped to the ground and burst from the trees, acutely aware of the three soldiers on the beach now aiming rifles at her back. She kept her focus on the shocked faces of João and Vidigal. It was the most emotion she'd ever seen on Vidigal's face. She pressed her advantage.

"Your Royal Highness," Maria said, bowing low, "there's a problem with the queen. I've been sent by her maid to ask you back to the convent."

The lie came to her as she said it. From what she'd seen, problems with the queen seemed a regular yet serious enough occurrence to make the Prince Regent return immediately. That was her first plan, get Prince João to return to the palace. If that failed, she'd delay and pray Victoria was on her way with soldiers.

"A woman in pants?" The Prince Regent widened his already bulging eyes. "Cariocas truly have the most fascinating customs."

Maria ignored the condescending tone and pressed, "Your Highness, the queen needs you immediately. Her servant, Victoria, the daughter of her former surgeon, sent me to bring you back to her."

"The little tonic girl?"

"Yes, Your Highness." She was genuinely surprised the Prince Regent knew who Victoria was, more or less.

"Her Majesty has great affection for the tonic—"

Shots exploded around Maria. She dropped into crouch. All six soldiers slumped to the sand. Three Bats, hidden behind a half-finished section of wall on the second floor, held smoking rifles aimed at the soldiers behind Maria. Two stepped from the tree line on opposite sides of Prince João, who gaped like a beached fish at his dead soldiers. Vidigal reloaded his smoking pistol.

"I had to cut you off, Highness. I have more important things to do with my time than listen to lies about the queen's tonic girl." Vidigal touched his temple as if feeling the first pains of a headache. He turned his attention to Maria. "Did you honestly believe I wouldn't recognize you? And did you think that after coaxing the prince all the way out here, I'd let him turn around and ride home?"

Her heart pounded as she counted five rifles, all empty, Vidigal's still empty pistol, probably five more loaded pistols on the Bats, six whips. Knives? Maybe in their boots, but she couldn't know for sure. She had her whip, one knife in her boot, the soldiers' rifles which she hoped to god were loaded and ready to fire.

And Isabel.

"Well," she said casually to Vidigal, "I always try to hope for the best."

"A strategy that seems to keep getting you in trouble."

"Not if I also plan for the worst."

Maria's whip sliced through the air toward Vidigal, who leapt aside. He whirled around, unfurling his own whip. "You missed," he hissed.

"No. I didn't."

A crack split the air. One of the wooden posts supporting the roof splintered and gave way. A shower of clay tiles and wooden beams crashed down. The Bats on the second floor leapt off the building to the sand. The roof collapsed.

The Bats guarding the Prince Regent watched the demolition. Isabel swung from the tree, planting a foot squarely in each of their backs. They pitched forward, sand filling their gaping mouths.

Isabel grabbed Prince João by the arm and dragged him forward. "Don't make it easy for them. Run!"

He stumbled toward Maria, Isabel covering his back. Two Bats spit sand. Of the three Bats scrambling away from the collapsing building, one clutched a knee and crawled. Vidigal loaded his pistol. Maria sent it flying with a flick of her whip.

Clutching his bleeding hand, Vidigal fixed his black eyes on Maria.

"Move!" Maria bellowed at the prince. Royalty or not, she wasn't going to let this bumbling oaf get her sister killed. "Get to one of the boats. We'll hold them off."

The prince eyed the water. "Oh no, the sea's quite dangerous. Too many sharks and lobsters."

Maria snatched the lapel of his jacket and stood nose to nose with the Prince Regent of Portugal. "Do you know what's more dangerous than a lobster? Six armed men determined to murder you. Get in the damn boat, or I'm feeding you to the sharks myself."

Prince João stumbled towards the water muttering pleas to either the Virgin Mary or crustaceans. Maria couldn't tell and didn't care. She was focused on stalling the Bats long enough for the prince to row out to sea. She prayed for Victoria and a platoon of soldiers to burst from the trees.

"Any more brilliant ideas?" Isabel called.

"I'm out of buildings to demolish. Your turn."

"Finally! I've got the two by the trees. Since we've already bonded." Isabel twirled her daggers and dashed up the sand.

She smiled and shouted, "Don't take things personally and overreact."

"I never overreact. I fully commit."

Maria lashed at the feet of the Bats in Isabel's path. Sand sprayed into their faces. The men sputtered, giving her sister time to drop one with a kick to the gut. Still in a crouch, Isabel twirled and stood up behind the one Bat still standing. Her knives flashed in the sunlight.

Vidigal's shouts drew Maria's attention. Spit flew as he roared orders to catch the regent at all cost. Maria planted herself between the two uninjured Bats and Prince João.

One charged with his rifle's bayonet pointed at her chest. She easily wrapped her whip around his leg and dropped him to the sand, but she saw he'd been a diversion. The fourth Bat and Vidigal had loaded their pistols. They aimed at her.

She sent a spray of sand into Vidigal's face then dove aside. She rolled in the sand and scrambled to stand. The ground gave way beneath her feet. She was in the soft sand between the forest and high tide—the worst possible spot to fight from. Vidigal had higher and firmer ground.

Isabel's shout sent lightning through her limbs. The Bats retreated beyond the reach of her whip and began reloading their rifles. Vidigal grinned, holding eye contact with Maria despite the morning sun beaming over the horizon. She charged towards the Bats.

A rifle cracked. The Bats ducked. A shot hit the wall over their heads. A high-pitched voice shrieked "Meu Deus!"

Victoria, in boots and black riding breeches, staggered from the kickback of a fallen soldier's rifle. There had never been a sight sweeter than the dainty maid with a big gun in her hand. Rubbing her shoulder, Victoria dropped the rifle then reached for the next soldier's weapon. She heaved it up and fired again. The Bats and Vidigal scattered, taking cover among the rubble. Maria sprinted for the soldiers lying along the shore. She scooped up a rifle and fired, catching a Bat in the shoulder.

Isabel appeared beside Maria and snatched her own rifl e. "I'm glad I didn't kill Victoria that fi rst day she came to visit."

"You mean you're glad I stopped you from killing her," Maria said, grinning. "You mean to say I was right and off er your thanks?"

Isabel snorted and fired. "You're not nearly as humble as everyone thinks."

Victoria fired the third and final rifle. She was out of shots. "Isabel, she needs help. I'll cover you."

Isabel charged back to the tree line and Victoria. Maria fi red her last shot, barely missing Vidigal. She cursed. One Bat stepped out from behind the collapsed roof and aimed at Victoria. Isabel sent a dagger into his stomach. Victoria drew a sword off the fallen offi cer and launched herself at the nearest Bat. She easily parried his dagger and lunged.

Next to Victoria, Isabel was a blur of red skirt and silver blades. Maria abandoned the empty rifl es and moved in close, attacking with her whip. She spun the handle of her whip knocking one Bat out cold. Together, the three friends drove Vidigal and his remaining men back to the tree line.

"Where are the soldiers?" Maria panted. Her shoulder ached. Her legs burned from running in the sand. Her shirt clung to her back, and sweat stung her eyes.

"There was a miscommunication," Victoria said, parrying a bayonet.

"Is anyone coming?" Maria tried to keep her voice even.

"Yes, but he's running late." Victoria glanced down the beach. "Or back in jail."

"Jail? You were supposed to bring soldiers, not criminals!"

Victoria kicked her opponent away and turned to Maria. "You assured me he was not a criminal. Diamond smuggling excluded."

Maria staggered back from the words. She looked in the same direction Victoria had glanced, and beneath the grunts, the clang of metal, and Isabel's laughter, Maria heard the low thud of hooves. Lots of hooves.

"Look out!" Maria bellowed. She snatched Isabel by the shirt and pulled her against a thick tree trunk.

A team of mules burst out of the forest and charged past them onto the beach. The stamping and braying drowned out the swearing of Vidigal and whatever men were still standing. Maria didn't know how many. Her eyes followed the mules. Riding alongside and directing the team, Mateus sat high on Tempest.

Her heart leapt into her throat and smothered her voice. Mateus gave a few sharp whistles, cracked his whip, and turned the team in a graceful, sweeping arc before they reached the water. It was beautiful. He was beautiful. And he was free.

Maria started toward him then froze. She tore her eyes away from Mateus, back to the chaos in front of her. She couldn't lose focus. When the mules charged through, she lost track of the Bats. One lame Bat cowered behind rubble. One lay with a knife in his gut.

A touch on the shoulder cut off her assessment.

Isabel smiled, her black eyes shining. "Victoria and I can handle the Bats."

"I can't—"

"We've got this. Go."

For once, she didn't argue. She ran toward the sea, kicking up plumes of sands. Mateus peeled Tempest away from the team and galloped toward her. Almost in arms reach, he swung to the ground and tipped his hat. Maria knew what she wanted most in the world. Her body trembled, from more than the exertion of battle. She grabbed Mateus with both hands and pulled him into a kiss. Their lips met. She felt the surprise in his body melt into joy as his arms tightened around her.

She pulled back from the kiss but held onto his shirt. "You're late."

"I escape imminent execution, and that's all you have to say?"

"Thanks for bringing my horse." She pulled him in for another kiss. A perfect moment played out to the sounds of rolling waves, clashing swords, and Isabel cursing a Bat's entire family down to the dog. She wouldn't change a thing.

Maria stepped away, grinning, and swung into Tempest's saddle. She nodded to the rifles and soldiers lying on the sand. "I've got to be the cavalry. Could you give me some cover?"

"Shoot some Bats? This day keeps getting better." The pure happiness on his face pulled a laugh from her lips. That happiness was worth fighting for.

Mateus reloaded, and Maria spurred Tempest down the beach. She circled the mules, whip cracking, and drove them back toward Victoria and Isabel, who faced four remaining Bats.

Mateus fired. Three remaining Bats.

She yelled a warning, and Isabel yanked Victoria aside. The mules charged into the Bats. She drove Tempest straight at one. Her first strike disarmed him. Her second blow with the butt of her whip as she rode by dropped him to the sand.

Maria brought Tempest around. Victoria and Isabel each fought a single Bat. She started to regroup the mules when a sharp whistle pierced the air. Mateus waved frantically from next to a rowboat. Maria kicked Tempest into a gallop, spraying sand in her wake. "What's wrong?"

Mateus pointed into the rowboat. "Is he supposed to be here?"

Frowning, Maria dismounted and stared in disbelief at the Prince Regent curled into a ball on the boat floor and sucking on a chicken leg. "What are you still doing here? You were supposed to row the damn boat to the dock in front of the palace!"

Prince João peeked over the lip of the boat. "Young woman, I have been waiting for a rescue."

"What the hell do you think we're doing?"

"I cannot leave without an escort."

She grit her teeth and turned to Isabel and Victoria who battled one final Bat.

"He's still here!" she bellowed. "His Majesty's waiting for a proper escort."

Isabel's eyes bugged out. Her sister spoke to Victoria with a wild flourish of hand gestures. Victoria shook her head then landed a thrust to the Bat's shoulder. He dropped his dagger.

"Victoria said we still have to save him!" Isabel shouted.

Maria huffed through her nose. Unbelievable. If he died, it'd be his own royal fault. "Your Majesty—"

"Your Highness. My lady mother is the queen and thus addressed as Your Majesty."

"Senhor, I don't care. I need you to stay in this boat. Don't move. We'll round up the men who tried to murder you, then escort you back to the palace, alive and unharmed." The last words were an order to herself. She forced herself to let go of the whip. She caught Mateus's smile. "What?"

"You're brilliant."

For an instant, Mateus filled all her senses, then the buzzing exploded in her mind. Time slowed. A flash of movement in the corner of her eye. Maria unfurled her whip. Victoria assessed a wounded and restrained Bat. Isabel stood a few feet back, poised to throw a dagger at the Bat's chest.

A few feet away, Vidigal aimed a rifle at Isabel's back.

Under Rio's summer sun, Maria went cold. Her vision tunneled in. How could she have lost track of him? How could she have been so careless?

She ran. Vidigal cocked the hammer. Her sister was in reach. She could stop this. She had to. She didn't get Mateus back in order to lose her sister. Maria sent her whip flying, and the Bat sighted down the barrel. She caught Isabel by the arm and jerked her sideways, as Vidigal turned.

With her whip tangled around Isabel and her last burst of energy spent, Maria stared down the barrel of the rifle. A puff of smoke. Her skin tore, and she understood.

Isabel had been a decoy.

Chapter
Twenty-Five

Isabel

A shot fired. The whip around her arm went slack, and Maria dropped to the sand.

"Maria!" Isabel screamed.

She tore the whip off her arm. Rage consumed her. It drowned out the shouts of Mateus and blurred Victoria running toward Maria. Isabel saw only the stooped man in a dark coat holding a smoking rifle.

With a shriek, Isabel launched herself at Vidigal.

Vidigal swung the rifle like a bludgeon. Isabel deflected it to the side. She slashed the back of his hand. The rifle hit the ground. He leapt back but recovered quickly, drawing his own daggers. Rumor claimed he was an excellent knife fighter. She hoped so. She didn't want it to be quick.

Isabel's rage drove her forward, slashing in fluid motions at Vidigal's chest, hands, forearms. He staggered back, blocked, and tried to counter. Isabel spun under his strikes or let them slip to the side with a twist.

Vidigal stabbed the air where Isabel's shoulder had been a second before. She slashed down across his elbow. He howled.

"You filthy, little bastard," he spit.

"You say *little* like it's a bad thing," she panted. "Why don't people realize it's better to be the smaller target?"

Isabel called up every injustice she'd witnessed Vidigal and his Bats deliver. A public whipping for whistling. A beating for dancing samba. A day in the stocks for worshipping at a Candomblé shrine. Torture and execution of innocent men. All so he could gain favor and power. Her hatred dulled the stitch in her side and ache in her arms.

Vidigal stumbled in the soft sand, and Isabel struck. She whirled, her skirt flaring out, and slashed the back of his knee. The major crumpled. Isabel placed the point of her dagger at his throat.

"Want to beg for mercy?" she growled, pressing the knife into his leathery skin.

"Do you?" Vidigal glared up at her. "I am the only person keeping the savages from devouring each other. Kill me, and the city will rot to the core."

"You think a lot of yourself."

He sneered, unimpressed by the blade against his Adam's apple. "No. I think very little of my countrymen. We are violent and lazy. We're animals, and you discipline animals with a stick. Our population needs to be purified. I will not apologize for trying to give Rio a strong monarch willing to suppress the rabble."

Every word fueled her rage. He'd judged an entire city, *his own city*, guilty and had appointed himself savior. He thought of her family as a pack of animals, totally expendable. Isabel's hand shook with hatred, but she didn't strike.

More than hurting him, she wanted to prove Vidigal wrong. If she slit the throat of an unarmed man on a deserted beach, she'd confirm his worst opinions. If she killed in blind hate, she was an animal. She wouldn't give him the satisfaction.

"When you shot my sister, that wasn't for Rio. That was for you. You wanted her to die. Like I want you to die, but unlike you, I'm not an animal." Isabel drew back, leaving a drop of ruby blood on Vidigal's neck. "I'm not going to kill you."

Vidigal spit on Isabel's boot. "I refuse to be grateful for some half-breed—"

She slammed the butt of her knife into his head. The Bat commander plummeted to the sand. She flipped his head to the side with the toe of her boot so he could breathe, then turned to the shore. Victoria and Mateus smiled at her. Maria, sitting on the sand with a ban-daged arm, raised an eyebrow.

Her sister's critical gaze was the most beautiful sight in all of Rio. Relief rolled over her. For a moment, she believed her sister was dead. It had been the single most terrifying moment of her life, but rather than race to her sister's side, Isabel tossed her sweat-coated hair over her shoulder.

"I said I wouldn't kill him. Not that I would listen to his bullshit."

Maria laughed loudest of them all.

She strolled over to the group. "One of you can tie him up. I don't want the temptation. There's a chance I'll change my mind and slit his throat."

"I'll do it," Mateus offered, helping Maria to her feet. "I don't want to be accused of not doing my share."

Isabel hugged him. "I'm happy to see you. The beard has to go."

"I know. I know. Dito's already offered his services." Mateus waved her off and headed up the beach with rope borrowed off a sailboat.

When he was out of earshot, she turned to her sister. "When's the wedding date?"

"I just got shot," Maria protested.

"You can't rush it. I need enough time to make you a fabulous dress."

Isabel pulled her sister close and held her until the rifle shot no longer echoed in her ears, and the image of Maria falling could be pushed aside to haunt her some other time.

"Oof. The arm."

"Oh, sorry," Isabel released her sister. She tossed her hair and shook off the melancholy. Victory called for laughter, not tears, so she flashed a bright smile. "It doesn't look that bad. Not bad enough to get you out of doing laundry."

"And dishes, cooking, shopping."

"I'm not doing laundry and dishes," Isabel protested.

"I can help," Victoria spoke up. She twisted her fingers nervously. "I could come stay with you. Just to help while Maria recovers."

"Yes," Isabel cried. She glanced at Maria who nodded. "Of course you're going to stay with us. You're family now." She threw an arm around her sister and newest friend. "*That* is how you rescue a prince!"

"Speaking of. . ." Maria pointed to a sailboat where a large rump stuck above the side.

"Your Highness!" Victoria shrieked and rushed to the boat.

Isabel rolled her eyes nearly out of her head. "He cowered in the boat the whole time? Next time there's a coup, I'm killing everyone involved and making myself queen."

"I don't see you sitting in a chair for two hours every night while nobles kiss your hand," Maria said.

"It would depend on the food they served."

Victoria steadied the Prince Regent as he clambered out of the boat. He tripped. Isabel reached out to keep Victoria from being crushed, but the Portuguese girl proved stronger than she looked. The future king got settled on his feet and looked around.

"Is my carriage here?"

"I'm afraid your driver and servant are dead," Isabel said. "I found them when I was scouting the area."

Prince João opened and closed his mouth. She pictured a bored frog.

"The major truly wanted me dead." Prince João spoke slowly as if realizing the truth for the first time.

"Yes, Your Highness," Victoria said softly. "But Major Vidigal and his men have been subdued. You're safe now, and we'll make sure you are escorted back to the palace."

His Highness squinted at Victoria. "I know you! You give the queen her tonics. Your father was Her Majesty's doctor." Victoria curtsied in affirmation. The prince pointed between Isabel and Maria. "You know these girls here?"

"Yes, Your Highness. They're my friends. We uncovered evidence of Vidigal's intention in his journal."

"Oh dear, I'm going to need to eat something before I hear all this." Prince João swatted away Victoria's words like flies. "I simply must be returned to the palace."

Victoria looked at Maria. "Can you sail?"

Before Maria could answer, Isabel spoke up. A fabulous idea materialized in her head and she couldn't let the opportunity slip away. "I'll take the Prince Regent home."

"How? Neither of us can sail," Maria protested. "What are you going to do? Throw him over my horse's saddle?"

"No. I'm going to drive his carriage."

Ten minutes later, Isabel sat high above the ground clutching the reins of the royal horses. Victoria gripped the seat next to her while His Royal Highness sat inside the carriage doing whatever he damn well pleased. Probably scrounging for a forgotten wedge of cheese.

The carriage slammed into a dip in the road and popped out the other side. Victoria gasped. Isabel grit her teeth. She may have been a bit hasty to take on this particular challenge.

"Don't worry," she assured Victoria. "Things will smooth out once we get back into the city." At least she hoped. She'd spent most of the last five years on horseback, but steering a team of four horses pulling a carriage was more of a challenge than she was willing to admit.

Maria and Mateus stayed behind to secure the Bats still alive. They told Prince João someone would remain on the beach until he sent soldiers back to collect the traitors, but in truth, Maria and Mateus would disappear with the mules and Vidigal long before the soldiers arrived.

Everyone agreed Vidigal couldn't be given over to the royal guard. They didn't know who he'd paid off with the diamonds. Not even Victoria, who trusted in the honor of the royal guard, believed Vidigal would remain in prison for long. He was too well connected, so other arrangements had to be made. As far as the Prince Regent was concerned, they'd tell him that Vidigal fled into the forest seriously injured. People who did that kind of thing usually weren't seen again.

They'd won. Mateus was free, and they had more than enough evidence to get him a full pardon. The Prince Regent lived to eat another chicken leg. Vidigal wouldn't be able to terrorize another person, and her sister had a wedding in the near future, even if she couldn't admit it out loud yet. Isabel's laughter rang through the forest canopy.

"What's so funny?" Victoria asked.

"When I got back to Rio a week ago, I thought I'd be cooking and selling sweets until the next trek."

"I'm sorry, Isabel."

"Sorry?" She nearly dropped the reins to clap with glee. "This has been the greatest week of my life! That's why I love Rio. Anything can happen."

"But Mateus won't be able to stay here. Too many royal guards have a personal vendetta against him. And maybe Maria, too. Don't you think he should leave?"

Victoria's question knocked Isabel off her victory pedestal. She had a point. Even after the Prince Regent pardoned him—which would be the least he could do — all the Bats, soldiers, and anyone who'd helped send him to jail could resent his freedom. People with power didn't like being corrected. Mateus wasn't safe in Rio, but Isabel didn't want to leave.

If she refused to leave, would Maria stay with her?

She would if Isabel asked her. Maria had spent her entire life in service to others, protecting Isabel and their mother, taking over their father's mule train, providing not just for the two of them but also her team and their families, saving Mateus from execution, stopping a coup. She collected stories, while Maria collected responsibilities. The only reason she'd always been able to follow every impulse and give into every whim was because her sister came behind to pay the bill. Isabel intended to solve this problem on her own.

"I'm sorry," Victoria murmured. "I didn't mean to ruin the celebration. It's a question for tomorrow."

"It'll take more than a question about housing arrangements to ruin this day. I'm driving the Prince Regent into town." Isabel forced a smile and flicked the reins. They rolled into downtown Rio, and she waved to the gawking crowds as they passed.

"What are you doing?" Victoria squeaked.

"Enjoying myself." She blew a kiss to a gaping priest, and Victoria gasped. Isabel elbowed her friend. "Come on. When was the last time you did something just because it was fun? You should try it. Now's the time. You're quite fetching in those breeches." Victoria looked ready to fling herself from the moving carriage, so Isabel held a hand up in surrender. "I'll stop teasing, but you could stop worrying. We won."

"We're not done yet," Victoria warned. "His Highness isn't back at the palace. We haven't given him the journal. He hasn't officially pardoned us. Technically, we're still wanted criminals with the Prince Regent's carriage."

"No, technically *you're* the criminal. I had nothing to do with breaking Mateus out of jail." Victoria's jaw dropped, and Isabel burst out laughing. Humor was clearly one subject Victoria had not studied. "I'm joking. Of course, the Prince Regent will pardon you. Especially once we tell him how you were the one who suspected Vidigal in the first place."

"I've got to get that journal." Victoria's leg bounced up and down.

"Why did you leave it in the queen's room?"

"Because I wasn't going to carry it into the middle of a violent coup," Victoria huffed. "Stop. I'm getting down here."

"We're still two streets from the palace," she protested, pulling the reins.

"The streets are too crowded. I can run faster than you can drive." Victoria climbed to the ground. "I'll meet you in the throne room."

"That is the greatest sentence ever spoken to me." She slapped the reins, and the carriage jerked forward. "Hurry up. It's never a good idea to leave me alone with soldiers for too long. They usually end up unconscious."

Chapter
Twenty-Six

Victoria

Victoria leapt up the stairs to the queen's chambers. She wanted to race through the streets of Rio screaming in triumph. Well, perhaps not screaming and only if the street wasn't too crowded. She imagined the shock of the other maids when she walked in with a torn shirt and dust-covered breeches and laughed. She wore the uniform of dragon hunters and monster slayers. With her chin high and boots tracking mud, Victoria marched into the queen's chamber.

The sitting room was empty.

The queen's bedroom door was ajar. Normally Her Majesty dressed later in the morning, and Victoria marveled at her luck. Not having to explain her appearance made the errand easier. She tiptoed to the desk and retrieved the journal.

But the bedroom door called to her. The queen had been Victoria's sole responsibility for close to a decade, and one morning's adventure couldn't sever that bond. A compulsive need to check on Her Majesty drew her back. She'd just peek.

Victoria crept to the bedroom and peered through the crack. Her Majesty slept soundly and—

She swung the door open and stared wide-eyed at Princess Carlota Joaquina perched on the bed next to the sleeping monarch.

Carlota Joaquina assessed the stunned Victoria with an arched eyebrow. "Is that how Her Majesty's attendants are dressing now? Standards have slipped further than I thought."

"Oh, I…I'm so sorry, Your Highness." Victoria reached to lift her skirt but grabbed only air. "There was an incident early this morning."

"What incident requires a maid in Her Majesty's service to dress like a stable boy?"

Victoria straightened, the story of the Prince Regent's rescue on her lips, but Carlota Joaquina's ferocious glare stole her words. Victoria wondered if the princess would be pleased to hear her husband lived.

"Is there something you would like to say, girl?"

"Yes, of course. Your Highness, I. . ." But the longer Victoria held Carlota Joaquina's gaze, the less certain she was that Her Highness would celebrate the averted coup. A list of all the names she'd overheard Carlota Joaquina call the Prince Regent would fill several pages. Soggy toadstool. The Prince Repugnant. Gluttonous mollusk. She couldn't say with any certainty that Carlota Joaquina would pick her husband over her lover.

Victoria realized she still held Vidigal's journal. How much did he tell the princess? She needed to get to Isabel. They hadn't won yet, not until Prince João and the journal were both safely in the hands of the palace guards. She backed into the sitting room.

"Are you trying to slip away? Feeling a little guilty?" Carlota Joaquina rose from the queen's side.

Victoria considered running. With her limp, the princess would never catch her, but fleeing would require turning her back on her future queen. Victoria was more likely to tame a jaguar.

"Guilty? No, Your Highness."

"Then you are not in the least sorry for failing to give Her Majesty my gift?"

A stone dropped in the pit of her stomach. "I'm sorry, Your Highness. Your gift?" What had she missed? She was always so careful in her procedures, in her duties.

"The tonic."

"The tonic?" Victoria groped through the chaos of thoughts tumbling around her head and remembered the princess peeling an orange, recounting her life story, and giving her a small bottle of tonic for Her Majesty. The surreal scene in Carlota Joaquina's sitting room seemed from the distant past. She'd put the bottle in a cabinet in the sitting room and not given it a second thought.

"I apologize, Your Highness. Her Majesty was sleeping last night when I returned, and I did not think it necessary to wake her for a dose."

"Oh, you're a doctor now?" A smirk twitched Carlota Joaquina's lips. "You can ignore my surgeon's advice to administer the tonic?"

"No, Your Highness, of course not. My apologies." Victoria dropped another awkward curtsey. "It's time for the queen's breakfast. I'll give the first dose now."

Victoria went straight to the medicine cabinet. Carlota Joaquina followed and stopped at the window, observing the morning bustle on the street below. Her father would have disapproved of waking an old lady to force-feed her medicine she might not need, but an extra dose of tonic seemed a small price to get the princess back to her own chamber.

The piercing cry of an enthusiastic newspaper seller came from under the open window. The princess scoffed. "These people don't need newspapers. They need character. They need a moral compass."

Victoria's stomach clenched at the familiar words. She'd heard them before. Not heard. Read. She'd read those exact words only the night before.

Vidigal's journal lay on her desk. Victoria looked from the journal to the bottle of tonic clutched in her hand then to Princess Carlota Joaquina.

Slowly, the pieces clicked together, illuminating the whole traitorous picture. With all her strength, she hurled the bottle of tonic against the wall. The shards of glass glinted in the tropical sunlight like diamonds. The silence in the room drowned out the clamor of the city.

Victoria turned away from the remains of her palace life and glared at the princess. "How could you?"

"How dare you question me!" Carlota Joaquina growled back. She stalked towards Victoria.

"I know about you and Major Vidigal! How could you side with that horrible man over your country and your prince?" Victoria's voice broke. This ungrateful woman had threatened her queen. "Are you so lonely and miserable you would kill a woman who's been a second mother to you? All because Vidigal asked you?"

"Why would I do anything for that insignificant man?"

Victoria frowned in confusion. "Because you're having an affair."

"An affair? With that mongrel?" Carlota Joaquina's lip curled back in disgust. "God, never. You think I could be seduced by that flea? That is the single greatest insult I've ever received."

Panic flowed through her. She grasped, trying to clarify her theory. "I've seen the two of you passing notes. I know about his coup. How could you betray Portugal?"

The backhand snapped Victoria's head back.

"I'm saving Portugal." Each word was a declaration. Carlota Joaquina straightened and lifted what little chin she had. "It's not Vidigal's coup. It's mine."

Her knees buckled. They hadn't won. The real monster was alive and well and in line for the throne. No one would believe her. Like the soldiers in the prison. They'd call her crazy.

Carlota Joaquina seemed to agree because she held Victoria's gaze and smiled. "Being banished to the countryside of Portugal made it difficult to act before we sailed. After we arrived in Rio, I knew I'd have better luck while we're living on top of each other in this pathetic hovel."

Victoria heard the words but didn't understand them. "Why? The Prince Regent is your husband. You're going to be queen."

"I'm NOTHING!" Carlota Joaquina roared. She clutched the sides of Victoria's face bringing her own close enough that Victoria could taste the orange on her breath. "Do you know what it's like to sit next to a fool, an oaf, a fat, reeking coward and watch him make decision after decision that drives the empire closer to collapse and you must remain silent? Do you know what it's like to see ruin coming but have all your warnings and counsel ignored?" Carlota Joaquina dug her thumbnail into Victoria's throbbing cheek. She let out a whimper.

The noise made Carlota Joaquina draw back, but she held onto Victoria's face. "No, you wouldn't know but maybe you can imagine. Imagine watching the men adorned with titles and medals scampering away from Napoleon like rats and knowing, *knowing*, that you could do better, but you would never be allowed to prove it. Imagine that, surgeon's daughter, and tell me, how long could you live with that knowledge before acting?"

"Forever," Victoria replied. Carlota Joaquina pushed Victoria's head aside and stalked away in disgust. "I'd live with it forever because my ambition isn't worth innocent people's lives."

"Your beloved queen is not innocent. No monarch is ever innocent."

"I'm not talking about Her Majesty. What about the men Vidigal murdered?" Surely, the princess could understand that. She couldn't be behind the deaths. She couldn't have stood by, unblinking, as Vidigal snuffed out blameless lives.

"Smugglers?" scoffed the princess.

"What about their families left without security? They had children. And there's a man, a muleteer, who's scheduled to be executed for one of Vidigal's murders. They're all innocent. I would never think I was worth their lives."

"Because *you're* not." Carlota Joaquina sized Victoria up with the same eye she chose her mounts. "You're soft, but you're not a fool. You've got your father's brains. It's why I let you train with my daughters all those years ago. I suspected you were smarter than the lot of weak-minded princesses I birthed. And I was right. Naturally. Of all the people in this palace, you figured out my plan, and I would like to know how."

Carlota Joaquina drew a knife from her boot, and Victoria realized the princess stood between her and the door to the hall.

Victoria needed to distract the princess until someone returned to the chamber. It was almost time for the queen's morning prayers. Some servant would arrive to prepare Her Majesty, then guards to escort her to the litter.

She dropped her gaze to the floor and twisted her fingers. "I saw you and Vidigal passing notes, and yesterday I heard him tell you that you'd have something to celebrate. When I saw the diamond he gave you, it made me suspicious. I found out where his private office is and went there last night. I found his journal. He wrote everything down. I was going to go to the Prince Regent while the queen is at prayer."

Carlota Joaquina crept towards Victoria. "Unlike the prince you apparently love so much, I'm not fool enough to believe that story. It doesn't explain why a princess holding a diamond would make you suspicious or why you care about a young muleteer scheduled for execution. Victoria, who have you been talking to?"

The menace in Carlota Joaquina's voice painted a vivid picture of what would happen to Maria and Isabel if Victoria surrendered their names. She pursed her lips and set her shoulders. Portugal be damned if this royal thought she'd betray her friends. Not after everything they'd done for her, everything they'd taught her. "I've spoken to no one."

"Fine. Be stubborn like your father." Carlota Joaquina's heavy step gave an ominous thud on the floorboards. "I should have expected his daughter to be equally ungrateful."

What did that mean? Her father had never been anything but gracious and respectful. "What did you do to him?" Victoria whispered.

"Only gave him the opportunity to be counselor to the ruling monarch of Portugal."

Memories rushed back. Carlota Joaquina's generosity to her and confidence in her father, a complete change in attitude, her father's death, Carlota Joaquina's banishment from court in Lisbon. "This isn't your first attempt to seize the throne." This woman ruined her entire life for more power. "My father refused to help you. Did he turn you in? Did you kill him?"

The princess barked a laugh. "Don't be ridiculous. I don't kill people. I have people who kill for me. But sometimes a princess can only trust herself to finish a job."

Carlota Joaquina lunged forward. Victoria watched the knife. She didn't notice Carlota Joaquina's free hand until it dug into her hair. She was yanked off-balance and propelled toward the open window. Victoria snagged the edge of a bookcase and dug her nails into the wood. Carlota Joaquina jerked her head back. Pain tore a scream from her. She lashed out at Carlota Joaquina with the only weapon she had, the truth.

"Killing me won't matter," Victoria gasped. "You've already lost. João is alive."

"Lies," she spat.

"No. The attack in Botafogo failed. Vidigal was taken. You've failed for the second time."

Carlota Joaquina's grip slackened and a howl of rage ripped from the princess. She wrenched Victoria from the bookcase. The second of hesitation had been all Victoria needed. She slammed the spine of a book into Carlota Joaquina's face. The blow sent her reeling backwards. The princess steadied herself in the bedroom doorway.

Rage burned across Carlota Joaquina's face. Her nostrils fl ared. Victoria tensed, expecting the princess to charge.

"That sniveling coward will be the ruin of the empire! I will not stand aside and—"

Victoria heard a thunk. Carlota Joaquina slid to the fl oor, revealing Queen Maria with a bedpan brandished like a club, her night dress stained with sweat, and silver hair spilling over her shoulders. "What a hideous way to be woken. The roosters are demure in comparison."

"Your Majesty," Victoria curtsied, switched to a bow, felt absurd, and went back to a skirt-less curtsy. As if summoned by the plight of a woman in breeches, Maria dropped in through the window.

Her friend raised an eyebrow at the sight of the queen standing over the unconscious princess. "I saw the bitch trying to throw you out the window, but it seems I didn't need to hurry."

"My dear Victoria, you need your own receiving room," the queen cackled.

"I apologize, Your Majesty," Victoria stuttered, recovering her voice, but not convinced the scene in front of her wasn't a dream. "This is my friend, Maria."

"Another Maria! My God we Portuguese lack imagination when it comes to names."

"I'm Brazilian," Maria corrected.

"Same empire." The queen waved away any possible differences between the two lands.

Victoria crept up to the queen's side as if approaching an animal equally likely to kiss or eat your hand. "Your Majesty, we met Maria during the excursion to the new palace. In the jungle. Maria helped stop Vidigal and saved His Royal Highness."

"Still killing snakes then, girl?"

"I try to stay busy, Your Majesty." Maria grinned, clearly enjoying the exchange. "I see you've bagged one yourself."

"We Maria's are a formidable lot, are we not?"

"Always." Maria tipped her head. She examined the queen as if trying to untangle a knot by sight alone then turned to Victoria. "I thought you said she was mad?"

"Well, that is. . . was my father's diagnosis."

"I'm certainly mad," the queen interrupted. She tugged at the ruby ring on Carlota Joaquina's limp hand. "As a young woman, I saw my dear Lisbon decimated. The earth shook, the ocean flooded the streets, and a fire burned anything leftover. I saw tens of thousands die. I've since buried my husband, my only daughter, and my first-born son. My heir has a wife who spends her days plotting to murder him and steal his throne. My girl, if you've seen as much as I have and aren't mad, you're crazy."

The queen pushed the ruby ring over her own swollen knuckles and held it up to the light. "I think I'll have this back. Never expect a dog to change by giving it presents for bad behavior."

Victoria stared at the queen in wonder. It was the most the queen had spoken in her seven years of service, and she wondered how much wisdom she'd mistaken for madness.

The door to the hall swung open and slammed against the wall.

"Isabel!" Victoria cried, delighted to see her friend leading a party that included the Prince Regent. At the head of a group of soldiers with knives drawn, her friend looked like a warrior princess from legend, and Victoria wished she were a poet to preserve the moment.

"We've been waiting for you. There was already a group of soldiers in the throne room and this man. . ." Isabel pointed over her shoulder at the seething officer Victoria had left in the stocks. "Nossa Senhora! He really wants to shoot you. What did you do to him?"

"I bested him in a sword fight and left him locked in the stocks of his own prison."

"I'm so proud of you!" Isabel cried, clapping her hands. She noticed her sister by the window and marched across the room in a huff. "Didn't we talk about sneaking into the queen's chamber without me?"

"It was an emergency," Maria said.

"Mother!" Prince João waddled to the queen. "Are you all right? What's happened?"

"Another great story that I was left out of," Isabel muttered.

Instead of accepting her son's outstretched hands, Queen Maria dropped the bedpan in them. "I told you that bitch was trying to kill us."

Victoria cringed while Maria smirked and Isabel gaped.

Prince João's shoulders sagged. "I thought she'd been behaving. So many years have gone by without any attempts."

"She's tried to kill you before?" Isabel asked the prince, incredulous.

Maria arched an eyebrow. "What did you do that made her want to?"

The queen barked a laugh. "My dear Maria, if you meet a man you don't want to kill after one conversation, marry him."

"That's my plan, Your Majesty."

"I'm sorry, mother," Prince João cut in. "To whom are you speaking? *Your* name is Maria. Who is this girl?"

"I am Queen Maria of Portugal," the white-haired monarch declared, "and João, my son, give these young ladies whatever they want."

Isabel's eyes lit up, but Maria's hand shot in front of her sister's open mouth. The muleteer hurriedly said, "Four full pardons would be greatly appreciated."

"Done. João, see to it." Her Majesty shuffled toward her bedroom. "Now, it's time for my morning prayers. Come, Victoria. Everyone else get the hell out unless you want to see an ancient monarch naked."

Victoria offered the queen her arm. She straightened and lifted her chin, proud to have the trust of the first queen of Portugal. The officer muttered a curse at her back, and she smiled. Surely Rio had a few fencing instructors. She looked forward to restarting her lessons.

The queen sighed. "At least we'll soon be able to ship that Spanish cow to her own house at Botafogo."

Victoria bit her lip. "About the princess's residence, Your Majesty. I'm afraid there's been an accident."

Chapter
Twenty-Seven

Maria

Her boots sank into the sand along the shore of Guanabara Bay. Maria tipped her head to the sun and let the morning light warm her face. Victoria and Isabel's laughter drowned out the sound of the waves. They were both barefoot and walking in the frigid surf.

A wave lapped Victoria's toes, making her shriek. "Why is it so cold? It's too hot here for the water to be this cold."

"Aren't you the one who walks on frozen water?" Maria teased.

"Not in bare feet." Victoria scurried away from the next wave.

"How does a person walk on water?" Mateus asked.

"It's a Portuguese thing," Maria told him. She leaned against his shoulder, breathing in his scent of leather and sea.

In the two days since thwarting a coup, meeting the entire royal family, and receiving a parcel of pardons, she'd only taken her eyes off Mateus to sleep, and even then she'd put up a valiant fight against exhaustion. Watching the rise and fall of his chest as he slept calmed her.

They hadn't discussed it. Mateus simply came home with Isabel and Maria with no expectation other than to be close by. Isabel insisted Mateus needed a hammock after a week sleeping on a cell fl oor, and since Maria was injured, he would take hers. She could sleep on the fl oor. Mateus protested until Isabel threw a knife at his head. It was always safer not to argue with Isabel.

Victoria still planned on moving in with them, after training new maids to serve the queen overnight. Their family had doubled in size, and Maria needed to look for a bigger house. But that chore could wait until after a walk on the beach.

Her sister craned her neck to scan the launch boats along the beach. Sailors loaded cargo of sugar, coffee, and gold destined for ports in Europe.

"Want to stand on my shoulders?" Mateus teased. Isabel stuck her tongue out, making him laugh. Maria's heart squeezed at the sound. The fear of losing him still clung to her thoughts. Every moment of joy brought another wave of relief.

Mateus dodged a blow from Isabel's hat. "I'm only trying to help."

"You did enough by shaving the beard. We've got it from here."

"Got what? Who's *we*?" Maria asked. Her sister's tone sounded an alarm. Victoria bit back a smile. "I knew the two of you were hiding something. What are you planning? I hate surprises."

Victoria held up her hands in surrender. "It's Isabel's plan. I merely provided consultation."

"Isabel is planning? And keeping a secret? A lot can change in a week," Mateus said. This time he twisted away from Isabel's punch. "Careful now. I have an injured lady at my side."

"Call me that again, and I will drown you," Maria growled, although the grip she had on Mateus's arm robbed her threat of any force.

The prince's surgeon examined her injury at the command of the queen and declared the bullet only grazed the skin. He still ordered her to rest the arm for two weeks. The surgeon's attempt to put her arm in a sling was stopped cold by an unblinking glare. In the end, she settled for a bandage with minimal grumbling.

"Don't worry. You'll be back to whipping men into shape in a few days," Mateus consoled her. He leaned down and kissed her. It was quick, neither wanted to turn heads, but the light brush of his lips on hers was enough to make her stomach flip.

Maria knew how close she'd come to a life without him and not because of murdered smugglers or corrupt officials. She'd been consumed with knowing what everyone around her needed and hadn't spared a thought for what she wanted for herself. And she'd been afraid.

She doubted the fear would ever disappear entirely. No matter how she prepared and planned, every trail ended eventually. There would be more sleepless nights and heartache, but the alternative was to give up, sit down, and wait to die. A captain didn't give up. She knew the risks and forged ahead then reaped the rewards along the way. She'd walk at Mateus's side as long as she could and bask in every minute of that happiness.

"Nossa Senhora. Lisbon, you're the same color as a cooked shrimp. Look at her!" Isabel threw an arm around their friend, playfully poking her cheek.

"We have got to get you a hat," Maria said.

"We can always steal one from him. It wouldn't be the first time…Ahoy, Tomasinho." Isabel waved at the tall American walking towards them.

Hat in hand, Thomas Sumpter bowed his head. "I'm honored to be in the presence of the saviors of the Portuguese monarchy." He replaced his hat and held his hand out to Mateus. "You must be Senhor Carvalho."

Mateus hesitated before taking the outstretched hand. "And you are?"

"Thomas Sumpter, from Philadelphia."

"An American." Mateus accepted the handshake still frowning.

Thomas smiled. "Yes, I had the pleasure of helping your friends during a rather thrilling chase through these streets. I shall never forget how effective mangos are against British marines."

Mateus looked at Maria. She shrugged. "You got out of jail two days ago. I haven't had time to tell you everything."

"Well, the trip will give you plenty of time to recount the entire adventure," Thomas said.

"What trip?" Maria frowned. Isabel and Victoria keeping a secret. Thomas appearing on the beach. She was enjoying the walk less and less.

"They don't know?" Thomas looked at Isabel.

"What trip?" Maria repeated, turning to her sister.

"The one I've planned for you." Isabel gave a tight smile, and Maria realized she was nervous. Her little sister who slayed caimans and corrupt city officials without blinking vibrated like a plucked guitar string.

"Isabel—" Maria started, but Isabel held up her hand.

"It's the trip you've been thinking about since the court arrived. Because even though we all have full pardons, you're not safe. The Bats were disbanded but not banished. Now they're jobless and mad as vipers. They hate the fact Mateus was released and even though Prince João publicly announced Vidigal's treachery, they blame the two of you for everything. I know because I trailed some of them." Isabel waved away the scolding on Maria's lips. "Too late. It's done. So sooner or later the Bats are going to get revenge. And as miserably boring as I think coffee farming in Bahia would be, it's better than always looking over your shoulder or getting stabbed in the back."

Isabel pulled the tarp off a cart behind Thomas. There were all of Maria's and Mateus's possessions, neatly packed and piled in the cart.

"Isabel, what have you done?" Maria gasped.

"We got you ready for a trip. Don't worry. Victoria handled the packing. I think your head wraps are organized by color and fabric type."

"As are the shirts, pants, and I even found your dress from the anniversary ball." Victoria pointed at various chests. "There's also Mateus's clothes, boots, toilette set for you both, cooking ware, and dry goods. Although, Mr. Sumpter has assured me there will be plenty of food aboard."

"Mr. Sumpter?" Maria blinked as though she'd taken a blow to the head. Luggage. The coffee farm. A ship.

Isabel grinned. "That was my part. I talked Tomasinho into giving up two passages on one of his ships."

In unison, Maria and Mateus turned to Thomas.

"What good is having ships at your disposal if you can't get passage for two friends?" Thomas said. "And to be clear, your sister didn't need to persuade me. I was glad to help. One of my ships sails for Salvador today, and there's room for the two of you."

"Meu Deus, Isabel," Mateus murmured.

Maria stared at the cart in silence. After a moment, she lifted her eyes to Isabel. "Only *two* passages?" She knew what it meant and couldn't believe they'd reached that crossroads so soon. She'd never known a life without her sister.

Isabel squeezed Maria's hands in both of hers. "I know you've stayed in Rio because of me and the team. You think it's your duty to take care of us and support the mule train Papa built, but what do *you* want Maria?"

Maria hesitated. She knew the life she wanted, but admitting it aloud scared her more than a dozen vengeful Bats. She took a deep breath and looked into her sister's eyes.

"I'm tired. I'd like to sleep in the same bed for more than two weeks. And I think I'd like to build something of my own. Like Papa did. But not a mule train. I want to stay put for a while." She said the words as though confessing her darkest secret, but the moment the words were out, a knot in her chest unraveled.

"That's what I thought, and you're too young to feel tired. You'll have white hair by thirty. Thank god you've already found a man." Isabel laughed, blinking back her tears. "You and Mateus are going to Bahia. You're going to grow plants and raise chickens and kids, and I'm going to be the muleteer."

"You want to run the team?" Mateus asked.

Isabel put her fists on her hips. "I believe I've proven myself when all hell breaks loose, and I want a chance to lead. I know I can. I've already talked to the team, and as long as they keep their jobs, they're happy to follow me. Zé's going to be my second."

"But Dom Joaquim? He won't work with Berto." Maria shook her head in confusion. It could never work. Joaquim owned the mines, mules, and all the supplies. He allowed Mateus to lead the train only because Mateus had worked with her father.

"Actually the owner of the train knows I'll be the captain," Isabel said.

"You. . . How?"

"I bought the train," Thomas announced. "Dom Joaquim was happy to be rid of it. The mines in Minas are drying up, and he was eager to unload the train while still profitable."

She must have misheard. Only a mentally ill individual would do this for them. "You bought a mule train that won't turn a profit for a group of strangers?" Maria didn't know if the American was generous, lying, or the worst businessman in the world.

"I don't believe the decision is as generous or suspicious as it sounds," Thomas said. "The mines are drying up, but I think Brazil has much more to offer than gold and diamonds. The country will only continue to expand with the court here. There's miles of land ready to be farmed. The climate means the growing season is year round. Brazil hasn't even begun to show the world what it has to offer. And an experienced muleteer will be necessary to get all those goods to port."

"I'm that experienced muleteer he's referring to," Isabel added, her face glowing with pride.

Maria put a hand on her sister's shoulder. Isabel would be an incredible captain. She didn't doubt her ability, but she'd promised their parents to look after Isabel. Leaving broke those promises. She couldn't live with that guilt. "You will make a great muleteer. You were meant for life on the trail, but I can't leave you alone."

"You won't be. I'm going, too." Victoria smiled.

"You're leaving the queen?" Maria said. The surprises kept coming. Emotions layered on top of one another, and she didn't know how to feel.

"Even with Carlota Joaquina moving to Botafogo soon, I can't stay in the palace. I have great affection for Her Majesty, but it was never my dream to be a servant. When we set sail from Lisbon, I imagined cataloguing the flora in Brazil. I want to study medicinal uses for plants here and use the medical training my father taught me. On the trail, I can do both."

"It will be an adventure." Isabel winked at Victoria. "A very well-organized and thoroughly documented adventure, and I'll finally have someone else who can tend everyone's wounds."

"You didn't want to give us any room to argue," Mateus said.

"No," Isabel replied.

Thomas cleared his throat and gestured to the loaded cart. "I apologize for interrupting, but the ship will sail on the morning tide. We need to load your belongings now." He looked around the group. "If we're loading them?"

Maria's hand shot out and gripped Isabel's arm. "I can't abandon my family."

"You're not," Isabel assured her. "I'm choosing to stay in Rio, and it won't be forever. The mines will dry up eventually, so you'd better have a room ready for me."

"For both of us," Victoria added. "We can help with the children."

"Victoria can help with the children."

"Forget children. I haven't even gotten on the damn boat yet," Maria said. She turned to Mateus.

"I'll go where you lead, captain," he said.

They all looked to her for an answer.

She stepped back from Isabel, and the muleteer captain did a final assessment. Her sister had a Portuguese maid on her right, an American merchant on her left, and a cart with her entire life packed and ready to sail at their backs. She had promised to look out for her little sister, and the young woman in front of her, armed with freshly sharpened blades and flanked by the beginning of her own team, was a job well done. Time to load up and move on.

Maria turned to Thomas. "Let's move these trunks before we lose the tide."

Isabel wrapped her arms around Maria's waist. Mateus stepped back to let the sisters have their goodbye. Maria hugged her sister with all her strength, ignoring the pain in her injured arm. She whispered, "I love you. And I will always come if you ask. You know that."

"I love you. And don't be insulted when I'm a better muleteer than you."

Maria laughed and squeezed tighter.

Isabel broke away first, wiping her eyes. "I hoped you wouldn't be stubborn and asked some people to help load up your things." She waved at a group of people down the beach.

Benedito broke from the group and sprinted into Maria's arms. She suddenly found herself surrounded by her entire team. The men exchanged laughter and back slaps with Mateus, teasing him on escaping prison only to go off and get married.

"No one is married yet," Maria barked.

"Will you please wear a dress for the ceremony?" Dona Antonia dabbed her eyes. "It would make your mama happy."

Maria smiled. "Everyone keeps talking about a wedding. There have been no proposals."

"How long are you going to keep me waiting?" Mateus brushed his lips against her cheek. "Well, men, I get to ask you to load up one more time."

Mateus and the team began hauling chests from the cart to the waiting launch on the beach. Thomas and Benedito joined them, the boy trying out a few English phrases. Antonia added a basket filled with fruits, cheese, and dried meat. She had canteens filled with her best port. The women gathered to the side while their friends loaded Maria's life into the row boat.

"Maria, I wanted to thank you," Victoria said. "Thank you for trusting me and trusting *in* me. I'll forever be grateful you dropped through Her Majesty's window."

Maria embraced her friend. "Thank *you*. You know you're family now?"

"I'm honored you feel that way."

"Stop, Victoria," Isabel interrupted. "Didn't you hear? We're family. *Santa Valentina*."

"All right, I've never heard of Valentina. You made that one up," Maria accused.

"I did not. *Santa Valentina* was burned alive in the year three hundred and eight."

"Wait," Victoria grabbed Isabel's arm. "All the saint names you call…you know each one?"

"I sure as hell wouldn't ask for help from a stranger." Isabel looked aghast at the thought. "When I was little, I asked the priest to teach me all the women saints people have forgotten. While Nossa Senhora is bogged down with a dozen requests an hour from every person in Rio, my saints have a lot more time on their hands. I figure that works in my favor." She patted Victoria on the shoulder. "You'll want to learn a few before we go out on the trail."

"Are you all going to stand around gossiping all day or help?" Benedito called from the boat.

A melancholy silence settled over the friends. Maria focused on the crates to ignore the tightness in her chest. Sorrow and joy and anticipation fought in her head.

As Thomas and Mateus set the last trunk inside the boat, Maria marveled, "Isabel when did you start planning this?"

"While driving the Prince Regent's carriage back from Botafogo."

"Is that why you were so terrible at driving? You were distracted?" Victoria asked.

"I didn't hear His Highness complaining," Isabel retorted. "I'd already sent Dito to fetch Thomas. I thought we might need a quick way out of Rio in the unlikely event we lost and Prince João ended up dead. Vidigal seemed like the kind of man who held a grudge."

"*Seemed?*" Thomas frowned at Isabel. "I thought Major Vidigal was taken into custody along with the Bats who participated in the coup."

"Don't worry, Tomasinho. I didn't murder anybody. Vidigal's alive and in custody. Just not Portugal's," Isabel said.

"We didn't trust the soldiers or guardsmen to leave Vidigal imprisoned, and we happen to know one or two morally flexible captains in need of some deck hands," Maria explained.

"You shipped him off with pirates?" Thomas asked, not bothering to hide his shock.

"Under a mixed captain sailing for Jamaica." Isabel clapped her hands in delight. "He's going to hate it."

"Jamaica was my idea, when we couldn't find a ship sailing for Angola," Victoria chimed in.

A smile had been spreading across Thomas's face as he listened to the women. He lifted his hat and bowed deeply. "I pledge this day to never cross any of you ladies or any member of your families."

"Words to live by," Mateus agreed. "Meu amor, we have to go before the tide changes."

"Wait!" Isabel shrieked. She leapt into the cart and came out with a large cooking pot. "You're forgetting the most important thing. All fixed and full as ever. You'll need it to start your farm."

"You know the ship has plenty of pots?" Thomas offered.

Maria accepted the pot Victoria broke, now repaired and filled with their savings of diamonds. She smiled at Thomas. "This particular pot has a special place in my family."

Maria turned to her friends. Her family. She embraced Benedito and Dona Antonia. She quietly asked Antonia to watch out for Isabel and Victoria. She shook hands with every member of her team. Zé squeezed her shoulder. "Your father would be proud. I think you track better than he did."

"Good luck with your new family," Maria said. She couldn't say more because there weren't words to express what the compliment meant to her.

Maria drew Isabel and Victoria into a final hug. For a minute, they were a mass of arms and bent heads. Victoria wiped tears away, and Isabel's eyes shone. Maria said her goodbyes with dry eyes. She wasn't leaving Isabel alone. They had a new sister. A muleteer had to read people as well as she read the trail, and Maria knew Victoria's loyalty ran as deep as the ocean. Isabel would never be alone.

And she had Mateus.

As the launch hit the water and rocked among the waves, Maria didn't feel sad. For the first time in a long time, her stomach knotted not in worry but anticipation. A sea voyage, a new city, a life as a farmer, maybe as a wife. New adventures awaited.

"Maria," Isabel shouted. "Get my room ready."

"Don't get my team killed," she shouted back.

"Victoria will patch them up," her sister yelled. Victoria's eyes widened in horror, and Isabel's laughter rang out across the bay.

They leaned against the deck railing and watched Rio de Janeiro slip away. She could make out Isabel and Victoria on the beach waving. Maria waved back until the city slipped out of sight behind Sugar Loaf.

Mateus **wrapped** an arm around her shoulder. "Do you think we'll ever come back?"

Maria smiled. Would they? She had all she wanted. Her love, her team's safety, her sister's **blessing**. What more could call to her?

A ship sailed past into Guanabara Bay. The sailors around her raised their caps in salute to the incoming crew. Maria joined them, waving in welcome and goodbye. The boom of cannon vibrated the deck under her feet, and for the first time, Maria imagined the twenty-**one** guns fired for her. A farewell and an invitation to return. Her home and her family would be waiting.

She leaned her head against Mateus's shoulder.

"We'll be back. There's always a reason to return to Rio."

Discussion Questions

1. Maria, Isabel, and Victoria are different races, classes, and cultures. How does each woman's background help the group achieve their goals? What skills and knowledge does each woman possess that are a result of her race, culture, or community? How does diversity of perspective and experience help in any kind of decision making?

2. Given their differences, what brings the women together? Why do Maria and Isabel choose to trust Victoria and vice versa? What similarities allow them to connect and relate to one other?

3. While friendships can start based on shared interests or circumstances, building and maintaining friendships requires conscious action. What choices do Maria, Isabel, and Victoria each make that strengthen their relationships with the others? What action does each woman take that proves she values her relationship with the others?

4. In addition to saving Mateus and the Prince Regent, each woman has their own emotional arc through the story. Maria opens her heart. Isabel learns self-control. Victoria finds her confidence. What were the key moments of each woman's journey that taught her these lessons? How did her relationship with the other two help that character grow?

5. Predator versus prey is a key symbol throughout the story. Who or what is the predator(s)? Who is the prey? Does this change during the story? What does the title mean to you now?

6. Power is an important theme in the story. What different kinds of power come into play? Who do you think has the most power? Who wields their power most effectively? Compare and contrast the different types of power Maria, Princess Carlotta Joaquina, and Vidigal have and do not have.

7. Who or what is the primary antagonist in the story? Is there more than one? Does it change depending on the POV character?

8. Maria wields a whip. Isabel carries daggers. And Victoria uses a sword. What does each woman's choice of weapon reveal about her background and personality?

9. According to the UN Refugee Agency, a refugee today is "someone who has to flee his or her country because of persecution, war, or violence." There is an implied vulnerability in the status of refugees and some who flee are specifically excluded from

claiming the status, such as war criminals. In your opinion, do the Portuguese who fled Napoleon's invasion qualify as refugees? Why or why not? Is there a distinction between the Court and Portuguese citizens such as Victoria?

10. The population of Rio de Janeiro in 1808 is estimated to have been two-thirds people of color. Brazil never had codified laws preventing intermarriage between races, and the people of Rio had more than twenty distinct racial categories to describe all the mixes of people. How does this compare to definitions and concepts of race in your city and culture's histories? Is race a primary descriptor in your culture, or is it something else such as religion or ethnicity?

11. How does the author evoke place throughout the story? Give some specific examples of sensory details that bring Rio de Janeiro to life. What words and specific scenery details differentiate Rio from other 19th century settings you've read about?

Author's Note

"How much of this is true?" That's the question I always ask after consuming a work of historical fiction, and given the near total absence of Brazil from US curriculums and popular culture, I imagine quite a few people are thinking "Did this really happen?" and "Why have I never heard about this?"

In answer to the first question, yes, it happened. While my Tropical Three Musketeers (that's how I think of Maria, Isabel, and Victoria) are fictional, the world and people around them were very real. The Portuguese royal family fled Napoleon to Brazil and arrived in Rio de Janeiro on March 7, 1808.

As for the second question, whatever the explanations, it really is our loss. When I moved to Rio after college, I knew almost nothing about Brazil except it was the birthplace of Pelé and "The Girl from Ipanema." I remember driving through Rio with my now-husband shortly after arriving, and he pointed to a beautiful mansion, holding up valiantly against the salty air. "That's where President Vargas committed suicide." He said it so nonchalantly, like pointing out the best barbecue place. "Brazil had a president who committed suicide? How?" He shot himself through the heart.

A version of this scene repeated itself regularly during my first years in Rio. My husband would point out a site of some incredible moment of history, and I would feel shocked and a little betrayed by my education for never having heard about it. This is where Brazil's royal family had their last ball days before the monarchy ended. This is Maracanã, site of the most attended soccer game in history with 200,000 spectators. This is where the Portuguese royal family lived when they arrived in Rio.

Here I want to emphasize I wrote a story about Rio de Janeiro. Not Brazil. While Rio and the court's arrival are important pieces of Brazilian history, saying this book is about Brazil is like saying *The Secret Life of Bees* is a book about the United States. Technically yes, in a very broad sense, but no one is going to have a good idea of jazz-age Chicago or present day Miami from reading *The Secret Life of Bees*. The same is true for *Jaguars and Other Game*. Brazil is home to the largest Japanese diaspora in the world. Candomblé is a commonly practiced religion in Bahia, while they celebrate Oktoberfest in Santa Catarina. A story set over the course of one week in one city cannot give an accurate picture of a country that evolved over five hundred years with people from every continent, so I humbly beg the publishing industry to give us more stories set in Brazil. We're missing out.

Okay. Now that we've managed expectations, Rio de Janeiro.

Before the land became known as Rio de Janeiro, the area was home to various tribes within the Tupi-Guarani linguistic group. The Portuguese arrived in 1500 and were bringing Africans as slaves by the mid 16th century. They officially founded the city of São

Sebastião do Rio de Janeiro on March 1, 1565, making Rio a multiracial and multi-cultural city for two hundred fifty years before Prince João and his 10,000-strong entourage showed up on the beach.

I based the personalities and beliefs of my royal family and officials on historical evidence. Vidigal skulked around Rio terrorizing his fellow *Cariocas* (natives of Rio de Janeiro city) with brutal policing tactics. Prince João hid in his room during thunderstorms, nibbling on the chicken breasts he kept in the pocket of a jacket. The specific coup attempt in *Jaguars* is fictional, but Carlota Joaquina did participate in five conspiracies over the course of twenty-five years. The woman could hold a grudge. There's no consensus on what plagued Queen Maria. Some historians have suggested she suffered from porphyria, but more contemporary research suggests a severe form of bipolar disease. We do know that she had "horrific" screaming fits, which were documented in the letters of guests with the bad luck to have rooms near the queen.

Honestly, writing the royal family was almost effortless. Centuries of inbreeding combined with absolute power does not result in emotionally stable and self-aware individuals. They were a decidedly dysfunctional family and brought all their drama across the Atlantic. The poor people of Rio had no choice but to deal with it.

Between the chases and fight scenes, I tried to show how the Court's arrival disrupted the daily lives of Cariocas. Shortage of food and goods. An explosion in construction that changed the landscape around the city. New rules and expectations. At the time *Jaguars* is set, Rio was transitioning from colonial to imperial. The old wasn't working, but the new hadn't yet developed to take its place.

If you're interested in learning more about this unique period in history, I recommend *1808: The Flight of the Emperor* by Laurentino Gomes. The English translation was my foundational source for this story. The book reads like a narrative, an absolutely insane comedy of the absurd. Someday I'll write a story about how all 60,000 volumes of the royal library were frantically packed in fourteen carts, hauled to the wharf, then forgotten on the docks as the court sailed off to Brazil. Don't worry book lovers. The library eventually made it to Rio three years later.

Another source that directly inspired characters and scenes was a Portuguese translation of *Voyage Pittoresque et Historique au Brésil* by Jean-Baptiste Debret. A French painter invited to Rio as part of an artistic mission, Debret lived in Brazil from 1816 to 1831, and his paintings and sketches depict daily life for Brazilians of all colors and social backgrounds. He viewed Brazil through a colonialist lens, exemplified by personal commentary on his paintings such as "The Guarani woman chose to flee during the night rather than be brought back to the city as a captive. How silly of the natives not to see the benefits of being kidnapped and enslaved." (I'm paraphrasing, but the sentiment is accurate.) But if you ignore his words and focus on the scenes he recreated, the streets of Rio come to life with the shouts of street vendors, the morning gossip while in line for a bowl of angu, and the clink of a young barber's basin and knives as he hustles for customers. Search Debret's paintings and you'll find my inspiration for Dito.

While the boy in Debret's painting is probably Black Brazilian, Dito in this story is mixed race, Guarani and Black Brazilian. The racial hierarchies of Imperial Rio de Janeiro were incredibly complex. Separate categories and terms existed for the children of two white Brazilian parents, two Black Brazilian parents, two white Portuguese parents, two Native Americans who lived outside cities according to traditional culture, two Native American parents who had adopted European traditions and lived in the city, one white Brazilian parent and one Black Brazilian parent, one mixed Black/white parent and one Native American parent, one Black African parent and one mixed Native/white parent. Each group was a distinct racial category and occupied different spaces in the social hierarchy.

At the time of the court's arrival in Rio, historians estimate the population was two-thirds people of color. Maria, Isabel, and Victoria were specifically chosen to represent the diverse population that existed in Rio. Their races and cultural backgrounds are not in service of a trend or a reimagining. They are historically accurate.

However, I have admittedly taken some liberties with other historical facts. Sometimes I did it to avoid a misunderstanding when crossing cultures. In Brazil, Prince João is never referred to using the Portuguese word *principe*. He is Dom João VI. I chose to use the title "Prince" instead of "Dom" because I thought most English-speaking Americans would translate Dom as "Lord."

Sometimes I changed historical fact to serve the story. In 1809, the palace where the royal family lived was undergoing significant expansion and renovations. The palace in *Jaguars* matches the layout of the Imperial Palace in 1818 because I wanted my girls to crash a ball but did not want them sneaking through a construction site.

Of all the changes to fact I made, the most important is the presence of Valongo wharf.

Valongo was the largest slave port in the Americas. Before the importation of slaves was finally outlawed in Brazil in 1831, historians estimate between 900,000 and 1 million Africans were brought to Rio de Janeiro. Valongo was built because Rio's elite complained about the smell, and officials worried about disease spreading from all the corpses unloaded off the ships. They decided to build a new port on the outskirt of downtown, which operated for twenty years. Officials buried the port before the arrival of Empress Teresa in 1843, and it remained hidden and mostly forgotten until unearthed **accidentally** in 2011 during renovation of the area.

Construction on Valongo began in 1811, but the port appears completed in my Rio of 1809. Valongo is one of the most signifi cant and horrifi c places in the history of the Americas, yet it's barely known out-side of academic circles. While the recently excavated wharf has been designated a UNESCO World Heritage Site, currently there is no museum or visitor's center, just a few graffi tied plaques. I made the decision for it to appear in *Jaguars* to help in the smallest way bring Valongo into public awareness and discussion.

Finally, from time to time throughout writing *Jaguars and Other Game*, people questioned the historical accuracy of a woman muleteer. I admit I never found evidence of mule train led by a woman. I chose that profession because of the skills Maria and Isabel would learn from the work and the access they would have to diamonds.

However, a woman earning her own income and fighting for her right to work in 1809 Rio is not fiction. While researching, I came across a single page that told how in the 1790s the *quitandeiras* were banned from selling their goods in a particular square. They banded together, women of color with no formal education and few financial resources, and collectively sued the city government for their right to sell in a public space. They won. That's why I don't believe Maria's business sense and entrepreneurial spirit are improbable or that Isabel couldn't have been a charming, expert saleswoman or that women and girls can't triumph over impossible odds when they join forces and work together. That's just fact.

Acknowledgements

Full confession. I've never actually read the acknowledgements of a book. That's hundreds of pages of unacknowledged acknowledgements. Now that I have to write mine, my ignorance of the form and general lack of sentimentality has me scrambling.

For a debut novel, I don't think it's a stretch to say every person who pointed me to a library book or defined a literary term or explained a piece of Brazilian history contributed to making me the person who could write this story. First novels require conscious and meticulous application of knowledge ranging from vocabulary to human empathy. Nothing is rote. There's no muscle memory. I take none of my skills or the people who gave them to me for granted.

But I'm short on time. Ms. Marvel starts streaming this week, so I'll limit my written thanks to those who gave advice specific to this story and people likely to ask me to my face why they weren't mentioned. But please know, my appreciation extends to so many not named here.

Thank you to my family. To my mom for believing whole-heartedly my first drafts are as good as anything you can find in a bookstore. Every artist needs a cheerleader blinded by love to banish their own doubts. To my stepmom for being my fi rst editor, correcting all my work from middle school short stories to a high school essay on *Atlas Shrugged* to the earliest drafts of my fi rst attempt at a novel. (I really apologize for using up moments of your life on that Ayn Rand essay, btw.) You're my lifelong English teacher. And my Dad. Thank you for being one of my best friends. I love you guys!

Thank you to my agent, Kaitlyn Johnson. Thank you for taking a chance on a story set during a time and place nobody in the U.S. has heard of. Thank you for reading my story and saying "You don't write for teenagers. You write for adults," which is probably the most profound, impactful, and accurate feedback on my writing I've received. I don't know if my writing deserves years of unpaid labor, but I'm thrilled you did.

Of course, a huge thanks to the entire team at Orange Blossom, especially my amazing editor, Arielle Haughee. You signed me thinking about where you could get Portuguese speakers to help organize events in Brazil. I'm humbled you thought my story was worth that effort. Thank you for your spot-on edits. I'm not exaggerating when I say everything I write from now on will be better because of you.

Jaguars was made infinitely better by feedback from early readers. Allie Hine, your comments led directly to *the* key plot twist. Laura-Ann Jacobs, our discussions about transracial adoption and your recommendation for best book battle scene were both critical to bringing Isabel to life. Mayken Brunings, my first beta reader not related to me. Befriending you is one of the truly good things to come out of my time on Twitter.

Bárbara Morais and Solaine Chioro, muito, muito, muito obrigada! Thank you for the invaluable feedback on race and culture in Brazil and calling me out on my missteps. It is such an honor to have your input for this book, and the queasy feeling in my stomach during the days it took me to work up the courage to open your emails and read feedback from *published authors* was totally worth it.

Lindsay Ely and Kip Wilson, amazing authors and PitchWars mentors. You took the time to send detailed feedback despite the fact I wasn't your mentee. Feedback I used to make *Jaguars* better. Thank you for your encouragement. I won't forget the lessons on craft and helping those coming up behind you.

Finally, my husband and my daughter. The people who have to live with me.

Alceu, I could never have written this story without marrying you. You introduced me to Brazil and your hometown of Rio de Janeiro. Over fifteen years of discussions and travel with you, I've learned your country's rich history, politics, and geography. You're always happy to hear about whatever unbelievable historical fact I just read and eager to invest in ridiculous quantities of books for research. You were and are my historical and cultural adviser, my sounding board, and therapist who heard every one of my fears and frustrations.

And throughout a decade of writing with only rejections to show for it, you always respected my writing as work. When I quit teaching and stayed home at my computer, you still considered that time work. Each conference and workshop registration fee was an investment in a career that you had absolute faith would come to fruition.

I am so grateful our daughter has you as an example of what a partner is. I'm just a little worried you've set the bar impossibly high. Thank you. This book and every book that comes after is possible because of your love and respect.

My daughter. Even if you were old enough to read this, you probably wouldn't since I ignored your advice and didn't put dragons in it. Your existence taught me the self-discipline necessary to finish a novel. Wanting to teach by example made me keep writing as rejections piled up over years. Your brutal honesty, "Have you made any money from your stories yet, Mommy?" gave me the existential crisis I needed to call myself a true artist. Thank you, sweet girl, for being patient and understanding when Mommy was at home but working and couldn't play. I love you both so much.

About the Author

Originally from Atlanta, Georgia, Brynn Barineau graduated from American University with a bachelor's in international studies and master's in international communication. She moved to her husband's native Rio de Janeiro after college with too many sweaters and not enough Portuguese and began writing as a way to process life in a new country. Her fiction is rooted in the power and possibilities of relationships across cultures. She's now back in Atlanta rediscovering her hometown with her Brazilian-American family.

brynnbarineau.com
facebook.com/brynnbarineauauthor
@brynnbarineau

If you enjoyed this book, please consider leaving a review on Amazon or GoodReads. It helps the author sell more books!

Check out other books by
Orange Blossom Publishing: